CONSPIRACY IN KIEV

ZONDERVAN

Conspiracy in Kiev
Copyright © 2008 by Noel Hynd

This title is also available as a Zondervan ebook.
Visit www.zondervan.com/ebooks.

This title is also available in a Zondervan audio edition.
Visit www.zondervan.fm.

Requests for information should be addressed to:

Zondervan, *Grand Rapids, Michigan 49530*

Library of Congress Cataloging-in-Publication Data

Hynd, Noel.
      Conspiracy in Kiev / Noel Hynd.
         p. cm. — (The Russian trilogy ; bk. 1.)
      ISBN 978-0-310-27871-9 (pbk.)
      1. United States. Federal Bureau of Investigation—Officials and
employees—Fiction. 2. Shooters of firearms—Fiction. 3. Conspiracies—Fiction. 4. Life
change events—Fiction. I. Title.
PS3558.Y54C66 2008
813'.54—dc22

                                  2008018529

Edited by Andy Meisenheimer and Bob Hudson
Interior design by Christine Orejuela-Winkelman
Photography by Stuck in Customs

Printed in the United States of America

09 10 11 12 13 14 • 26 25 24 23 22 21 20 19 18 17 16 15 14 13 12 11 10 9 8 7 6 5 4

NOEL HYND
CONSPIRACY IN KIEV

THE RUSSIAN TRILOGY — BOOK ONE

ZONDERVAN®

ZONDERVAN.com/
AUTHORTRACKER
follow your favorite authors

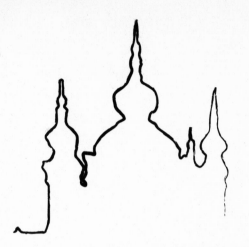

For my good friend Thomas H. Ochiltree.
Thanks for so many years of wit and wisdom,
inspiration and laughter.

Every culture has its distinctive and normal system of government. Yours is democracy, moderated by corruption. Ours is totalitarianism, moderated by assassination.

—Unknown Russian diplomat

PART ONE

ONE

The late-evening cognac and cigar were indulgences that Daniel had come to enjoy. So each evening at ten, on fiendishly cold nights like this one, he would set out on foot to the lively restaurant at the corner. It was Friday, January 2, two days into the New Year. He wouldn't be in Paris for much longer, so he might as well enjoy each evening. Even he didn't know which evening would be his last.

His small apartment was on the rue du Bourg Tibourg in the Marais district, not far from the Hôtel de Ville, which was no hotel, but Paris's majestic city hall. The neighborhood, which stretched across the third and fourth *arrondissements* on Paris's Right Bank, had been the city's most exclusive neighborhood in the seventeenth century. It had deteriorated into a sordid slum two generations ago, one of the tougher sections of the city for the Parisian police when they bothered to go into it.

Now all that had again changed. The Marais had been gentrified and rebuilt during the reign of President François Mitterrand — a regal Socialist, said by critics to be "the last French king" — in the 1970s. It was now a lively place in the first decade of the twenty-first century, a favorite of tourists, busy during the day with art galleries, museums, quirky shops, and restaurants. And it still had its distinctive flavor; several small shops and stores that catered to the older Jewish residents of the area, Holocaust survivors, and their descendants.

His favorite café, L'étincelle — "the spark" in French — anchored the square that connected the rue du Bourg Tibourg with the rue de Rivoli. This was not the tourist rue de Rivoli with the arcades that ran on one side of the Tuileries and along the Louvre, but its extension that ultimately turned into the rue Saint-Antoine and wound up in the place de la Bastille. There were few tourists here.

Daniel trudged past the South American café on the near corner, affecting the awkward hesitant gait of an old man. The night was frigid, unusual even for Paris in January. He pulled his overcoat tight.

He stepped past some remaining patches of ice. His breath was a small cloud in front of him. Twenty degrees Fahrenheit. It felt colder.

His gray whiskers, a two-week growth of beard, shielded his face. He looked like an old rabbi, which was ironic, but not exactly an accident. Below the beard, he wore the white clerical collar of a priest. Under the bulky coat rested a silver cross with the body of Christ, the unmistakable sign of a Roman Catholic.

Just a few more steps and Daniel was in the restaurant.

The Spark was appropriately named. It was a bright place with a pleasant staff. One of the waitresses spotted him as he entered. Irène. She was a trim girl in her early twenties, articulate, pretty, and friendly. Like the rest of the staff she zipped around in a brown T-shirt bearing the restaurant's logo and a snug pair of jeans.

Why, if he were a younger man, he mused, watching her ... and if he weren't a priest ...

Not a priest. The thought amused him.

She had an interesting exotic face. Daniel was a student of faces. He pegged her as half French, half Algerian. Irène reminded him of this French-Algerian singer he liked named Nadiya or the American singer Norah Jones.

"*Bon soir, mon Père,*" she said. "Hello, Father."

"*Bon soir, Irène,*" he answered.

He had been here often enough to know the staff and their names. He pulled off his wool coat, gloves, and scarf. The restaurant smelled good. It was a good life he was living these weeks in Paris. He liked this part of the day where he could sit in a bustling place, pick up on the energy of the young people around him, and be alone with his thoughts.

"Sit anywhere you like," she said.

He nodded. He scanned. He spotted the American woman at a table by herself. Well, fortune was smiling on him. He would not be alone this evening. Rosa, as she had introduced herself on a prior evening. She was a professor of some sort, or so she said. Single, she had said, and appreciative of some unthreatening companionship as the day ended. She had never given her last name and he had never asked it.

She had held him in conversations about philosophy and theology for the last two evenings and didn't seem to have any ulterior motives, something against which Daniel was always watchful. Surely she wouldn't mind having company again. He knew he wouldn't. It was tough these days to even find a woman who could tolerate a cigar, much less a cigar smoked by a priest.

She was seated near the door. She smiled when she saw him.

He approached her table. "Mind if I join you?" he asked.

They spoke English, his with a trace of an accent that suggested eastern or south central Europe. Hers was American, flat as corn country. When she had asked about his accent, he had explained that his roots were in Hungary.

"I was a boy in Budapest," he had recounted. "That's where my parents had lived until 1956. When the Russian tanks rolled in, they fled to England and then Canada."

"Where did you go to seminary?" she had asked.

"Montréal. That's how I speak French."

She, in turn, explained that she had grown up in Kansas but now lived in New York City. He knew all about New York, it turned out. He entertained her with stories. She did likewise.

This evening, as always, Daniel folded his overcoat and placed it neatly on an extra chair at their table. He sat down. Irène brought him a cognac, gave him a cute smile, and quickly left to attend other tables.

"You're sure my cigar doesn't bother you?" Daniel asked his table companion.

"Not at all."

They fell into a conversation easily. He noticed that she was watching his hands.

She was drinking a Coca-Cola with a twist of lemon. There was music playing again tonight, so loud that one had to raise one's voice just to be heard. A friendly din. Lots of conversation in several languages, lots of glasses clinking and plates clattering. L'étincelle was a cheerful upbeat joint.

A few minutes into their conversation, she raised a hand and waved to a man who came in the door and surveyed the place.

"Oh! There's a friend of mine!" she said. "He's going to join us."

Daniel didn't like that. For no reason, or for *every* reason, he didn't like it at all. He had an acute antenna, and he sensed something was wrong. He looked at the stranger with a stare that could bore a hole in a cinderblock wall.

But before Daniel could object, the newcomer slid into the extra chair, the one closest to the door. Daniel took him to be American before he even opened his mouth. He looked like a businessman of some sort. Another sign of trouble.

There was an awkward moment. The man looked at Daniel with intent dark eyes. Rosa offered no introduction. That in and of itself was enough of a further clue.

Three strikes and—

"What?" Daniel asked, looking back and forth, hoping he might be wrong.

"You're not an old man, Father Daniel," she said.

"You're not my friends," he answered.

"And you're not a priest," the man said. "You're not even Catholic."

Daniel moved his hand quickly under his jacket, reaching for the gun that he carried for just such moments. But Rosa thrust her hand roughly after his, momentarily deflecting his grasp and minimizing any possibility that he might defend himself.

At the same time, the newcomer, quickly and professionally, reached across the table with a small snub-nosed handgun. He pressed it right to Daniel's chest and he pulled the trigger.

The gun erupted with an ear-splitting *bang*. It was barely audible above the noise of the restaurant, though diners at some tables started to look around.

Daniel's face showed shock, then outrage. Then all that dissolved with accelerating pain. The bullet had smashed the sternum at the midpoint of his chest. The gunman followed his advantage with a second shot. Another powerful *bang*. He squeezed that one off so quickly and accurately that it passed directly through Daniel's heart.

The woman braced his body and steadied it so that Daniel didn't tumble. Instead, with a helpful little push, Daniel slid forward, his body slumping onto the table as if he were drunk.

The gunman pocketed his weapon and rose to his feet. Rosa did the same. They used their hands to shield their faces and moved quickly to the door. Only as they were going through it did they start to hear a commotion behind them. Loud agitated conversation built into shouting.

Several seconds later young Irène came to the table to see what was wrong.

She saw the shattered brandy glass under Daniel's lifeless head. She saw his unfocused eyes and his blood mixing with the cognac on the table.

Her hands flew to her face and she started to scream. The evening manager, a fit young man named Gerard, rushed over. But by this time, Daniel's two acquaintances had disappeared into the dark side streets and alleys.

They were gone into the icy night, leaving their victim behind.

TWO

As the same cold midwinter gripped the eastern United States, Alexandra LaDuca sat at her desk in Washington DC, at a few minutes past nine in the morning. Her desk, and her job, was at the main building of the United States Department of the Treasury on Pennsylvania Avenue and Fifteenth Street.

She pondered the fraudulent document before her, received via the US mail by a citizen who had brought a complaint to the Treasury Department. It was not that Alex hadn't seen thousands of similar pitches, and it was not that she hadn't heard sob stories from people who had been similarly swindled. And it wasn't that such chicanery so violated her sense of decency and fair play.

No, what bothered her most was that anyone would be so venal as to make a living through such outright crookery ... and that any victim would be gullible enough to fall for it. The correspondence was on a fancy letterhead:

> FOREIGN REMITTANCE DEPARTMENT
> CENTRAL CREDIT BANK OF NIGERIA
> TINUBU SQUARE, VICTORIA ISLAND
> LAGOS, NIGERIA

There was the first duet of lies. There existed nowhere on the planet, Alex knew, any such department or any such bank. She sometimes wondered if Lagos existed, other than in her own bad dreams. But she knew Lagos did exist because she had spent a couple of weeks there a year earlier investigating a similar fraud. The only success of the previous trip had been in what *hadn't* happened. She had successfully avoided getting killed.

The scam continued:

> Dear Sir/Madam,
>
> IMMEDIATE CONTRACT PAYMENT CONTRACT #: MAV/NNPC/FGN/ MIN/009 / NEXT OF KIN FUND/ US$16.3M

From the records of outstanding Next of Kin
Fund due for payment with the Federal Government of Nigeria, your name was discovered on the
list of the outstanding payments who have not
yet received their funds.

We wish to inform you that your payment is
being processed. We will release said funds to
you *immediately* as soon as you respond to this
letter. Also note that from records in my file
your outstanding payment is US$16,300,000. Kindly
reconfirm to me the followings:

Your full name.

Phone, fax and mobile number . . .

Yeah, sure. Sixteen million bucks in an offer as phony as a uni-
corn with a three dollar bill on its nose. She simmered. She had seen
enough of these to last a lifetime.

Alex LaDuca, at age twenty-nine, worked as a senior investigator with a little-publicized agency of the US Treasury: the Financial
Crimes Enforcement Network, or FinCen. The agency enforced laws
against domestic and international financial crimes that targeted US
citizens and corporations. She was actually a special agent of the FBI
but on loan to FinCen to combat international financial fraud.

Her boss was a stocky little man named Mike Gamburian from Boston. His office featured a mural of a triumphant Fenway Park in October of 2004, a moment when the Red Sox finally won something. The
New York employees who worked for him, in grudging good humor,
claimed the mural created "a hostile work environment." Aside from
that, Gamburian was a genial fellow and not unpleasant to work for.

Alex was one of FinCen's shrewdest investigators, as well as one of
the toughest. She was also the youngest to have "senior" status. And
she didn't lack for assignments. With the proliferation of the Internet,
fraud had gone global and high tech. Financial fraud was a growth
industry.

The shameless scam continued . . .

As soon as this information is received, your
payment will be made to you in A Certified Bank

Draft or wired to your nominated bank account
directly from Central Bank of Nigeria.

   You can mail me on my direct email address ...

Yeah, Alex thought, shaking her head. Don't even try to phone because a phone call can be traced. She skipped ahead. It was signed,

Regards,

Dr. Samuel Ifraim
Executive Governor,
Central Credit Bank of Nigeria
(CCBN)

Right. Sure. A fake name with a fake doctorate. And the "CC" in the CCBN might just as easily stand for Crooks and Criminals.

The scam was known at FinCen as a 419, named after a widely unenforced section of the Nigerian criminal code. Millions of these stinky little con jobs circulated across the globe each year, most emanating from West Africa.

They were all the same. They claimed that due to certain circumstances — disbursement of will proceeds, sale of a business, sale of cheap crude oil, a winning email address in an Internet lottery, or something similarly unlikely — a bank needed help to transfer this money to the lucky recipient's account in the United States. If the recipient assisted them he or she would be entitled to a percentage of the funds.

If contacted, the scam artists would request thousands of dollars for various costs that were required before the lucky winner got the share of the funds. Of course, the victim's payment went through but — surprise — the transfer of riches never happened.

The scam was as widespread as it was shameless. In 2002 the US Department of Justice had gained a court order to open all mail from Nigeria passing through JFK airport in New York. Around seventy-five percent had involved scam offers. Much of it even bore counterfeit postage.

And then there had been her nightmarish trip to Lagos the previous year. A mission from the United States Treasury had sought to present evidence that much of the swindling was being done with the apparent complicity of the Nigerian government.

The hosts in Lagos didn't take well to that theory. While the Americans were meeting with representatives of the government, their hotel rooms were sacked and trashed. Their clothes were taken, their suitcases slashed, and death threats scrawled on the walls. Of five staff cars used by Treasury representatives and belonging to the US Embassy, three were stolen and one was chopped apart with a chain saw while their meeting was in progress. A fifth blew up, killing their Nigerian chauffeur.

So much for a little international fieldwork. Most members of the delegation felt lucky to touch down again physically unharmed on American soil.

Alex filed the paperwork before her. The 419s would be around for as long as people would fall for them. The fight against them would continue. But in the absence of follow-up at the source — when a foreign government might be aiding the perpetrators — they could only be contained, not defeated. Not that she was going to ignore them. She wasn't above a personal vendetta or two for criminals who deserved to be put out of business. She had a long memory for such things and could be stubborn as a bulldog once she got her teeth into a case.

But she had more immediate dragons to slay. There was a messy business involving untaxed wine imports from France. There was a perplexing matter about some art stolen by the Nazis from a wealthy Jewish collector who had died in the Holocaust; a Swiss bank denied culpability despite the fact that a looted Pissarro had been hanging in the New York office of the bank president for the last thirty years. And then there was a whole sheaf of various non-419 Internet frauds that seemed to be associated with an online casino operation in Costa Rica.

If human beings invested the same ingenuity in eradicating disease and hunger that they did in swindling each other, the world might be a better place ... and she might happily be in another line of work, one that would have put her on the front lines in the fight against worldwide oppression, ignorance, disease, hunger, and poverty, causes she felt were compatible with her guiding principles.

Sometimes she thought she should have become a doctor. She would have been an excellent one and could easily have become one.

But human beings didn't manifest such ingenuity and Alex hadn't become a doctor. So she did what she could. She enjoyed sticking up for victims. Out in the field, she had several teams of investigators who worked for her. The day was young. It was time to see what cases were shaping up for arrests or prosecution. She dug in for a day of combat, matching wits with various crooks across the world and on the Internet.

THREE

The electronic surveillance team in Washington was a perfect combination of four elements: speed, efficiency, intelligence, and the refusal to ask questions. And today they even had one convenient coincidence tossed in.

Carlos was the tech guy and the lookout. He turned up in a uniform that bore the markings of one of the local cable companies. Janet was his cohort, but she arrived independently and in street clothes, which in this weather meant a parka, a denim mini, and woolen leggings. She looked like any other pretty young twenty-something. Their target this morning was an apartment in a residential complex on Calvert Avenue and Twenty-fourth Street, opposite the sprawling art deco Shoreham Hotel, now the Omni Shoreham, and just a few blocks from the Woodley Park Metro station.

There was nothing special about the bugging. It was a routine job as long as the victim was at work. Tuesdays were good for this sort of thing.

Carlos arrived first, at about ten in the morning. He had the proper paperwork—routine maintenance on the cable system—and got a free pass from the building's superintendent. He went to work in the basement, checking the cable lines, the phone lines, the power. He located the setups for the targeted apartment on the fifth floor.

Duck soup. This was easy.

On a previous visit Carlos had stolen a passkey that worked for all apartments. The black-bag keepers back at his agency congratulated him on his good work and made a copy. Carlos returned the original before anyone knew it was out of the building.

They had files back at the agency's headquarters for hundreds of buildings and hotels in DC, completely legal under the classified sections of the Homeland Security Act of 2005. So this would be a snap as long as no one who really *did* work for the cable people turned up. But that didn't happen this morning.

Carlos's specialty was rigging radio frequencies to go through the main electrical wiring of the building. Then, from a car within two blocks, a tuner could home in on the specific apartment and the "easy listening" was officially "on the air." Carlos was never a listener. That was done by higher-ups.

Carlos moved quickly from the electric grid to the junction box for the telephones in Calvert Arms Apartments. He could see from the electronic blowback on the phone lines that most people used cordless phones, including his target. So Carlos dropped a chip on the fifth floor apartment he wanted.

Job done. He flipped open his cell phone and called Janet.

"I'm just about finished," he said. "Got ten minutes?"

Two blocks away, she was sitting in a car cheerfully working *Naruto: Ultimate Ninja 2* on her PSP. "Sure," she said. "See you on the flip side."

Here was today's happy coincidence: Janet's uncle lived in the building. He was an overeducated but charming old coot who had worked for the State Department for the better part of three decades as a foreign service officer. He had served in numerous embassies in Europe and Latin America, as well as in the department's building in Washington's "Foggy Bottom" district, again alternating between European and Latin American affairs.

Janet was used to coming by unannounced, sometimes to drop off DVDs or groceries. Her uncle never minded and rather liked the young skirt rustling by, even if it was look-don't-touch.

Janet moved fast. Her whole job was about working fast.

She was in the lobby seven minutes later, carrying a small bag with two new DVDs for her uncle. She blew past the doorman with a big smile and a crack of Juicy Fruit. She zipped up to the fifth floor. She found Carlos in the utility closet near the elevator, studying the cable wires.

"Ready?" she said.

"Let's go," he said. He handed her a pair of mini-transmitters. She tossed off her parka and stashed it with him in the closet.

The baby transmitters were the size of old-style soda bottle caps. They were stick-ons, marvelous little instruments, imported from Singapore by the US government at a cost of five bucks each. They could monitor conversations in the apartment in one file. At the same time, in another file they could eavesdrop on the data from even a perfectly configured — and supposedly secure — wireless computer network. They could also pick off the radio emissions of a computer monitor. Their operational life was one year. They had an ultrahigh-pitched whine, which only a few people could hear. Otherwise, they were fine. Unless discovered. Unless someone's dog went nuts-o.

In addition to the work Carlos had done in the basement, he reckoned he might as well drop these babies on the victim. They were a safety net. If one system of electronic ears failed, the other would likely be up.

Now Carlos and Janet set to work. They slipped latex gloves onto their hands. Carlos killed the elevators and stood lookout. Janet used the passkey to enter the target apartment.

No one home. No pets. No alarms. The break-in trifecta!

She took stock quickly. It was a woman's apartment. Normal kitchen and dining area. Living room filled with bookcases. This victim read a lot; maybe that was part of her problem and why she was getting a wire dropped on her. People who read a lot were always suspicious.

There were books in different languages and a travel poster in Russian with a picture of Gorbachev or Yeltsin. Janet could never tell those two eighties Russian guys apart. One had a weird bald head and looked like someone had smashed a strawberry on it; the other dude had too much white hair, like a polar bear. One stood on top of a tank to put down a coup and the other one did a Pizza Hut commercial. Who cared who was who? Why not a poster of Lenin saying, *Workers of the World, Shop Till You Drop!*?

Near the music system, under the Russian poster, there were scattered a ton of CDs. Many of them foreign. How much more subversive could it get?

There was a coffee table in the living room. Janet stuck her hand under its lower shelf, six inches above the floor. She positioned one of the bugs on the underside of the shelf and stuck it in place.

There! Done!

She went to the bedroom. She looked around quickly. She saw a few photos of the resident with a guy. She was wrapped up in his arms at some beach somewhere. Whoa! The lady looked good in a Speedo two-piece and the guy was six-pack hunky; she looked like a real estate agent and he looked like a lifeguard. Didn't really look like subversives, but troublemakers frequently don't. Keep it moving. These two must have done something or they wouldn't be on the bug list.

Janet got to her knees in the bedroom.

The second transmitter fit perfectly under the headboard of the bed. Janet smirked as she fixed it in nicely. Bedroom bugs were endlessly entertaining.

She jumped back to her feet. Test time. Using her cell phone, Janet accessed both transmitters and primed them. They worked perfectly.

Great. Keep moving.

Another thirty-six seconds and she was out of the apartment and into the hall. Less than three minutes had passed. She gave a thumbs-up to Carlos, who was still standing guard.

No words were spoken.

Carlos went back to the elevators and turned them on. Janet popped into her uncle's place and dropped off the DVDs. She'd get her feedback this evening as, again by coincidence, she was planning to come over for dinner and some tutoring on a graduate history course she was taking.

She retrieved her parka from the utility closet.

In another five minutes, she was crossing the lobby to leave. The doorman winked at her. She smiled and winked back. Secretly she was grossed out. He was probably three times her age.

A *rich* older man, well, *that* would be something else! But a doorman . . . ? No way!

Carlos was already back out to the street via the service entrance.

They rendezvoused in the car shortly thereafter. Their day was going well. They just had one other job that day. Considering they were funded by the taxpayers, they were an outstanding example of governmental efficiency.

FOUR

Outside, another unusually cold winter evening chilled the city of Washington. In her office, Alex shut down her primary desktop. She checked the email on her secondary computer, the one that carried classified material, and spotted a message that had come in minutes earlier. The sender wasn't anyone she recognized. She grimaced. "I'm never going to get out of here today," she whispered to herself. She clicked her mouse to open the email. Hopefully it was something she could dispatch easily.

The correspondence opened. Might have known.

For her eyes only:

```
THIS IS A CONFIDENTIAL COMMUNICATION FROM THE
GOVERNMENT OF THE UNITED STATES OF AMERICA AND
IS INTENDED FOR THE ADDRESSEE ONLY. IF YOU HAVE
RECEIVED THIS EMAIL IN ERROR PLEASE IMMEDIATELY
DELETE THE EMAIL AND ANY ATTACHMENTS WITHOUT
READING OR OPENING THEM.
```

"Yeah, sure," she muttered, slightly louder. She had lately developed the habit of speaking to the computer, usually insultingly, when she was not happy with what was on the screen. The final hours of a long day often brought forth the habit.

But there was no changing the message. She had been summoned to a specially arranged meeting at the State Department the next morning. Main Building on C Street NW, only about a twenty minute walk from Treasury along Pennsylvania Avenue and then down Twenty-first Street. Room 6776 B. No further details. She was to be there at 8:00 a.m.

She stared at the text for a moment. Was this email official or some sort of late hours after work prank? The State Department?

Streamlined and reorganized in 2007, FinCen was a division of Treasury, which interfaced with other American intelligence agencies:

the FBI, the National Intelligence Service, the CIA, the recently over-hauled Immigration and Naturalization Service. It was through this connection that Alex knew a man named Robert Timmons. Timmons was an agent of the United States Secret Service, assigned to the Presidential Protection Detail at the White House. He was also her fiancé, the wedding scheduled for the following July. On Alex's left hand, she wore the diamond that Robert had given her.

The Presidential Protective Detail, these days known as "Einstein Duty." All the presidents had their nicknames among the men and women of the Secret Service who guarded them. Clinton had been "Elvis." Clinton's successor, Bush 43, had been the "Shrub." This president, newly elected the previous November, was Einstein, a tribute to not how smart the president was, but how smart the president *thought* the president was. That, and a certain distracted way with clothing.

A slight smile crossed her lips as she reconsidered this email.

Maybe . . .

She picked up the phone. She called Robert at the White House.

In addition to being one of the new president's bodyguards, Timmons was also a liaison officer between the United States Secret Service and foreign protective services. He wasn't above sending her an amusing personal message disguised as a work document. He came on the line. His tone said all business.

"Hey," she said. "Is this the Black Dog?"

His tone softened and changed as he recognized her voice.

"Hey," he answered. "That's what some people call me."

"Know anything about this meeting I've been summoned to tomorrow morning?"

A pause, then, "I know all about it," he said.

"Why do *you* know all about it and *I* don't?" she asked. "Or is this a trick to get me to call you so we can have a late dinner?"

"I'll accept the late dinner," he said, "but the State Department thing is legit." A pause, then, "Think Orange Revolution."

A beat, then she had it. "Ukraine? The old Soviet Republic?"

"Bingo. Presidential visit to Kiev in one month. I hope your passport is current."

"The passport is current, but *I'm* not. Can't you scratch my name off the list?"

"I suppose I could have, but I didn't."

"After nearly getting blown apart in Lagos, the only place I wish to travel to is the gym. Right now." She glanced at her watch. Almost 7:00 p.m.

He was silent on the line.

"Then, Greek food later?" he asked.

"Why not?" Her tone was one of resignation. "Maybe I can impale myself on one of the skewers. Or better, I'll impale you for not knocking my name out of contention."

"Perfect," he answered. "I'll see you at the Athenian at ten."

"Bring flowers," she said. "I'm furious with you."

"I wouldn't dare arrive without them," he said.

Alexandra and Robert had first met four years earlier in Washington.

Their respective employers required that they continue their "second language" studies. So both had signed up for advanced Spanish literature at Georgetown University.

They read bizarre but intriguing South American novels in the original Spanish, which they both spoke fluently. Characters could talk directly to angels, demons, and sometimes even God. They sprouted wings and flew. They wore magic rings, mated with wild animals, and slipped in and out of various universes.

Alex and Robert hit it off right away, bonding over shared experiences: rural blue-collar work — Alex had worked on a cattle ranch as a teenager, Robert put himself through college working on a dairy farm during summers in Michigan, feeding the livestock, hauling hay, shoveling manure, and taking the occasional dead calf out for burial. A few weeks after the course ended, the Secret Service assigned Robert to Seattle, then to San Francisco, while Alex worked out of FBI bureaus in Philadelphia and New York. They did not see each other for three years. Later, in 2006, when Robert was assigned to the White House and she had taken a job at Treasury, he tracked her down.

He was a Secret Service agent, but he was also a guy with a golden Labrador retriever named Terminator, whom he referred to as "my kid from a previous relationship." He was Alex's chess partner, a guy who wore a Detroit Tigers cap at home while he watched sports on TV, often reading a new book at the same time. He was a four-handicap golfer and an amateur guitarist. Unlike anyone else she knew in law enforcement, he could play the opening riffs from Led Zep's "Black Dog." This had given him a great nickname in his class at the Secret Service Academy in Turco, Georgia.

Black Dog.

Many of his peers still continued the nickname. It was often his code name on assignments. Alex though it was funny. In many ways, Robert was as white bread as it got. And he sure wasn't any dog. Hence the nickname, perfect in its imperfection.

Time out: Washington insiders knew Secret Service personnel to be very arrogant. Touchy. Showy. Difficult to deal with because they always put agency agenda in front of everything, even personal relationships.

Time back in: "People ask me what it's like to date a Secret Service agent," Alex would tell people. "I always say, 'I'm not dating a Secret Service agent, I'm dating Robert Timmons.'"

Time out again: Secret Service people were also known to be the best shots in the federal service. According to folklore, they could knock a cigarette out of a chickadee's beak at fifty feet and still leave their little feathered pal chirping. The bird shouldn't have been puffing on a butt anyway.

Time back in: On the pistol range, Alex was better than Robert, something he grudgingly admitted and admired.

So the relationship worked. He was everything to her and vice versa. He was also something that no one else had ever been, the one person who was always there for her and accepted her exactly the way she was. He was also the guy she went to church with on the Sunday mornings when he wasn't on duty, which was something very special to her.

They were completely compatible.

He set up a chessboard at her apartment. He liked the figures from the Civil War and they always had a game in progress. Sometimes when he would stop by they would do two moves each or four or six, the game ongoing day-to-day.

He loved leaving affectionate or funny notes for her to find, nestled into towels, under a piece on the chess board, in the medicine cabinet, in the freezer, on a window.

Anywhere.

Then, while away, he would send her emails suggesting where to look for the notes. "Look inside the Rice Chex box," said one. "You might want to look behind the television," said another.

He could not travel without calling her. If they could, and they always managed some way, they always had a last kiss before he went out of town on an assignment.

They both shared a soft spot for country music, to the horror of many of their eastern friends. Heartfelt white soul music by people whose names could be reversed and they'd still work just fine-and-perfect, good buddy: Travis Randy, Tritt Travis, Black Clint, Paisley Brad, Gill Vince.

Even Chicks Dixie.

"Waffle House music," Robert called it. But he admitted that he liked it too, with particular attention to early Cash Johnny.

Waffle House music. Robert always made her laugh, but they had had their serious talks, too, both before and after deciding to get married. Robert had talked with her once about dying young.

"If I'm going to go to my grave early, 'in the line of fire' isn't a bad way," he said. He told her that if something should happen to him after they married, she should allow a new husband to find her. It was all hypothetical, of course. Neither of them ever thought disaster would really strike. Horrible things like that only happened to other people.

FIVE

A lex drove to the gym on Eighteenth Street and Avenue M.

In the women's locker room, she changed from her office attire — "the monkey suit," she called it — into trim dark shorts with a Treasury Department insignia, a sports bra, and a loose-fitting white T-shirt with the likeness of U2 — the Irish band, not the Ike-era spy plane — across the front.

She went to the second floor and spotted some friends shooting hoops, including a close friend, Laura Chapman, who worked at the White House as a liaison between Secret Service and other protective agencies. Laura, a former Secret Service agent herself, now had her own agency and department.

Alex and Laura worked their way into a co-ed game, along with two other women. The gym was warm, noisy but not deafening. Two other games were in process on nearby courts. Runners thundered around the track overhead, and somewhere in one of the side rooms a martial arts class was in session. A local George Washington University kid carried the whistle, wore a striped shirt, and reffed the pickup hoops. He called a good game.

Recently, two new guys had worked into the rotation. She didn't know much about them. A wiry guy named Fred, who looked like a banker: all arms and elbows and jerky movements. The other players called him, "Head and Shoulders." Another new guy was Juan, a muscular Latino who was a law student at GW. At five foot six, he was a tall dwarf in basketball terms — shorter than both female players. But he made it up in speed and court savvy. The star of the game this night, however, was another regular gym rat, a strapping big guy from North Carolina named Benjamin.

Alex liked Ben, though she knew him only from the gym. He'd been a marine gunnery sergeant in Iraq where a remote control roadside bomb in Anwar Province had taken off his leg below the knee.

Now he had a prosthesis for a right leg. He was in the process of getting his life back together.

Ben was the slowest guy on the court, but at six four was also the tallest in more ways than one. He played center for Alex's team and played it with a huge heart. From her guard position, Alex loved to feed him quick high passes that he'd pick off with his huge hands and slam into the hoop. The half-court helped him.

On this night, Alex's team won 29 – 25. Ben had a dozen. Alex had five, including a swished trey from the corner.

After the game, she toweled off, went to the weight room, worked out, ran laps, and was finished. She grabbed her stuff, headed back to the lockers and showered quickly. She changed into casual clothes and joined Robert for dinner, arriving a few minutes after ten at the Athenian in Georgetown.

The Athenian was a small, dimly lit Greek seafood place, red and white checkered tablecloths with a small candle on each table. The place was owned by a hulking mustached guy named Gus.

Gus was an émigré from Cyprus, a moody quick-tempered sort but an admirable host. Gus liked to pour free glasses of ouzo for his favored guests, which included anyone who displayed a reverence for Maria Callas, the Aegean, or a knowledge of soccer.

Gus was a fervent DC United man, but also followed, for reasons known only to himself, Barcelona FC and Chelsea via Gol TV. There were team photos and other colorful regalia around the place to bear witness.

Gus liked straight-arrow law-enforcement people. When Robert or Alex called ahead for a reservation, Gus always had a quiet table waiting and made sure the wine was chilled and the fish was cooked perfectly with the right herbs and a generous plate of rice and vegetables on the side. And so it went on this particular evening.

Robert had remembered the flowers, which Alex received with a kiss and a smile. Still, however, the idea of another high-anxiety trip abroad was something about which she was less than enthusiastic. The discussion went there quickly.

"And more language lessons?" she asked. "What's this? My penalty for already speaking five fluently?"

"I hear Ukrainian is similar to Russian."

"Similar but different. Like a tiger to a mountain lion."

"Look, tomorrow morning you'll get a briefing. If you want to say no, you'll get the chance."

Alex and Robert split a sea bass that Gus had grilled to perfection. Midway through the meal, Alexandra looked up and saw a man at the end of the bar whom she thought she recognized.

She caught him watching her. Rather than smile or acknowledge her, he looked away.

She was always noticing details: where someone stood, what they wore, who was present, who wasn't. She knew the man at the bar hadn't been there when she came in. She remembered that the far end of the bar had been empty.

So he had come in after her. Or had followed her.

Her hand went to Robert's. She was about to give him a signal, to ask him to check the guy out. But Gus wandered to their table to chat.

Gus embarked on one of his tamer political rants, something to do with a Michael Moore film. Alex nodded and refrained from joining in. Robert listened patiently. Alex watched the man at the bar while Gus was speaking, using the mirror above the bottles. The man kept watching her.

It wasn't her imagination, she decided. He was watching her and she had seen him before. But where? When their eyes hit head-on a third time, he finished his drink and hurried out.

Gus talked them into the baklava for dessert. Alex was glad she had spent the time in the gym. Gus's baklava was delicious but portions were huge. Gus left their table. Alex turned to her fiancé. "There was a man at the bar watching me," she said.

"Can't say I blame him."

"This isn't funny, Black Dog."

Robert looked to the bar. "Where is he?"

"He just left."

"Okay, if he comes back in, I'll pull the jealous boyfriend thing and shoot him. We might have to delay the wedding for twelve years while I serve the manslaughter charge."

"That's not where I'm going with this."

"Okay, *you* shoot him."

"Not funny," she said. "He was watching me as if he had a reason. He just left. Fifteen seconds ago."

His eyes slid to the doorway. "Okay," he said. He got to his feet, went quickly to the door, opened it, and stepped out into the cold.

He was back in a minute. He sat down.

"Sorry. No one," he said. "Just the usual muggers, junkies, and car thieves."

"Not in this neighborhood," she said.

"Okay. I didn't see anyone."

She settled slightly. "Thanks for looking."

Being with Robert relaxed Alex, but through the whole evening there was only one thing she could think about.

Ukraine. She began to ask more questions.

"Look, normally they'd leave you alone after the Lagos trip," he said. "But you know how the government works. Turn down the mission they want you to do and you don't get the next one that *you* want to do."

There was another quiet moment as she simmered. "Next you'll tell me it's not dangerous."

"It's *very* dangerous."

"So why don't they get one of those big six-foot-six guys in your department, the ones who block the view of the president when the prez is dumb enough to go shaking hands in hostile-action places like New York and Philadelphia?"

"They need a woman for this and all of the six-six ones are currently playing pro basketball."

"Very funny," she said. "Look, what do they want me to do? Go undercover at a night club in Odessa, swing around a pole, and listen in on gangsters?"

"I'd love to see that," he said.

"Well, you won't. And neither will anyone else."

"Presidential visit," he said. "That makes it top priority. The personnel computer spit out your name as someone who spoke Russian as well as the other major European languages. I saw your name because the list went by the Secret Service. They're probably going to want you to learn some Ukrainian too."

She groaned. "I was planning to spend the next few weeks planning a wedding, sitting around with my husband-to-be, going to movies, and maybe reading a trashy novel or two."

He shrugged. "Sorry," he said.

The more she thought about it this evening, the more the concept bothered her. She made a mini-decision. She would listen politely at State the next morning and then give them a firm but polite, "No way!"

There. That settled that.

Who was in charge of her life, anyway?

Her or them?

SIX

Alex returned home, picking up her mail in the lobby, giving a friendly nod to the concierge. She fumbled with two bags, flowers, and mail as she walked past.

Alex lived alone in a one-bedroom apartment in a modern building called Calvert Arms Apartments on Calvert Avenue and Twenty-fourth Street, in the Cleveland Park neighborhood in the northwest quadrant of the city. It was a comfortable quiet building built in the mid-sixties, filled with young single people — students, interns, people just starting their first job out of college, and government retirees.

She waited at the elevator. It was stopped on the fifth floor. It seemed to be permanently stopped, as if someone was saying a long-winded good-bye.

She grew impatient. The elevator began to descend slowly.

Five, four, three ...

She knew everyone on her floor, at least by sight. Who was making her day longer than it had to be?

Two, one ...

The twin doors of the elevator opened. Out stepped a young woman who could hardly have been older than her early twenties, very pretty in a heavy parka and tight jeans. A student at one of Washington's numerous colleges, Alex figured.

Students, along with career-beginners, were the Calvert Arms' bread and butter. They coexisted with the old women in their seventies, eighties, or even nineties who had moved into the place when it opened forty years ago. At that time they had been middle-aged empty-nesters. Time had passed. They were still empty-nesters, just twice as old. Their ex- or late husbands had been pushing up daisies for decades.

The younger girl hurried to the front door. Alex stepped into the elevator and rode to the fifth floor.

Her neighbor across the hall had started out as a friendly nodding acquaintance and ended up becoming a good friend in a fatherly kind of way. He was a scholarly sixty-year-old who had worked for the State Department for twenty-eight years. Now he was a retired diplomat who played catchy pop music from Latin America each morning as she was on her way to work. The Calvert Arms was pretty well insulated, but you could hear music in the hallway through the doors.

Alex had on occasion met him going into or coming out of his apartment and had struck up a conversation in the laundry room, commenting on his choices. She too liked Lucero and the late Rocío Dúrcal. One day she couldn't help asking, "Do you only listen to women singers?"

"Absolutely," he replied. "My virtual harem."

That conversation and similar exchanges had let to a curious kind of friendship with a man who could be friendly but was self-contained, seemingly content with his virtual harem. He had few visitors. They spoke only Spanish with each other and his was easily a match for hers. She called him Don Tomás, though he was no Latin. He had invited her and Robert in for brunch one Sunday. They had been fascinated by his collection of art deco prints from the 1920s and 1930s, notably some beautifully preserved works of the French artist Tamara de Lempicka. They were all stylized pictures of beautiful women.

"Another part of your virtual harem?" she had asked.

Don Tomás had replied in the most relaxed manner imaginable, "Absolutely."

This evening no sound from the vocal part of the virtual harem was coming through the door as she passed. She hoped nothing had happened to him.

She glanced at her mail and dumped it on the dining table. Then she stood perfectly still. Was everything exactly as she had left it? Was there something that she sensed, but could not quite put a finger on? Alex was unsure. Coupled with the appearance of the man at the bar in the Athenian, the evening had taken on a strange spin. Or was she just overanxious about a Ukraine trip that she didn't want to make?

She sighed. She dismissed it. She placed the flowers in a vase.

She was in bed by midnight. She set the alarm for 6:00 a.m. Then, as she settled in to sleep, her eyes shot open. A realization hit her.

The man she had seen at the bar in the Athenian?

He was Fred, one of the two newcomers at the gym. Away from the gym, in a Burberry raincoat instead of basketball togs, she hadn't recognized him. Chances were that he couldn't figure out why he thought he knew her. Well, now she could relax. At least she knew why she recognized him and from where.

She closed her eyes. Minutes after her head hit the pillow, she was sleeping soundly.

SEVEN

The next morning at 7:54 a.m., Alexandra walked through the entrance to Room 6776 B at the main building of the United States State Department, a vast complex covering two city blocks. To come in out of the cold she used the Twenty-first Street entrance, which had been built in the 1930s as the War Department for the US Army.

The handsome marble-clad art deco lobby had a curious mural featuring peaceful Americans at work and prayer. They were surrounded by protective soldiers in gas masks, cannons, and then-new-fangled four engine bombers. Out of embarrassment at the martial theme, the State Department had long hidden the picture behind a curtain, but later more tolerant minds had prevailed.

Alex's meeting was not in that part of the building but in the much larger part built onto the original structure under Eisenhower. The two components had different floor plans that Alex always found disorienting when she paid a visit.

She arrived in a small conference chamber with a circular table and six chairs.

The room tone was flat. Soundproofing. It was like being in a clinic for hearing aids. One window with double glass overlooked an inner courtyard with a statue of Atlas holding up the globe.

At the desk, a small, trim man adjusted his spectacles but did not look up. He had a mop of gray hair and a reddish face. He wore a crimson tie and a cream-colored shirt. He was flanked by a half-finished container of Starbucks, the tall one with the full day's caffeine punch. He had a look to him that she thought she recognized, one of those surly old State Department retirees who get called back for special assignments.

"Alexandra LaDuca," he said, finally glancing up. "Good morning."

"Good morning," she said. "Yes. I'm Alex."

He stood. He was a smaller man than she had initially thought, not much more than five foot four. Over the years, she had learned to be wary of tiny people who might harbor king-sized complexes.

"I'm Michael Cerny. State Department. Please sit," he said. He indicated that she could take any seat at the table.

"I'm afraid I don't even know what this is about," she said. She sat, choosing a seat that allowed several empty chairs between them.

"Doesn't matter," he said. "This is the government. We're soldiers, aren't we? We march forward. Orders."

"Sometimes," she said.

"Sometimes," he agreed.

"I suppose you better bring me up to date," she said. "Explain where I'll be marching. You talk and I'll listen."

"Quite," he said. "Excellent. Tell me. Water? Coffee? Tea?" he asked. There was a service on a side table, which held all three.

"Just some water," she said.

He fetched it. She glanced around the room. One reading chair. Reading lamps. Prints from second-rate paintings. Landscapes meant to offend no one. Bookcases without a single book. Michael Cerny sat down again.

He related that he was actually retired from the State Department after thirty-five years but had returned for a special ten-week assignment. She was off to a good start, assuming he could be believed. She had called that one perfectly.

"Well," he said at length. "You have an overseas mission coming up. The president is going to Ukraine," he said. "Official state visit. Arriving February fifteenth."

She glanced at a calendar. It was January seventh. The trip was five weeks and two days away.

Cerny kept talking. He was, he explained immodestly, an expert on Ukraine, having done two tours in the capital, Kiev, and one in Washington on the Kiev desk, the office that handled Ukraine.

"I'm not an expert on that part of the world," she said. "The Ukraine."

"I suppose then, that's where we should start," he said, "with terminology. They don't call it that with the definite article any more," he said, his tone almost professorial. "Let's backtrack a little. In English, the country was formerly usually referred to with the definite article.

The Ukraine, as in *the* Netherlands or *the* Congo or *the* Sudan. However, usage without the article is more frequent since the country's independence."

"Thanks for the tip," she said.

"Don't mention it. The modern name of the country is derived from the term *ukraina* in the sense of 'borderland, frontier region, or marches,'" he said. "Not that you care, but these meanings can be derived from the Proto-Slavic root *kraj-*, meaning 'edge, border.' In Russian, a modern parallel for this might be — "

"The Russian word *okraina*," she said. "Meaning 'outskirts' and *kraj* meaning 'border district.' I speak Russian fluently."

"Your language skills are the major reason you're here," he said.

She sipped some water.

"But why do I make the point?" he asked. "Because Ukraine has always been exactly that. A border district. A frontier. A dangerous unruly place. Europe ends there and Asia begins. Asia begins there and Europe ends. One could put forth the theory that civilization sometimes ends there and chaos begins."

Alex smiled. Cerny was coming across as a windbag, but at least he was an entertaining and knowledgeable windbag.

"Now," he continued, "I'm not so dumb as to think that you don't pick up rumors within the government, same as everyone else," he said. "Particularly with a fiancé who is employed by the Secret Service. So you probably knew already about the visit."

"I'd heard a few rumors," she admitted.

"Of course you have," he said. "In any event, the intent of the trip is to bolster the pro-Western regime elected in the *pomaranchevya revolutsia*, the 'Orange Revolution' of 2004 and 2005. A secondary intent is for the president to look good here at home. We should get a good reception there." He switched gears again. "I also note in your c.v. that you're a member of a Christian church."

"That's a private matter, but yes, I am."

"Then this should appeal to you. The Orange Revolution was widely supported by the Christian churches of the region."

"Fine, but it's not just a Christian thing," she said. "Anything that threw off the old-style Soviet way of doing things would have its appeal to any fair-minded people, wouldn't it? Religious freedom is for everyone, or did I misread the Constitution?"

"Point well taken," he allowed. "You're rather a live wire, aren't you?"

"I like to believe in what I'm doing, particularly if I'm doing it for my country. I might be a little strange in that respect."

"I can respect that," he said. "So let me refresh your memory on events from southeastern Europe from the past few years. The Orange Revolution."

Cerny spoke without notes. Alex listened intently, matching Cerny's official account of events with what she remembered from the news.

The Orange Revolution was a series of protests and political events in Ukraine from November 2004 to January 2005, in the immediate aftermath of the run-off vote of the 2004 Ukrainian presidential election.

The 2004 presidential election in Ukraine had featured two main candidates. One was sitting Prime Minister Viktor Yanukovych, supported by Leonid Kuchma, the outgoing president. The opposition candidate was Viktor Yushchenko, leader of the Our Ukraine faction in the Ukrainian parliament, also a former prime minister.

The election, which Cerny had observed personally, was held in a highly charged atmosphere, with Yanukovych and the outgoing president's administration using their control of the government for intimidation of Yushchenko and his supporters. In September 2004 Yushchenko suffered dioxin poisoning under mysterious circumstances. While he survived and returned to the campaign trail, the poisoning undermined his health and altered his appearance dramatically.

"To this day, Yushchenko's face remains disfigured," Cerny added without emotion. Orange, he continued, was originally adopted by the Viktor Yushchenko's insurgent camp as the signifying color of his election campaign. "Later the color gave name to an entire series of political terms, such as *the Oranges* for his supporters. When the mass protests grew, and especially when they brought about political change in the country, the term *Orange Revolution* came to represent the entire series of events."

Protests began on the eve of the second round of voting, Cerny remembered, as the official count differed markedly from exit-poll results. The latter gave Viktor Yushchenko an eleven percent lead, while official results gave the election win to Yanukovych by three percent.

Yanukovych's supporters claimed that Yushchenko's connections to the anti-incumbent Ukrainian media explained this disparity. But the Yushchenko team publicized evidence of many incidents of electoral fraud in favor of the government-backed Yanukovych, events witnessed by many local and foreign observers.

The Yushchenko campaign publicly called for protest on the dawn of election day, November 21, 2004, when allegations of fraud began to spread. Beginning on November 22, 2004, massive protests started in cities across Ukraine. The largest, in Kiev's Maidan Nezalezhnosti, Independence Square, attracted a half million participants, who on November 23, 2004, peacefully marched in front of the headquarters of the Verkhovna Rada, the Ukrainian parliament, many wearing orange or carrying orange flags, the color of Yushchenko's campaign coalition.

"I remember them chanting, hundreds of thousands of Ukrainians filling Kiev's Independence Square on the evening of November 22. *'Razom nas bahato! Nas ne podolaty!'* 'Together we are many. We cannot be defeated.'"

Emerging from a sea of orange, the mantra signaled the rise of a skilled political opposition group and a determined middle class that had come together to stop the ruling elite from falsifying an election and hijacking Ukraine's presidency.

The Ukrainian capital, Kiev, was the focal point with thousands of protesters demonstrating daily. Nationwide, the democratic revolution was highlighted by a series of acts of civil disobedience, sit-ins, and general strikes organized by the opposition movement.

Over the next seventeen days, through harsh cold and sleet, millions of Ukrainians staged nationwide nonviolent protests. The entire world watched, riveted by this outpouring of the people's will in a country whose international image had been warped by its corrupt rulers. The nationwide protests succeeded when the results of the original run-off were annulled, and a revote was ordered by Ukraine's Supreme Court.

Under intense scrutiny by domestic and international observers, the second run-off was declared to be "fair and free." The final results showed a clear victory for Yushchenko. Yushchenko was declared the official winner and with his inauguration on January 23, 2005, in Kiev, the Orange Revolution had peacefully reached its successful conclusion. Similarly, by the time Yushchenko's victory was announced, the Orange Revolution had set a major new landmark in the post-communist history of Eastern Europe, a seismic shift westward in the geopolitics of the region.

"Now, in terms of an impending presidential visit, particularly with a new president in office, normally we have a bigger planning stage. But the president is adamant. Political statement, diplomatic statement. All the usual bull. It means we have the normal three months of preparation and only one month to do it."

"How do I fit in?" she asked.

"Rather perfectly," he answered. "Your c.v. is very impressive," he said. "You should see some of the people I've had to prep. Dumb as doorknobs would be both an understatement, as well as an insult to the world of doorknobs." He paused. "So. Would you be willing to accept a temporary assignment to Ukraine?"

She sighed. "Only if you talk me into it," she said.

"Well, the Ukrainians are wonderful people, warm and much deserving of any help we can bring them. They've been oppressed for centuries, most recently by Soviet Russian Communism. Fascinating place, rich in history and culture."

"Keep going," she said.

He paused, taking a glance down at her c.v. again. His tone changed.

"Look," he said. "The assignment will call on your previous experience in undercover work. It presupposes an ability to learn functional Ukrainian in one month and have the pre-existing knowledge of Russian. So this, right here, is your opportunity to get out of jail free."

"How?"

"You can avoid the assignment by being unable to pass the basic language requirement in Russian. Follow what I'm saying?"

"Yes. But I'm fluent in Russian and everyone who knows me knows that."

"We have two other agents we can interview. They're not as quali-fied as you, but it's an imperfect world. We can talk to them."

She pondered it for a moment.

"I came here this morning with the intent of declining this assign-ment," she said. "But it's also not in my nature to back away from challenges."

He let a moment pass. "That's in your c.v. too," he said.

"So tell me more about the assignment," she said. "I'll listen."

He smiled in response. "Let's talk about you. It's one thing to read a c.v., quite another to learn personally about someone who might take an important job."

"What are you asking for?" she asked.

"Tell me about yourself," Cerny said. "How you came to be here. How you're so good as an investigator, with a firearm, and in so many languages. I'm fascinated."

She opened her mouth to answer. Before she could speak a word, he added one more request. "Explain it to me in Russian," he said. "I'd like to hear you speak."

Alex fumbled at first. Not withstanding that souvenir poster in her living room, she hadn't spoken Russian in years.

But she began.

Her Russian kicked in quickly.

EIGHT

Spanish was spoken in my home," she said. "My mother was from Mexico City and was a devout Roman Catholic. She moved to Southern California in her twenties to marry my father. He was an aircraft worker with McDonnell-Douglas. His parents had been from southern Italy and had come to America in the 1920s."

"But if he was Italian, they didn't speak Spanish to each other," Cerny observed.

"No," Alex said with a smile. "Of course not. But I used to visit my grandparents, *los abuelos mexicanos*, during summers. And I loved listening to the Latino pop stations out of Los Angeles and San Diego. By seven years old, I was completely bilingual. Then there was church Bible study. I was raised as a Protestant. My father's choice to convert — because it was 'more American.' But my mom insisted one Sunday a month on taking me to 'her' church. It was a traditional Roman Catholic one in Santa Clarita. They spoke Spanish and Latin there. When I first heard Latin, I wanted to study it. My dad didn't object. He just stayed home to watch the Raiders and Dodgers."

Cerny laughed. "Sounds like *my* dad," he said, still in Russian.

Alex continued. Her father had died in an auto accident in the summer of 1993 when she was fourteen. While Alex settled into her faith and found solace there, her mother settled into an alcoholic depression. Alex buried herself in schoolwork. A year later, her mother's health worsened. Alex went to Mexico for a year to live with an aunt and their family. Her fluency in Spanish gelled. "I read voraciously in two languages," she said. "Histories. Biographies. Novellas. Journals about *el beisbol* or *el fútbol*. Anything."

She came back overprepared for her own school system, she explained. A local guidance counselor in California had ties to the East Coast. When her mother's illness worsened, Alex was sent to a rigorous boarding school in Connecticut on full scholarship.

The school allowed her to excel. She branched from Spanish into

French. She won a summer internship in Europe. Off she went to work in the rural Camargue region on a ranch in southern France, an area famous for prized bulls, wild ponies, and a pounding summer sun.

"You know what? I turned into a French cowgirl," she said with a laugh. "And I loved every minute of it. The local people had a wonderfully unique culture. Distinctly Mediterranean. After six weeks, I came home and without even realizing it, I was fluent in a third language."

"So where did the Italian come from?" Cerny asked.

"That was easy," she said. "My dad was from Sicily, as I said. I wanted to know about his culture too. I started studying on my own, but since I knew Spanish and French and had had some Latin, it was very easy. I was lucky and won another summer internship the following year, this time in art history and Italian literature."

Cerny laughed. "I'm not sure how 'lucky' that was," he said. "Obviously you had a gift and studied hard."

"What's the old saying?" she asked, stumbling a little and trying to translate into Russian. " 'Luck is the confluence of hard work and opportunity?' I spent three weeks in Rome and another three in Paris."

She was fascinated at the time, she recalled, by the work of the Italian poet Dante, whose *Divine Comedy* consigned deathbed confessors to the first circle of Purgatory. She switched into Italian. "During life they made God wait for them. So after death, they must wait for God."

Cerny blinked. She knew she had him. A personal first for Alex, switching from Russian to quote into sixteenth-century Italian.

Returning to Russian, she described how during her senior year at boarding school, she won a prestigious state university scholarship in California. It was a remarkable achievement, and yet she would always associate her senior year with tragedy. Two days after her eighteenth birthday, one week before graduation, her mother died.

The funeral was in Veracruz. She attended the funeral and missed her own graduation, which at the time barely seemed to matter. She was now on her own. She spent two years at the University of California at Berkeley where she was one of the more conservative students. It was a lonely stretch, by her own admission. She had many acquaintances but made few close friends. She joined a local Episcopal church, formally transferring from her old Methodist church. "It felt more comfortable," she recalled, "almost as if it were midway between my father's faith and my mom's."

Though she skipped over it here with Michael Cerny, as she entered her early twenties, Alex had transformed from a cute but shy teenage girl into an attractive young woman. She had attained her adult height of five foot seven, but all the sports and training through the years had given her a strong, lean but feminine body. And she had acquired an ample amount of self-confidence and self-assurance to go with it.

She had her mother's dark Spanish eyes and brown hair. She dated occasionally but there was never anything serious. She tried smoking but quit quickly. She dabbled in liquor but kept it in moderation. She tried pot once at a party and didn't care for it or its foggy-headed lifestyle. So she never touched weed again or any harder drugs, either, but she had acquaintances who dabbled in both.

She supported herself through work-study jobs and her scholarship. She played soccer for the freshman women's team at Berkeley and ran track. After two years, she transferred to UCLA. She selected an undergraduate major in business and finance and found herself surrounded by a coterie of unusual friends. Many students were foreign, Asian and European. Many were American.

Her political views came more into focus at this time too. She disliked the right when it became intolerant and bigoted. She disliked the left when it strayed into cuckooland. She liked to think she was of the reasonable center, able to listen to an argument from either side and make her own judgments accordingly.

At this time, she was also finding that her abilities in language combined with a business major were opening doors for her, not the least of which was even more financial aid for her academics.

"When I was at UCLA," she said, "I started Russian, then accelerated my study by taking a summer semester in Moscow. It was an exciting place to be, during the Gorbachev era, perestroika, and all that."

Cerny nodded. "Have any Russian boyfriends?" he asked.

"Is that any of your business?"

"No. Just curious."

"An American girl in Moscow who spoke Russian?" She laughed. "I got a lot of offers," she said, "but didn't accept very many of them. Too much vodka, водка, too many late nights at the Café Pushkin after going to the clubs, can interfere with a girl's studies."

He raised an eyebrow in mild disbelief. "Sure," he said. Then he moved on.

The following summer, she worked in New York for a big time entrepreneur named Joseph Collins. She worked in his international finance section. Her work was so diligent that he took personal note of her. Collins promised her a job after university, if she was interested.

She switched her course of study to a five-year program that led to a master's. By the time the University of California awarded her an MA, she was fluent in five languages, had a thorough understanding of modern European politics, art, and history, and had a master's degree in finance.

After UCLA she turned down an offer to return to New York and work for Joseph Collins, who was expanding his business in Latin America. Instead, she wanted to stay in California. She worked for Wells Fargo for eighteen months in one of their international divisions, overseeing *hipotecas* — mortgages — in the Latin community.

She used her Spanish daily.

"I was bored stiff," she said. "But I stumbled across a few cases of bank fraud in the mortgage division. So I grew interested in law enforcement. I applied for a job with the FBI."

"And they hired you," Cerny said.

"About two weeks later," she said. "I filled an immediate need."

The FBI sent her to their academy in Virginia. She excelled at all aspects of her training, from the book-learning to firearms to the bone-crunching unarmed combat.

She advanced quickly. Her linguistic skills were of immense value. She was assigned to Internet rackets and bank frauds in her first years, initially working out of the Newark, New Jersey, office, then moving around the country on a case-to-case basis.

She was socially traditional as an adult, which meant she didn't have affairs all over the place, same as she had been as a student. But she liked looking good. She wore sharp suits, blouses and skirts that appealed to men. She worked hard at the gym to maintain a good physique. So her clothes flattered her, and she chose them carefully, same as the men she went out with.

In recounting this part of her life to her interviewer, small scenes in her past played out in her mind. She had realized as an adult that her late father had had his quirks. He had not been a faithful churchgoer but he had been a believer nonetheless. At Alex's twelfth birthday, her father had given her the small gold cross on a delicate gold chain that she continued to wear around her neck. It was the only thing of substance that he had given her that she still owned. As jewelry went, it was modest, more meaningful in what it represented than its actual monetary worth. But she had worn it now for almost eighteen years.

Wear it in good health, he had told her, in good health and in good fortune.

So far, she always had.

And over the years, she had even developed this inadvertent habit of taking the cross between her thumb and forefinger; she would hold it and touch it thoughtfully at times when somehow she sought guidance or when she was deep in thought. For whatever reason, emotional, spiritual, or just plain quirk of habit, it comforted her. The cross was something that had once been in her father's hand. It represented both his and her beliefs and kept his spirit close.

"Someday," her dad had once said to her many years ago, "your faith will be challenged. You'll think it has been destroyed. You'll think your world has come to an end. That's when this cross will mean more to you than you'll ever know. When that happens, find your way back to the cross."

This advice had come from a casual Methodist who wasn't the best at showing up for Sunday services. Faith survived, she had concluded, in some strange dark places. It was a conversation she would never forget. Ever since that day, the small gold cross had been part of her.

Sitting in the small office at the State Department, her thoughts came back to the present. As she sat in front of Michael Cerny and concluded her dialogue in rapid now-excellent Russian, she realized she was fingering the small gold cross as she spoke.

If it bothered him, he didn't mention it. But she knew he had noticed.

"That's really about it," she said with a shrug and a smile, switching back to English. "What else can I tell you?"

NINE

Extraordinary," Cerny finally said, following Alex back to English.
"Thank you," she answered. "But let's get real. I don't speak any
Ukrainian. Drop me down in Odessa and I'd be unable to find either
the bathroom or the railroad station."

"Oh, I disagree," he answered. "You speak Russian. Odessa is an
almost one-hundred percent Russian-speaking city. It was part of Russia until given to the Ukrainian Soviet Socialist Republic by Khrushchev in the early fifties as a PR move," Cerny said.

"Touché," she said. "I warned you I didn't know the area."

Cerny enjoyed scoring the point. Then he got back to business.

"Under normal circumstances, I wouldn't think a three-week crash
course in Ukrainian language and culture would do much good," he
said. "But you're not the normal student and you're not being primed
for a normal task. How much do you know about the relationship between the Russian and Ukrainian languages?" he asked.

"I know they have a similar grammar, a common root, and a similar vocabulary, while sounding quite different," she said. "I traveled
in eastern Hungary and Poland the summer I was in Russia. I heard
some Ukrainian near the borders. I could understand a little. They're
similar, much like French and Spanish are similar."

"Good start," he said. "Assume that Ukrainian assumes the role of
Spanish in your analogy and Russian is in the role of French. The river
that runs through Kiev is known in Russian as the Dnieper. The *dn-YEH-
per*. In Ukrainian it's the Dnipro, the *dnee-PRO*. When I was there Kiev
was almost entirely a Russian-speaking city. I suspect that it remains
so despite efforts by the new government to promote Ukrainian."

"When were you there?" she asked.

"From 1996 to 2005," he said. "Due to Soviet dominance, every
Ukrainian, at least in Kiev and the eastern Ukraine, is usually able
to speak Russian fluently even if he regards Ukrainian as his native
language. I would have meetings at the foreign ministry and speak in

Ukrainian, and then on the way out, my interlocutor would turn to his secretary and speak in Russian. Typical."

Alex nodded.

Cerny continued. "How much do you know about the great famine of the 1930s in Ukraine — the so-called 'fake famine'?"

"Again, I'm not an expert," she said, "but I've read my history."

In truth, she knew quite a bit. The 1930s were the bleakest years in Ukraine's modern history. The famine of 1932 and 1933 killed up to ten million people. Largely unknown beyond Europe, the famine was still called the 'fake famine' by older Ukrainians. Fake, because it was manufactured in Moscow and didn't have to happen.

The Ukraine had normally been a fertile agricultural region. But the harvests of those years were confiscated by the Soviet Red Army under orders from Joseph Stalin, the Soviet dictator. Under the new policy of Soviet agricultural collectivization in the 1930s, all grain from collective farms in Ukraine was shipped back to Russia, leaving millions of Ukrainians to starve to death. It was part of a brutal campaign by Stalin to force Ukrainian peasants to join collective farms while local farmers resisted all such collectivization. It was an era when almost all food disappeared from the rural areas of Ukraine. Children disappeared as cannibalism became widespread. About a quarter of Ukraine's population was wiped out.

The Ukrainian famine, or *Holodomor*, was one of the largest national catastrophes of the Ukrainian nation in modern history. While the famine in Ukraine was a part of a wider famine that also affected other regions of the USSR, the name *Holodomor* was specifically applied to the events that took place in territories populated by ethnic Ukrainians. It was sometimes referred to as the Ukrainian Genocide, implying that the famine was engineered by the Soviets, specifically targeting the Ukrainian people to destroy the Ukrainian nation as a political factor and social entity. Some modern-day revisionists and apologists suggest that natural causes such as weather, inadequate harvest, and insufficient traction power were also among the reasons that contributed to the origins of famine and its severity. Yet the truth was that Moscow initiated a policy of death by forced starvation, all for the greater glory of the godless Soviet Communism.

To Alex it was just one more example of the suffering and atrocities of that part of the world. The Nazis had killed nearly one and a half million Jews in Ukraine after their invasion of the Soviet Union in June 1941. But with few exceptions, most notably the 1941 slaughter of nearly thirty-four thousand Jews in the Babi Yar ravine in Kiev, much of that history had gone untold. Alex shuddered. So much of the twentieth century had been a testament to man's inhumanity to man, a complete loss of any moral compass.

Thinking about all of this today in a room with Michael Cerny, Alex felt her indignation rising, three quarters of a century later. Anyone could say or think whatever they wanted about Christians, but true Christians sent missionaries all over the world to help *feed* people, not starve or murder them.

"*Holodomor* in Ukrainian means 'death by hunger,'" said Cerny, bringing it back to the 1930s. "In central Kiev there is a monument to those who perished in the *Holodomor*. The president of the United States is going to lay a wreath at the base of that monument."

"In my humble opinion, long overdue," Alex said.

"It's also a controversial gesture. The Russians still deny that the fake famine was official policy. Never mind the fact that there are documents in Moscow above Stalin's signature ordering the Red Army to shoot anyone caught hiding food."

It was hard to comprehend. The Soviet policy of that era was as mind numbing and satanic as the extermination camps of Nazi Germany or the attacks on the civilians at the World Trade Center on September 11.

Cerny leaned down to a briefcase beside him. "I'm glad you seem to be a sympathetic soul," he said. "I'm going to give you some reading. For right here, right now," he said. "The first thing you need to know is the current political situation vis-à-vis Ukraine and Russia. Under Vladimir Putin, who's basically a gangster, Russia is under its worst dictator since Stalin."

"You think he's *that* bad? Worse than Khrushchev?"

"'Vlad the Impaler Lite,' we call him. Look, you be the judge," Cerny said. "Putin has allowed Gazprom, the state gas company, to raise its own army. He had the editor of *Izvestia* fired for publishing accurate accounts of the Beslan school hostage crisis. And now he's founded these ideological youth groups called *Nashi* to do the pro-Putin brainwashing of the first generation to come of age in post-Soviet Russia. They look like all those sick little Aryans in the Hitler Youth of the 1930s. On top of that, he's out of official power as president, but still runs the country. You decide."

"You make a solid case," Alex said.

"But how does that affect us? Today. With the president going to Ukraine?" Cerny asked. "The Russians have never accepted the idea of an independent Ukraine. But Ukraine is about to join NATO. There are groups of fanatically pro-Russian, pro-Putin young Ukrainians who are opposed to this. They've vowed to cause trouble, probably when our president visits the monument to the victims of the famine. The president is visiting to maintain a visibility in support of the pro-Western elements, not the least of which are the members of the many Christian churches in Ukraine."

Alex was always smart enough to listen to an expert on anything.

"Why would ethnic Ukrainians support the Russians?" she asked.

"While there are Ukrainians who are strongly committed to Ukrainian independence from Russian influence, there are others who actually regarded Ukraine's past as one of partnership with Russia in what was a superpower," he answered.

"Despite the famine?"

"Despite the famine," Cerny said. "The Russians hoped to eventually turn the Ukrainians into Russians, something not all that difficult given the relative similarity of the languages and cultures, including the common Orthodox faith prior to the Russian Revolution. The Russians ruthlessly repressed any stirrings of Ukrainian nationalism but offered 'little brother' status in return. An ambitious young Ukrainian who bought into the concept could wind up in the Politburo in Moscow. Ukraine's first president, Leonid Kuchma, was actually the boss of the factory that made the ICBM's that were the Soviet Union's nuclear deterrent."

"But there is Ukrainian nationalism? Right?" Alex asked.

"Absolutely. It is centered in western Ukraine, where the Austro-Hungarian Empire let Ukrainians be Ukrainians as long as they were loyal to the emperor in Vienna. But the tension between Ukrainian nationalists and 'Russophiles' is a basic fault line that runs through the country. And it has implications for the US. The Ukrainian nationalists want a Western-oriented Ukraine, one that joins the European Union and NATO. The Russophiles don't necessarily want to reestablish the Soviet Union, but they want a close 'special relationship' with Russia."

Cerny had organized some hard-copy reading for her. He had a briefing booklet, a blue-jacketed document of several dozen pages folded into something with a blue cover that looked like an old-fashioned examination book. He placed it on the table. Then he gave her another half dozen books.

She knew the drill. It was a day of background preparation.

"Choose a comfortable place to read," he said, motioning to the sofa and the chairs. He glanced at his watch. "Take the rest of the day with this stuff. Let's meet back here at 4:30 this afternoon, and we'll speak further. How's that?"

"That would work," she said.

Alexandra broke the official seal on the table. She scanned the stiff opening pages that warned of dire legal sanctions for blabbing what she was about to read.

Cerny slid a paper along the desktop in her direction. "The confidentiality agreement," he said. "If you please . . ."

He slid a fountain pen along with the paper.

She picked up the pen and looked for the space for her signature.

"You might wish to read it first," Cerny said. "Always a good idea, you know."

She was midway through the form already. At the top was the usual "steam-rollered eagle," the flattened bird that was the Great Seal of the United States.

Olive leaves in one talon and the arrows in the other. Then the content:

```
I, Alexandra LaDuca, have today read the declara-
tions of USSD Intelligence dossier UK-3-122a-2008.
I resolve and warrant that I will not divulge
any part of this report. . . .
```

Blah, blah. . . .

She scanned to the end. The normal crap that no one paid much attention to. Probably everything in the documents had already been in the *New York Times* anyway.

She signed.

Cerny left the room. Alexandra stayed at the conference table and began to read.

TEN

At first it was mostly issues of taxation, import fees and quotas and copyrights. Dull stuff, which she plowed through in the morning. Then she moved to the more incendiary stuff and started it during the afternoon.

A remorseless image of Ukraine came through: one of the most corrupt places on earth. Late in the day, one particular topic heading seized her, and the subsequent document seemed to sum up everything else she had read.

Partners in Extortion:
Criminals and Public Officials

The most pernicious element of organized crime in Ukraine is the alliance among former Communist Party elite, members of the law enforcement, security apparatuses, and gangs of professional criminals. Much crime in Ukraine combines government officials' access to information or goods with the use or threat of force by organized criminals.

Crime and corruption had soared in Ukraine over the past decade. Since gaining independence during the Gorbachev era, the corruption of the Soviet years had been replaced by energetic gangs of organized criminals.

In the summer of 2004, several American corporations had considered investing a total of two billion dollars in Ukraine, mostly in the appliance field. After investigating carefully, each of the corporations decided that the business environment there was fraught with both financial and physical danger.

Drug traffickers, particularly those involved with heroin, laundered money through casinos, exchange bureaus, and state banks.

The banks provided criminal groups with information about businesses' profitability and assets, which the gangsters used to extort money from them.

Criminals and public officials often colluded. The extortion was imaginative. Criminals, for example, extorted money from businesses by threatening to sell the information they illegally obtained from banks to the tax police. In turn, tax officials sold their information about businesses with crime groups in return for a share of the money the crime groups extorted from the same businesses.

Alex continued reading.

> Infiltration by criminals into Ukrainian legislatures remains rampant. More than thirty members of the Parliament might be tried on criminal charges if they were to be stripped of their governmental immunity. Fifty-four legislators, at minimum, elected to local political bodies, also have criminal backgrounds. The problem of corruption extends to the highest levels of government in Ukraine. Ukraine's prime minister in 1996 - 97, reportedly made tens of millions of dollars annually through his company's license to import natural gas and oil.
>
> [Case officer's note: The former prime minister is also suspected of having stolen $2 million in state funds and stashed some $4 million in a Swiss bank during his premiership. In February 1999 Ukraine's Supreme Council stripped the former premier of his parliamentary immunity, and a warrant was issued for his arrest. He is currently incarcerated in the United States. See also, UK-2-356-2006.]

Alex moved along. There was a section on the growing narcotics problem in the newly independent state.

> Ukraine has become a significant conduit for Afghani and Southwest Asian heroin bound for European and American markets. . . .

A dismal feeling started to creep over her. Ukraine made Lagos look like Disneyworld. Why was she spending her life with such things?

She flipped to the final pages, absorbing quickly.

> The main trafficking routes are (1) the sea-
> ports of Odessa and Sevastopol; (2) Transdnies-
> tria is often mentioned as a high-risk region
> for drug trafficking. The drug is stockpiled in
> this region for further trafficking to Ukraine
> and Romania. The drug continues by air from the
> military airport next to Tiraspol or by trucks
> toward the north of Moldova and then contin-
> ues to Poland, Lithuania, or Latvia. The route
> continues in Transdniestria, reenters Ukraine
> at Chernivtsy to move westward to Hungary and
> Romania. (3) There is an important transit from
> the eastern border of Ukraine with Russia. The
> trucks from Northern Caucasus cross the border
> at Taganrog, Luhansk, and Kharkiv en route to
> Hungary and Slovakia. (4) Another transit route
> goes through the eastern border of Belarus with
> Russia since there is no control of this border
> with Russia. . . .

Ukraine lacked adequate law enforcement and an independent judiciary which might be able to block the influence of organized crime. Alex's eye settled on a concluding sentence, a masterpiece of understatement.

> Institutionalized Ukrainian corruption is
> perceived as the worst in the world. This is no
> small accomplishment.

Nigeria, but worse. Oh, Lord …

She finished the document. She closed the briefing book and settled back to think. A few moments later, the door opened and Michael Cerny reappeared.

He poured himself a fresh container of coffee and sat down. "Now

I need to mention something else," he said. "*Ask* you, actually. Up until this moment in time, have you ever heard of something called 'The Caspian Group'?"

"No. Should I have?"

"Maybe, maybe not," he answered. "But that's why you're here. They're based in Kiev. They're a private equity firm. Almost all of their investments are related to government contracts in Ukraine and in the United States. They cozy up to the proper people in both governments, take a financial position in an industry, then move into the industry."

He took a long drink of coffee.

"Let me illustrate to you how it's structured," he continued. "Picture a triangle with the three corners anchored by the politicians on one, the military on the second corner, and the oil and gas industries on the third. Then picture a second triangle, interconnected with the first. Concentric perhaps. Now assume that one triangle is an American one and the second is Ukrainian. Then figure that the two triangles, for financial purposes, are interlocked and service each other. Any corner can connect with any other corner. Follow?"

"Of course I do," she said. "But what's the big deal? The world runs on the oil and gas business. I'm sure the triangle is filled with venal overpaid self-serving people making their fortunes off the backs of ordinary folks. Deplorable, but nothing new."

He broke open a new file, which he pushed before her.

"I'm going to give you this to take away," he said. "An FBI dossier on Caspian Industries. Examine what Caspian Industries is doing. A lot of money and a lot of product disappear into thin air, escaping taxation completely. See the problem?"

"Yes," she said.

"When you go to Ukraine," he said, "you're going to meet this man." He reached into his pocket and pulled out a picture. He handed her the photograph. "Say hello to Yuri Federov."

Alex looked at an eight-by-ten surveillance shot of three men, all of whom had the Russian wise-guy look to them. They were seated at a table in a night club. There were women at the table who looked as if they were being paid to be there, one way or another. Everyone was smoking. The men had short haircuts, almost shaved heads, and wore silk suits with open collars. A Eurotrash night out. There was a stage show going on in the background. More women, but not much clothing.

Cerny leaned forward and pointed an index finger at the man in the center.

The man was a thick-browed thug with wide shoulders, a lantern jaw, and a hard dark pair of eyes. He wore some sort of a medallion at his open neck. Alex could see that it was no companion piece for the gold cross she wore around hers. She fingered her own neckwear for a moment.

"Yuri Federov is probably one of the most dangerous men in the world," Cerny said. "And certainly no friend of the United States."

"Where was the picture taken?" she asked.

"Paris. A night club somewhere near the Place Pigalle where he had interests."

"When?"

"Late last year. December."

"Who are the others in the picture?" Alex asked. "Are they important too?"

"Since you inquired," Cerny said, "the one on the left is Marko Marchenko. The one on the right, a man named Michael Kozlov. A couple of gangsters. You don't have to worry about either of them." He paused. "Former business partners of Federov. They disappeared, and now he owns full interest in the club. Draw your own conclusions."

"Thanks. I will. But I'm sure you have more details."

"Kozlov's remains were found in an industrial furnace in Toulon, in the south of France. Marchenko was found in the River Seine outside of Paris. He was in sixteen feet of water, but his feet had been wired to a diesel engine block. According to the autopsy, he had been alive when he was dumped from a bridge. Then again, apparently Marchenko had been alive when he was shoved into the furnace."

She handed the pictures back. Cerny placed them in the files he was giving her.

"Federov," Alex asked. "Is he Russian mob or Ukrainian?"

"He's a blend of both. Worst aspects of each. Ethnically he's Russian, socially he's a Uke. Maybe if you can get close enough you can ask him that question. We wouldn't mind knowing what he considers himself."

"How close am I going to get?"

"As close as you can," Cerny said. "And I should warn you. This guy knows how to turn on the charm. For whatever reason, a lot of women find Federov irresistible."

She laughed. "An over-steroided gangster isn't exactly my dream date."

If Cerny was amused or encouraged, he wasn't showing either.

"Yuri Federov owes the United States government about ten million dollars in personal taxes," Cerny said, "and that's just the beginning of it. Then there are the corporate taxes and a long list of criminal activities just since we last deported him."

"And?" she asked.

"He has agreed to meet with a representative of our government to discuss the issues," Cerny said. "That's where you come in. One of the most dangerous men in the world. Federov is your assignment."

ELEVEN

In Rome, an American couple known as Chuck and Susan were looking for a taxi. They had stumbled out of a late-night watering hole in the medieval neighborhood of Trastevere shortly after 3:00 a.m. on January 8.

It had been quite an evening, starting with "ladies night" at Sloppy Sam's, a popular pub on Campo dei Fiori. In front of the commemorative statue of the philosopher Giordano Bruno, who was condemned to death by the Catholic Church for heresy in 1600, beefy shirtless male bartenders had served up discounted shots of Sambucco. Susan loved to sit at the bar, knock back the Sambucco, and ogle the guys, while Chuck worked the room for single women. Then Susan and Chuck had moved on to the Zeta Lounge around the corner. There a reveler could have all one could drink for one low price, and usually did. The Zeta was also well known as a pick-up joint for couples looking for a special sort of excitement.

Giordano Bruno, the philosopher, would have had much to ponder if he could have seen his old neighborhood and the debauchery that took place there nightly. But there wasn't much old Giordano could do about it, other than roll in his grave for another few hundred years.

There was a taxi sitting down the block from the Zeta Lounge when Susan and Chuck emerged. The cab's meter was off, the driver with a mobile phone to his ear, talking furtively.

Secrets. Chuck and Susan had plenty of secrets.

First off, it was the secretive nature of their work and the European nightlife Susan and Chuck loved most. That and the risqué thrills. The thump of the clubs late at night, the dancing, the drinking, living for the moment. The lasting friendships among those who worked in the clubs in London, Paris, and Rome. The casual assignations when couples would pair off, including each of them without each other.

Then there was their professional life.

Their current assignments would soon have them in one of the old Soviet republics again where it was even colder and nastier. Oh, well, they were making a good career out of their involvement in this international cloak-and-dagger stuff.

They had money stashed in Switzerland, New York, and the Bahamas. If they weren't doing it, they reasoned, someone else would be, just not as well. So they continued on. Across the street an American tourist was barking through a souvenir-shop megaphone asking a woman to hike up her skirt, eliciting laughs from his friends and, surprisingly, the woman herself, who was equally soused. Chuck was amused.

The sidewalk was terrible. Ice everywhere. Chuck checked the shadows in the doorways nearby. He was always on his guard. He never knew when someone would step out of such shadows and, from some grievance in a complex past, raise a weapon. He always had an eye out for anyone who might recognize them and know them by their real names. There would be no end to the inconvenience that would cause.

They were partners in a gray world, a world of the political underground, half-formed conspiracies, plots, and counterplots. They thought of themselves as warriors for a good cause. The truth was, they were closer to foot soldiers, and the validity of the cause was open to argument.

Their last work project, the one in Paris, had ended in complete disaster. So they weren't celebrating this evening. They were trying to forget.

Chuck led Susan to the single waiting cab. He and Susan had a local woman in tow, someone they had met at the club. The woman had called her roommate and left a message, or so she said. She was staying over with "a friend" that night. So as she dropped her own cell phone into her purse, she was at liberty.

Chuck approached the cab. The driver looked up. A face that could have belonged to one of Caesar's centurions. Drawn, unshaven, and tired.

"Le Grand Hotel," Chuck said. He spoke good Italian but an American accent was noticeable.

It made perfect sense. A hotel with a French name in the heart of Rome. Back in the 1890s when the hotel had been named, the French motif had suggested elegance, as if the Romans didn't have enough on their own. Yet the hotel was still the most luxurious in Rome. "*Vittorio Orlando Strada, numero tre,*" he continued.

The driver replied with a grumble. He was still gabbing into his own cell phone. "*Non in servizio,*" he answered, pointing to the roof of the cab. "Off duty."

"I'm never off duty, so why should you be?" Chuck said. "I'll make it worth your while."

The cabbie looked at him as if he didn't understand. The Italians were good at that. Chuck dug around his pocket and came up with something the driver *would* understand.

An American fifty-dollar bill. Nice and crisp. Ulysses S. Grant in one of his sober moments.

"This is yours on top of whatever's on the meter."

The cabbie hesitated. Then, "*Va bene,*" he said.

The cabbie put his hand on the fifty. Chuck eyed the vehicle from end to end, trying to assess any potential danger.

Standard Roman cab. A white Mercedes with a fresh dent in the driver's side front door. Brand new and it had already collided with the rest of the city.

He dug deeply into the cabbie's eyes. Standard sorehead Roman cabbie.

"I'm getting cold," the second woman said, stamping her feet briskly, holding her legs tightly together against a sharp breeze. "Are we going somewhere or not?"

"Okay," Chuck concluded. He released the fifty. They huddled into the taxi, the three of them in the back seat, Chuck on the far end, Susan in the middle, their new friend on the end. The cabbie pulled away from the curb.

Chuck eyed the hack license that the driver displayed on the dashboard. More bad vibes: The name was Italian but the face was something more Eastern. Still, one saw just about everything these days in the capitals of Western Europe.

Maybe Chuck was growing too paranoid. Maybe he had spent too much time in the back alleys and out of the sunlight for his government. Maybe he was too old for this sort of thing. Sometimes he didn't even recall what name or identity he was using.

From that point, the ride was over in a few seconds.

It was past 3:15 a.m. The streets that were busy by day were deserted now. On the wet asphalt of the via Piemonte, the driver suddenly took a sharp turn down a narrow dark side street. Chuck saw that there was a larger car a quarter of the way down the street, blocking passage. The cabbie pulled up hard and brought the taxi to an unsteady jolting halt.

Then in the fraction of a second before anything happened, Chuck knew that he was a dead man and Susan wouldn't fare much better. Another car screeched up behind them. Chuck heard car doors open and slam shut. At the same time, his lateral vision caught the movement of a fourth man emerging from between two parked cars to the side.

Chuck started yelling. Loud, accusatory, and profane.

Chuck and Susan felt the weight of their own cab change as both the driver and the woman, knowing what was happening, bolted and fled, leaving their doors open.

Susan's voice, high and anguished, "What the—?"

Chuck's voice followed close, frenzied. "It's a trap!" he screamed.

With one hand, Chuck worked his door handle. It was locked.

His other hand groped for a gun, the one that he had chosen not to carry that night because so many of the clubs did searches. In his peripheral vision, he saw two men swiftly approaching the car. Dressed in black, they pulled down their ski masks, stealthy and efficient as a pair of urban panthers.

In his last moments, Chuck noticed that one of the men had an obvious nervous tic under the ski mask. And he recognized their weapons, Sig Sauer P226s. But he didn't have time to think about any of it. All he could think about was how the enemy had known that somehow he was unarmed that night. Then, in a final realization, that came together in his mind also. The woman they had met in the club. She had fixed their execution via her cell phone.

The gunmen lifted their weapons. Silencers.

In a final reflex for life, Chuck smashed his huge body against the car door to his side. It didn't budge. He swung an elbow and shattered the window. The glass tore into his sleeve and slashed his arm as the rest of the window poured to the asphalt. He groped wildly for the outer door handle and worked it.

No luck. The cab was a high tech roach motel. The door wasn't going anywhere and neither was Chuck.

The gunmen raised their weapons. Chuck and Susan raised their arms to protect themselves. They heard little past the first shots as their bodies exploded in searing pain.

The first volley of bullets tore into their arms.

Their screams and their blood filled the night. The next volley of shots ripped into their heads and necks. The rear door lock finally gave way when bullets tore apart the locking mechanism.

Chuck's body fell face down onto the street, his legs remaining in the taxi. Susan's body remained huddled against Chuck's but convulsed with each of a half dozen hits from the assassins' weapons. Their bodies were still moving slightly when one of the gunmen stepped forward and pumped two final bullets into each of their heads.

Then, working swiftly, the assassins dragged their bodies from the taxi to the van behind them. They loaded the corpses into the truck. As the gunmen disappeared into the night, one of the follow-up crew threw a gallon of gasoline on the stolen taxi. Then he threw a match. A mini-inferno followed; lights started to go on around the block and the team of killers fled the scene of the executions.

TWELVE

A few hours after the sun rose in Washington, Alex sat in her office at Treasury and received the official word from her boss, Mike Gamburian. She was to reassign every other case on her docket and immerse herself in Ukrainian language and background immediately. She would have two days to wrap up current operations and complete their reassignment to others. Half the cases she was happy to be rid of. And strangely enough, she was quickly coming around on the idea of getting back out into the field.

"As a precaution, you should visit the firing range again," Michael Cerny had also said, walking Alex to her car earlier in the day. "Colosimo's. You know the place, right?"

"I know it."

"Do you still have a weapon in good working order, or should we requisition a new one for you?"

She had grown up around long weapons and had trained meticulously with handguns during her years with the FBI. But since she had come over to FinCen, target practice had been an extracurricular that she hadn't had much time for. Frankly, she had always enjoyed it and had missed not doing it. She was good at it.

"I have a Glock 9," she said. "It's only two years old."

"Excellent. I suppose you use it to keep the squirrels out of the bird feeder in your off hours."

"How did you know?"

"We know everything. Federal permit still valid?"

"If you know everything, you should know that."

"I'll take that as a yes," he said.

"Good idea."

"Then you're in business. I doubt that you'll see anything other than a few ceremonial cannons going off in Kiev," Cerny said, "but one can never be too cautious. Keep in mind, you won't be able to travel with your Glock. So if you need one in Ukraine, your control officer will need to deliver it to you."

"I understand," Alex answered.

"I do admire your attitude," he said.

And in truth, with recurring images of the chainsawed auto in Lagos still in her mind, the opportunity to hit the firing range again could do no harm. Might as well pack some heat if she was going to a dangerous place. And during a presidential visit, the more friendly weapons in the area, the safer the president would be. At least, that was the theory.

To end the same day, Michael Cerny took Alex to another room in the State Department. There he introduced Alex to the woman who was to be her Ukrainian language instructor over the next two weeks.

Her name was Olga Liashko, and she was built like one of those Soviet tractors from the mid-1950s. She was a large thick woman, taller than Alex by half a head, wider by the same amount. She was somewhere in her sixties and had grown up during the Soviet era. It stood to reason that she hadn't led the easiest or happiest of lives. She had been raised in a military family from Odessa and spoke Ukrainian natively.

A mass of gray hair framed Olga's bulky face. The whites of her eyes were more pinkish than white, and she had heavy bags beneath both. She wore a work shirt like a blazer and had on a pair of men's painter's pants. Her stomach was low and chunky like an old man's. An idle but amusing thought shot back to Alex. A girlfriend in college used to call the condition Dunlap's disease. Her belly "done lapped" over her belt.

"Olga has been with us since emigrating in 1982," Cerny said helpfully. "She's FSI's top Ukrainian gal," he said, referring to the Foreign Service Institute. "None better. Knows the language forward and back. Her dad was in the military in the big war. Olga will be your tutor. You start tomorrow afternoon."

Olga said nothing. Instead, she stared disapprovingly at the younger woman, running her gaze up and down. Alex was six inches shorter, and half her weight.

"Very nice to meet you," Alex said.

"Be prepared yourself to work hard, study hard, and including nights I advise you," Olga said. It was clear which language Olga would be teaching and which one she wouldn't.

The teacher handed Alex a Ukrainian language textbook. More homework. Cerny had arranged a special room in the State Department for the lessons so that they wouldn't have to go out to FSI in Virginia. He gave the room location.

Alex flicked through the book. It looked even more tedious than she had reckoned. Olga must have read her mind, because she snorted.

Alex looked up. She could tell: Olga didn't just have a chip on her big round shoulder, she had a couple of chips on each with plenty of room to spare.

Where does the government find these people? Alex wondered.

Wondered, but didn't ask.

"I'm looking forward to the lessons," Alex said.

It was that most unusual of statements for her: an outright lie.

THIRTEEN

At 8:00 that evening, Alex presented herself to Colosimo's. She checked in with her federal permit and waited for her turn on the firing range. She had not used her weapon for several months. She purchased a new box of nine-millimeter ammunition. She had a respectful relationship with firearms — she had drawn her weapon many times but had never had to fire one against another human being. She prayed that she never would.

But she knew she could, if necessary. Her possession of a weapon in the line of duty for the FBI had been a professional necessity. She might have been dead without it. And tonight, she just plain felt like blasting away at some paper targets.

At half past the hour, in a heavy white UCLA sweatshirt, her new basketball sneakers, and a pair of red Umbro soccer shorts, she took her place on a firing line. Trim, twenty-nine, and with long legs that seemed chiseled from all the workouts, she drew the usual set of approving and admiring glances from the predominantly male clientele.

Though flattered, she ignored it. She also made sure she also had her goggles and an anti-noise headset. An agent she knew had once practiced on a range without the ear protection and been cursed with permanent ringing in the ears from then on. Heaven knew there was no apparel sexier than those two items.

She opted for bull's eye targets, the old-fashioned ones with concentric circles, rather than a man-shaped target. The target was twenty-five yards away. Before shooting, she fiddled with the two adjusting screws across the top sight until they appeared to be fixed just right.

The range was warm. She ditched the sweatshirt and was down to a blue and gold UCLA T-shirt. Much more comfortable.

She hadn't held the Glock for several weeks. It felt different in her hand, as if it were ready to fight her. She adopted the ungainly squatting position that had been standard for shooters for the past several decades, raised the pistol in both hands, held it forward, and focused on the sights with her right eye; she didn't close the left, but paid no attention to what it saw, not that anyone ever can aim a pistol in a quick draw combat situation.

Front sight. Front sight.

That was the key, one FBI instructor had told her once, the rock upon which the Church of Almighty Handguns was built. A shooter had to see the front sight and let the target remain hazy in the background.

Otherwise, might as well call in an air strike.

So, front sight, front sight.

In the notch of the rear sight, a frame, she saw the bull's eye of the target.

Her hand was steady. She squeezed the trigger, fighting the temptation to flinch. Even under the headset, the blast of the weapon was frightful. The recoil was less than expected, however, and her aim had been near perfect on the first shot. Not bad after a long layoff.

She fired six more rounds quickly and succinctly.

She brought the target forward.

Wow! She was pleased. Pretty good for a chick who hadn't fired a shot in many weeks. Three hits right in the center. The others were off by less than an inch. She should do this for a living.

She sent the target back and reloaded, firing another seven rounds. Even better. One shot on the perimeter of the smallest circle, the others within it.

A real life shootout didn't usually allow the luxury of a studied methodical aim, so she quickly graduated to a more challenging shooting pattern. She would raise the weapon quickly, no time to aim, and try to hit the center of the target.

This she did with great skill as well.

She had, in fact, forgotten how good she was at this. She continued on the range for another twenty minutes. Her skills were in excellent shape, she decided. She was more than pleased.

She went through two boxes of ammunition. Seventy-two shots, then stopped. She didn't want her wrist to be sore the next day. She had done enough. She turned.

An even larger group of guys was watching her, their jaws open in admiration. Must have been a dozen of them. When she caught them looking, she was at first slightly resentful, then almost embarrassed.

Then they gave her an impromptu round of applause and a couple of "good ol' boy" whoops of approval. She was their type of female, at least for the moment. She shook her head, laughed, and accepted the compliments.

"Beginner's luck," she said, carefully locking her weapon in its case.

"Yeah. Some beginner," one of the younger guys said knowingly.

"Do they all shoot like that at UCLA?" another one asked.

"Only on the basketball court. Have a good evening, boys," she said.

And she disappeared.

FOURTEEN

She phoned Robert from her car. He was home, following a difficult shift at the White House. Some wacko had breached the security at one of the side fences by climbing over and making a run for the Rose Garden.

The nut case hadn't gotten more than twenty feet when he was tackled. But such occurrences always ramped up the anxiety level of the entire Presidential Protection Detail. And of course, investigations had to follow and the breach needed to be studied. One never knew whether one small incident was a prelude to something larger. In the post–9/11 world, acute paranoia was the new normal.

"So I'll bring dinner over. How's that?" she asked Robert. "We'll have dinner; then I have to scoot. I have this Ukrainian stuff to study and a final FBI report to read."

"Dinner would be great," he said.

She picked up some Thai takeout for dinner after leaving Colosimo's. Robert lived at a big apartment complex on Dupont Circle, a building known as the Bang Bang Hotel because there were so many well-armed government security people living there and so many single women. It was two blocks away from the Iraqi consulate.

They split dinner. They lingered together for a while afterward, but Alex was back at her place by midnight.

She showered and spent half an hour looking at her Ukrainian books and working with one of Olga's CDs. What an unforgiving language. Not like French with its charm, English with its complexities, Italian with its musicality, or Spanish with its history. But the tough parts — the existence of "perfective" and "imperfective" and the whole tangle relating to verbs of motion — were the same as in Russian, so at least Alex wasn't starting cold.

To ingratiate herself with her teacher, she made a point of memorizing several phrases in the fifth chapter. She found that she could concoct a primitive conversation with reasonable ease.

Ja vpershe u vashij krajini. I'm in your country for the first time.
Ne serdytesja na mene. Please, don't be angry with me.

Toward 1:00 a.m., she thought she heard a sound at her front door, almost like someone trying the knob. Cautiously, she went to the door and looked through the peephole. She relaxed. It was her neighbor, Don Tomás, the retired diplomat, wandering in, a little tipsy, humming a Lucero tune, his keys clicking against his own door.

She rechecked her own locks. She brewed a decaf cup of tea. She settled down at her kitchen table, positioning herself where she could see the door.

There was one final task at hand for the evening. She needed to read the final file she had been given, the FBI dossier on The Caspian Group.

She settled in and took the first step toward knowing Yuri Federov too well.

FIFTEEN

FBI Document UK-2008-5AR-2a
Subject: Ukraine> Organized Crime> Overview>
Caspian Group> Federov, Yuri
Initial report date: June 19, 2005
Amended: (7 times, most recently:) March 12,
2008
Source: Federal Bureau of Investigation, Wash-
ington DC
Status: Highly Classified; AA-2
Author: S.A. Diane Liu, FBI, New York, Southern
District

The Caspian Group (TCG) is a Ukrainian energy
conglomerate doing business with Western Europe
and the United States and presumably Asia. The
latter market will warrant careful scrutiny in
the future.

The unofficial head of operations of TCG is
a Ukrainian of Russian extraction named Yuri
Federov. Almost uniquely, TCG functions without
actual incorporation within Ukraine.

Their assets exceed one billion dollars (See
Chart 56-2008a-1). They invest in all financial
sectors common to entities that do business with
governments and the military. Additionally, they
have positions in all criminal enterprises in
Ukraine, including heroin and trafficking in
women.

TCG's young enforcers were trained by veterans
of the Soviet war in Afghanistan. They are infa-
mous for their extreme brutality. Their victims

are usually business people who have balked at extortion demands. Victims have been known to have been repeatedly stabbed and tortured, then mutilated before they are butchered. Others have been fitted with concrete cinderblocks and thrown live into the Desna River. The wave of terror has been so hideous that it has scared many of the competing crime groups away from doing business in Ukraine. . . .

Since the collapse of Communism, українка мафія, "ukrainka mafia," the Ukrainian Mafia, has become bigger, more brutal, and better armed. It is now as wealthy as any Russian crime cartel. It wields the same worldwide influence as its major counterparts in Colombia. The Ukrainian Mafia traffics narcotics, currency, human sex slaves, handguns, carbines, submachine guns, antiaircraft missiles, helicopters, plutonium, and enriched uranium.

{Editor's note: In 2006, Deputy Assistant Director Kevin Fosterman, then the FBI's supervisor in charge of organized crime, warned Congress that the Ukrainian mob, which had 37 crime syndicates operating in 24 North American cities, had "an outstanding chance" of becoming "the most dangerous crime group in the United States.". . .}

In the United States, the activities of the Ukrainian mob alarm all law-enforcement agencies. By 1996, the Ukrainian Mafia had supplanted the Cubans as one of the top crime groups in South Florida and has supplanted many established African American and Sicilian interests in Detroit, Chicago, Philadelphia, St. Louis, and New York. . .

Until recently, the most powerful Ukrainian crime figure in the United States was Yuri

Federov. In November of 2004, undercover surveillance {*Note: Court wiretap approved 10/29/04
by Hon. Ira J. Cohen, 2nd Circuit Court, Brooklyn,
NY* . . .} Federov boasted of his brutish past,
but he also mentioned his charitable activities
and described numerous fund-raisers that he had
held for Catholic charities at a restaurant and
Brooklyn night club he owned called Old Odessa.

Federov is a nonpracticing Eastern Orthodox
Christian but holds Israeli citizenship. He in-
sists that he never stole from religious organizations. But according to statements he made
to undercover agents for the New York City Police Department, the "overhead" for these events
tended to reach eighty cents of every dollar.

Federov has always manifested the qualities
of a mobster. He is greedy. He stole tip money
from the strippers at his clubs. He is ruth-
less. He once forced a woman to drink bleach as
punishment for an unknown transgression. He is
ambitious. He brokered the complicated negotia-
tion involving the transfer of a Russian military submarine to Cali-based Colombian narco-
traffickers.

(**Note:** See www.usdoj.gov/dea/pubs/his-
tory/1999 - 2003.html—2006 - 03 - 07)

The unwavering point here is that there is
no transaction *too large or too small* {Italics
mine—Diane Liu 092507} to escape his interests
if a profit can be obtained. Special attention
should be paid to his emerging business connections with a shell corporation named Park Enterprises, based in Taipei, *believed to be a conduit
for business with North Korea.* . . . {Italics again
mine—Diane Liu 092507}

Federov was born in 1965 in Odessa, a Black

Sea port that was once the Marseilles of the Soviet Union. When he was three, he moved with his
mother and his father to Rivno, a small city in
the western Ukraine. He sang in a boy's choir and
participated in a boxing program set up by the
Soviet military. His father was a professional
thief and prosperous dealer in the Ukrainian
black market. He'd trade stolen merchandise for
choice cuts of meat, theatre tickets, and fresh
vegetables. His father's brother was a successful
actor in Moscow.

In 1980, when Federov was fifteen, his father
had the word "Jew" stamped in the family's passports even though they weren't Jewish. Then he
managed to move the family to Israel and gain
Israeli citizenship. Before leaving Ukraine, the
Federovs converted their money into diamonds.
They stashed some in shoes with hollow heels
and hid the rest in secret compartments in a
specially built piano, which they shipped to
Israel.

In the late 1970s, the Soviet government was
under diplomatic pressure to let Jews freely
emigrate. In response, the Brehznev government
searched their Gulag for Jewish criminals and
allowed them to leave for America. Many were
"recent converts." More than forty thousand Russian Jews settled in Brighton Beach, a section
of Brooklyn, New York. Most were sound citizens. But the criminals among them resumed their
careers. By the time Federov arrived in 1992,
Brighton Beach had already become the seat of
the *Organizatsiya*, the Russian Jewish mob. Using
his Russian ties, Yuri Federov fit in immediately and flourished. . . .

In addition to his "normal" criminal activities, Federov has a habit of brutalizing women.

"This is cultural," he once explained to an undercover FBI agent, following an arrest in 1996. "In Russia, it is manly to beat women. In the stories of Dostoyevsky, Chekhov, and Gorky, to beat a woman is normal. Then you do something like that in America, something that you grew up with, and you're arrested for domestic violence! It makes no sense."

In an incident taped by the FBI and the DEA from a surveillance apartment across the street from Old Odessa, Federov once chased a girl-friend out of the club and hit her repeatedly with a hammer. On another occasion, he allegedly pounded a female dancer's head against the door of his black Cadillac Escalade until the window broke and the vehicle was covered with blood. No charges were filed in either case.

Federov regularly abused his two daughters and his common-law wife, Tanya, an Estonian Jew whom he met in Israel. When the police arrived at their home in response to 911 calls, the wife was sometimes found huddled inside a locked car with her daughters or hiding in a closet. Tanya later vanished and is presumed dead. His daughters have changed their last name and live with a second cousin in Toronto. . .

Following one instance of domestic violence in Brooklyn, Federov was arrested. The arresting officer, who knew who he was, referred to him as "a filthy *(expletives deleted)* Russian Jew gangster." Federov, though handcuffed, bit off the upper half of the officer's ear. He beat the domestic abuse charge when his wife disappeared. But for assaulting a police officer, he drew four years in a New York State prison. (See NY Criminal Docket #98-CD-456-2) It was the first time Federov had been convicted of a felony. . . .

Criminals with Israeli passports have a sanc-
tuary that other criminals don't. It is extremely
difficult to extradite Israeli nationals, Israel
being the self-proclaimed "land of opportunity,"
at least in theory. It is *not* difficult, however,
to deport Israeli citizens (e.g., *USA vs. Meyer
Lansky*, usdj 020472).

Thus in 1999, the United States government
confiscated Federov's traceable assets in the
United States (estimated at two million dollars)
and deported him to Israel.

But as he departed, his enthusiasm for the
land he was leaving was undiminished. "I love
America!" Federov said to a federal marshal
who escorted him to his departing flight. "The
people are stupid, the government protects rich
people and the police are corrupt. It is so
easy to steal here! Even your big elections are
stolen!"

Federov stayed in Tel Aviv for one month,
then moved back to Ukraine. {*Note: Surveillance
conducted by French and Israeli intelligence
partnerships. See CIA File No. 2006-SF-345-c.*} He
quickly became the guiding force behind The Caspian Group. He has survived several attempts on
his life since 2003 from various competitors and
other parties who might have a positive interest in his death. He has also always been known
to strike back forcibly at those who have struck
at him. . . .

Through his normal tactics of terror, extortion, and intimidation, he has become wealthy
again. The company (TCG) keeps no official records. Reputedly, Federov has a highly disciplined mind and a photographic memory. He keeps
all financial records in his head. . . .

The extent and degree of Yuri Federov's in-fluence in Ukraine, particularly in government circles, is unknown at this time but is also considered to be almost without limit. . . .

Federov should be considered dangerous at all times. Under no circumstances should he be underestimated. . . .

Attention should be paid to the fact that Federov, while on top of the Ukrainian under-world, has many competitors who would benefit with his demise and who might have an interest in his premature death. . . .

SIXTEEN

When Constanza d'Amico awoke in Rome the morning of January 9, her head was pounding. She was trying hard not to think about the direction her life was taking. But she couldn't help it.

She lay in bed with her eyes open. The sun penetrated the drawn blinds in her bedroom, spilling little slashes of sunlight across the room. The clock at her bedside said 9:12 a.m.

Her stomach churned. Her nerves wouldn't settle. Her mouth tasted like cigarettes. Then, next to her in her bed, she was aware of light snoring.

Oh, yeah. She was married.

Beside her, Rocco, her husband, slept fitfully. She had arrived home before he did in the early morning hours, and he had crawled into bed next to her.

Not unusual. Rocco was a musician, a guitarist for a techno-pop band that had a modest following around the city. He often came poling in shortly before dawn, usually smelling of sweat, booze, and cigarettes, sometimes smelling of cheap perfume, but never smelling of nothing. He would set the clock radio in their bedroom for 2:00 p.m. the following afternoon. He would set it LOUD with a heavy metal American CD. The intense volume of music was the only thing that could rouse him.

Whatever. Constanza had given up caring and always made plans to be out of the apartment when the music blasted on. She and Rocco had been married for four years and had started to go their separate ways. He was particularly repulsive, she had come to learn, when he crawled out of bed in the early afternoon after his usual night of debauchery. So she arranged each day to miss those golden moments.

She edged up in bed and looked at him. How could she ever have made such a mistake? She could only see half his head since he was facing away from her. But that was enough. Dark, dirty hair. No shirt. Unshaven for a week.

She sighed. Her head pounded. What a life. There was a time when she had been philosophical about it. No matter where you are, there you are. Recently, however, she had become more proactive about her fate.

Her future: she decided she wanted to have one.

Extra work. Specialty jobs. Some significant income on the side. Like the previous night. Stash some money, put together enough to take off. Make sure she had a passport that was good to go on a moment's notice — or more than one passport if she could work it right. Make sure no one could ever find her. She could start again under a new name. After all, some bad people might come looking for her.

Maybe she could even get to America. She had heard that in the cities of the United States a woman could pay off certain priests and get a marriage annulled. Well, she decided, she would do that and find a way to stay in America.

It would be a new life, and it would be all hers.

But first, that horrible headache, the one that threatened to define the new day.

The buzz in her head graduated to a full firestorm. Time to go proactive on that too.

She had some Vicodin stashed in her purse, thanks to an amateur pharmacist she knew from some of the clubs. The Vike and a Red Bull would get the day off to a good start.

Got to get up. Got to get moving.

A few more weeks and she'd be out of this nightmare.

She rose. Above her bed, a halfwit movie poster in Swedish, not even framed, just tacked to the wall to cover some cracks and peeling paint.

Cheech and Chong — de korsikanska bröderna.

She eyed the poster in anger. Stuff like that had destroyed her life. Set her on the wrong path. Well, not much longer. Not much longer.

She stepped over her dress and shoes from the night before. She lurched uncomfortably into the bathroom, stared at herself in the mirror and winced. She looked awful and felt worse. But her life was a mess. She took her clothes off and turned on the shower.

She walked to the next room. She was in the habit of stashing her purse somewhere so that her husband wouldn't filch money. Her head was hurting badly. Where had she hidden the purse this time? It took a moment to remember.

Then she found it. It had been under a pile of shoes in the front closet.

She found the Vicodin. She went to the refrigerator and found the Red Bull.

So far, so good.

On the kitchen counter, she found some bread. It was yesterday's, half a loaf of good stuff from the corner *panetteria*. But it was unwrapped and half stale. Her pig of a husband must have come in late with the post-gig munchies. You'd think he could at least rewrap the food. But no.

She had given up complaining. On the walls of the apartment were several pictures of her a few years earlier when her career as a model had been taking off. Print ads in glossy magazines. Her on the runways of Rome. For two years, everything had been crackling with excitement. Then it all crashed, about the time she met Rocco and started spending too much time out late. She started to look too tired and dissipated for morning shoots. The business went away to younger, thinner, fresher girls. It never came back. Now, as she stood in her apartment surrounded by the glossy ghosts of the recent past, all she wanted was to get out, which was what the income on the side was all about.

There was a soft knock on the apartment door. The sound startled her. Everything startled her these days. She kept still. Then the soft knocking came again, followed by a familiar voice in accented Italian.

"Constanza, ci sei?" Constanza, are you there?

She recognized the voice. She moved to the door. The last thing she wanted was for one of her butch male friends to wake her husband. There would be explaining that she didn't wish to do, plus arguments and sour recriminations. Fortunately, Rocco slept through early mornings as if he were hibernating.

She leaned to the door.

She peeked through the eyehole. Two male figures shifting nervously, an empty hallway behind them. One with a twitchy left eye, one in wraparound shades. They must have slipped by the old woman,

Masiella, who kept guard downstairs. Masiella was deaf as a doorknob and not much smarter.

"*Eccomi*," she answered. "I'm here."

Twitchy Eye switched to English. "Open us the door. We have you the money," he said. Twitchy was a good-looking guy, but he spoke no language perfectly.

"Let me get my robe," she said, her voice very low.

She quickstepped into the bathroom where the warm water continued to run in the shower. She found a robe and pulled it on, tying the sash around her waist.

She returned to the door, turned the bolts, undid a chain, and unlocked it.

Two men stepped in. She embraced the first one, Twitchy Eye. The second man shut the door. "Anyone else here?" the first man asked.

"My husband," she said, her voice barely above a whisper. "He's sleeping."

The nervous eye was on overdrive now, blinking, twitching, worse than she had ever seen it. He gave the second man a nod. "Okay," he said.

"So? Where's my money?" Constanza asked.

"Don't be so anxious," he said. And she saw him give a slight nod to the second man. Then he turned back to her. "It's in my pocket," he said, indicating to a spot within his jacket. "Give me a kiss first."

She glanced as he beckoned to his jacket, open to show a black and white camo T-shirt that showed off the muscles of his chest. She also saw he was wearing a gun, not unusual. And he had an envelope, as promised, in his inside pocket.

She grinned slightly. She saw what she wanted. She saw, in fact, a great deal of what she wanted in comparison to the geeky husband who slumbered noisily in the next room. Well, today she would have to content herself with the *denaro*, the *cinquecento dollari* that she had been promised. Five hundred bucks of blood money.

She leaned to him and reached in, bringing her body close to his. The man leaned forward to savor the closeness and the scent of her body. She winked at him as she reached into his coat. Why not? They had been lovers once recently, though no one else knew that. Flirtatiously, he planted a gentle kiss on the lips, something she did not resist.

Then he did something rougher than usual and something that was highly unexpected.

He held her tightly at the left wrist, then used his other hand to hold her other wrist. He held her arms downward against her body, making the upper half of her body highly vulnerable. All this, while continuing to press his face to hers. Her robe loosened slightly, something she was okay with at first but then began to resist.

Then the first man withdrew his lips and the second man removed something from his pocket, something that Constanza soon realized was a silk cord. With incredible dexterity, and hardly allowing her a moment to struggle, the second man looped the cord over her head and around her throat. The cord went tight quickly, faster than she could utter a word. It was so tight that it cut into the flesh and almost disappeared.

She tried to kick but they overpowered her. Twitchy Eye let go of her wrists and stepped back impassively to watch her die.

She saw him mouth some words. "I'm sorry, Connie. I'm sorry." He shrugged. The young woman's fingers dug into her own flesh to fight for her life.

As the cord went tight, her face darkened with compressed blood. Then the blood began to run from the wounds at her throat. Her wrists went free, her eyes bulged, and after a brief struggle, all the strength drained from her body. First there was pain. Horribly searing pain. Her legs folded, her body sagged, and an earthly darkness descended upon her. The pain went away.

The killers released her. Her body hit the floor.

The first man gave a nod to the second. It was Twitchy Eye's turn now.

He drew his pistol. He disappeared into the bedroom where there were still sounds of sleep from Rocco. There were two large reports from a high-caliber pistol. Then a third to make sure the job was done.

Twitchy Eye reappeared.

No more snoring sounds. Just some gurgling.

"*Finito?*" asked the first man.

"*Finito*," Twitchy Eye answered.

"*È certo?*"

"His brains are against the wall if you want to go look."

Twitchy Eye went into the bathroom. Using a washcloth to preclude leaving any finger prints, he turned off the water. No point in presiding over a flood that would bring the *carabinieri* here days before they otherwise might be summoned.

Their business there concluded, the two men left the apartment. They were in separate cars leaving Italy before the sun rose to the midpoint of the sky.

SEVENTEEN

Alex LaDuca and Michael Cerny sat at a round table in the office at the State Department office he had reserved for such meetings.

They had been together for two hours. It was already past 11:00 a.m. His background briefing on Yuri Federov and The Caspian Group neared conclusion. The forefront of Alex's mind was teeming with new information and ideas as Cerny moved his discussion of Federov in a final direction.

"He has one soft spot," Cerny said. "One Achilles heel."

"I can hardly wait to hear what that is."

"He has a passion for highly educated Western women."

"I was up till 2:00 a.m. reading the FBI file," Alex answered. "He's a pig, a murderer, and a gangster."

"That would be accurate."

"I don't know why any educated Western woman would want anything to do with him. And if you don't mind a little vengeful Old Testament spunkiness," she continued, "his soul should burn in hell someday."

"Look," Cerny said, "I like your take-no-prisoners spirit, but let's be constructive. Your assignment will be to discuss issues pertaining to The Caspian Group and US Taxation. As mentioned, Federov owes the US millions in unpaid taxes. Just getting him to file the proper forms would be a victory."

She felt a wave of indignation building. "And what's my *real* assignment?"

"Stay with him every moment you can. Barely let him out of your sight for the duration of your trip, particularly while the president is there. Find out everything you possibly can."

He fell silent. She felt there was more on the way. She waited.

"It wouldn't bother us if you got to know him as well as a woman could," he said.

Then he smirked. There was a nasty pause.

"Are you asking me to *seduce* him?"

"If you choose to do that," he said, "even if it were only an occasional relationship. At your rank you're eligible for performance pay. Bonuses."

Alex steamed. She glared at Cerny. He raised his eyebrows. "Why don't I just walk out of here right now?" she asked.

"I was expecting that question by the end of this briefing," he said, "but it's my job to put this proposition before you. It's not coming from me; it's coming from your government. Sometimes dirty work has to be done for the greater good."

"You people are disgusting. Why don't you hire a hooker?"

"Not to put too keen an edge on it, Alex, but if we could find one who was a security specialist, spoke five languages, could master a crash course in Ukrainian in a month, and could take care of herself and *possibly* come back in one piece, which, since you like honesty, the last part wouldn't be essential, we probably would. But we can't. So there. We're asking you."

There was a moment that passed between them in tense silence.

"Have someone else do your dirty work. And have me fired if you wish," she said.

"Not at all. And once again, you've just demonstrated why you're perfect for this assignment. Alex, really! We need you to do it. You don't have to get physical with him, but we do want you to be with him. Constantly."

She seethed. "Why?" she pressed.

"I can't answer that. I don't even know, myself. We want you to watch him every moment," he said. "Every inch of the way. We want to know exactly where he is. Just shadow him. Promise him anything. Find out whatever you can about him, his business, his associates. Anything from how he used to beat up his bimbos in Brooklyn to whether he's selling Pepsi-Cola and *Playboy* to the North Koreans. You're our one person who will keep him interested. Your country is counting on you."

She found herself fingering the gold cross again. Her thoughts went far away as she disappeared into herself. A long silence passed between them.

He waited.

"I'll take the assignment. I'll make the trip," she said, "but I'll do things on my own terms. And if your sleazebag Bolshevik narco-gangster puts his hands on me I'll break both his filthy wrists."

"See? That's what we like about you. Righteous indignation. You're perfect for this."

"Those are my conditions."

"All right," he said. "It's a deal."

EIGHTEEN

Later in the day, Alex went to Human Resources where she sat for a series of photographs, changing her blouse for each new photo. She rearranged her hair slightly with each picture so that no two shots were too much alike or appeared to have been taken at the same time. New IDs were being made and new photos were in order. It was yet another indication that this was no ordinary trip.

In the early afternoon, back in her office at FinCen, Alex completed the reassignment of her current caseload to other investigators at FinCen. After lunch she returned to a newly assigned room in the State Department.

Her language instructor, Olga, arrived at a few minutes past four. Olga led Alex through some preliminary ground rules for the study of Ukrainian. The teacher seemed pleased that Alex had a solid grasp of Russian. That gave her entry into Ukrainian. Alex felt like a graduate student getting tutored for a final.

The trouble was, her heart wasn't completely in it.

She found herself thinking about her assignment that night when she worked out at the gym. There was no basketball that evening, but she did spot a few of the players: Jack, who was an accountant for the IRS; Laura, her old buddy who worked at the White House; and Ben, who was running laps on his prosthesis.

From the locker room afterward she phoned Robert on her cell phone. He wasn't home yet either.

"Want to grab a pizza?" she asked.

"I'd like to grab you, instead," he answered. "Or maybe the pizza and then you."

"I've got cold beer in the fridge," she said. It was the first time all day Alex felt relaxed. Robert had that effect on her.

"It's a deal," he said.

There was a Chicago-style pizza place called Jean & Luca's not far from Dupont Circle where he lived. He said he'd swing by there, get a thick pie, and drive it over to her place.

He did.

She had an ulterior motive this evening, however, and elaborated when they broke open the pie and the beer.

"How would you feel about running a couple of names across your files?" she asked.

"What files?"

"The Secret Service ones that will tell you where someone in the government works."

"Where are you going with this?"

"Michael Cerny, who recruited me for this Ukrainian assignment," she said. "And this three-hundred-pound woman named Olga Liashko. I want to know if they have any CIA links."

"Come on," he said.

"No. Really. Something about them doesn't smell quite right."

He considered it.

"Michael Cerny's been with the State Department for several years. I've known him for six years. I've never heard of any CIA affiliation."

"That doesn't mean he's *not* connected to the CIA," she said. "You know that as well as I do. Look, there's an awful lot of this that doesn't make sense."

She was angry. Indignant. She kept going. "Listen, Robert, what are they asking me to *really* accomplish? They're practically asking me to share a shower and a bedroom with this repulsive East Bloc hoodlum. I don't know what they think I can find out that all their intelligence hasn't already given them."

"I don't know the answers," he said. "I agree with you, but I don't have any answers."

"I don't like Cerny and I don't like this Ukrainian steamroller he works with," Alex said. "So why don't you just be the man I know and love and run a check?"

He finished one square slice of pie and started another. He nodded thoughtfully.

"I can't do it myself," he said. "I don't have the authorization. But I can call in a favor. I won't have an answer right away, but I'll see what I can do. How's that?"

She leaned across the table and kissed him.

"That would be perfect," she said.

NINETEEN

The *Lt. de polizia* Gian Antonio Rizzo stood with his arms folded across his chest in the small cluttered apartment on the via Donorfio. A tall lean man with dark hair and sharp features, Lt. Rizzo of the Roman city police felt a deep disgust, an outrage, that fed upon the deeply cynical outlook on life that he had developed over the decades.

Lt. Rizzo had had more than enough of the type of scene that lay before him. At age fifty-five, he was contemplating retirement toward the middle of the summer. His final day at this underpaid unappreciated job could not come soon enough. Of course, he still had an enterprise or two on the side, but who knew about that?

Downstairs at the doorway to the street, a crowd gathered. Here, upstairs, police had strung crime scene tape in the hallway. Police techies vacuumed everything for fibers. Forensic photographers took digital shots of everything while busily trampling the rest of the crime scene.

Rizzo's brown eyes slid uneasily over the death chamber. The *carabinieri* who busily assisted him, as well as his own detectives from Rome's homicide squad, had no question about the emotions sizzling within him.

"*Pervertitidi! Degenerati!*" Rizzo said. "Scum! You know what makes me mad? Having to spend time investigating what these people do to each other. Maybe we should let them kill one another, hey? Then these foreign parasites — *questi scrocconi stranieri* — would stop coming to Roma. Wouldn't that be better for everyone?"

In the lieutenant's opinion, there was a struggle under way for the soul of Rome. On one side were the forces of restraint, lawfulness, etiquette, and cultural preservation. On the other, the unswerving desire to use the ancient city for permissiveness, debauchery, and the commission of international crime.

Lt. Rizzo saw it every night on off-duty strolls through the Campo dei Fiori and the Piazza Navona. Why, just two evenings earlier witnesses in overlooking apartments had reported seeing two people shot and killed around the corner from where Julius Caesar used to address the forum, their bodies whisked away afterwards.

The case had landed on his desk and it was most unwelcome.

Well, the city had changed a bit since Caesar's day, and not necessarily for the better. So Rizzo, who felt himself a guardian of public decency, looked around this room and felt his blood pressure rising.

More murder. More crime. More drugs.

"*Incredibile!*" Rizzo growled as those under his command went about their business. "This is a country that can't form a government to last longer than the soccer season and can't do anything about all these foreign degenerates either!"

With retirement beckoning, Rizzo was increasingly free with his opinions. The forensic technicians busied themselves with the details of the double homicide. Why take issue? They agreed with him, anyway. Even his assistant, Stephano DiPetri, knew enough to ignore him.

The dead woman was on the floor of the living room, her arms and legs a tangle, a robe half on, half off, the upper part of it caked with blood. Her face was blue from strangulation, her eyes frozen wide in the pain of her death. Her throat looked as if it had been perforated with a butcher's knife.

Lt. Rizzo walked to the next room. There, a man, who appeared to have been a musician, had been shot to death while sleeping. He had a couple of guitars by the bed, a collection of sheet music, and the inevitable marijuana paraphernalia, none of which was going to be much use to him now.

The first and second bullets had passed through him. The third had blown apart his skull. Nasty splatter. A crime scene pick-four: Skin, hair, tissues, bone in every direction.

It wasn't pretty.

The pillow and the worn mattress had caught most of the blood, which was good for the cleanup squad. But his left eye was ruptured and half out of his head, which would make their task messier. And at least the remains of the bullets had already been recovered. That was another good part.

The really grisly detail, aside from the homicides themselves, had been the discovery. For a solid day, starting at two in the afternoon, the dead man's clock radio had blasted some vile American music.

The downstairs neighbors, after a sleepless night and much pounding on the ceiling, indignantly phoned the *proprietario* over the excessive noise. The landlord had raised the *portiera*, the deaf-as-a-haddock old Signora Massiella.

Signora Massiella had used her passkey to enter the apartment. She had pushed the door open. The door had stopped against the dead woman on the floor.

Then she screamed and fled, crossing herself several times as she ran. She called the police. The *carabinieri* arrived and then summoned the homicide people, which included Lt. Rizzo. Rizzo brought in his attitude, of which he had plenty.

Rizzo stood at the foot of the bed, surveying the death scene and not feeling much compassion. He glanced at the disgraceful film poster above the body, one that turned immorality drug addiction into a joke.

Cheech and Chong. *The Corsican Brothers*. Who was kidding whom? If one of these potheads wanted to meet some *real* Corsican brothers, Rizzo could arrange it. And as for this dead guy being a singer-musician, well, Sinatra and Pavarotti had been singers. Gino Paoli was a singer. The current pop star Zucherro was a singer. This guy was just a dead guy.

Nearby, detectives went through drawers. They found enough illicit pharmaceuticals and "head" equipment to equip a small store.

Rizzo had an opinion: victims like these brought such things upon themselves. So why then should he, Lt. Rizzo, have to spend his life sorting out a mess like this? Elsewhere in Rome there were good God-fearing *local* people who were also victims, good Italian working people who battled every day against immigrants and street thugs. Those *genti* deserved his attention more than this international trash, didn't they?

A young policeman with chubby cheeks stood next to the lieutenant. His name was Quinzani. In his squad room it was frequently said that Quinzani looked like a hamster in a police uniform. He was of the municipal police and not the homicide brigade. This was his first serious crime scene, and up until now, everyone made fun of him.

He was frightened not just of his boss and the hardened old *bastardi* of the homicide brigade, but he was also scared stiff just of being there. "*Signor Lieutenant?*" the young man asked.

Rizzo's thoughts were far away at the moment. He liked to tell people that his distant cousin had been police commissioner and then mayor in Philadelphia. It was a good story and played well with his fellow cops, usually accompanied by one of his diatribes about the scheming American government and their outlaw intelligence services that operated across Europe. There was no doubt in anyone's mind that Rizzo, despite his likings for Americans personally, loathed anything to do with the US government.

Then again, on a recent trip to America, Gian Antonio Rizzo had had himself photographed in front of the mural of the world famous Frank Rizzo at the Italian market in South Philly. And if you asked him, the two *paesani* had a strong facial resemblance! Aside from that, like many excellent stories, this one had no basis in truth.

His thoughts drifted further, and he wondered what his mistress, Sophie, a nice young French woman in her late thirties, was doing. Sophie worked in a dress store near the Piazza San Marco, dealing with pretty feminine things and cultivated customers, while he was engaged in this muck.

"*Signor Lieutenant? Scusi?*" young Quinzani repeated.

"*Cosa che?*" snapped the lieutenant, breaking out of his reverie.

"*Guardi, signor Lieutenant, per favor,*" the young policeman said. "I found this."

"*Dove?*" he asked. Where?

"In an envelope. Behind some books," the young man said, "in the living room."

A hand covered in a surgical glove extended three passports to the lieutenant, plus a thick handful of Euros and dollars.

Rizzo looked around for DiPetri. The man was gone, as usual, leaving Rizzo to the mercy of this overanxious young laddie. Rizzo eyed the passports and the money.

"Let me see this," Rizzo said.

He put the money in his pocket for safekeeping. He would turn it over at headquarters. Or maybe he'd take Sophie out to dinner. He'd decide later.

Then he looked at the passports: an American one and two Canadian ones.

The lieutenant didn't grasp the significance at first.

Then he opened the top one. The picture showed the woman who lay dead on the floor. Her name on the passport was Angelina Mercoli. Then he opened the next one, issued in Ottawa in 2006. Same woman, different picture. Now her name was Diana Gilberti. A trend emerged. He looked at the third. Now the dead girl had born in Toronto and her name was Lana Bissoni.

He looked at the passports, at their bindings and their printing. Good fakes but fakes nonetheless. Probably good enough to cross a porous border. Not good enough for entry into the United States, Japan, or China but workable for almost anywhere in Europe. Once you got into a country of the European Union you could travel freely to any other, with a handful of exceptions like Great Britain. Such as Italy, where they were now.

He grunted as young Quinzani looked over his shoulder.

He closed the passports, then looked down. He drew a breath. His blood pressure must have been three hundred over two hundred right at that moment, he reasoned. He was going to have to learn to calm down, or he'd have a stroke and Sophie would end up with some young punk her own age who didn't deserve her.

He focused: first this had looked like a drug hit or some snap of jealousy among lowlifes. But now there were fake passports. No way Rizzo was going to be able to sweep this one away.

This case was going to be a pain. What was this city coming to anyway? Rome was starting to remind him of the wide-open city of the seventies where the loathsome Red Brigades and their criminal friends had the whole country in fear.

Rizzo looked back to Quinzani. He gave the young man a nod and was suddenly back on his game. "What's happening with the old woman downstairs?" Rizzo asked. "That old deaf woman who lives by the elevator and always has her door open? Was that her name? *La portiera*?"

"Massiella," Quinzani answered.

"Are they talking to the old *vacca*? Did she see anything? Does she remember anyone enter yesterday morning?"

"She says she doesn't always have her hearing aid in," Quinzani said. "She's very frightened. She says these people had a lot of visitors she didn't like, but she never asked questions."

"*Altro che!*" Rizzo answered. "Of course. That's always *our* job, eh? To ask the bloody questions?"

"*Si, signor Lieutenant.*"

Rizzo thought for a moment. "Is there anyone in particular she remembers?"

"*No, signor Lieutenant.*"

"No. Of course not," he fumed. He thought further. "All right. Good work for now. Maybe you'll have my job someday soon because I'm old and senile."

"*Si, signor Lieutenant.*"

"Oh, you think so, do you?" Rizzo snapped.

"Yes, sir. I mean, no, I don't, sir. I mean I never considered it, sir."

Rizzo winked at him. "Go do your job, *ragazzo*," he said gently. "And I'll do mine." He actually liked young Quinzani. For a kid, he was okay.

The young man looked at his superior with uncertainty. Then he gave a nod and a slight smile, not knowing what else to say.

Rizzo knew what to say, however, but it was wildly profane. So, defender of public morals that he was, he kept it deep inside.

TWENTY

A week passed. Busy days for Alex, not happy days. The weekend became inseparable from the week. Robert drew Sunday duty as well, this time at the Secret Service Training Center at Beltsville, Maryland.

The Beltsville complex was officially known as the James J. Rowley Training Center. It had a fake town, driving courses, helipad with a helicopter, bunkers, an obstacle course, twelve miles of roads, caves, a simulated airport apron, an "instinctive" firing range, a protective driver training course, a K-9 training area, and outdoor training and tactical response areas. Best of all, the center had six miles of paved roadways where the Secret Service Mountain Bike Patrol could drill. Once during a previous administration a president had been off on a seventy-five minute bike ride while Homeland Security had been on Red alert. No one bothered to tell the president. So here was where Robert got to wear what Alex jokingly always called "his sexiest outfit." The helmet, the colorful red, white, and blue USA bike shirt, the black bike shorts, the SIDI shoes, and a nifty little Beretta 9000S on his hip.

For Alex, more prosaic stuff: language lessons on top of language lessons, then back to the firing range, where at least she could blow off some steam.

Then back to language lessons. Robert went on an overnight trip with the president to Boston. Nasty hecklers intruded on the motorcade. Lots of street scuffling and placard waving. Irritating but innocuous. "Typical Boston," Robert said.

No big deal. No significant incidents. Fifteen arrests, including a drunk with a carton of eggs he wanted to hurl. The new American president had then continued on to Kansas to do some political fundraising with the party faithful. Corn country was more receptive and respectful. Or maybe the president hadn't worn out the newly elected welcome just yet.

For Alex on day eight, Olga droned on far into each afternoon of instruction, her grasp on Ukrainian strong as a bull, her grip of English somewhere short of perfect, even after all these decades in the West. Privately, Alex and Robert had nicknamed Olga, "the baroness of the Black Sea."

"Another terminology point," Olga said, as Alex stifled a yawn. "You so will have noticed and perhaps been mystificated by the fact the name of the capital city on the embassy website is spelled K-y-i-v," she said. "Why is it this?" she asked.

"I have no idea," Alex answered. *Mystificated*, indeed.

"Of course, you do not. But we are about to discuss and you will learn," Olga said. "Ukrainian, like Russian, has two *i* sounds. A short *i* sound like in 'prick' and a long *i* sound like the French *I* or like the English *ee* in 'needy.'"

Alex's mind was drifting. She was maxed on this stuff. "Uh huh," she said.

Olga, bless her, must have realized this because, just to be mean, she started to amp up the small killer details about the Cyrillic alphabet.

A soft knock and then the door opened. Michael Cerny came into the room with a nod and a smile. He seated himself at the table, saying nothing. He was carrying a green interoffice folder that was tied shut.

"Olga, my dear," Cerny interrupted gently, "I need to talk to Alex for a moment. Why don't you take a break?"

Without speaking, Olga stood and marched out the door. She looked angry. The door closed with a high profile.

Cerny rolled his eyes when she was gone. "Having fun?" he asked.

"She's brutal," Alex said. "Who's side is that woman on anyway? Is she trying to get me there in one piece or kill me first?"

"Now, now," he said with a smirk.

"Thanks for rescuing me. I needed a break."

Alex leaned back in her chair.

"Thought you might," Cerny said. He opened the green folder. Alex waited.

"Alex," he said, reaching into it, "let me show you some things. We've set you up quite nicely."

"Set me up?"

From the folder, Cerny pulled a variety of IDs in the name of Anna Marie Tavares, all with photographs of Alex. The most impressive was the US passport. It looked just like standard government-issue because it was. But it had been backdated to reflect an issue in 2007. Entry stamps had been impressed into it from Ireland, France, and Mexico.

"Please memorize your new date of birth," he said, "as well as your location. I know there's a lot on your plate right now, so we took your normal birthday, October 20, and cut it in half. Ten twenty becomes five ten. May 10. Get it?"

A pause as she shook the remnants of the day's Ukrainian lesson out of the forefront of her mind. "Got it," she said.

She examined the passport.

"We made you a year younger and set the birthplace as Los Angeles," Cerny continued. "You look young and LA would fit with the 'Tavares' name."

Alex looked at one of the photographs that she had sat for a day previously. She had gone undercover with the FBI, but the thoroughness of this was impressive even by law enforcement standards.

"If you have monograms on anything," Cerny said, "be sure not to bring it. Same with magazines with labels or books with your name in it. If you want an address book, create a new one. Better, don't even bring one."

"Uh huh," she said.

"Notice those travel stamps," he said. "Ireland, France, and Mexico. You've been to all three places. Have cover stories for your trips. Note the days of entry and exit. Just in case you're ever quizzed."

"Why would I be?" she asked.

"Ukraine is an old Soviet republic," he said. "Paranoia is still the *plat du jour*. Nice mixed metaphor, right?"

She didn't answer.

Cerny began opening envelopes and pulled out supporting material.

There was a Maryland driver's license, valid, he claimed, which employed the second picture that had been taken the day before. Then there were a trio of credit cards: Discover, Visa, and American Express, plus a bank ATM card.

"All of these are live credit cards," he said. "We have a special relationship with a bank in northern Virginia, which issues these. However, you're only to use the Visa if you see fit. You can expense up to five thousand dollars on it, no questions asked, so buy yourself a nice fake Cartier watch in Kiev if you have the chance. They do great work on counterfeit brand names in Eastern Europe, so might as well take advantage."

"That's perfectly illegal, you know," she said.

"Of course it is, but who cares?" he answered blithely. "You can score some nice stuff before some rival gangsters put them out of business."

She tried to ignore the point. She examined the credit cards individually.

"The other cards are 'fly traps,' " he said, continuing. "If used, they will function up to two hundred dollars but will issue an immediate alert that something has happened to you. They will only work in an ATM that takes photographs. If primed, they will send a picture immediately to the State Department as to the location plus the photo of the user. If they're used anywhere else, they're a distress signal and a squad of marines in civilian clothes will probably come looking for you and want to kill someone just to make their trip worthwhile. Understand?"

"Clever," she said.

"It *is* clever, isn't it? The latest thing," Cerny said with some pride.

He gave her a trio of pens, three different shades of ink.

"You might want to sign everything, the passport and the cards. Don't use the same pen on any two cards. Use a ballpoint on the passport, and be sure when you sign to sign 'Anna Tavares.' Do it now right in front of me so I can see it, then give me one more Anna Tavares signature for your passport application so we have a record."

She did what was asked. She looked up.

"So, what's your name?" he asked.

"Anna Tavares."

"When were you born, Anna?"

"May 10, 1979."

"Really? Where?"

"In Los Angeles."

"*En español*," he pressed. "*Ahora mismo.*"

"*El diez de mayo, mil novecientos setenta y nueve a Los Angeles.*"

"*Muy bien*," he said. "Now in Ukrainian."

She threw it back to him. He was pleased.

"I have your plane tickets too, Anna," he said. "They're e-tickets, but you need the invoices. You're flying Air France to Paris, connecting to Kiev. You will depart on February sixth and arrive in Kiev on the seventh. That's ten days in advance of the president's arrival. Excited?"

"Completely overwhelmed."

"Don't be," he said.

"I assume I'm in all the proper computers as Anna," she said. "If anyone checks these?" Alex asked.

"Absolutely," Cerny answered. "Which reminds me." He opened a final envelope. "Commerce Department ID. It's your cover. Plus some supporting nonsense. Library cards, health club membership. BS stuff, but the type of things a lady would have in her purse. Which reminds me again. Do you have an old purse you can use?"

She opened her mouth to answer. He answered his own question before she could.

"Well, you do now," he said. He had a worn Couch purse, complete with attached change purse. A nice leather Couch billfold actually, but with the proper wear on it.

"Would you like a gun when you're in Ukraine?"

"Why would someone from Commerce be carrying a gun?" she asked.

"Because it's Ukraine," he answered. "Don't ask logical questions about an illogical place."

"I'll think about it," she said.

"Have it your way," he said. "If you want one when you get there, talk to Richard Friedman. He's with the State Department there. He'll also be meeting you at the airplane. He'll know you as Anna, by the way. Don't confuse anyone with the truth. The truth never does anyone any good for trips like this. Truth is confusing."

"I know."

He paused. "I'm told that you've been putting in your time at the firing range. Good scores too, from what I've seen."

"Are you watching everything I do?"

"Just enough. You should be happy that we keep an eye on you. Think of us as guardian angels, all right? Anyway, congratulations on the good shooting. It's a shame to have a fine skill and not use it. Are you sure you don't want a gun in Ukraine? We can get you a Glock."

"I said I'd think about it."

"Okay. Any more questions for now?"

She looked at everything that had been given to her.

"No," she said.

"Good."

"Why? You got something more for me?" she asked.

"Don't I always?"

"Then let's have it," she said.

"Ever heard of a man named Georgiy Gongadze?" he asked.

"I don't think so," she said. "Someone else I'm going to meet?"

"Not if you're lucky," he said. "Gongadze was a Ukrainian journalist. In April 2000, he founded a news website, *Ukrayinska Pravda*. Ukrainian Truth, it meant, but unlike the old Soviet-style Pravda it really was the truth. The website specialized in political news and commentary, focusing particularly on President Kuchma, the country's wealthy 'oligarchs,' and the official media."

"Sounds like he went looking for trouble," she said.

"He did. And in a place like Ukraine, trouble isn't hard to find."

In June 2000, Cerny continued, Gongadze complained that he had been forced into hiding because of harassment from the secret police. He said he and his family were being followed, that his staff were being harassed, and that the SBU, the successor of the KGB, was spreading a rumor that he was wanted on a murder charge.

"Gongadze disappeared in September of 2000," Cerny said. "Opposition politicians reported that the disappearance had coincided with Gongadze receiving documents on corruption within the president's own entourage. The Ukrainian parliament set up an inquiry run by a special commission. Neither investigation produced any results.

"Two months later," Cerny continued, "a body was found in a forest in the Taraschanskyi Raion district, forty miles outside Kiev. The corpse had been decapitated and doused in acid to make identification more difficult."

Alex cringed. She could never get over man's limitless cruelty. "The corpse was Gongadze, I assume," she said.

"Oh, yes," Cerny said. "A group of journalists identified the remains. His wife confirmed the same a few weeks later. But the government didn't officially acknowledge that the body was that of Gongadze until the following February and did not definitively confirm it until as late as March 2003.

"The affair became an international crisis for the Ukrainian government during 2001. There were rumors of Ukrainian suspension from the Council of Europe. Mass demonstrations erupted in Kiev. The protests were forcibly broken up by the police.

"In May 2001, Interior Minister Yuri Smirnov announced that the murder had been solved. Conveniently, both of the alleged killers were now dead. The claim was so outrageous that it was dismissed by the government's own prosecutor-general. Mass protests again broke out in Kiev and other Ukrainian cities in September 2002 to mark the second anniversary of Gongadze's death. The demonstrators again called for Kuchma's resignation, but the protests again failed to achieve their goal, with police breaking up the protesters' camp.

"The prosecutor of the Tarascha district, where Gongadze's body was found, was convicted in May 2003 for abuse of office and falsification of evidence," Cerny said. "He was found guilty of forging documents and negligence in the investigation and was sentenced to two-and-a-half years in prison. However, he was immediately released due to a provision of Ukraine's amnesty laws.

"In June 2004, the government claimed that a gangster identified only as 'K' had confessed to Gongadze's murder, although there was no independent confirmation of the claim. Then a key witness died of spinal injuries sustained while in police custody.

"Gongadze's death became a major issue in the 2004 Ukrainian presidential election," said Cerny. "The opposition candidate, Viktor

Yushchenko, pledged to solve the case if he became president. Yushchenko did become president following the subsequent Orange Revolution and immediately launched a new investigation."

"Are you trying to scare me off this trip?" Alex asked.

"Not at all. I'm reminding you what you're getting into. Ukraine is a dangerous, wide-open place. Exciting and endlessly interesting, but dangerous and wide open. 'Frontier,' remember?"

"Well, at least they're paying lip service to democracy," she said.

"Ukraine's a plutocracy. No matter which side is in power, many things continue the same way they've gone on since before the time of the Cossacks. The corruption, the gangsterism never changes."

"I'll be careful," she said.

He paused for a second. "I skipped one detail," he said.

She waited.

"The Ukrainian underworld plays very dirty and they play for keeps. The acid bath and the decapitation that Gongadze received?" Cerny said. "They did it to him while he was still alive."

She let it sink in for a moment, then, "If you want me to participate in a CIA operation," she asked, "why didn't you just tell me that? And why don't you tell me what you really want to know about Yuri Federov instead of putting me through all this crap?"

"Everything will make sense eventually," he said. "Any scrap of information you get out of him could prove very useful, particularly on the range of his businesses and foreign trade partners. And if everything goes well, you'll never see me again afterward."

"I wouldn't mind if you disappeared right now for the rest of this evening," she said. It was almost 6:00 p.m. She was beat.

"I'm about to," he answered.

"You mean I can go home now?"

He laughed. "Don't be silly," he said. "The night is young."

He stood and went to the door. He knocked.

A moment later, Olga entered with all the delicacy of a Panzer division. She had a one-liter bottle of Classic Coke in one hand and a large bag of pork rinds in the other, ready to continue well into the evening.

"Now," Olga said. "You tell me personal stuff. Why you go to Ukraine. Who you are. Personal stuff. In Ukrainian, hey?"

"In Ukrainian?"

"Yes," Olga said, sitting back. "Pork rind?" she offered. "They very good."

Alex sighed and began.

TWENTY-ONE

On the first day of February, four evenings before her departure, Alex opted to go to the gym. She fell into her usual game of pick-up basketball. Robert went to the same gym to lift weights. As was his habit, as he cooled down, he watched Alex's game.

Alex was the playmaker for her team, the point guard who handled the ball and set the tone. He liked to watch her compete, her body strong but feminine, quick and agile, with solid strategy behind each move.

This evening, the other team had added yet another new player, a young man with a University of Kentucky T-shirt. He had been a varsity reserve forward for a successful team in the SEC. The new kid was very good. The game was a struggle. Alex's team kept fighting from behind. Ben and the Kentucky kid constantly battling under the hoop. Alex's team stayed within three or four points the whole time.

With thirty seconds to go, Alex had scored a dozen points. Ben had twenty-six. But their team remained down by three. Alex sank a short jump shot with twelve seconds to go on the clock. Then, as the other side prepared to kill the clock, Alex faked going back down court, turned quickly and cut directly in front of the new player, figuring the in-bounds pass would be to him.

She had a clear shot from the outside, about ten feet from the basket, but she threw Ben a laserlike eye-high pass. Ben followed with a short jump shot, getting as high as he could on his one good leg, over the reach of the off-balance backpedaling Kentucky kid. Their team had its first lead of the night, 34 – 33. Three seconds later the opponents threw up a desperation shot that went off the offensive backboard, as time ran out.

The winning players mobbed each other in celebration. Ben, with big powerful arms, looked to Alex who had stolen the ball and fed him the great pass. He hoisted Alex up in jubilation, hugged her tightly, bussed her cheek, and swung her around before setting her down again and passing along hugs to other hot sweaty survivors of the game: Laura, Fred, Juan.

When Alex met Robert a few minutes later, he seemed distant. When they met in the gym's lobby after showers, she asked what was bothering him and he explained.

"I didn't care much for the way that big guy with the missing leg picked you up and swung you around," he said.

"Who? Ben?"

"If that's his name."

"That's his name, and he doesn't have a *missing* leg. He has a prosthesis."

"You know what I mean."

There was silence as they walked out of the gym to their cars.

At first she was miffed. Then she tried to explain it away.

"It wasn't anything," Alex said to him. "Ben is an Iraq war vet and he's just getting his head straight again. He didn't mean anything by it. After what he went through in that insane war, I'm happy to have him as a teammate. I'm happy to see he can still play basketball."

"I just didn't like it," Robert repeated. "Him grabbing you like that. He doesn't own you."

"Do *you*?"

"That's not my point."

They stopped just outside the door. The night was sharply cold, but dry.

"Then what *is* your point? Jealousy?" she asked. "Be honest."

"Maybe. Yes."

She thought about it. As was their habit, even if she didn't agree with him, she wanted to see his side of things. His feelings.

"All right," she said. "Look, when I see Ben next, I'll tell him that my fiancé saw the touchy stuff and didn't like it."

"Why don't you tell him that you didn't like it, either?"

She felt herself start to grow angry again, one of the first times there had ever been any contention between them.

"The truth is," she said, "I didn't mind. I didn't think anything of it. Laura Chapman was in the game too. She hugged me afterwards too, and Ben hugged her and Laura has a boyfriend, too. It's not like Laura and I are taking showers together with Ben handing us the soap."

"It's okay if Laura gives you a hug. It's not okay if a guy does it."

"You're being crazy." She turned and walked toward her car.

"I'm telling you about something that bothers me," he said, following. "I would think that would be important to you."

She thought about it. They arrived at her car. Now she just wanted to defuse the issue.

"Okay, okay," she said. "When I see Ben I'll tell him you didn't like what you saw, and I didn't like it either, and he should never do it again."

"Thank you. You tell him that."

"I promise," she said. A pause. "Okay?"

A longer pause. "Okay," he finally said.

He kissed her good night. They left separately.

The next morning her cell phone rang on the way to work. She was driving on Connecticut Avenue, a few blocks from Treasury.

She looked at the phone's screen and recognized Robert's number. She answered.

"Hello," he said. "Me."

"Hello, you."

"I'm sorry," he said. "You don't have to say anything to Ben."

"I don't mind," she said as she drove. "I'll do it if you want me to."

"No," he said. "I *don't* want you to. It's okay. It's done. It never happened."

"If you say so," she said.

She was pulling into Treasury parking, normally only available to the most senior employees, but Cerny had arranged a spot for her. She showed her government pass. It opened the gate. A guard waved her through.

"I say so," he said. "I'm fine with everything. I love you."

"Love you too."

"Let's go to the Athenian tonight, okay?"

"Looking forward to it," she answered.

Her fiancé could get a little testy, a bit territorial, a bit overprotective at times. She already knew that. But sound reason would always prevail. There was never any reason for him to get jealous. But what stayed with her was an underlying subtext. In his eyes, in his spirit, he seemed to have a premonition of some sort. A sense of danger. Maybe of potential loss. Or maybe he sensed something imperfect that was in the air and yet to come.

The worst part about it was that she shared the same feeling. There was somewhere hanging out there the notion that a third party could somehow do something that could come between them, separate them, take that perfect partner away from the other. It was a horrible sensation. But was it really there? Or were their worst fears just wandering around like sprits or phantoms, looking to settle somewhere?

TWENTY-TWO

On her final day before departure, Alex had lunch with her boss, Mike. He wished her well and expressed the fear that she might be permanently assigned outside his department. She reassured him that if that were the case, she had heard nothing about it. Nor was she inclined to stay with this sort of assignment. She was anxious to do a one-time-only job and return to what passed for a normal life.

In the afternoon there was a final torturous Ukrainian lesson from the baroness. Then in the late afternoon, a final briefing from Michael Cerny on Ukrainian politics. "There's been tyranny, criminal behavior, and instability for a thousand years. Probably more. No point to expect much different now," he said.

"Thanks for the cheerful worldview," she said.

"I'm a realist, so don't mention it," Cerny answered. "I'll try to say hello before you leave tomorrow. If I miss you, don't worry about it."

She left the office at 6:00 p.m. and went to the gym, partly out of habit, partly because exercise released tension.

She showered, went home, and changed into some casual clothes. Robert picked her up at 9:00 p.m.

They went out to a nice place for dinner, a French place they liked in the Adams Morgan neighborhood, just a fifteen-minute walk across the Duke Ellington Bridge that spanned Rock Creek Park. La Fourchette on the Eighteenth Street Strip. Great food, but not at all formal, with a genuine French woman keeping an eagle eye on guest satisfaction.

Robert was irritated by a reassignment within the White House. His duties hadn't changed but his partner had. The Service had brought in a ballistics expert named Reynolds Martin to accompany the president on the impending trip and join the small army of assigned agents. Robert was assigned to partner with Martin, whose behind-the-back nickname was "Jimmy Neutron."

"The boy genius," Robert said, as he glanced at the menu. "Or at least he thinks he is."

Alex managed to laugh.

"Anyway, after the trip, he's back to the Denver office, so I don't have to deal with him for too long."

"Single guy?" she asked.

"Family. He's got a wife in Colorado Springs and a girl. Tina. Age eight."

"Jimmy Neutron," she said. "That's funny. I like that."

They both laughed. "To tell you the truth, he doesn't seem like a bad guy to me. Other people have had their issues though. Here," he said, picking up the wine list and handing it to her. "You read French and you know what I like. Pick something out."

She picked out a Côtes du Rhône, four years old, and ordered a couple of steaks. Why not? They had a great dinner and got gently buzzed.

After dinner, they went back to his place for a dessert and some coffee.

He had a small gift for her.

He had visited one of the better-known jewelers in Washington, an extension of a big New York store. He had picked out an inauspicious but pretty bracelet for her; a strand of rolled silver threaded with gold. It came in the store's normal blue box with a white ribbon.

She opened the box and immediately let him place it on her wrist.

"Just one more thing for me to remove on our wedding night," he teased her. They laughed together and embraced.

"Wear it in Ukraine," he said. "When I see you in Kiev I'm going to look for it."

"It's a promise," she said.

"You also have to promise to return safely," he said. "I don't like the fact that you'll be there for three days on your own."

"I'll be okay."

"I don't like Cerny either," he said.

She was startled. "I thought he was your friend," she said.

"No. I only *know* him. Met him twice. I don't have anything against him, but he's an acquaintance, not a friend."

"Did you ever have a chance to—?"

"Oh, yeah I ran their names against the personnel computers," he said. "I didn't find anything that I didn't already know."

She asked directly. "Is he CIA or not? And that battle-ax who works with him. Countess von Olga. What about her?"

"No entries on her," he said. "If he's CIA, he's at a high enough level so that my own access to it is blocked. I can't find anything further than that. But that doesn't address the 'blue card-green card' situation," he said.

"What's that?"

"Back in 1992 after the CIA was hit with major budget cuts, they started contracting out a lot of special assignments. A CIA officer could turn in retirement papers and his blue ID badge one day and go to work for a military contractor the next day. He or she would come back into the same Langley building with a green ID the next morning at a higher salary but with no government oversight. After September of 2001, the outsourcing went completely nuts. Green-badge bosses were recruiting blue-badge employees right in the CIA cafeteria."

"And no one stopped it?"

"Who would stop it during that era? Figure that the federal budget includes about five hundred million for intelligence gathering, but now the CIA only gets one percent of that. The Pentagon gets the rest and pays the military contractors. The taxpayers get three times as high a bill, but if there's a screwup, the Pentagon 'classifies' it so no one can investigate. So even if Cerny has a State Department ID, who knows who's really running his operation?"

"Got it."

"Take it from there."

"Got it," she said again, nodding, and not reassured in the least.

She arrived home past 1:00 a.m. She organized her apartment, wrote out checks to pay bills, and dropped them in the mail chute in the hallway.

She walked back into her own apartment, closed the door, stopped, and listened.

There was something about her own place that was giving her the creeps these days. She couldn't place it, but it was there.

She stood perfectly still and cocked her head.

Man, this was driving her nuts.

There *was* something! There absolutely *was*!

She put her ear to the wall, then the floor. She opened the window and listened. She couldn't find it. She went out to the hall and then she picked up on it.

She looked at her watch. Okay. It was late. So to be safe, she went back into her apartment and found her Glock. She loaded it and put it in a holster. She pulled on her UCLA sweatshirt so the gun wouldn't be visible and went for a walk.

Out the door. Down the hall. Past the utility closet that the phone and cable people used to repair things when the service was screwed up.

Down the stairs. Onto the floor below her. Then down to the third floor.

Then she had it.

Two apartments under her.

Music. Voices. Whoever lived there was jamming late. She sighed. It was bad manners to be making such a racket at a late hour.

Okay. She was turning into a nut case. Her nerves were shot for this undercover assignment and this proved it. Worse, she realized that there was something else unsettled in her spirit too.

She went back upstairs and crashed into bed, leaving the Glock on the bedside table and the final packing to the next morning. There would be one unscheduled stop tomorrow morning and no one she worked with would know about it.

TWENTY-THREE

On the morning of her departure for Kiev, Alex drove to her parish, St. John's Episcopal Church on Lafayette Square. St. John's was a tall building from the early 1800s, with a handsome white steeple and light yellow exterior. There were white columns at the entrance and stone steps leading upwards. The church was on a busy urban corner, two blocks from the White House. Many presidents had worshiped here.

She was lucky with parking, finding a place less than two blocks away. The morning was cold, but there was no precipitation. The sun, in fact, was breaking through clouds for the first time in several days.

Alex had joined St. John's when she came back to Washington after accepting her job at Treasury. She felt comfortable here. The atmosphere mixed just the right amount of Protestant tradition and reverence with inclusiveness.

She found her way to a pew halfway down the center aisle.

She knew most of her friends would smirk at her habit, her belief, her "superstition," as they might call it. She knew what people sometimes said about "faith" behind her back, but it was a free country and she felt comfortable with her beliefs.

She felt better being here. There were a handful of other people in the church, including an assistant pastor who recognized her, nodded, and gave her a warm smile. There were a few tourists at the front.

She prayed for Robert. She prayed that God would watch over her. She could hear her own words echo in the old church, and she didn't care who else could hear her if the Almighty could.

She prayed so hard that her eyes almost hurt and began to tear. She prayed as if the act of supplication was something new, or something renewed or reborn. She prayed to Jesus and to God. And then she realized something about herself and about the present.

She was deeply frightened for one of the first times in her adult life. She deeply feared something about this trip, and there was no way now to back out.

She prayed out loud and she listened and she didn't hear anything in return except the distant drone of DC traffic in the distance.

Then she sat up. She felt better. She drew a deep breath and composed herself.

In a few hours her taxi would arrive.

She had done everything she could to prepare for this trip.

Whatever God's plan was for her, she told herself, she would have to go down that road.

She was finally ready to travel.

TWENTY-FOUR

Lt. Rizzo parked his car in the entrance area to Le Grand Hotel on the via Vittorio Emanuelle. He brushed away the doorman, flashing his police credentials. For a moment, the career cop stood in front of the hotel and took in the grandeur of the place.

Le Grand Hotel was more luxurious than any other in Rome. Not even the Excelsior or the Eden could match its excesses. Its only drawback was the gritty Stazione Termini nearby, the Roman railway station, a bustling intersection of business people, excited travelers, pickpockets, creeps, hookers, and weirdoes. But once inside Le Grand Hotel, all thoughts of trains and of the people at the station vanished.

The lobby was resplendent with sparkling Murano glass chandeliers, white columns, marble busts, and grinning cherubs, a lavish but tasteful explosion of French and Italian styles in muted gold and pastels. Rizzo had been in a few of the bedrooms over the years, on official business and otherwise, and remembered them being recently restored in what the hotel called the "Barocco" style, a mongrel blend of baroque and rococo.

Everywhere one stepped there were plush carpeted floors. Everywhere one glanced, antiques and artwork. Everywhere one turned, a different hand-painted fresco showing a Roman scene. The place had come a long way since 1890 when it first opened, and its luxurious pitch had included a private bath and two electric lights in every room.

Rizzo sighed as he waited for his contact, Signor Virgil Bruni, in the lobby. To stay in a place like this for more than an hour, Rizzo reflected, a man had to be really rich. No, not really rich, *filthy* rich. Royalty rich. American movie star rich. Internet rich. Russian gangster rich. Even the local mafia guys would gasp at the prices here. What was it? Five hundred Euros a night for a room by the elevator? Eight hundred American dollars. Ouch!

Rizzo's connection was the hotel's day manager, an old friend. As he continued to wait, Rizzo surveyed the clientele, the men in designer suits, the jeweled, bronzed women in their two-thousand-Euro suits with their daring miniskirts, their beautiful skin and perfect figures, and their long sleek legs. Outside, the sports cars and Benzes of Rome's international set glided past Rizzo's dented Fiat.

Wealth, privilege, beauty, sin, and sex came so easily to these people, Rizzo mused. And what had they ever done to deserve it? Many of the men had been born into it. Others had stolen it. A few had been fortunate and earned it. Then the women had latched onto it. What was it that some French writer had written a century ago? Behind every great fortune there is a crime?

Rizzo's old man had been in an America POW camp in Sicily, then been a worker in a Fiat brake plant in the north. It had always been Lt. Rizzo's plan to rise above his police job and join these people who frequented this hotel, to live a life of expensive meals, good clothes, and beautiful women.

He had done his job diligently over the years, but his final goals had been elusive. The system had shut him out. Lieutenants in the homicide brigades of Europe were not welcome in these social climes. They were, in fact, often a nuisance. Rizzo felt as if these people had intentionally excluded him from their cozy well-heeled little clubs. So he hated these people who surrounded him this morning. He hated them with a passion. He would have loved nothing more than to bring a few more of them back down to earth before he retired.

Rizzo settled in at one of the small tables in the lobby. He eyed the whole scene before him, but mostly he eyed a trio of women who were sitting at a nearby table having morning tea. Wealthy Arabs in expensive suits, he guessed. Or maybe Iranians. Who could tell the difference these days?

Rizzo listened to them. They were speaking English. On the table in front of him was a ceramic ashtray with the hotel's logo. He picked it up and examined it. Clean, sturdy, and new.

No one was looking. He slipped it into his coat pocket. It would be perfect for a cigar at home. At least he would have a souvenir of this trip to the hotel. In fact, he now owned a piece of the joint.

A well-modulated voice came from over his shoulder. *"Gian Antonio?"* it asked.

Rizzo turned and looked. It was Virgil Bruni, his contact, and no, Rizzo hadn't been caught palming the ashtray. Or if he had been, his friend was going to let it slide.

Bruni was a small man, modest and unassuming, with a ring of close-cropped dark hair around the shiny dome of his bald head. Bruni's eyes gleamed with pleasure upon seeing his old chum. It had been two years, maybe three. He approached graciously and extended a hand.

"Hello, Virgil," Rizzo said softly. He stood.

Virgil. Named for a classic Roman poet and contemporary of Christ, Bruni had become a manager of breakfasts, banquets, bidets, and bathtubs. And he had done quite well at it, judging by his Armani suit.

Bruni slid into the other seat at the small table. Rizzo sat again.

"I wanted to alert you to something," Bruni said after the opening pleasantries and summoning coffee for both of them. He spoke in subdued tones below the other conversations in the lobby. "About ten days ago, we had two guests here. Americans, I believe. They checked in, went out one night, and no one has seen them since."

"They skipped out on the bill?" Rizzo asked.

"No, no. They deposited cash when they checked in. Ten thousand dollars American, seven thousand Euros. Not unusual for our clients. But the amount suggests that they planned a longer stay. They did in fact have a reservation for twelve days."

"Did they cause trouble of some sort?"

"Not for us. Maybe for themselves."

"It's wonderful to see you, Virgil," Rizzo said, "but would you mind coming to the point?"

Two demitasses arrived.

"Sometimes guests register and only use the hotel during the day," Bruni continued, "as you know. They find more interesting accommodations at night. This couple just went out and disappeared. I have the details."

The couple had arrived the fourth of January, Bruni explained, a

Sunday. The security cameras in the hotel had images of them until the seventh, a Wednesday. .

"Their room was undisturbed between Thursday the eighth and Wednesday the fourteenth," Bruni recalled. "Our cleaning staff is instructed to keep track of such things."

Rizzo was thinking furiously, trying to leap ahead of Bruni to see where this was going. Until he made that leap, however, the coffee was excellent and up to the hotel's high standards. Bruni sipped with his pinky aloft.

"We naturally keep passport records," Bruni said. "Records and numbers. We photocopy the personal pages of the passports. We don't tell guests. But we do it for our security."

"Of course," said Rizzo, who felt the world would be a safer place if more people spied on each other.

Bruni reached to a business-sized envelope from his inside suit pocket.

"Take a look. You may keep this. See if it means anything to you," Bruni suggested. Bruni then presented copies of the passport pages, including photographs.

Names: Peter Glick and Edythe Osuna. They had checked in as man and wife, despite the different names on the passports. It was not the hotel's policy to question such matters.

Rizzo looked at the information carefully. "The names are unfamiliar to me," Rizzo said.

"I see," Bruni said.

"Should they be familiar?" Rizzo asked.

"When the couple had been gone for six days," Bruni said, "we alerted the American embassy. At first there was no interest. A young assistant counsel said to call back in a week. But just to be sure, I left the names of the people and the passport numbers. In case some other report came in, an accident or something."

Rizzo finished his coffee.

"Then, about an hour later," Bruni continued, "some very unpleasant security people from the American embassy showed up. Barged right through the revolving door, they did. Four of them. A bunch of gorillas. I dealt with them myself. They acted as if we'd made these people go missing ourselves. They sat me down, questioned me as if I had done something. They said they'd break down the door to the room if they weren't admitted. Security people. Stood right over there by the front desk," he said, indicating. "Highly confrontational. Raised an awful scene in the lobby until I took them into my office. Demanded to get into the room. Threatened me if I didn't go along with everything."

"Did you admit them? To the room?"

Bruni seemed ill at ease with his decision. "Yes. I did. I was within my rights, as the deposit had run out. As had the reservation." He paused. "I watched them as they went through the room. They tried to get me to leave, but I said I couldn't do that. I said I'd let them remove things from the suite, but if they threw me out I would call the local police. They didn't want that. It was all very '*unofficial*' while being very much '*official*,' if you know what I mean."

Rizzo's eyes narrowed. He knew *exactly* what Bruni meant. Rizzo had locked horns in his police capacity with some embassies and foreign governments before when the foreigners had tried to keep their dirty laundry out of sight. It was always confrontational eventually and never a good experience. Rizzo, in fact, knew his way around embassies, foreign governments, and security people far better than any of his peers imagined, not that he was boasting about it.

"They went around the room with big trash bags," Bruni continued. "Took everything. Clothes. Cameras. Books. DVDs. Came across a small cache of weapons. A pair of handguns, it looked like, maybe three, which they tried to keep me from seeing. Believe me, the more I saw, the more I felt they were taking care of a problem for me. In a way they did. By this time, I just wanted Glick and Osuna, or whoever they were, out of our hotel. We needed the room for incoming arrivals too, of course."

"Of course. They're a bunch of arrogant pigs, the Americans."

"Here's the strange part, though," Virgil Bruni said, his own coffee now sitting ignored by his elbow. "When they were finished, they went around the room with cleaning material," he said. "Scrubbed everything down. That pine scented crap that Americans love so much. Smells like snowcapped toilet seats. They were removing all fingerprints, any possible DNA. That's when I knew not to ask any more questions. I should just be glad these people were out of the hotel."

"True enough," Rizzo said.

"But it caused me to think," Bruni said. "And I haven't stopped thinking. I went back and looked in the newspapers. You remember that story about two people who got shot one night on the via Donofrio?"

"Of course I do. It's my case."

"I knew it was your case," Bruni said. "I saw your name in the papers. That's why I phoned you. You see, the seventh, that was also the night when Signor and Signora Glick disappeared," Bruni said. "Same night that couple got shot down and their bodies whisked away, according to rumor. What do you think of that?"

Bruni lifted his demitasse cup again and sipped.

"I find it quite remarkable," Rizzo said after several seconds. "*Grazie mille*. But I'm not sure how it helps me with anything. And that was many days ago. Why do you bring it to my attention just now?"

Bruni shrugged. "It's been bothering me," he said. "They seemed like a nice couple. Somewhere, they might have family."

A moment passed. Then one of the Persian women spilled some tea.

"Excuse me, Gian Antonio," Bruni said abruptly.

Then Bruni, officious as always, grabbed a cloth napkin. He moved quickly to assist.

TWENTY-FIVE

The Air France Airbus gave a violent shudder. Alex blinked and was awake, her heart jumping suddenly. She glanced around. They were on their descent into Kiev and had hit a pocket of extreme turbulence.

The bumpiness continued and Alex drew a breath. The plane was banking now, moving through a layer of clouds, its left wing tipped toward earth, the right wing toward heaven. She peered out the window into an infinity of cottony white.

The aircraft descended below the cloud cover. The landscape below came into view. And there was Kiev, the ancient city of Kievan Rus, the early medieval monarchy that represented the glory of Ukrainian history until it was sacked by the Mongols, giving the Russians, who stole the name, their chance to shine. The city stretched out before her, a bluish silvery gray vision in deep, deep winter as the afternoon died. For a fleeting moment, even as a light snow fell, everything was very clear, the colors of the city stark and intense. It looked like a Vermeer landscape.

They flew just below a thick layer of angry low clouds above the city of two and a half million people. Below, the River Dnipro was impacted with ice. Bridges laced the river. She could see traffic moving among the old buildings. Bare trees stood like skeletons along the boulevards, the naked dark branches extended like grasping arms and hands. The gilded domes of the old Ukrainian churches reached for the sky and glimmered with the final flickers of afternoon light. From her seat on the Airbus, Alex could make out Independence Square — formerly Lenin Square — and the huge statue of the Archangel Michael, the city's patron saint, golden wings extended a halo behind his head. Michael dominated the square, much as a statue of Lenin once had.

To Alex's right, in the distance, she could also see the huge statue of Rodina Mat, the Soviet vision of the motherland, celebrating the victory and sacrifices of the Great Patriotic War. The statue of a woman reminiscent of the Stature of Liberty, except Lady Liberty held a torch and Rodina Mat held a sword and a shield.

Alex had done her homework. She knew the statue was eight stories high and stood above a museum to the Great Patriotic War, known in the West as World War II. Alex also knew that Rodina was done in titanium. The rumor was that she wasn't too steady on her pins these days. Like much of what the Soviets had built over seventy-five years, Rodina too might take a hard fall sometime soon.

Eight stories high, a sample of Soviet subtlety.

A sword and a shield, a sample of Stalinist philosophy.

An even bigger statue had once been planned, one of Stalin, who was to stand over the new Metro where it entered a tunnel after crossing the river on a bridge, just like the Colossus of Rhodes. But underground water had delayed completion of the tunnel, and happily for almost everyone, Uncle Joe had kicked the bucket before the statue could be built.

The plane leveled out and finished its descent, passing over the outskirts of the city. In twenty minutes, the Air France jet was at the gate. Alex was on her feet, reminding herself of the details to her new identity and ready to disembark after seventeen hours from Washington.

TWENTY-SIX

Alex's arrival in Kiev was not at an airport gate but down steps to an ordinary bus. An icy blast of cold met her. It wasn't much warmer inside the bus as the door remained open for several minutes.

Welcome to Kiev — just like Chicago, except even colder and even more corrupt.

Alex passed through Ukrainian customs. Then she moved to immigration.

She stood quietly and watched the Ukrainian officer scan her passport. He waited for something on a computer screen.

What? Was this whole thing going to blow up right at the start? The reality of her situation hit home; she was entering Ukraine illegally. Sometimes there were long prison sentences for people who did such things, just so others wouldn't.

She had been undercover before but had never passed from one country to another with a fraudulent identity. She had planned for this moment and prepared for it. But still, her palms moistened. Her blouse stuck to her ribs. She felt as if a monarch butterfly was fluttering around in her stomach.

Oh, Lord! The officer was looking at the screen too long. Much too long.

It went through her head: something had glitched with the passport. Some chunk of old Soviet style computer science had pegged her fake documents.

She turned and scanned the room. No one she knew. Nowhere to run.

The immigration officer frowned. The sweat poured off her. Now it felt as if a dozen butterflies were doing a bizarre mating dance in her stomach.

He was a nice-looking man in his mid twenties. Clean cut, fair-skinned, and blond. Looked a little like a cop or a guy she'd gone to college with, which made it all the more weird. He refused to smile.

His blue eyes slid from the computer screen to her. He spoke Ukrainian.

"*Dyplomat?*" he asked.

"*Tak,*" she said. Yes.

She fumbled slightly but pressed on. "Diplomat, sort of. United States Department of Commerce," she said.

"You are Anna Tavares?"

A beat. "I am Anna Tavares."

Still in Ukrainian: "You are *sure* you are Miss Anna Tavares?"

She couldn't tell if he was flirting or trying to catch a spy. She stayed with it.

"Who else would I be?" she asked, trying to make a joke of it.

He closed her passport and placed it on the desk in front of her, out of her reach. He switched to English. "You will now please wait," he said. "I call superior officers."

"What!? Why!?"

"Because for you, this passport, I must."

He looked to his left. Two security people approached, black uniforms, blue and yellow trim. Guns. Police clubs. A dog the size of a Volkswagen. A large man and a larger matron who looked like Olga's steroidal big sister. Their eyes were on her; they hulked in her direction and they didn't look happy. Her head snapped back to the immigration officer.

"What's the problem?" she said. "What have I done wrong?"

Her nerves were in open revolt against her common sense now. She wanted to be anywhere else in the world than here. In the back of Alex's mind, a prayer had kicked in.

The young man turned back to her. "There is no problem," the officer said. "Our country's courtesy to you. You are an American diplomat. We will escort you past the long lines."

"Oh …"

Her insides completely unraveled.

"Have a good stay, Anna Tavares," he said, returning to English and giving her a smile. He opened her passport, stamped her entry, and pushed it back in her direction. Then he winked at her. "American women are always so beautiful," he said.

"Thank you," she answered.

Her jaw closed tight. She took back her passport. The two security people then, with the utmost politeness, bypassed a hundred other travelers, led her through an official portal, and guided her into the reception area.

There she found herself face-to-face with a young man holding a piece of paper with *US Commerce* on it. She approached him and smiled.

"Anna Tavares?" he said.

"That's me. A bit frazzled. But me."

"I'm Richard Friedman. I'm with the commercial attaché's office. I'm also your control officer while you're here. Welcome to Kiev."

"Thank you."

They shook hands. He grabbed her bags.

Friedman was about her age, maybe a shade older, likeable, with a round face, glasses, and a smart look through the eyes. He wore a suit and tie beneath an open overcoat.

He carried her luggage and guided her to a waiting car and driver.

The car was French, a Peugeot, perky, deep green, and brand new. In contrast, the driver, Stosh, was a brooding Ukrainian in his fifties with a short gray beard and a three-inch scar across his left temple.

"Everything go well at immigration?" Friedman asked.

"Perfectly."

"Glad to hear it, Anna. It doesn't always. They're usually a pretty sour bunch. Still paranoid from the Soviet era. Always looking for spies."

"Imagine that," she said. "Well, if I see any I'll let them know."

They both laughed.

TWENTY-SEVEN

Soon they were rolling toward Kiev. Alex was in the back seat with Friedman, a pair of attaché cases on the seat between them.

She peered out the window, missing nothing, taking in a city she had never seen before today. The road was straight as an arrow and flat as an ironing board, with pine trees interspersed with surprisingly large houses and entrances to gated developments.

"The new rich," Friedman said, noticing her interest in what was beyond the car windows. "The FSNs tell me this all used to be forest up until independence. Now a lot of locals have gotten rich and foreign money has moved in."

"FSNs?" she asked.

"Foreign Service Nationals," he said. "Local people employed by the embassy."

She nodded. "How long have you been here?" she asked.

"Me?" Friedman answered, "Two years. The department just extended me, so I'll be here three more. I don't mind. My last posting was Yemen. At least this is in Europe."

Her nerves were still returning to earth from the immigration incident. And she was worn out by two long back-to-back flights.

The road led to a long bridge that it shared with a metro line and then climbed up onto a bluff. There sat most of Kiev, largely separate from its river.

They were in a surprisingly picturesque city, the city she had glimpsed from her airplane, with intricately styled old buildings from before the Russian Revolution of 1917. The ancient was mixed with a smattering of small stores and new structures.

Then the older buildings ended. Alex, Friedman, and their driver were in the middle of Stalinist "wedding cake" architecture, a style characterized by massive buildings as expressions of Communist state power, intimidation of the masses via steel, concrete, and glass. The combination of overwhelming size, patriotic decoration as mural decoration, and traditional motifs had always been the most vivid examples of Soviet architecture.

"This is Khreshchatyk," Friedman said. "Just Khreshchatyk, not Khreshchatyk Avenue or Street or Boulevard. It's like Broadway in New York."

"It's unreal," Alex said. She felt as if she were seeing a city from another era, another world. In a way, she was.

"Most of Kiev was spared in the big war because the Germans crossed the river elsewhere," Friedman said. "But the Russian NKVD, the KGB's predecessor, booby-trapped the buildings on Khreshchatyk with dynamite. They figured the Germans would use them. Then they blew them all up with the German soldiers in them. Wicked, huh? After the war the street was rebuilt to Stalin's taste." He pointed to a massive, ornate building with terra cotta tiles. "See how high the portal is, the square columns, the windows suggesting twenty-five foot ceilings? Architecture designed to intimidate."

Strangely enough, the buildings today looked harmless to Alex, with people strolling peacefully beside them. Time had exorcised some of the political demons.

Stalin was gone. So was Lenin, so were Khrushchev and Brezhnev, Andropov and Chernenko. The curtain had been pulled away, and the Soviet wizards of yore were no longer objects of fear. The current day people, she knew, were a different story.

Friedman lifted his eyes to the driver. "No one misses the Russians, right, Stosh?"

The comment elicited an amused sneer out of Stosh, the driver, who didn't answer further, but studied the rearview mirror as he listened in.

"Oh, by the way," Friedman said, reaching, into his overcoat pocket. He found a new cell phone and gave it to her. "This will work here. It's programmed with all the numbers you need, and there's a Ukrainian SIM card in it. Keep it with you."

She took it and riffled through the numbers index. She dropped it in her own overcoat pocket. "Thanks," she said.

Their car pulled up in front of one of the old Stalinist buildings. They were on a plaza at the very end of the street before the street disappeared down a steep hill. The rectangular building had an active revolving front door and a galaxy of foreign flags above the door.

"Your hotel, the Dnipro," Friedman said, stressing the final syllable, saying Dni*pro*. "Same name as the river, which in Russian is the Dnieper."

Dusk was settling in and the hotel had lit its blue and red neon sign. Stosh jumped out. So did Friedman. The driver's eyes were still checking out something back on the road.

"The place used to be a typical Communist 'prestige hotel,' which is to say it used to be a total dump," Friedman said. "Foreign money has fixed it up though, from what I hear. If you don't like it, we can move you. Let me know."

"I will."

The driver picked Alex's two pieces of luggage out of the trunk and waited while Friedman's conversation ensued with Alex. The cold was biting. Alex pulled on a pair of gloves from her pocket.

"You're right next to a park with a very interesting monument," Friedman said to her. "Take a look."

She glanced. More gross Soviet Commie artwork. Two muscular bare-chested men, oversized, sixteen feet high each, crossing a hammer and a sickle, one holding each. Compared to this, the Rocky statue in Philadelphia was an exercise in delicacy and subtlety. In a perverse kind of way, the bad sculpture in front of her made her think of Robert and his liking for the sensitive bronzes of Rodin and the canvases of Renoir.

"Monstrous, huh?" Friedman mused. "It was put there by Khrushchev on the four hundredth anniversary of the Treaty of Pereyaslav. The Ukrainians thought they were allying themselves to Russia, and Russia thought the Ukrainians were giving themselves over to the Russians. I don't have to tell you who got the dirty end of the stick. That's how it goes in this part of the world. Even when you're not screwed, you are."

"I'm surprised the sculpture hasn't been removed, now that Ukraine is independent," Alex said, giving it a final glance and turning away.

"This is a complicated country," Friedman replied.

"I understand there could be trouble when the president visits," she said.

He snorted slightly. "If it happens, it happens. We take every safe-guard we can, but you can't be on Red Alert twenty-four hours every day of your life. Know what I mean?"

"I know," she said. "Is there anything on my schedule yet for tomorrow?"

"I *do* know the answer to that," Friedman said. "The ambassador wishes to greet you himself. We're enormously busy with the preparations for the presidential visit, but I know he has some time scheduled for you."

"I look forward to meeting him."

"We'll pick you up at nine," he said. "Same car. Stosh is my normal driver."

"Perfect."

Stosh gave her a low quiet bow.

"Tomorrow you'll be in briefings all day," Friedman said. "There's a reception at the ambassador's residence in the evening. You'll find an invitation in your welcome kit here," he said, handing over a folder he had brought with him.

She knew from her visit to Nigeria that every US embassy provided guests with such kits, including maps of the city and little phrase-books. "The day afterward, you'll have more briefings in the morning. Then there's a 'Ukrainian businessman' on your schedule for the afternoon and evening," Friedman continued. "Yuri Federov."

They started to move toward the front door of the hotel.

A doorman intercepted them to help with the bags.

"I'm sure you're familiar with the name," Friedman said.

A hesitation, then she said. "I know who he is. Back in Washington, they enrolled me in a 'Thug of the Month' club. He's my thug this month."

Friedman laughed slightly and had a knowing look in his eye.

"Impossible not to know that name," he said. "Well, an assignment's an assignment. You've even got a number for him in your cell phone. Good luck."

Stosh pulled on Friedman's sleeve. Friedman stopped as the doorman went ahead with the bags. In a low voice, Stosh spoke to Friedman in Ukrainian.

Alex listened. Friedman answered in Ukrainian, not terribly alarmed.

"What was that all about?" Alex asked after they had passed into the lobby.

"Stosh says we were followed over here. Two men in a Mercedes. I didn't see them, but he was watching. He says they're gangsters. Whoop-dee-do." He paused. "Don't worry, it happens all the time. I can't go to the airport without a tail. No big deal. And don't be put off by something like that. The Ukrainians like Americans. They want to do business with us, most of them. Of course, after the Russians, we'd look good to anyone."

"Thanks," Alex said.

"For what?"

"For telling me honestly what your driver said. I listened in. I understood."

"Very good," Friedman said with a raised eyebrow. "Smart. Don't trust anyone. You'll do well here." He handed her the attaché case. "Open this when you have a chance," he said.

She hefted it in her hand. It was heavy.

"Vodka," he said.

"Vodka," she repeated with a smile. "Or maybe something even better."

Fifteen minutes later, having checked in, she opened the attaché case. Within it, was a box, the wrong shape for a vodka bottle, but wrapped in bright red paper, the color of blood.

She worked away the wrapping. The contents of the box were nothing she could drink; the box came unhinged and clicked open. There was a small pistol within.

Welcome to Ukraine. The piece was a Walther PPK 9 mm short. She checked it to make sure it wasn't loaded. It wasn't. She hefted it in her hand. It was slim and sleek and would carry well beneath a jacket or coat. And she knew it could pack a lethal wallop if necessary.

The PPK commonly chambered 7.65 mm auto rounds. It could carry seven in the magazine plus one chambered if one wanted to live — or die — with the notion of it accidentally going off. For security services, this version, the 9 mm short was a better choice. It could hit harder than the 7.65 mm. Because the cartridges were fatter, however, only six 9 mm short bullets could be carried in the magazine, plus one in the chamber if desired. Like its larger counterpart, the Walther P38, the PPK also had a double-action trigger to permit a fast first shot.

The gun was favored by many armed agencies, including the fictional ones of James Bond. But in the real world the weapon was known to suffer metal fatigue and malfunction. Thirty years earlier, this had nearly ended in disaster for Britain's Princess Anne when her bodyguard's PPK jammed during a hijack attempt in 1974. He took three bullets himself but lived to tell about it.

But at least it was compact. With it, a dozen bullets and a nylon holster, the type a woman can attach to a belt and wear under a jacket.

Someone somewhere was thinking of everything.

That, or someone somewhere expected some serious trouble.

TWENTY-EIGHT

In the evening, Alex had dinner by herself in the hotel restaurant. The food was ordinary but wasn't bad either; the ex-Soviet states still had a ways to go for business travelers and tourists. The restaurant was on the top floor of the hotel. Though night had fallen she could see the lights of part of the city below.

Afterward she asked the desk staff if the neighborhood was safe for a single woman. "Most times, but not always," a girl at the front desk advised. A man at the desk advised Alex to stay visible in the park.

She took her cell phone and, just in case, tucked the loaded Walther into the pocket of the heavy coat she had brought. American women were always targets in places like this. Fortunately, she had also brought a pair of durable boots that looked good yet were warm. She walked out into a freezing night for air. There was ice all over the sidewalks and public square.

She could see floodlights and a monument in nearby Khreschatyk Park. She walked toward it, stepping carefully through the ice and encrusted snow. There was little traffic; compared to an American city, Kiev was eerily quiet.

Before her, growing larger as she approached, was a rainbow-shaped arch, reminiscent of the Gateway Arch in St. Louis, Missouri, but smaller. She arrived there and put her knowledge of Ukrainian language to good use. More pre-*glasnost* propaganda in granite and steel. The sculptures had gone up in 1982.

The Friendship Arch, read the sign.

Underneath the Friendship Arch there were two statues, both illuminated. One to her right was in granite and showed a huddled mass of peasants. It commemorated the great treaty of 1664, the one that sold the soul of Ukraine to Russia. The one to her left was the statue Friedman had pointed out on the ride in from the airport. It was made of bronze and depicted two workers, one Russian and one Ukrainian, as they held aloft the Soviet Order of Friendship of Peoples.

A harsh wind kicked up and bit through her coat. It must have been fifteen degrees but the wind chill made it feel even colder. Her face stung from the icy air. She wrapped a scarf around her throat and the lower part of her face.

She gazed at the monuments, feeling very alone as she looked at them. They were creepy in their oppressiveness combined with the deep silence. She was happy that she could leave this place in a few days and return to an America where she could vote as she wished, think as she wished, and worship as she wished. Some people would have called her an old fashioned flag-waver, and she was as aware of her own country's faults and shortcomings as anyone. But no one was putting up official statues trying to tell her what to think, and even if someone did, she was under no obligation to look at it.

The extreme cold continued to penetrate her overcoat. She remained tired from the travel. She turned to walk back to the hotel.

She smacked into a huge man in a great sheepskin coat and a massive fur cap pulled low above his eyes, a heavy woolen scarf wrapped around his face. Her heart jumped into her throat. She would have fallen, except he reached an arm out and held her. She could only see his eyes and the bridge of his nose. She knew immediately that she had been incredibly careless to let a stranger get so close to her in a place like this.

His eyes bored into her. He looked like he had stepped out of the Czar's army of a century earlier. He had arrived quietly beside her, coming up out of the ground or the shadows or God knew where.

Then she realized he was not releasing her.

"*Zakordónna?*" he asked. Foreign?

Crunch time for her knowledge of Ukrainian. Sink or swim. No backups here and no interpreter either.

"*Mozhlývo,*" she answered. Maybe.

"*Frantsúz'ka? Anhlíys'ka? Amerykánka?*" he pressed. French? English? American?

She reached for a phrase from Mistress Olga.

"*Ne váshe dílo!*" she said. Mind your own business. Always a useful phrase to have ready. She pulled away, but he held her coat, his grip tight as a vice, an iron fist in a leather glove.

A moment passed. She was a heartbeat away from attempting to kick free and reaching for her weapon at the same time.

Then his grip eased. He laughed. She steadied herself. He released her.

"A monument to 'friendship,' yes?" he said, now switching into Russian, indicating the monument: "Дружба."

She couldn't help herself in replying. "Friendship enforced by the tanks of the Soviet Red Army," she said, throwing the same language back at him.

His dark eyes took on a deep burn. Her remark had touched something.

He nodded toward the statue of the workers. "Soviet Order of Friendship," he said. "In Ukraine, we call that the 'Yoke of Oppression.'"

Another moment passed. He looked both ways, dropped his hands into his pocket, and laughed. Then he slowly turned and walked away into the night. Despite the bright lights illuminating the monuments, her visitor knew where the shadows were. He did not look back as he walked away. Then he was gone, as quietly as he had arrived.

TWENTY-NINE

Rome. Quarter to seven in the morning under a cold gray drizzle. A police car bearing Lt. Gian Antonio Rizzo and his assistant, Stephano DiPetri, drew up outside an inauspicious steel door on the via LoBrutti. The building was set among two warehouses and a closed factory.

The two policemen jumped out. Rizzo walked at a quick pace. He knew this place too well. DiPetri followed close behind, pulling his coat close against the elements.

Miserable weather. A miserable place. There was a sign beside the door. It read, *"L'Obitorio Municipale — Città di Roma."*

Rizzo pulled the door open. He barged purposefully into the municipal morgue. For the next half hour, he and his assistant stood in a basement chamber that was barely warmer than the outside air. Noxious fumes assaulted their nostrils, the scent of death and chemicals everywhere. They eventually stood over two marble slabs where a pair of decomposing bodies in yellow canvas bags were set forth for their examination.

An emissary of the mortuary's office presided. He was a chubby bearded man named Bernardo Santangelo, pleasant and jovial, considering his line of work, well known for his unending courtesy and attention to detail. A meticulous well-groomed man, he looked more like a jolly chef than a technician of mortality. In his handsome pudginess, he moved like a big pampered cat.

Nearby, with her arms folded behind her back, stood a young assistant, Neomie, a woman with dark hair, thick glasses, and a complexion as pale as the resident cadavers. Rizzo gave her a quick glance and a nod. Neomie couldn't hold a candle to Sophie, so Rizzo's attention bounced back to the business at hand.

Like the corpses, Neomie remained silent.

Lt. Rizzo had worked with Bernardo Santangelo previously and knew him to be an intelligent man who did his wretched job with an air of earnestness. Santangelo adjusted the thermostat in the room to below freezing before he began to talk.

"We may now proceed," Santangelo said. "Please open the bags." Neomie unzipped first one bag and then the other.

Rizzo winced. DiPetri retched. Neomie ignored them and the dead folks.

Rizzo had seen many corpses in his career, including those of people he had known personally. But these were particularly horrendous. There had been just enough time since death — perhaps a couple of weeks, he assessed — for advanced discoloration and decomposition to set in. Death had been caused by gunshot, and the gunshots had raked the heads, necks, and upper chests, and caused particularly horrific effects.

The bodies were those of a man and a woman. Half of the woman's face had been hammered away by bullets and the remaining eye socket was filled with brains and blood. The man's face had been smashed in by gunfire so brutally that the features almost looked as if they had been turned inside out.

Gravely, his voice muted to low tones, Santangelo explained how the man and woman came to lie in his place of business.

A band of children had been playing near some old Roman ruins in the campground at Villa di Plinio. Rizzo knew the area. It was a sandy swampy region twenty kilometers east of Rome and two kilometers south of the massive airport at Fiumicino. It was a place where unusual things were known to surface.

The *bambini piccoli* had been kicking a soccer ball when it bounced into the marshes. The ball rolled to rest against *qualcosa non comune* — something unusual — sticking up out of the ground, something that looked like a broken branch of a tree or a strange piece of driftwood that had washed up from the Mediterranean.

The children pushed away the wet dirt and dead grass. They discovered that the "something unusual" was the arm of a human being. The arm was attached to the rest of a decomposing body, that of a man. The body had been stripped of clothing, jewelry, or any other pieces of identification.

The children ran off and told their parents. One of the fathers phoned his brother, who was a policeman in Castel Fusano on the

Mediterranean coast. The brother drove to the area, saw the body with his own eyes, and used his cell phone to file a report.

The local police discovered that the dead man had been buried with a female companion, one body stacked up on top of the other. It was as if those getting rid of the bodies had been too lazy — or in too much of a hurry — to dig two graves and weigh them down with stones, the normal procedure in the area.

Not long afterward, federal police were called, notably the anti-Mafia brigade. The Castel Fusano police were happy to get rid of the remains.

The bodies were shipped to Rome where they were stored here in the central *obitorio* where more experienced technicians could examine them. They were also frozen at a temperature of thirteen degrees below zero centigrade to arrest the decomposition and assist the forensics units.

Lt. Rizzo listened to all this very thoughtfully, saying nothing until Santangelo had finished. Then, "Have these victims been identified yet?" Rizzo asked.

"No," Santangelo answered. "We received them here only two days ago. We have some leads that may help us soon, however. Perhaps within the next day or two."

"Then why did you phone me?" Rizzo asked.

"Please follow me, if you would," Santangelo said.

Neomie rezipped the bags and summoned more help from the next room. The team at the morgue would return the bodies back to their own deep freeze.

Santangelo walked his visitors to a computer at a desk in an adjoining office. He sat his guests down at chairs which afforded a view of the screen. A few entries on the keyboard and Santangelo brought up the information that he wanted.

On a split screen, there were photographs of bullet fragments, courtesy of the central Roman police CSI records. Thumbnails first, then enlarged images.

A CSI techie who had been working on recent crimes had been looking for links among several shootings in the central and southern parts of Italy. The techie had grouped the homicides in the area in the last month by weapons and then, among the gun crimes, matched the subgroups by caliber. He had struck gold.

"The ammunition on the left," Santangelo explained, "are the bullets that were used in the shooting in Rome," he said. "The musician and a young woman. I believe you were the ranking investigating officer at that scene."

"Yes, I was," Rizzo said. "The musician was a local guitarist with links to local drug traffickers. The young woman had three passports. We've determined that she was a Canadian named Lana Bissoni from Toronto. She was the signatory on the apartment. How and why she had three passports is a question as yet unanswered."

Santangelo nodded.

"But here is what should interest you, Gian Antonio," Santangelo said. "The fragments on the right were recovered from the bodies in the marshes," Santangelo said. "If you look carefully, you'll see that they match the fragments shown on the left. These four murders are linked. Find the person or people who committed one of these crimes and most likely you've resolved the other case as well."

For the first time since he had stood in the cluttered apartment on the Via Donorfio, Rizzo began to grasp the possible scope of the various murders before him. Could it be that there were not two sets of two, but rather one set of four?

That, in and of itself, suggested a methodology, as well as motivations that were not easy to explain. The fact that the dead girl at the musician's apartment had three passports suggested some sort of international spin—dirty international business or espionage of some sort. And then there had been precision execution of two Americans on the streets of Rome the evening before the musician and the girl. Now, this carnage in front of him, plus where their corpses had been dumped, suggested killers who did this for a living, not for amusement or as a hobby.

He lost himself in thought for a moment, trying to tie it together. Gut instincts? His guts were exploding with them.

"How long can you keep these bodies here?" Rizzo finally asked. "I'll probably require further tests and examinations."

"Under the law, if they remain unclaimed, and if you get me the proper papers," Santangelo said, "forty-five days."

Rizzo then went into an adjoining room and filed the proper warrants.

"Now do me one more favor, if you would," Rizzo said as he placed his fountain pen back into his pocket.

"What would that be?" Santangelo asked.

"If anyone else expresses any interest in these corpses, if there are any inquiries out of the ordinary, please give me a call immediately."

THIRTY

Gian Antonio Rizzo sat quietly in his car. His assistant DiPetri drove silently through the cluttered Roman roads back to his office on the via Trafficante.

All right. Bernardo had given him something more that he could work with, although the next part of pulling things together was not yet in sight.

Traffic was jammed. Morning rush hour in Rome. DiPetri was muttering about the truck in front of them. Rizzo had half a mind to tell DiPetri to slap the flashing blue light on top of the car and drive up on the damned sidewalk if necessary, but just get them out of there.

Why didn't DiPetri think about the blue light and the siren? Because DiPetri didn't care, that was why.

Increasingly, DiPetri irritated Rizzo. It had been a long time since DiPetri had contributed in any way to a case. DiPetri was burned out worse than he was. He had been a good cop years ago, but few people could remember that. These days, he had two loves: drinking and fishing. Some day, they were going to find DiPetri dead in a bathtub of beer with a drunken tuna fish.

On the other hand, the traffic jam afforded Rizzo time to think outside of the office. At least DiPetri could be counted on to keep his trap shut.

Rizzo pondered a new angle. As far as the ballistic links were concerned, the lieutenant had another idea that might play out. There were a couple of younger people working in the homicide bureau these days, a couple of new hires and a pair of interns from the university. They were amiable kids in his opinion, both the boys and the girls. The boys had funny haircuts that looked like someone had used an electric mixer and whipped up their hair like meringues. But the girls dressed cute and Rizzo liked to flirt with them.

No contact. Just harmless flirting. Nothing wrong with that.

The real value of these kids, however, was their willingness to crunch statistics and poke around various computer systems. They knew all the new computer games and websites and could hack just about anything. Not just in Rome, but for a few Euros on the side they could even hack Interpol across Europe and some of the American sites in Washington and Virginia.

So, good. He would feed this new information to the kids in the office. He would do it individually with each of them, the girls first, so that each would think he or she was working on something special. Then he'd see where that would take them.

Who knew? He might get lucky.

After twenty minutes of sitting in traffic, which seemed like twenty days, DiPetri broke the silence in the car.

"I've got an idea," DiPetri said. "Let's get out of here."

He turned on the siren, threw the blue flasher onto the roof, and jumped the car onto the sidewalk. He navigated an armada of frightened pedestrians and within a minute had accessed the main boulevard, pointed back to headquarters.

"Good thinking," Rizzo said sullenly. "What would I do without you?"

Rizzo, however, was already thinking ahead. He had a plan.

He was going to make a return trip to the *obitorio municipale* and this time not with this fool at his side.

THIRTY-ONE

The air of the hotel room chilled Alex's face and shoulders. Her eyes opened and her sleepy gaze went to the window.

Morning. February 8.

Outdoors, across Kiev, a heavy snow was falling.

Alex gradually remembered where she was. She rose and went to the window. She watched the flakes, dark and silvery, falling obliquely against the city. Traffic moved, but slowly, leaving tire tracks on the streets and boulevards. The morning was bright gray. The snow was everywhere, across the rooftops, upon the bare trees, on the sidewalks, on the monuments, and upon the crosses that topped the many churches.

She looked at a clock and felt the overwhelming need to talk to Robert, even though it was midnight in Washington.

She phoned and got lucky. She reached him on his cell phone, waking him. "Hey," she said.

"Hey." There was a pause. "You okay?" he asked. "Everything all right?"

"Yeah. Fine. Just wanted to hear your voice."

Her own voice cracked slightly.

She was thrilled to hear his voice, and yet it made her homesick at the same time. He mentioned that he was still assigned to his new partner for the trip but that things were working out better than expected.

"That's good," she said. "Yeah. Good. Real good."

"What's wrong?" he asked.

"Nothing's wrong." There was a pause. "I'm just missing you," she said. "A lot."

"I'll be there when?" he asked sleepily. "Three days?"

"Yeah. Three days."

Three days projected into the future had never seemed so long a prospect. But she felt strengthened by hearing his voice.

"I love you and miss you," she said. She stood at her window and looked out on the snowy square, which was busy with people. There was also a trio of policemen with automatic weapons. She scanned for the man who had confronted her the previous night, but she saw no one who might be him.

"Same," he answered. "I love you and miss you. You sure there's nothing wrong?"

"I'm sure," she said. And now, hearing him, nothing was wrong. "Travel safe, okay?"

"It's Air Force One," he said. "Government of the United States of America. Greatest nation on earth. You know what that means, right? Every inch of the aircraft, construction, maintenance, fuel, hey ... it's all done by the lowest bidder or a political pal."

He managed to get her to laugh. She told him she loved him again and how much she missed him. He was her mentor, her love, and often her inspiration. Sometimes the miles, the distance, the separation were too much to bear.

She told him she looked forward to his arrival. He said the same. When the conversation ended, she put down the phone and sat quietly for several minutes, a bittersweet feeling in her chest.

Then she rallied her spirits. The man in the square had spooked her even more than she had realized. But now he seemed like nothing more than a bad dream.

She ordered coffee and a light breakfast sent to her room. She ate as she dressed. She was downstairs in front of the hotel to meet her driver punctually at 8:00 a.m., even with jetlag. The snow felt surprisingly good on her face. She had a minute to enjoy it, then her car and driver arrived.

Friedman again, with Stosh, the everyday designated driver.

As the snow continued, they drove to the US Embassy which was on the outskirts of downtown Kiev. They passed through a front gate with guards and heavy fortifications. The building was in gray brick, with ornamental pilasters on the front, a mongrel of a building.

"Not exactly our first choice of a structure," Friedman said as they arrived and stepped out of the car. He added with a smile, "It was once the headquarters of the Communist Party organization for this district of Kiev. When independence came, the old-line Reds went into the real estate business and sold us the lousy building. Then they went out the day after the money was transferred, imported a planeload of blondes from Estonia and Lithuania, and had Stolichnaya orgies with the profits. Some Marxists, huh?"

Alex laughed. "Did they want to be paid in rubles or dollars?" she asked.

Friedman laughed in turn. "What do you think, Anna? *Dollars.* No one ever said they were stupid. And most of those blondes were pretty great looking, I must admit."

"Typical," she said with a smile.

Alex was surprised how compact the building was. "Got to admit, I've seen larger embassies," she said.

"We're enormously overcrowded," he answered. "There's a new complex being constructed, but it won't be finished for a few years. Meanwhile, we're cramped. No one foresaw how important Ukraine could be if *glasnost* happened. So now we're stuck with our usual bad foreign policy planning. It's depressing if you think about it, so I don't think about it."

They walked in the front entrance. Two marine guards stood by. Friedman had a fresh ID for Alex. She brushed snow off her shoulders in the front entrance hall.

When word had come to the embassy in Kiev six weeks earlier of an impending presidential visit, the embassy faced three challenges. One, making sure that the president regarded the visit as a success, both substantively and organizationally. Two, making sure the organizational details were flawless. And three, ensuring that the visit actually met what the ambassador regarded as American objectives in the country.

Ambassador Jerome Drake had announced that he would be the control officer for the visit. He was a political appointee in his final posting before retirement. But Drake had also spent a career in the Foreign Service. He was unusual in that regard, in that he was wealthy, a crony of the president, *and* had had experience in the diplomatic field. His family had amassed a fortune in aluminum siding in the 1960s, and Drake had used the fortune wisely.

"In some ways, Ambassador Drake is 'bulletproof' because of his relationship with the president," Friedman explained to Alex in private shortly after their arrival that morning. "And he was bulletproof for congressional approval because he had been a generous donor to both political parties."

"Money talks," Alex said.

"It doesn't just talk, it's multilingual," Friedman answered. "Same as you."

Friedman then introduced Alex to his own boss, Charles Krimm, the chief political officer at the embassy.

"Oh yes, of course," Krimm said. "You're the lucky party in charge of keeping tabs on our favorite local hoodlum, Yuri Federov."

"Apparently so," Alex answered.

"Don't spend much time with him alone. We'll never see you again."

"Thanks."

"Good luck, Anna," he said. "You'll need it." He rushed off. Within minutes of arrival, Alex had the impression of the embassy in Kiev as a place in constant motion, the impending presidential visit being the cause.

Then, briefly in a hallway, Friedman introduced Alex to the ambassador himself, Jerome Drake. Drake was a tall, thick, lumbering bear of a man, about sixty with a moonish face — Grizzly Adams in a three-piece suit. He was known as a man of dry humor and a quick tongue.

Like Krimm, Drake seemed preoccupied. Yet Alex also immediately picked up the notion that he was more interested in her as a new female on the premises than in what she was doing there.

"We're having one of the countdown meetings in fifteen minutes," Friedman said. "That's why everyone seems slammed. You should sit in on it."

"Sit in on what? The slamming?" she joked.

"No," Friedman said with a grin. "The countdown meeting."

During the weeks that had preceded Alex's arrival, there had been back-and-forth between Washington and the embassy on the details of the program for the president, but the White House had remained in the driver's seat. It took advice but the trip was the president's visit and his staff's call. As the schedule had begun to take shape, appointments were made of two officers for each "event." Since this all-hands-on-deck event was draining embassy personnel resources, these were junior officers.

Everyone got sucked in. An "event officer" was responsible for organizing each event, working with a Ukrainian counterpart assigned to the visit. The event officer knew everything about the event. There was also an embassy "site officer" for each event whose job was to know everything about the locale where the event would take place, including but not limited to the location of the toilets.

Then there was the presidential "advance" team. They were mostly young White House staffers, sons and daughters of heavy political contributors, who descended on the embassy with the mission of ensuring a perfect experience for the president.

"Some of the advance people are okay; most are a pain in the butt," Friedman said sotto voce as he and Alex entered a large conference room on the third floor. "They arrived weeks ago and insisted on running through every event time after time. They were accompanied by a 'site officer' and an 'event officer,' both based in Washington."

"Do they know what they're doing?" Alex asked.

"Let's just say Ambassador Drake can't stand them."

"What do you think of them?"

"No comment."

"Thought so," she said.

The meeting began when Ambassador Drake finally rambled into the conference room. The ambassador mostly listened over the course of the next ninety minutes. Charles Krimm, the political officer, ran the meeting. There were forty staffers present, plus the entire advance team from the White House, who hogged all the seats at the large table in the center of the room. Other attendees sat in chairs scattered around the room. As the newcomer, Alex selected one of the more remote seats against a wall. Friedman sat with her and looked as if he was trying to stay clear of the meeting entirely.

Yet among the assembled staff, Alex found a genuine nonpartisan feeling, even though the president was from the extreme wing of the reigning political party. It was, after all, the boss who was coming and the boss represented the United States of America. But then again, Alex found the diplomatic enclave on high anxiety and high alert. As Michael

Cerny had suggested back in Washington, there was plenty of opposition to the president's impending appearance.

"We're still picking up a lot of rumors of trouble," Krimm said.

He expanded.

The most persistent rumor, the same one that Cerny had mentioned in Washington: A group of pro-Russian Ukrainians, the *filorusski*, were determined to stop the proposed NATO alliance by any means possible. Even worse, according to intelligence that local CIA people had picked up, within this group there was one fanatical subgroup that had now decided to assassinate the new president of the US during the state visit. Their goal: to torpedo US-Ukraine relations and thus Ukraine's membership application for NATO.

The ambassador then interjected one of his few remarks of the morning.

"I should stress," Drake said, "that this is *not* part of the official Russian program these days. Putin may be a bastard, but these days, he's *our* bastard. So the Russians are looking at the big picture of future Russia-US relations. The feelings of Vladimir Putin, no matter what you think of him as a clone of Uncle Joe, echo the alliances of World War II when America, the arsenal of democracy, allied itself with Soviet Bolshevism to battle Hitler. All of you, please keep that in mind."

"We won that one, didn't we?" Krimm asked, trying to lighten the mood. "The big set-to with our Russian friends."

"Yes," Drake answered without missing a beat. "First in 1945 and then in 1986. I suppose the next one will be in 2027, but I don't expect to be around for it."

To Alex, political alliances never ceased to have an Alice in Wonderland aspect. They adjourned for lunch.

At 2:00 that afternoon, an associated meeting convened, planning out the itinerary for the president while in Kiev. This time, the ambassador was absent.

On any occasion, a visit by an American president to a counterpart in a foreign country was largely a media show. The purpose was always to demonstrate the "close ties" between the United States and the host country. This was accomplished by symbolic acts, all staged with the media in mind.

"To review," Krimm said, "while in Kiev the president will have three events, all of which will occupy the day after arrival. By evening the president will depart."

Alex then learned the full details of the three events for the first time. There would be a meeting with the Ukrainian president in the morning. Attendance at a Christian church service would follow. Then there would be the laying of a wreath at the memorial for the victims of the *Holodomor*, the enforced famine of the 1930s.

"Then, we have no scheduled fourth event," Krimm said to mild laughter. "The president will get the executive butt out of the country as fast as possible."

From what was said, Alex saw quickly that the trip from the cathedral to the memorial was the problem. It was no more than several hundred yards, and there was no way to make sure the area was completely secure. The Ukrainian security services would have no qualms about occupying apartments and roofs.

"But are these guys dependable?" asked one of the more belligerent members of the advance team. "Come on. How can we count on them?"

"We *can't* count on them," Krimm said. "We just hope they do their job and our security people will assume they won't. No protection is infallible. There's always risk."

Back in Washington, Krimm explained further, the US president had been warned of the problems but refused to cancel the visit or change the program. The Secret Service was apoplectic, as was the CIA bureau chief in the Ukraine. Alex felt herself cringe slightly at the mention of the Secret Service and the potential dangers that lurked in Kiev.

But the president wouldn't budge. The ambassador was an old pal as well as a political crony. Ambassador Drake had assured safety. The president further insisted that it would be an affront *not* to visit the monument. The president was not one to shy away from a high profile political date, laden with political positives — the least of which was the defender-of-liberty-around-the-world role — particularly in a new administration. So both venues remained in the official program.

Alex leaned to Friedman and whispered. "If there's no way to secure the appearance at the monument," she asked, "the president shouldn't do it. Or am I missing something?"

Friedman winced.

"The advance team and the president's spin doctors are still fighting with the Secret Service about that one," he said. "The spin doctors love the image of a head-bowed president walking across a large square with the Ukrainian counterpart. Yet that's the most vulnerable moment. What the heck can we do?"

"Then they should avoid it," she said, thinking of the safety of both Robert and the president.

"Try telling *them* that," Friedman said. "The security people know that it's impossible to completely secure the public square. Somewhere there's going to have to be a compromise of some sort. And we've only got three days to find the compromise."

"Great," she said.

"Politicians take dumb chances all the time," Friedman said, almost a little too loud, since a few heads turned in their direction. "Ninety-nine-point-nine percent of the time they get away with them."

THIRTY-TWO

Virgil Bruni, assistant manager of one of the finest hotels in Europe, had an invitation that evening also. Gian Antonio Rizzo picked him up at 6:30 in the evening and drove him to the municipal morgue, where Bernardo Santangelo, the cheerful, chubby mortician, waited.

By arrangement, Rizzo walked Bruni back to the vaults where unidentified bodies were kept. Two corpses were removed from their freezer vaults and brought to marble slabs for inspection. Rizzo barely spoke, and neither did Santangelo. They had been down this path many times before.

Despite the cold within the viewing chamber, Bruni looked as if he were about to break a sweat. Rizzo moved quickly, however. There was no point to prolong the agony.

Santangelo personally unzipped the body bags. Then he presented the partially decomposed bullet-smashed faces of two murder victims to the dapper little hotel manager.

Bruni gasped. Then for a fraction of a second, Bruni swayed and appeared as if he might faint. Rizzo held out a hand and steadied him.

"Well, then?" Rizzo asked. "Were these unfortunate ones — *questi disgraziati* — your guests?"

Several seconds passed before Bruni could answer, not because he didn't know the answer, but because he had to get past his horror. Never before had he seen anything like this happen to someone he had known personally, however briefly.

"Yes," he finally said, his voice barely audible. "They were."

Rizzo nodded to Santangelo, who rezipped the bags. The evening trip to the morgue was a resounding success.

THIRTY-THREE

Alex returned to her hotel after her first working day at the embassy in Kiev. Her initial meeting with Yuri Federov had been pushed back a day. No reason given.

It was Ukraine. Reasons weren't necessary.

She would not have the luxury of staying in this evening and relaxing, however, since a social event had been scheduled at the ambassador's residence. The event was the ambassador's reception in honor of the most unpopular people currently in the embassy, the White House Advance team. All embassy officers were "invited," including those like Alex who were on temporary assignment, albeit in *Godfather* style — an invitation that could not be refused.

From the clothes she had brought with her, Alex picked out a pale green travel dress with three-quarter sleeves and a scooped neckline. The material was clingy and followed her shape nicely, stopping two or three inches above the knee.

Richard Friedman picked up Alex at the hotel. Once again, Stosh, Freedman's driver was at the wheel. Their car guided them through the quiet cold streets of Kiev. A light snow fell.

The ambassador's residence was in a neighborhood called Podil, upstream from the main part of Kiev. Podil was the old merchant's quarter when the river was used for trade; there was still a station for tourist riverboats there, the "River Station," and Podil was filled with the former houses of such merchants. In the streetlights Alex could see that many of the old mansions had been gentrified.

When they arrived, Alex found "the Residence," which was how embassy personnel always referred to the place where the ambassador lived, to be a modest mansion, a comfortable old building with an appealingly livable quality. There was a staircase leading from the sidewalk to the front, but the actual entrance was in a courtyard in the back for security purposes.

"I guess we're early," Alex said. The only people present were embassy personnel.

"Standard practice," Friedman said. "It's like the crew of a warship going to action stations as the enemy approaches. Don't forget this is work."

"But it's also a party, right?"

"Free food and booze, but you have to earn it."

"Doing what?"

"Depends." Friedman nodded in the direction of a young man. "For instance, Bill Katzmann there is a JO who has pulled receiving-line duty."

"Which consists of ...?"

"... keeping the line moving. There will be three hundred guests. If each one spent five minutes talking to the ambassador that would be about twenty-five hours. So guests are expected to be content with a handshake and maybe a 'glad you could come.'"

"Are they?"

"Most understand, but some don't and want to have a real conversation. So Bill's job will be to wait for a break in the conversation and politely say, 'This way, sir,' or something like that. The problem is when an ambassador doesn't understand the drill because he's a political appointee new to the game or who doesn't want to play it. I was in Bonn under Arthur Burns, a good ambassador but also a very chatty person. At the Fourth of July reception, where there are over a thousand guests, the line slowed to a crawl, with some guests waiting in it for three hours."

"Did any just give up and leave?" Alex asked

"No way. An invitation to the Residence is always the hottest ticket in town. Everyone wants to say, 'As I told the American ambassador ...,' even if in reality the exchange was one sentence each. In Bonn, not to be invited to the Fourth of July and be seen there was a major humiliation for anyone who thought he was someone. The pathetic cases were noninvitees whose secretaries would call to ask about the invitation that had apparently been lost in the mail."

Alex laughed. "How are the guests selected?"

"That's the job of the section chiefs. Each section is tasked with providing suggestions for the guest list. These are the people they regularly come into contact with. The guest list is weighted toward the interests of the visiting Americans. For instance, if the guest of honor is a high-ranking Treasury official, the guest list will be heavy with people from the Economic Ministry and so on."

At this point, Ambassador Drake appeared and moved around, shaking the hands of the embassy personnel present. Eventually, he came back to Alex, whom he remembered from that morning. He took her hand and held it.

"Beautiful dress," he said, eyeing her head to toe. "Lovely color."

"Thank you," she said.

"Most of the women around here are built like beer trucks," he said. "You're closer to a Ferrari. A breath of fresh air. Don't quote me."

In her peripheral view, Friedman rolled his eyes.

"You flatter me unnecessarily," Alex said.

"It's my pleasure to do so," Drake said. Politically incorrect as he was, Drake got away with his flirtations through a natural charm. His manner was engaging and amiable. After extending a few extra words of welcome, he released Alex and moved on.

"Well, you're fitting right in," Friedman said with a smirk.

"Is he always such a flirt?"

"He's got an eye for the ladies. Wait till he has a few drinks. He's like a nice old dog who still chases cars. I don't know what he'd do if he caught one."

"I know the type," she said.

"Hey, I've got to go to action stations soon so let me wrap up," Friedman said. "In addition to the officer on the receiving line, other JOs are supposed to look out for guests who don't mingle but just stay with their wives looking on, and engage them in conversation. Then there are officers who go to the most important guests and lead them up to the guests of honor and introduce them. And finally, officers are supposed to use the opportunity to chat up their contacts, asking how things are in their areas and so on."

"And the ambassador?" Alex asked.

"After the line shuts down, when the flow of guests has trickled off, he can turn things over to the DCM, who'll be in the line next to him, along with relevant section chiefs, including me, unfortunately.

The ambassador stands in the crowd and talks with the people brought up to him or who come to him of their own accord. Again, if an unimportant guest has glommed onto the ambassador, our officer will engage said guest in conversation while the ambassador smiles to that guest and says; 'Delighted to talk with you,' and wanders off."

"So this is a *'party'*?" she laughed.

"It's a 'reception,'" he answered, "with all the stuffy implications that go with it."

"You like these things?"

"It's one of the things we're paid to do. Does a dentist mind looking into people's mouths? And as you 'mix and mingle' you can meet some interesting people outside your usual circle of contacts. It's the receiving line I hate."

Friedman glanced over to where the ambassador was already in place with the DCM and some other officers.

"Action stations!" Friedman said. "Have fun." He turned and took up his place in line. Not a moment too soon, for an early guest was walking through the door.

The event was a cocktail buffet. The food was very good. It was set forth on a table while white-jacketed waiters hired for the occasion took plates of it around the room. Heavy trays laden with drinks followed. There were three open bars, but by late in the evening they were barely necessary.

The party took on a Ukrainian flavor, much encouraged by the popular American ambassador. The Ukrainians, like the ancient Romans, liked to drink in toasts, two sides taking turns. Someone silenced the room toward ten in the evening and proposed the first toast of Ukrainian vodka. Friedman pushed a drink into Alex's hand.

When in Rome, Alex decided quickly, do as the Romans do.

"Guests are expected to shoot their shot," Friedman advised with a smile. "Sipping is wimpy. You okay with this?"

"Someone else is driving me back to the hotel, right?"

"Yes, and it won't be me."

Three toasts went back and fourth. Alex bailed after that. Two more followed. Ambassador Drake set the tone by conspicuously leading the consumption of shots. It was no surprise that he was popular among the locals and his staff, as well as whoever sold the vodka to the embassy.

Toward 11:30, the party was still going strong. Richard Friedman, somehow still sober, guided Alex over to Ambassador Drake. By this time, in addition to the shots, Drake had found too many of the heavy trays laden with drinks. Small talk followed. He addressed her as "Anna" and asked her when she would be meeting with Yuri Federov. She said the next afternoon. He nodded and soon began to mumble about how beautiful Alex was. He followed that by mentioning that his wife was out of town. Some of his aides exchanged glances.

Nearing midnight, Drake, wobbly, noisily drained a gin and tonic and looked around for another. An aide quickly found him one. His assistants seemed to enjoy getting him toasted. As he sipped his ninth drink of the evening, Drake surveyed the sea of young people who were still partying, the advance team, for whom the party was given. Here were all the young folks who had been making his life impossible for the last five weeks.

"The 'advance team,' " muttered the ambassador. "I've never cared for those little clowns. Anna? Know what my first run-in was with those people?"

Alex sipped her drink and waited. "What?" she finally asked.

"I was in Bonn twenty-two years ago, as chief of the Political/Internal Unit," the ambassador said. "I was the event officer to a boat trip on the Rhine that President Reagan and Chancellor Kohl of West Germany were taking. The 'romantic' part of the Rhine, the part with the mountains covered with vineyards with ruined castles on top, starts upriver, south of Bonn. The idea was for the president to fly down to Oberwesel — that's this picturesque little town where the romantic crap starts — and board the boat there, along with Kohl. They'd sail north and then get off."

Oberwesel, he explained, had no Nazi baggage from World War II and made for a great photo-op. Alex sipped and listened. Other members of the embassy staff gathered, carefully keeping away any members of the advance team.

"Now, every lousy little German town has a so-called Golden Book," the ambassador continued, "where honorary citizens are inscribed. Naturally, the mayor of Oberwesel wanted his filthy fifteen minutes of fame with a book signing next to the gangplank. So this clown from the Reagan advance team sneered, 'Out of the question,' except he used an extra word before 'question.' He cited security considerations and the need not to waste the president's time on what he called 'a bush-league event.' Well, I tried to advise this jerk of the symbolic importance of the Golden Book in Germany and the fact that the mayor belonged to Kohl's party, and I was told to 'keep it zipped.' "

The ambassador stirred his drink with a swizzle stick as he nursed along his story.

"Well, Helmut Kohl's whole career was based on networking and an incredible memory of people," Drake continued. "The man was like an elephant. He'd remember folks he'd met ten years earlier while soused at some podunk wine festival. So when the disappointed mayor called Kohl, the head of his party, Kohl apparently called Reagan personally. Of course, Mr. Reagan approved it. He loved stuff like that. The Golden Book was on. You can imagine how I relished this."

The ambassador grinned and lurched slightly. Alex, with a sweet and friendly smile, sidestepped his advance and escaped from under his thick arm.

"Anyway, when the event finally happened, there was press aboard the boat, but their access to Reagan and Kohl was supposed to be limited. Naturally, no good reporter abides by this kind of fence, and soon Mr. Reagan was chatting with them. A member of the advance, the same bozo who'd been giving me all the trouble, was *fuming* about this. So I went over to him. I said, 'President Reagan looks happy. Why aren't *you* happy?' The advance guy looked at me as if I'd punched him in the nuts. That the president could be content with something that hadn't been planned to the minute by his staff was incomprehensible." He paused. "Those advance people are mostly a bunch of weenies," he concluded. "They couldn't organize a cat fight in a bag."

As Alex and the embassy staff laughed, the ambassador finished his drink and found a final one on one of the last passing trays of the evening. Apparently, a wave of nostalgia hit him at the same time also.

"Ronald Reagan," he said. "I miss the man. Reagan looked the part, he acted the part. Hell, he *was* the part! Now *there* was a president!" he said.

And he drained the rest of his glass.

THIRTY-FOUR

Lt. Gian Antonio Rizzo stood in his office in Rome the next morning, the ninth of February. Around him at a rectangular table, he had grouped four of the best homicide detectives in his bureau. Rizzo was now attacking the two linked double-murder cases with a vengeance, while at the same time trying to keep a lid on the inquiries from his superiors, official and unofficial.

One of the four men around him had been recalled from a climbing vacation in Switzerland. A second detective, a woman, came back two weeks early from her maternity leave. Another man was taken off a juicy assignment involving a local radio personality whose drunken semiclad wife had recently "fallen off" a yacht—or was it *jumped* or *pushed?*—that belonged to a Marxist member of the Italian parliament. And the fourth had been on a winning streak at a high-rolling *chemin de fer* table at Monte Carlo when the call had come from Rome to report back to Bureau headquarters immediately.

Rizzo briefed them all. He asked them to not mention the linkage of these cases to anyone else in the department. In Rizzo's experience, if he felt that he had an advantage in an investigation, if he knew something that was not yet known by the public, he was one step ahead of the people he was looking for. He never wanted to tip his hand.

He showed the computer mockups of the bullet fragments and presented all of the photographs taken at the two crime scenes. He asked if any of the people at the table had any initial notions as to where this might lead, how these slayings might be linked.

No one volunteered anything.

"*Allora, bene,*" he continued. "The Mafia guys like their small caliber .22s. They like to use a silencer from close range. Two behind the ear, am I not right? The South American drug scum, Colombians for example, like machine pistols and they blow away the victims with a hundred shots."

His eyes roved the room. Not one of his detectives was willing to make contact.

"Our colonial friends the Ethiopians have no subtlety at all," he continued. "They drag you to a warehouse, put a tire around you while you scream for mercy, ignite you with gasoline, then stand there and gape. But what was *this* all about? *Who* is doing this? What type of criminals are we looking for? Could I see some life, *per favore*, some reaction from this table, or should I find four better detectives?"

The two interlocking questions were barely out of Rizzo's mouth when he realized that there would be no answer coming this morning. Business like this drove him crazy. Why had he even come in to work this morning? Sophie was off work today and they could have been spending the day together. Instead, he was chasing down the scum that brought crime to Italy while having to light a fire under those who should have been best equipped to help him.

"All right then," he said in conclusion. "Foolish me, who thought that we might have some angle on these cases this morning from the four of you. I will be in this office working sixteen-hour days on these cases. I will also be monitoring the four of you closely." Without consulting anyone's files, he added, "It is not by coincidence, that I've assembled the four of you. I notice that each of you has recently put in for a major promotion. I will be watching your progress very closely. Be assured that the cases I've put before you this morning will directly impact both promotions and demotions. We will have success or failure here, I don't know which. But as for your careers, I can promise you *repercussions!*"

He eyed them. "I want thorough reports from all of you by Friday of next week," he said. "I want potential leads and connections for these two cases. I don't care if you're up all night every night and have to work all weekend to get this done. I want progress."

Rizzo turned on his heel, left the conference room for the hallway outside, glowering in his usual bad humor.

Where were all the kids this morning, he wondered.

The interns. Maybe one of those bright kids would have something. They'd make great spies one day, those little imps, he thought.

But none did. Not today.

THIRTY-FIVE

Alex walked into a conference room at the embassy, followed by the two attachés who had been assigned to her. The first was Ellen Higgins, a dowdy middle-aged woman with thick glasses in a brown suit. The second was Phillip Ralston, whom Alex had met the previous day.

Ellen was the keener intellect of the two. She was a University of Chicago graduate and a skilled interpreter in Russian and Ukrainian. Ellen was also the official note taker. At every embassy meeting there was a note taker to draft the report on meetings, except in the case of the very rare "under four eyes" meetings that the bureaucracy dreaded. Recording devices were almost never allowed, since principals wanted to be able to deny any misspeaking.

Ralston was a wealthy man in his thirties who played at being a diplomat and had already spent much of his time talking about his home in New Canaan, Connecticut, as if anyone else was interested. Half an hour earlier, he had been laughing and showing pictures of the house back in the United States. Now, going into the meeting with Federov, he looked taut enough to explode.

They arrived in the conference room at the same time as the opposition.

The Ukrainians wore overcoats on top of suits. They seemed to have been carved from the same block of solid Russian stone. They smelled of tobacco and cologne.

Federov was the tall one in the middle, a thick jaw, very short hair, stubble across the chin much the same length. He was handsome the way a retired boxer is handsome, the wear and toughness suggesting survival and the survival suggesting a certain intense masculinity. His nose looked as if it had been broken once and bent out of shape, then broken a second time and pushed back in the right direction, probably without anesthetic either time.

Federov was six four. Imposing. Powerfully built. In American terms, the body of a tight end. He was a head taller than Alex was, with huge hands and a weightlifter's body, definitely more of a presence in person than he had been in the photographs. His teeth — the teeth that had bitten the ear off a Brooklyn cop — were yellowed but straight.

The stories came back to her: him abusing women in his night clubs, two wives "disappearing," and having people murdered almost for sport.

He was physically intimidating to her, but there was no way she was going to tip him off to that fact. He moved close to Alex, offering a hand, his dark eyes midway between a glare and a smile. She got the idea that he was mentally undressing her as he eyed her and she stifled a cringe — she tried to tell herself that she had dealt with more vile human beings than this and survived, but on second thought, she wasn't sure that she had.

Alex accepted his hand. It was firm, strong, and dry.

"I'm Yuri Federov," he said in Russian.

"I'm Anna Tavares. US Department of Commerce," she said, also in Russian.

He switched into Ukrainian, testing her already. "Aren't you going to say you're pleased to meet me?" he asked. "That would be the polite thing, Anna Tavares."

"It would also be a lie," she said in Ukrainian. "Let's be seated. We have a lot of business to discuss, so I appreciate your coming in."

Silently, she said a big thank-you — *velykyy diakuyu tobi* — to Olga. She had kept pace in Ukrainian, but was anxious to get out of it before betraying any weakness.

A smile crept across Federov's face with the slowness and deliberateness of sun breaking through the clouds on a mostly cloudy day. He introduced his two backups, Kaspar and Anatoli, no last names given. They looked like bookends or, more appropriately, the twin doors on the rear of a truck. They were husky and stocky. Alex assumed they were bodyguards of some sort. She further assumed that the metal detectors around the embassy's entrance had done their jobs and any artillery hauled over by Kaspar and Anatoli had been left outside.

Back to Russian. "Charmed," Federov said.

"Let's get to work," she said.

"I don't know what this meeting is about," he said.

"Well, as soon as it starts, I'll tell you," she said, gaining some traction.

He switched to English. "Then let's begin. I can express myself well in English, so we will speak your language."

"I speak Russian," she said in Russian, "and some Ukrainian. Mrs. Brown here is able to interpret and take notes. So any of the three languages are fine."

"I still prefer English," he said.

"That's fine," she said, relieved. The meeting began.

Alex guessed that Kaspar and Anatoli wouldn't have much to say in any language, particularly with the boss present. It turned out she was right.

They couldn't smile, and for all Alex knew, they couldn't read either, because when files were placed before everyone in the room to present the topics of the meeting, unlike their boss, they ignored them. Instead, they sat there beside their boss, their four hands folded on the table, staring at her as if someone were holding a gun on them.

"Why is there a note taker if we are anyway being recorded?" Federov asked.

"Who says we're being recorded?" Alex asked.

"Why *wouldn't* we be recorded?" he asked.

"I want to talk about The Caspian Group," she said.

He looked first to Kaspar and then to Anatoli. "What is The Caspian Group?" he asked. "I've never heard of it." His two peers understood enough to smile on cue.

"Mr. Federov," she said. "You're not a mystery to the United States government. You do millions of dollars of business that are subject to US taxation. You'll either pay your proper share or we will make certain that you no longer can do business in the US, even through one of your puppet companies. Am I being clear enough?"

He went through the same charade. He laughed slightly. He took out a pack of cigarettes and pulled one into his lips. She intentionally watched him until he had lit it and inhaled deeply. There were tattoos on the backs of his fingers, common with Russian hoods. The rest of his body, not that she wished to see it, would tell an even larger story, she knew.

"There's no smoking in this room," she said.

"I'm smoking," he said.

"And you're about to stop," she said.

He looked at his bodyguards and exchanged a shrug. They chortled.

"Something funny?" Alex asked.

"A lot is funny," he said.

"Put the cigarette out."

The look in his eyes mocked her. So did the contempt in his voice. "Yes, ma'am," he finally said.

He turned the cigarette around and tamped it down on his tongue without flinching. She was ready for the move and didn't bat an eyelash. He flicked the remains of the butt across the room.

"Very good," she said next. "Now. I want to talk about The Caspian Group."

"What is The Caspian Group?" he asked again.

"All right," she said. "We'll do it the hard way."

She held him in her gaze and flipped open the file in front of her.

She began to read aloud.

THIRTY-SIX

The destination of Mark McKinnon, an American with an important job in Rome, was a basement bar in Trastevere, a neighborhood of Rome, on the west bank of the Tiber, south of Vatican City, which felt more like a small Italian town than part of the capital city. Trastevere was a community of small streets lined with restaurants and café bars spilling out onto the narrow sidewalks. There were not so many tourists here, which was always nice for McKinnon. He didn't like to run into anyone he knew, other than the individual he might be looking for.

Normally four o'clock in the afternoon would be considered early to meet a contact for a drink and some chat. But McKinnon easily found one of his regular haunts for just such afternoon meetings. It was a small basement bar called San Christoforo, around the corner and down a few side streets from the Piazza di Santa Maria. McKinnon walked down four brick steps and pushed open a wooden door to a dark place, dimly lit with candles.

As he entered, a dozen spooky figures turned to eye him from the bar. For a few seconds, McKinnon allowed his eyes to adjust to the dim light.

Then, from a corner table shielded by shadows, rose a shy voice. "Mark?" it asked.

McKinnon turned.

In the corner sat a fit middle-aged Italian man behind a large glass of red wine, a small tray of bread sticks, and a votive candle.

"Please have a seat, my friend," the Italian said in softly accented but impeccable English.

The men shook hands. McKinnon seated himself. The bartender sauntered over and without speaking, set up a second glass and poured a bold young Chianti from a jug.

The Italian lifted his glass. "*Salud*," he said, with mock formality.

McKinnon grinned and reciprocated with a similar toast. There was a moment or two of small talk. These men knew each other well but only met when they absolutely had to — maybe once or twice a year at most, and almost always in this place. Two of the figures at the bar worked for the Italian man and were armed accordingly.

"Well," McKinnon finally said, "we seem to have a problem. A couple of our people have been murdered."

"So it appears," the Italian said.

"Can you help us?"

The Italian sipped more wine. "So it appears," he said again.

McKinnon started to laugh, exuding a sigh of relief at the same time. "I knew I could count on you," he said.

"So it appears," the Italian said a third time.

THIRTY-SEVEN

It took until Monday afternoon, February 12, before Federov would concede that he had an interest in a conglomerate called The Caspian Group, the bookkeeping of which existed only in his head. It took another two days for Alex to get him to concede that he might be liable for US taxes.

Alex's spirit's got another boost that day. Despite how busy Robert was with his own trip preparation, he had managed to send her a Valentine by courier.

Then on that same afternoon, the fourteenth, she started to wear Federov down as she documented everything she and the United States Department of Commerce knew on TCG. He finally allowed that his corporation might be inclined to file records with the US government and actually pay some taxes.

This he would do, he stressed, on one condition.

"What condition is that?" she asked.

"You accompany me to my favorite club in Kiev this evening, Miss Anna," he said. "You come alone and you are my guest. You do this for me, and I file corporate tax returns."

Ellen Higgins rolled her eyes. Phil Ralston looked away.

"That's a highly unusual bargain," Alex said.

"You're a highly unusual negotiator. Deal?"

An unsolicited offer that would make her trip a stunning success if Federov followed through. And her assignment was to stay with him as much as possible. In a distant part of her mind, she recalled Cerny's warning: Federov had a penchant for smart, beautiful, educated women.

"Well?" he asked. "I am tired of these discussions. You have convinced me. I will obey your tax laws. I will put our agreement in writing if we have one. Yes or no?"

All eyes were on her. "An agreement in writing would be excellent," she said.

"Then we will do it."

"Let's make a few things very clear," she answered, "The president of the United States arrives tomorrow and will be here for one overnight. My fiancé, who works in the White House, will be here too. My fiancé and I are going to be married in July."

"*Pozdoróvlennia*," Federov said. Congratulations.

"The day *after* tomorrow, *I* will also be leaving with the president."

"Yes. So? Then we should go out and celebrate the visit and your engagement," he said. "We will go to my favorite club and drink to your fiancé's safe arrival."

Federov's assistants' eyes were on her like those of a pair of terriers.

She thought about it further. "We draft a deal memo on receiving your corporate records and on proposed taxation. We do that this afternoon," she said. She glanced at her watch. It was 3:45 p.m.

"If it's complete by 6:00 p.m.," she said, "I'll go to your club with you."

"Excellent!" he said.

"I expect to be back at my hotel by midnight."

"Midnight is very early in Kiev. How about 3:00 a.m.?"

"This is completely inappropriate."

"All right. Midnight. But you wear the sexiest garment you have with you."

"I only brought normal clothes," she said.

"Pity," he said. His two guards laughed. She was getting angry.

"Will we get a deal memo drafted this afternoon?"

"Yes."

"You have your deal," she said.

"And you should have some new clothes," he said.

"But I don't," she parried. "If I had something worthy of a Kiev nightclub, I'd wear it, I promise you. But I don't, so, end of discussion."

He opened his hands and looked helpless to his bodyguards, who smirked.

"One of us has outwitted the other," he said with a tinge of regret.

"At no small effort."

The American staff called in two stenographers who successfully took a draft agreement from Federov. It was complete by 5:30.

"Great," Alex muttered to Richard Friedman when she reported to him at the end of the business day. "I've been here a week and I'm dating the worst gangster in town."

"He's only the worst temporarily," Friedman answered. "Putin is scheduled to visit after the president leaves."

"That makes me feel so much better about everything," Alex said.

She put the memo on file and sent it by secure fax back to Washington.

Then she returned to the hotel to change for an involuntary evening out.

Federov, meanwhile, was one step ahead of her.

When she arrived back in her hotel room, she discovered that Federov had sent over a change of clothing that she had unwittingly agreed to wear.

A new dress, a deep burgundy silk, from one of the top Italian designers, a low cut with a high hem, material that was as light as a feather. The type of thing that cost three thousand dollars in Rome, Paris, or New York. She tried it on and walked to the mirror and stopped short. The neckline was lower that anything she had ever worn in her life. The hem was at least ten inches above the knee. For several seconds she stared at herself, hardly believing what she saw. At first she thought, no way. She didn't dare wear it and wouldn't do it. She would pretend that she hadn't received it.

Then a change of mind came over her.

All right. She would live a little on the edge. If this was what it took to get a deal out of Comrade Federov, full speed ahead. Then she'd save the dress, wear it for Robert and let him go crazy over it. He could have his fun removing it from her. That also reminded her. She found the bracelet Robert had given her just before she had departed. She put it on her wrist. Part of Robert would be with her.

Meanwhile, if this was what Federov wanted, she'd let him have it.

THIRTY-EIGHT

It was not a Valentine's Day evening that Alex was looking forward to. In fact, she was downright unhappy with it.

Robert was already in transit with the Presidential Protection assignment out of Washington. He would arrive with the president the next afternoon. She and her fiancé had already made plans to meet in a restaurant near her hotel in the late afternoon, when his shift would be over. In the embassy, all other protective people had drawn assignments as security tightened around the president.

Yet suddenly, what Alex was doing was secondary to the entire trip. The goals of the American president were to get to the cathedral the next day, lay a wreath, and exit the country as quickly as possible. And trouble continued to hang in the air.

For a moment, at a few minutes before nine that evening, Alex knelt quietly in a quick prayer in her hotel room. Then she inserted a loaded magazine into her gun and packed it into her purse along with her cell phone. She wore the new dress that Federov had sent over. Against the cold, she pulled on a pair of boots and a heavy wool overcoat.

Two minutes later she was in the lobby. A Mercedes limousine was already waiting. Federov stepped out and beckoned. She sighed and went forward to the vehicle.

"Get in," he said. "We'll have a great evening."

The things she would do for her country.

Dancing with the stars. Dancing with the gangsters. Well, this was part of the assignment too. Find out as much about this thug as possible. Keep him in sight. Who knew? Maybe some tidbit she picked up could put him in jail for two hundred years. She could always hope.

They were alone in the back of the limousine, where it was warm. They spoke Russian. The vehicle began to move. There was much room in the backseat. Alex stretched out her legs, loosened her coat, and tried to get comfortable. After a moment Federov reached to her and opened the coat, pushing it aside. His eyes devoured her in her new dress.

"You are quite beautiful," Federov said.

She sighed. "I don't know where you're trying to go with all this, Federov—"

"Please call me Yuri," he interrupted.

"I don't know where you're trying to go with all this, but I explained to you, I'm engaged. I'm not interested in any relationship other than our professional one."

"I understand," he said.

"Do you?" She sounded skeptical.

"What am I doing wrong?" he said. "You are very safe. I'm making sure of that. And I am being a gentleman. We are conducting business, you and I. And so perhaps I like going out with a beautiful American woman seen on my arm? Is that so wrong?"

They came to a stoplight. The driver ignored the red and eased through with impunity.

"By itself, no," she answered.

"Then where's the problem?"

"We just need to understand each other."

"We do," he said. "So I need to understand something too?"

"What's that?"

"Why does your government want to kill me?" he asked. "And why do they use you as their instrument?"

"What?"

He repeated.

"I know of no plans to have you killed," she said.

"Of course. They would *use* you, not *tell* you."

"You're making me angry, Yuri. I'm not lying to you."

He studied her carefully and shifted gears. "Then maybe a kiss," he said. "One kiss."

"No."

"Maybe later."

"I doubt it," she said.

"Then you don't know the Russian system," he said. "If I can't get what I want the proper way, I steal it. When you're not looking, when you least expect it, I will have a kiss from you."

"I'll be on my guard," she said, trying to parry his advance and defuse it.

"I'm sure," he said with a laugh. "I'm sure."

He sat back and relaxed.

The driver took them through the snowy streets of Kiev and into a neighborhood that was lively with neon and flashing marquees. Alex tried to memorize the route but it was impossible. Federov kept her talking and she guessed that was the reason.

Clubs and bars were packed one next to another along a trendy urban strip. The car stopped in front of a place named Malikai's.

Federov's driver jumped out and opened the doors for them. Alex felt like a gun moll. A skin-headed bouncer guided them past a waiting line of people, and they entered the club. People seemed to know Yuri Federov. Everyone was quick to jump out of his way.

They walked down a flight of steps, through a dark corridor. Alex could barely hear above the blasting techno beat from the sound system.

"Is this a restaurant or a club?" she asked.

"Both," Federov answered.

But it wasn't that easy. *Restaurant*, Federov explained, meant bar in Ukraine, whereas *nightclub* meant restaurant and *bar* meant nightclub, which is where they were. And not to put too fine an edge on it, even though Malikai's was a nightclub, it also had a bar and restaurant.

"Very confusing, isn't it?" Alex said.

"Not as confusing as Russian-Ukrainian politics," he answered.

"Quite right," she agreed, still in Russian. "Politics works in strange ways," she said.

The noise in Malikai's was deafening. Federov had to incline his head so that Alex could shout into his ear. They moved past the line that stood waiting for a table. Federov obviously never waited to be seated.

"The owner, Malikai, is a friend," Yuri said. "His brother plays ice hockey in North America. We share a love for ice hockey. And beautiful Western women."

They obviously shared a love for something, because Malikai

himself turned up a moment later and embraced Yuri. Then Malikai turned and bellowed over the music.

"Natalka!"

Natalka, a hostess, materialized out of nowhere. She got another tight hug from Yuri too, one that lifted her straight off the ground. She was a trim woman in a sleek black dress and a ruby on the left side of her nose. She looked as if she was used to getting manhandled in this place and took it in stride in exchange for a solid paycheck.

The crowd on the floor parted for them, and Natalka led them to a semicircular front row table in a corner that was midway between a bar and a stage. One of Federov's friends was at the table, a man named Sergei with his own friend, Annette. Annette wore a gold minidress that was as short as Alex's. In a good American touch, she seemed to be knocking back a Jack and ginger. She also looked as if she were quite plastered already. Sergei had a pistol on his belt that he was making no effort to conceal.

In terms of booze, Federov didn't even have to order.

An ice bucket appeared, as did caviar, blinis, and a tray of hors d'oeuvres, presented by a mustached man in a red tunic who assisted Natalka. He said nothing but no one would have heard him if he did. Then, almost by magic, Natalka produced from nowhere a bottle of vodka that bore a blue and yellow Ukrainian label. She opened it with surgical precision, poured four generous shots, and plunged the bottle into the ice.

Alex scanned the room. Everything was all shined up. Lots of chrome and glass and glitter. The entire world looked as if it had been wiped down by a paper towel and a bottle of Armor All.

Federov proposed a toast to American-Ukrainian relations. Alex made sure that Federov drank first, then joined him. She was careful to eat along with the vodka. The liquor was powerful. It had a kick that could give liftoff to an aircraft. A buzz was setting in. Without even trying to, she was getting hammered.

"How do you mean that?" he asked. "What you said about politics being strange?"

After being exploited by the Russians for several generations, she explained, one would have thought the Ukrainians would be in a hundred percent agreement on getting rid of their old Soviet masters. Yet this was not so, as was already evident.

Federov met her comments with a shrug.

"Putin is a dictator and often seems like a gangster," she said. "Yet he has wide support."

"He has brought stability," he said.

"At the expense of freedom."

"You can't eat freedom and you can't spend it either."

"No," she said, "but to some degree the suppression of freedom is nothing more than a power grab. Putin has also turned the Russian Orthodox Church into an official state religion, harassing most of the other Christian denominations that flourished since glasnost. What's wrong with religious freedom?"

"Russia is not required to give freedom of religion," Federov answered with an indignant snort. "Russia is not the United States and neither is Ukraine. People here differ from Americans. Religious freedom is not a panacea. The Russian Orthodox Church was nearly destroyed during Stalin's rule and throughout the Soviet era. No Protestant churches would survive if ninety percent of their followers were annihilated. This is the main reason the Russian Church is worthy of respect and why Protestants must not preach in this country. And that's only for people who want their religion." He paused for a moment. "I am an atheist and most people I know are atheists. Atheism makes more sense."

"I don't agree with you at all."

"I don't expect you to."

"And I don't understand the Ukrainian relationship with Russia, either."

"Few Americans do."

"Then explain it to me," she challenged.

"Most Ukrainians accepted Communism as their fate or even believed in it," he said. "Most older people lived better under Communism. I know of a woman who was the conductor of a factory orchestra, one of many. The factory has long since been privatized, the orchestra dissolved, and the woman was demoted from a 'member of the intelligentsia' to someone living with her mother on the latter's tiny pension. Our friendship toward Russia is not a perversion of crazy people. It was an option that was attractive to people like the woman I've described, not to mention the Russian-speaking people in the eastern district oblasts and Crimea."

She had no response. She began to wonder if somehow she had been drugged.

Then he looked at her for a long second and appeared to be preparing to move the discussion to a new level. The noise in the joint was important as it allowed Federov to speak freely.

No listeners, no microphones.

He spoke Russian. "Have you ever heard of a pair of Americans named Peter Glick and Edythe Osuna?" he asked.

She asked him to repeat the names. He did. No recognition.

"New names to me," she said. "Should I know them?"

"Maybe," he said. "Maybe not. They are involved in this visit by your president."

"Part of the delegation?" she asked.

He laughed. "No. They're a pair of American spies," Yuri said. "They were recently retired."

For a moment she was taken aback, thinking his explanation was a joke of some sort. Then she realized it wasn't.

"I don't know them," she said. She wondered whatever other name they might be going by, but she let the opportunity slide by. "I'm afraid that's not my department. Spies," she said, slurring slightly. "I wouldn't know the first thing about them."

"Of course," he said without conviction.

THIRTY-NINE

Yuri had big hands, big ideas, and big talk. All three were all over the place. But he also had unending charm when he wanted to, and a certain rough magnetism. The briefings in Washington had touched upon that, but hadn't conveyed it completely.

Alex worked her gaze around the club and took stock. Students, pretty girls, athletic looking young men, a few high-ranking soldiers in uniform, and some diplomats. More pretty girls, in fact, hordes of beautiful women, plus a batch of local wise guys. Conspicuously missing: Kaspar and Anatoli, Federov's presumed bodyguards. Alex asked where they were.

"Why do you ask about them?" he asked.

"I would think you would have them with you," she said.

"Why?"

"Because you always seem to," she said.

He laughed. "Things are not as they appear. Kaspar and Anatoli," he said, "they are my 'mushrooms.' I keep them in the dark and feed them with manure."

"Lucky them," she said.

"You learn never to rely on or trust anyone fully," he said. "Your best friend today is your mortal enemy tomorrow, hey. That's the nature of my business. And if I weren't worse than everyone else, I wouldn't be alive to tell you that."

"Then why don't you get out of your businesses?" she asked.

"What would I do?"

"Count your money. I'm sure you have a lot hidden in various places. Switzerland. Cayman Islands. Monaco."

He laughed.

"What's funny?" she asked.

"You know me too well. Was that your briefing before you arrived or your intuition?"

"Both."

"I like smart women," he said. "I'd like a smart woman as a wife someday. Then maybe I would settle in Switzerland and become a farmer."

"You had a wife," she said. "You used to beat her."

"She wasn't a smart woman."

"That's why she was your wife. But you didn't have any right to beat her."

Surprisingly, his look went far away, then came back as he poured more drinks. "Yes, I used to think I had that right," he said. "Perhaps not. What about you?" he asked.

"What do you mean, what about me?"

"Would you marry a wealthy Russian man, a former gangster, and be the smart, rich wife of a Swiss farmer? Marry me and I will retire and grow cheese." His eyes twinkled in a devious way. "You would be Madame de la Gruyere, and I would make many babies with you."

She smiled grudgingly. "Is this part of your plan to seduce me tonight?"

He laughed. "Maybe. Or is it the vodka talking?"

"Either way, your plan isn't working."

"Shame on me. I must try harder."

"I've already found the man I want to marry," she said.

"See, I was right," he said.

"About what?"

"You're very smart."

The music was blasting, then came to a halt. An announcer introduced a singer in Ukrainian and French. Then, to much applause a drop-dead gorgeous blond girl appeared on stage. She wore a slick minidress, a silvery-blue satin that reflected the glitter of the club. It was clinging so tight to her that it looked like she'd put in on with a shoehorn.

She was about twenty, slim and feline. She had legs that wouldn't stop. Her voice was husky but smooth and velvety. She sang beautifully. Great to look at, great to listen to. She took a microphone and launched into a series of Tina Turner songs from the seventies and eighties. She performed from a stage that was elevated about three feet above the club floor.

Alex took her to be Estonian or Latvian, judging by the blond hair and cheekbones, though she worked under a French name. Yvonne-Marie Something-or-other. Now Alex was *really* feeling the vodka. She had once been to the Crazy Horse Saloon in Paris where drinks had always packed a similar wallop. She smothered another blini with caviar and decided life wasn't so bad after all, and maybe Federov wasn't, either.

Federov watched Yvonne-Marie with a smile and turned to Alex. "Do you like her? She used to be my girlfriend," he said.

"Really? For how long?" she asked. "A week?"

"One night," he said. It didn't sound like a joke.

Alex had never heard soul music sung by a six-foot blonde in a silver-blue mini before. But in the old Soviet republics, she well knew, anything was possible. Believe nothing that you hear and only half of what you see.

Yvonne-Marie then launched into a version of "Proud Mary" and the dance area filled to overflowing. Presumably the river they were rolling on was the Dnipro.

Alex scanned the room again. Everyone was carrying on, singing, dancing, shouting, groping, kissing. Alex looked closely and saw plenty of army or police haircuts in civilian clothing. A reminder to be careful. The distinction between those who enforce the law and those who break it was vague here at best. She felt her head spin slightly and missed Robert horribly.

Yuri forced another vodka on her. She got through half of it before she realized she was flying. For a moment she wondered again if the drinks were spiked, but she equally realized that they were all drinking from the same bottle. Yuri knocked back a third and a fourth shot. So did Sergei.

Alex cautioned herself. No more booze. She tried to make conversation, her mind rambling all the way back to the FBI dossier that she had read on Federov, and the warnings about him personally.

"Now we dance," Federov said.

"Oh no! Oh no," she protested.

"Oh yes!" he said, standing. He gave her an amazingly handsome smile.

"No," she said.

"Please," he begged.

"One dance, in exchange for answers to some questions," she bargained.

"Dance first," he said.

Several seconds pounded past her. The vodka loosened her inhibitions and wore down her reserve.

"All right," she said.

Federov took Alex by the hand and pulled her out onto the floor. The singer on stage moved quickly from Tina Turner to Whitney Houston and the next thing Alex knew she was breathlessly being swung around to the tune of "I Wanna Dance with Somebody." Remarkably, Federov could dance well. He knew how to lead. He knew how to hold a woman. The rest of the dancers cut them plenty of space, and too much of it was too much of a blur. Twice Alex was ready to stumble and Yuri's hand on her arm steadied her.

The song came to an end. Applause filled the room. The singer took a break, excusing herself in Russian, French, and English. Alex wobbled while Federov led her back to the table. He held her arm supportively as she slid into her seat.

She was sweating, not from nerves now, but exertion.

"See?" he said. "I'm not such a monster, hey?" he asked.

"I'll need more convincing than just a good tumble around a dance floor," she said.

"What else do you need?"

He poured two double shots of vodka. He knocked back his; she didn't dare touch hers. Meanwhile, Sergei and Annette were on another planet.

"What do you sell to the North Koreans?" Alex finally asked.

"What?"

"Pepsi-Cola or *Playboy*?" she asked, continuing Cerny's facetious comment of two weeks earlier. "Park Enterprises," she said, recalling the dossier. "What's that all about?"

He smiled. "Like much of what is in your files about me, this is not accurate," he said. "The government does business with Park, not me. As for *Playboy*, I would only want a copy if you were in it."

"You're much too fresh with too many drinks," she said.

"So if I'm fresh, slap me, hey?" he said.

"No."

"Why not?" he asked.

"I'm not going to give you an excuse to hit me back."

"I won't hit you back," he said with a gracious smile. "Slap me."

"No."

"Please?"

She started to laugh, her head spinning more rapidly by the second. Playfully, she raised her hand. He did nothing to deflect it or stop her. He gave her a nod. She brought her hand across his cheek, barely harder than a pat.

"There," she said.

He shook his head. "That wouldn't have broken the shell on an egg," he said. "Do it for real."

She hesitated, then, buoyed by the vodka, impulsively proceeded. She whacked him one at three quarters strength, hard enough to make some noise, hard enough to be heard at the adjoining table. People who saw it stopped talking and gazed with horror at how Federov, probably the most feared man in the place, would react.

With half a grimace and half a smile, Federov's mouth formed a perfect "O" for a second or two. His hand patted his cheek. He shook his head and laughed heartily. For a moment that was frozen in time, Alex looked at him in panic, thinking she had overstepped or blundered into a trap.

But he reached to her with his powerful arm and hugged her in congratulations. Then he removed his arm. His expression told everyone around that all this was in great fun, there would be no problems, no violence.

"I've never allowed a woman to slap me in public and get away with it," he said. "You are the first."

"And why is that?" she asked. "Why am I so privileged?"

"Because I say so," he said. "That's the only reason that would matter."

Then they both laughed. The whole table was laughing now. More vodka went around. By now, almost everyone was flying. Annette sat with her head slumped against Sergei's shoulder, her hands in his lap, and he had one arm slung around her in return. It looked like they were going to get to know each other better that night, if they didn't already.

Several minutes went by. The sound system kept the place at a high decibel level. Two traditional Ukrainian hits: "Summer of Sixty-Nine" and "The Wall". Bryan Adams and Pink Floyd. Glasnost on steroids. Yuri turned back to Alex who by now had moved onto some chicken dumplings, which were, like the live entertainment, better than they had any right to be.

He kept the conversation in English and resumed with some small talk. Weather, sports, and a few off-color jokes about Russian women. Then he eased into a few tidbits about local black markets and currency dealing.

Everything was grist for the mill for Alex. Little tidbits often filled out a big picture and she was amazed how much someone would talk after several shots of vodka just to show off his proficiency in English. Then again, she assumed he was throwing her information that he wanted her to know.

"What about you?" he finally asked. "Your assignment here in Kiev?"

"I think everything's been completed. Successfully," she added.

"Except for watching me," he said.

"What do you mean?" she asked.

"That's part of your assignment, is it not?" he asked. "Stay with me. You're keeping an eye on Federov."

She said nothing. He had hit the nail right on the head. But he had also primed something else that Alex found troubling about Federov. It wasn't his massive size, it wasn't his violent history and it wasn't his primitive attempts at seduction. It was the way he looked at her through his hard dark eyes. The look in his eyes was one of familiarity. It was as if he knew a great deal about her, much more than he should have, much more than she would have liked.

"Drink with me and tell me the truth," he said, "and I will drink with you and tell you the truth."

He poured himself another shot of vodka. Then he put her shot glass in her hand, wrapped her fingers around it and held it to her lips. She held the glass.

"*Pravda*," he said. The truth.

She put the glass to her lips and, with a nudge from Federov, threw back another shot.

"Yes," she said boldly. "My government asked me to do two things. Negotiate a tax agreement with you. And to watch you."

He laughed.

"That's good. That's good," he said. "I hope you enjoy watching me because I enjoy being watched by you. How's that?"

He nodded his huge head and seemed to want to say more. Alex, as her head whirled, leaned across him, reached for the vodka and poured him more. He seemed pleased and intrigued. He also caught the glimmer of her engagement ring as it passed.

With respect, he asked about her prospective husband. That gave her the opportunity to tell him all about Robert. In one way, she hoped it killed his mood, or his ideas. On another level, she hoped it wouldn't. Why not keep him talking?

He laughed again eventually.

"What?" she asked.

"I brought you here to seduce you," he said.

"I'm wearing an engagement ring."

"To some women that wouldn't matter."

"To this one, it does."

He nodded and laughed again. "What would your boyfriend say if he could see you right now?"

"Robert would be jealous," she said.

"What if he could see you in that dress?" Federov asked. "Showing all those lovely legs to every man in the club."

"He *will* see me in this dress. I'm going to wear it for him."

"Will you tell him you were here with me?"

"Probably."

"Let me kiss you anyway," he said.

"Not a good idea."

"What if I try?"

"Then I get up and leave, Yuri. Don't do it."

Out of the corner of her eye she saw a New York Rangers jersey hanging behind the bar, and she recalled what the owner had said about a brother playing ice hockey in North America. Then there was a pause. Mercifully, more food came and Natalka poured more booze. Alex sensed a little easing down of the passions on Yuri's part.

He thanked Natalka with a pat on her backside. Alex could barely believe what Eastern European women had to tolerate.

Yuri started a cigarette and maintained a stony silence. Music started again and Yvonne-Marie stood in the wings, which Alex could see from where she sat, waiting to come on again. The music was obviously important because it allowed Yuri to talk without anyone overhearing, not even Sergei and Annette who were preoccupied with each other.

Alex was reflexively fingering the little gold cross around her neck. Could her dad ever have imagined that the little cross would trek all the way to Kiev from Southern California? What would he have thought if he could have known?

Federov caught the gesture. "You're a Catholic?" he asked in English.

"I'm a Christian, yes," she said. "But I'm not a Catholic."

"You seem intelligent," he said. "How can you believe all that superstitious religious stuff?"

She moved her hand away from the cross.

"Maybe I have faith because I *am* intelligent," she said. "Ever thought of that?"

"No, I haven't."

"Then maybe you should," she answered. "There's a Christian remembrance service at the cathedral in two days. For the victims of the *Holodomor.* Come with me."

"Why should I?"

"It might do you some good."

"Business isn't done in Ukraine without bribes," he said. "Bribe me to go to church with you."

"Bribe you how?"

He shrugged. "With a kiss," he said.

She laughed. "You never give up, do you?" she said.

Federov gave some thought to something, it appeared. A full minute passed.

Then he spoke Russian again, like most of the crowd in the restaurant. She listened carefully.

"I'm going to do you a favor, anyway," he said finally. "I was going to do it later. After you had given me some pleasure. Instead, I'll do it now. I will give you two pieces of information. In return, perhaps you can be my honest broker on US taxes. If I have a problem, I will contact you for advice."

"I can't give you advice. I can only tell you what the law is."

"Understood," he said. And for the first time, it occurred to her that he wanted something. Or perhaps he even *needed* something.

"So what's this information?" she asked.

"When your president visits, there will be major trouble," he said.

"We've heard those rumors already."

"No," he said. "It is assured."

"Then what can we do to stop it?"

"Nothing," he said. "Terrible things have always happened in Ukraine. There is little control. There is a group of young men. Complete troublemakers. Terrorists. The pro-Russian Ukrainians, the *filorusski*. They will make trouble."

"Where can we find them?"

"I don't know. They are not my people or I would have them shot. I don't look for trouble from America. I seek to avoid it."

She considered it. "What's the other bit of information?" she asked.

"The two spies," he said. "The Americans named Peter Glick and Edythe Osuna?"

"I told you I don't know those names."

But he forged ahead. "Castel Fusano," he said.

"What's that?" she asked.

"That's where they are buried," he said, "in Italy. They tried to kill me, these two American hoodlum assassins. They failed and they were going to try again. So I had them killed first. My people in Rome took care of it."

In a flash, she knew he was telling her something significant.

Annette and Sergei were still pawing each other. Federov looked away, as casually as if it had just given a football score. He had nothing else to volunteer on the subject, and she had nothing else to ask.

Then he looked back at her and smiled. His eyes danced. And in that moment, in that good hard look that she had of his eyes, she knew something else.

He had been the man in the square the first night, the one who quietly moved up on her at the monument. She was nonplussed.

"That's all I have to tell you, my friend. Other than the fact that by the time you return to America, you will know I have done you a great favor."

She looked away for a moment. Federov grabbed the opportunity. He reached to her and turned her face toward him. Too much vodka. She didn't resist fast enough. He leaned over and, as he held her jaw gently with his strong hand, he gave her a long kiss on the lips.

She was so shocked, that for several seconds she didn't react.

Federov smiled. "See what happens when you drop your guard?" he asked. "Let that be a lesson."

She gathered her bearings. "I think," she said, "the evening is over."

"You gave me a kiss," he said. "Now I have to go to the church with you."

"That's fine," she said. "But for now, get me out of here."

"As you wish, Alexandra LaDuca," Federov said. "As you wish."

And for the second time within a minute, she was too stunned to react. There was no way he should have known her real name. No way! Federov, meanwhile, signaled for his driver.

FORTY

Early the next morning, Alex reported to the CIA station chief at the embassy and reported on her conversation with Federov the previous night, particularly pertaining to his discussion of a threat against the president.

The station chief listened politely, asked her a few questions, and made some handwritten notes.

"These stories are all over the city," he finally said. "We're doing everything we can, but at this point, the White House won't alter any part of the visit. There's nothing we can do except ramp up the security as tightly as possible."

"Isn't the White House being a bit foolish?" Alex asked.

"What else is new?" the station chief answered. "We'll let the president have the right photo-ops and get in and out of here as fast as possible."

"I just wanted to report what I'd heard," Alex said.

"That was the right thing to do. Thanks."

Air Force One arrived in Kiev from London at three eleven that same afternoon, the fifteenth. The trailing plane that carried the rest of the entourage including the "traveling press" arrived nineteen minutes later.

The American president was received at the airport by the president of Ukraine. There were plenty of smiles for the cameras. Ukrainian troops and police had secured the airport. The US Secret Service provided the inner ring of protection around the president.

A twenty-two vehicle motorcade took the president of the United States into Kiev. Thousands of onlookers lined the streets in subfreezing weather, some waving flags, some holding signs, most applauding with enthusiasm as snow flurries continued. The presidential limousine, which had been flown in two days earlier, moved at speeds close to fifty miles an hour. The route all the way to the hotel was cleared of other traffic.

Within an hour of arrival, the president was ensconced at the most secure hotel in the city, the Sebastopol. It was a time to relax in the suite with the White House advisers. The Secret Service advance team coordinated their protective details with the White House units that had arrived with the president.

Everything went smoothly in the first hours of the presidential visit. Not one detail had verged from the detailed prearranged plan. Yet rumors of potential trouble continued to sweep the frigid city.

Later that same day, Alex stood in the center of Mikhaeylevski Place and waited. Then, toward 6:15 in the evening, she saw two figures emerge from the heavily guarded Sebastopol Hotel.

She recognized Robert by his walk. She didn't know the other man with him, but she assumed he was Secret Service as well. On their breaks in foreign countries, the agents were never to be alone.

Robert waved to her. She walked toward him and they embraced.

"How's it going?" he asked.

"Okay," she said.

"How's the Commie gangster you're babysitting?" he asked. "Has he tried to hit on you yet?" he went on, trying to make a joke out of a trace of jealousy. "Let me know if I need to come over and shoot him."

"I've got him under control," she said, "but I don't know what State or Treasury thinks I can find out in two days that they don't know already."

"Who knows what they're up to?" he said with a shrug. "Half the time *they* don't know what they're doing. So how should *we* know? I'll be happy when we're out of this place."

"That makes two of us," she said.

"Make it three," said the other man said.

Robert introduced his friend, Agent Reynolds Martin, who was partnering on this trip. Martin was the southerner who had recently been added to the Presidential Protection Detail at the White House.

He was also the ballistics expert who had come along as part of the foreign security detail.

"My fiancée," Robert said of Alex. " 'Anna' we call her here, if you know what I mean. Next time you see her, she'll have another name."

"I know how the game works," Martin said, nodding. "They call me 'Jimmy Neutron' behind my back because they think I'm obnoxious. I'm not supposed to know."

They all laughed.

Robert placed a hand on his partner's shoulder. "Reynolds — I mean, Jimmy — is working out pretty well on the trip, after all," Robert said.

Martin laughed again.

"This guy keeps me calm," Special Agent Martin said, thrusting a thumb at Robert. "You caught yourself a good man."

Alex smiled. "Thank you. I know," she said.

"Anna is working for Commerce here. Or is it Treasury. Or is it State?" Robert said. "She's my future wife and even I can't keep the facts straight, much less the cover stories."

"Get used to it, brother," Martin said.

"Robert even got me the first half of a handcuff," she said, holding up the Tiffany bracelet.

"It's nice," Martin said. "And what you guys do with handcuffs on your own time is none of my business."

"The cuffs will match the ball and chain Robert gets," she said.

"Hey, speaking of families, let me show you something," Martin said. He reached into his pocket. "I just got this at the hotel souvenir stand," he said.

He pulled out, in brown wrapping paper, a set of nesting dolls. He showed how it worked. The outer doll was shaped like a small bowling pin with a painting of a smiling blond woman on it. Martin unscrewed the top part and showed an identical but smaller doll inside. And so it went until he got to a two-inch-tall figure of the same design which was solid and didn't unscrew.

"Clever, huh?" he asked. "Tina, that's my daughter, is going to love this."

"It's a *matryoshka* doll," Alex said.

"Yeah!" Jimmy Neutron said. "That's what the girl in the store called it. How do you say it?"

"*Matryoshka*," Alex repeated. "It's a traditional Russian doll. The symbol is that of all Russian women. They make them with the Russian leaders now too. The big outer doll looks like Gorbachev. You unscrew the interior ones and you work your way down through Khrushchev and Stalin to Lenin."

"Right," Martin said, catching on. "They should make an American one. It could start off with Madonna and Brittney Spears and work down to Michael Jackson."

He was already putting the doll back together and into its wrapping. And something else had taken Martin's attention. He was scanning the area and not with approval. "This square is a logistical nightmare," he said. "I have bad dreams about places like this."

"Who doesn't?" Robert asked.

"Tomorrow we have to get the president from St. Sophia's Cathedral to the wreath laying and then to the airport. Just look around," Martin said. "If there's an incident, here's where the problem will come. The advance team, the Secret Service, the ambassador, everybody's sweating bricks over this place."

He nodded to the buildings and structures in every direction, a rambling collection of windows, rooftops, and alleys. "See what I mean?"

She saw and understood. Where others saw quaint and architecturally fascinating old buildings, a professional bodyguard saw only the potential for trouble. Every angle for attack had to be blocked, every window closed, every rooftop covered, every manhole bolted down.

As they stood in the square together, savoring their few moments, Robert put an arm around Alex and held her tightly.

Martin was still looking around at the buildings again.

"With modern weaponry," he said slowly, "the official Secret Service Red Zone is four fifths of a mile. That's fourteen hundred yards, fourteen football fields lined up back to back. Sounds like a long way, but it isn't. A bullet from a modern high-velocity rifle can travel that distance in less than a second. That means, if the target is stationery, with a head bowed in prayer. Giving a speech, shaking a hand . . ."

His voice trailed off.

"God protect us," he said. "We need all the help we can get."

"We're going to need to have our own people on every rooftop," Robert said. "Helicopters overhead, security checkpoints, not a single window open anywhere that you can see from here."

"Almost impossible," said Martin.

"Think the president will cancel the appearance?" Alex asked.

Martin and Robert shook their heads.

"Einstein, that's the president," Martin said, "hasn't come this far just to have a couple of lousy pictures taken with a bunch of Bulgarian farmers and washerwomen. No way there's a cancellation now."

"We're not in Bulgaria. We're in Ukraine," Robert said, holding back his amusement.

"Yeah, right. *You* can tell the difference?" he asked.

"Not from the inside of a hotel," Robert allowed.

"We've tried to talk Einstein into wearing a bulletproof vest," Martin said, "but the boss won't listen. Like Kennedy ordering that the bulletproof bubble not be used on his limousine. Stubborn and egotistical. They all are, but I knew that already."

"And Reagan, Truman, and Ford," Robert continued. "The joker in the deck is always the president's desire, any politician's desire, to be in the center of all the attention."

Alex stifled a shiver. Martin caught it.

"The weather helps," Martin said. "Frigid weather makes a gun stock more rigid. The cold changes the vibratory patterns of the wood, the stock, the metal, and the finger on the trigger. Makes it more difficult."

"But who wants to even risk a lucky shot with a subsonic round?" Robert mused. "Two thousand feet per second at a weight of maybe 175 grains. Location, time, distance, temperature, weapon, mental stability of the shooter. Everything factors in."

"Someone could use a .50-caliber sniping rifle," Martin said. "Those are coin of the realm around here. Same type of weaponry the Soviets used in Afghanistan and the Americans used in Iraq."

"Actually, this country isn't as bad as a lot of them," Robert allowed.

Martin lit a cigarette and shivered.

"Did I ever tell you?" Martin asked, looking at both of them. "Two years ago I was on a special assignment with the Bureau of ATF. We were tracking some Serbs from New York City who were shipping rifles from the United States to the Balkans," he said. "They were buying the weapons in Ohio. I was undercover, and I went with one of their guys named Milo to a gun show in suburban Cincinnati. Milo had this Ford Explorer with a *Sportsmen for Bush* bumper sticker, and he could barely speak English. Of course I worked for Bush, and Bush couldn't speak English either," Martin said.

Robert grinned. He had worked for the last three presidents too but was always too politic to criticize any of them, even when they deserved it.

"Anyway, inside this auditorium in Covington, Kentucky, jeez, they had everything. AK-47s, M-16 assault rifles, sniper rifles, handguns, flat and round bullets, silencers, night scopes, knives, Japanese swords, muskets. Totally illegal but right out there in the open. Daggers, even a couple of antiaircraft guns, and some old junk from World War II. The most impressive gun, however, was the .50-caliber high-powered Barrett sniper rifle. That's the one the Serbs wanted."

"Did they get them?" Alex asked.

"The Barretts were going for six grand each," Martin said, "and Milo said this was just what his pals needed to take potshots at the Croatians and Albanians in Kosovo. But there's this other stand where a guy in a wheelchair and Cincinnati Bengals jersey was selling Chinese-made Barrett knock-offs for just $2,200. Milo asks how many he could get. The guys says, 'As long as you don't have a criminal record or live in the People's Republic of New York City, I can sell you as many as you can carry away.' Well, Milo *did* have a criminal record. Double homicide. But it was in Spain. So he was 'clean' in the US. He takes out thirty thousand dollars in cash and buys twenty rifles. He drives away and ships them out from Detroit by private courier the next day."

"You couldn't arrest him?" Alex asked.

"For what? It was all legal. We were just keeping an eye on it, figuring out their routes, who their players were. With those knock-off Barretts an amateur could probably hit a target from a mile away. He said he had armor-piercing, tracer, and incendiary .50-caliber bullets available too. So Milo buys a few boxes of those as well."

"That stuff could bring down a helicopter," Robert said.

"The weapons got shipped to Macedonia," Martin said. "But here's the wicked part. Know where three of those rifles eventually turned up? At an al-Qaeda training camp in Pakistan. Those rag-head terrorists are going to shoot at our marines, and it was a guy with a Carson Palmer jersey who helped get the firepower to them. What a world!"

Robert shook his head.

"Shows you what we got to look out for in this square tomorrow," Martin said. "Everything coming from everywhere. There's no way to handle an exposure like this perfectly; there's always something that can go wrong."

"We just try to get in and out fast," Robert said. "We can't be perfect but we can be speedy."

"Good luck," Alex said with a sigh.

She embraced Robert. They exchanged a long meaningful kiss, one she would remember for a long time.

Robert and his partner returned to the Sebastopol a few minutes later. His schedule called for him to remain on duty throughout the visit.

She had dinner with a few new friends from the embassy that night. Federov joined them but was remarkably tight lipped, unlike the previous evening, almost jittery. He did, however, renew his promise to attend the cathedral ceremony with Alex. She requested that he arrive at the embassy at 10:00 a.m., and they would proceed in an American vehicle. He agreed.

Back at her hotel at the end of the evening, for some reason, she slept better than she had in weeks.

FORTY-ONE

Rome, Friday morning, the sixteenth. Gian Antonio Rizzo was sizzling.

"*Nessuna cosa*," said Gina Adriotti, the fourth of Lt. Rizzo's expert homicide investigators. Nothing.

She closed the file she had been allowed to read. She raised her eyes to her superior and waited for the explosion. His three colleagues had done the same. But the explosion, for whatever reason, was not forthcoming. Not yet.

Instead, Lt. Rizzo walked to the window. He stood with his back to the room, surveying the morning traffic that connected onto the via Condotti and which would lead past the plush shopping distracts and the Italian parliament.

Rizzo felt like death warmed over. He was losing sleep and felt as if he was coming down with the flu. He was of two minds. On one hand, the four detectives in this room were the best that his department had to offer. On the other hand, they were overpaid thumb-sucking idiots who couldn't find the ocean from the end of the pier.

He managed to control himself. He had established the identity of the dead woman and the musician who had been murdered in the apartment above deaf old Signora Masiella. He had now linked the bodies in the marsh at Castel Fusano to the disappearance of an American couple from a Ritz hotel in Rome. But he, and those who worked for him, were now drawing a double blank.

Who were the Americans who had been murdered on the street?

And what was their link, if any, to the musician and his live-in girlfriend?

He turned. "All right then," he said, controlling himself. "We've done what we can and it has not been successful. But we need to do more. We need a link. A connection. Somewhere in this city someone knows something. What is the feeling in this room? Do we need more investigators? More shoe leather on the street? More money from the 'reptile fund' to buy an informer? Tell me. What is it we want?"

Again, no answers. Now Lt. Rizzo *was* about to explode. A moment later, however, there was a soft knock on the door.

One of the technicians from the lab, a girl named Mimi, a university student, had something interesting.

The sight of Mimi settled Rizzo down. She was a criminology student at the American University in Rome. Fluent in English and Italian, she was one of the four young interns to whom he had thrown some tidbits of information from Bernardo Santangelo.

Mimi had caught Rizzo's eye more than once in the past. Mimi sailed through life in the orbit of the magical girls of Sailor Moon. She had Technicolor hair, chopped short in a trendy fashion and streaked with red, blue, green, and yellow, like her favorite Japanese *manga* characters. Under her lab coat, she favored boldly colored miniskirts, school girl white socks, and low cut sneakers, also in keeping with the *anime* motif.

She didn't look like the type who would come bearing news that could kick a homicide investigation in a new direction. But then again, Rizzo knew, the Case Breakers never do, which is why he'd included her with such important information.

He always prized the people who could think outside the normal channels. On a day like this, he prized anyone who could think at all, and if Mimi had come up with something, well, it just proved that he was a genius and totally justified in flirting with all those younger females.

Magical girls, indeed.

"Yes, Mimi?" he asked.

She looked at the detectives at the table, two of which had been on the force longer than she had been alive, as had Lt. Rizzo. Ten professional eyes stared back at her in silence. Eight of them were hostile. Rizzo's were adoring.

"May I mention something?" she asked.

"Of course you may, Mimi," Rizzo said. "These officers are under my command. Anything you say to me I would relate to them immediately, and as you can probably tell, they are in dire need of all the help they can get. So please tell us what you have."

"Maybe it's nothing," she said, "but maybe it's something."

Mimi sat down at the table and Rizzo closed the door.

Mimi had been doing some research and some digging, she explained, trying to relate the ballistics tests that Rizzo had shown her to anything else going on in Europe. So, helpful young chick that Mimi was, she hacked into some English-language military sites just to check out some pictures of real sailors and see what else was there.

Penetrating fifty million dollars of US Defense Department software took Mimi six and a half minutes. The United States Naval Station at Rota, Spain, she discovered, had recently finished its part of an annual weapon and ammunition moving and tracking exercise called CAWDS.

Under the CAWDS, or Containerized Ammunition Weapons & Distribution System, several boatloads of small arms and ammunition had been moved in standard shipping containers by air and sea.

The exercise had started in September 2007 and had run through June 2008. Under the system, computerized, numerical micro-imprints had been placed on all equipment to further facilitate their tracking.

"It's a very complex process," Mimi said. "But as we all know," she said, "firearms examiners use a comparison microscope to determine whether or not a bullet was fired from a particular firearm. The comparison is based on the individual marking left on fired ammunition components that are unique to a particular firearm. That's how we have the linkage of the weapons used in these two cases that Lieutenant Rizzo is discussing."

"Good so far," Rizzo said. His instincts told him to trust her.

"But the CAWDS system suggests something further," she said. "Apparently one of the boxes of containerized ammunition disappeared from a United States Navy warehouse in Sardinia. Stolen, in other words. It was, or so it was believed, hijacked by members of the Sicilian Mafia who sold the contents on the black market."

Rizzo blinked rapidly several times. This was all taking on a bizarre geometry.

"The pistols involved had been inventoried at Rota, Spain," she said. "The guns were unique among their manufacture because the others of the same series have never been removed from their shipping containers. I ran an Internet check. They are all in the hands of the US Navy except this one crate that was stolen. One of these pistols was used in these two crimes."

Mimi pushed a printout in front of the detectives at the table. They leaned forward to see it.

"So?" Rizzo pressed. "Anything else?"

"*Si, Tenente*," Mimi said. "The rest of the pistols turned up in southeastern Europe," Mimi said, "in the hands of underworld people there. We know this from recent arrests. The stolen naval cargo seems to have been trafficked by an agency called The Caspian Group."

"Caspian?" Rizzo asked. "As in, the 'Caspian Sea'?"

"*Mafia ucraina*," Mimi said. "It's a supposition and I might be wrong. But you could link all four of these assassinations to gangsters from Kiev."

FORTY-TWO

At 11:00 a.m. on the dot, the gates of the US Embassy in Kiev swung open. The police escort emerged first, Ukrainian vehicles first, sirens blaring. A phalanx of police poured onto Kotsyubynskoho. Ukrainian flags flew on the front and rear of the cars. A few moments later, the president's limousine pulled out of the gates of the embassy compound. It moved onto Kotsyubynskoho, then followed the streets of Kiev, closely guarded by American vehicles.

Alex rode in the eighth car, an armour-enforced van. She had a window. Federov, who had arrived punctually at the embassy at 10:00, sat beside her in a middle seat.

"Still expecting trouble?" she asked him in Russian.

He didn't directly address the question. "I've told you everything I can," he said.

She turned away and watched history unfurl before her through bulletproof glass.

The streets again were lined with spectators. Again snow flurries swept across the city. Most spectators were cheering, craning their necks for a view of the lead car of the motorcade. There were many old people who had lived through the very hard times. They remembered Stalin and the war and never thought they would lay eyes on the leader of America, much less live in a more open society. There were younger people who remembered the Orange Revolution and still held dearly to its principles. There were middle-aged people who had lived through Ukrainian Communism and had accepted it as their fate or even believed in it. They mostly just remembered, all of them, huddled together against the frigid weather.

The motorcade crept through the city streets, an armada of Mercedes limousines, including empty backups in case of a disaster. They moved as quickly as safety would permit. At each crossroad there were heavily armed police and soldiers, Ukrainian and American, who secured the intersections and kept wary eyes peeled for trouble.

The trip to Kiev's Cathedral of St. Sophia was only a few blocks away. But more than twenty thousand people lined the way. Many were part of religious groups, pilgrims, Eastern Christians who had travelled to the city for the event, many just to see the American president. Many had camped out on the streets overnight and huddled together for warmth. Some raised crosses. Some waved the flags of their church. Others waved American flags, others Ukrainian. Some held Christian signs in English for the president to view.

John 12:24.

Matthew 19:34.

Long live America.

One bearded man in his early thirties stood out from the rest. He was wrapped in blankets and carried a placard in English. *Jesus is the answer!*

Federov, the sceptic, snorted slightly.

He spoke English now. "If Jesus is the answer," he said, "what was the question?"

"Does it matter?" she volleyed back. "*Any* question."

"Of course," he said.

For some reason, this man in blankets caught the attention of the president, who rolled down the window and waved, breath visible against the rush of cold air into the car. The crowd was delighted. Not too far away stood a delegation of Pentecostal churches from all over Ukraine. They stood not far from their devout brethren from evangelical churches all over the new nation. The Blessed Kingdom of God for all Nations in Ukraine. Thousands of people took up a chant in English. "Jesus is the answer. Jesus is the answer."

Then the motorcade came to a sudden stop. A radio crackled in the front of Alex's van. Two of the security people in the van stepped out. The president must have been looking for the groups of Christians because, to the horror of the Secret Service, the limo stopped and the president stepped out.

From the angle of her own vehicle, Alex could press her head against the window and see what was happening. Security people flooded the streets to mark a cordon for the president. The American leader moved toward the delirious crowd of Christians, making sure photographers could capture the moment, pushing to the first row and extending both hands. Clearly, the moment was important to the president. The crowd surged forward but was well controlled, euphoric. For a quarter of a minute, the president moved from right to left and touched as many hands as possible, then retreated to the limousine, waving and smiling, basking in the cheers.

Alex knew the history that lurked beneath the moment. When Ukraine had been under Soviet rule, the Orthodox Church had been totally subservient to the patriarchate of Moscow, its clergy fully infiltrated by the KGB. Say the wrong thing in confession, and expect to disappear. That had led to the Ukrainian diaspora to set up a rival patriarchate, which had now moved back to Ukraine. There had also been Eastern Rite Catholics, whose churches were given by the Communists to the Russian Orthodox Church. With the collapse of the Soviet Union, the churches enjoyed a new freedom, one that also allowed them to bicker with each other over formerly state-owned property.

The motorcade started again, then slowed as it passed the memorial to Mykhailo Hrushevskyi, first president of Ukraine, where those gathered prayed for the country's future.

Then the motorcade turned and moved toward St. Sophia's Cathedral. Alex craned her neck to watch the progress of the parade. Over the shoulders of the men riding in front of her, she first saw the cathedral, Sobor Sviatoyi Sofiyi, one of the city's best-known landmarks and a centerpiece of the old city's skyline, and the church complex that surrounded it.

The building, almost a thousand years old, was stunning, an example of Old Kiev architecture, Byzantine motifs, white walls and green or gold turrets, five in total. Each of the turrets were topped by a Christian cross in the three-tiered Orthodox fashion: a crosspiece representing the mocking inscription over Jesus, the cross itself, and a crosspiece pointing upward representing both the piece to which Jesus's feet were nailed and the hope of salvation.

The tallest turret, a separate tower in the manner of an Italian campanile, was also a bell tower. It rose a hundred feet into the cold blue sky. It was richly embellished with stuccowork, the details of which Alex could see more clearly as they drew closer. The tower, topped by a green turret and a cross, seemed to beckon to the visitors as they approached. Around the main cathedral, within the complex, were a scattered accumulation of former monastery buildings. Miraculously, they remained untouched despite the centuries of warfare that had raged around them, warfare that had reached its peak under Uncle Joe Stalin, who died before his plan to demolish the cathedral and its surroundings could be carried out.

The president's car stopped right in front of St. Sophia's.

A phalanx of tall security people surrounded the president as the trailing vehicles also stopped. Everyone moved briskly. Alex knew that another detachment of security people would come together inside the church. She had no idea where Robert was. She only knew he was among the president's inner circle.

She stepped out of her own van, Federov with her. She wondered what Robert would say to her later if he caught sight of her thuggish companion.

"I know the way," Federov said, indicating the church. "This will surprise you, but I have been in here."

"It *does* surprise me," she answered.

Alex entered and took a place, standing among the congregation, Federov edging into a pew as he stood beside her. Hundreds were already gathered within the church, an invitation-only event. Any ordinary Ukrainian would have been carefully selected, like a presidential "town meeting" in America. The congregation suddenly applauded the president's arrival. The president was having a great day pressing the flesh and meeting the people. Too bad none of them could vote in an election.

From where she stood, Alex admired the complex beauty of the church. Much of it made sense to her from the traditional churches she had gone to with her mother as a little girl. She scanned the mosaics and frescos by Byzantine masters that dated back to the eleventh century. Marvelous frescos decorated the walls, pillars, and vaults. The central part of the cathedral was decorated with a large mosaic depicting a praying Virgin Mary, which was about six feet high and consisted of stone and glass plates of various reds, greens, yellows, and blues. Other frescoes depicted the annunciation, various martyrdoms, and familiar scenes from the Holy Bible. The design was endlessly intricate and delicate, as if made by hands guided by angels.

The worshipers remained on their feet. An Orthodox priest presided. The ceremony began as soon as the president arrived at the front. The brief service took place in the front of the church, before a special memorial table, small and freestanding, with an upright crucifix on top. Nearby there were icons of the *Theotókos*—the Virgin Mary—and the Apostle John. Some members of the faithful had also lit candles, which burned quietly on the table.

Alex scanned the worshipers. She watched Federov. As she watched him, he turned her way and gave her a nod.

Alex turned her attention back to the presiding bishop. He swung a censer with hypnotic precision. The scent crept toward her: sandalwood with pine. She suppressed a vague smile from her past. Whenever someone burned incense in college, it meant they were smoking something funny.

The congregation held candles for the dead. One was passed to Alex. The wax was brittle in her hand, but the flame warm. The congregation remained standing and would do so for the entire ceremony.

A prayer from St. Basil. The priest intoned in Church Slavonic with a fluent English translation running concurrently for the honored guests.

"O Christ our God who art graciously pleased to accept our prayers for those who are imprisoned in Hades ... send down thy consolation," he said in a near chant. "Establish their souls in the mansions of our Redeemer; and graciously guide them into peace and pardon."

Alex closed her eyes for a moment and took in the sounds and scents. She felt very much at peace with the world around her. The priest continued. "But we who are living will bless thee, and will pray, and offer unto thee propitiatory prayers and sacrifices for their souls."

Alex opened her eyes, again watched the ceremony carefully. The memorial service had an air of penitence about it. In the Eastern Church, the prayers for the departed had a specific purpose: to pray for the repose of the departed, to comfort the living, and to remind those who remain behind of their own mortality and the brevity of this earthly life.

The priest continued again. "The Holy Sacrifice of Christ, brings great benefits to souls even after death, provided their sins can be pardoned in the life to come. However, the prayer for the dead must not be an excuse for not living a godly life on earth. The Church's prayer cannot save anyone who does not wish salvation or who never sought it during his lifetime."

Alex glanced at Federov. He was fidgeting, his eyes darting around. Was he looking out for someone or afraid someone might see him there and wonder if he had gotten religion? Well, no matter. Much as the insides of a church might have done him some good, she also understood why he felt ill at ease. Maybe the mural showing the descent into hell had made him nervous. It should have. She smiled.

There was a final musical interlude, a *troparion*, a short hymn of one stanza which the congregation sang in Ukrainian. Near the end of the music, members of the congregation either put out their candles or placed them in candle holders on the memorial table. Alex followed along and understood the symbolism. Each candle symbolized an individual soul, which, as it were, each person held in his own hand. She remembered long ago her mother whispering to her in Spanish the meaning. "The extinguishing of the candle is symbolic: every person will have to surrender his soul at the end of his life."

She had never forgotten.

Moments later, the service ended.

The president was now to quickly lay a wreath on the other side of Shevshenka Park—named for Ukraine's great poet Tara Shevschenko—from the cathedral. The controversial monument to the victims of Stalin's "artificial famine" stood there outside the Ukrainian Foreign Ministry.

If there was to be trouble, this is where it would happen. And yet, the day had already been so blessed. Federov remained at her side as they exited the cathedral.

"There," she said. "Was that so awful?"

"I prefer the clubs and the vodka," he answered. "Sexy women and loud music."

"I'm not surprised," she answered. "Maybe someday you'll learn to lift your eyes to the hills."

"What's that mean?" he asked.

Alex paused. "Nothing you'd understand right now."

Leaving the cathedral, Alex caught sight of Robert. He was in a tight cordon of agents around the president. She knew he saw her. But he stayed focused on his assignment as the president stepped back into the limo. Alex held up her hand and gave him a wave, just in case he could catch it out of the corner of his eye. He didn't. But in that short space of time, when she took her eyes off Federov to wave to Robert, Federov disappeared.

FORTY-THREE

She looked in every direction, but saw no Federov. Mentally, she beat herself up. How could he have slipped away so easily? How could she have been so foolish as to take her eyes off him, even for an instant?

But he was gone. Completely gone.

The president was already in the limo. Alex's driver signalled to her. The motorcade needed to move quickly. Still turning her head, looking everywhere, searching the crowds, she tried to find Federov.

No luck. She ducked into her van. The door slammed shut behind her. An instant later the van moved forward with a lurch. Far up ahead, Alex could see the president's limousine as it moved slowly away from the cathedral. It inched across the square while the president waved to cheering Ukrainians, and then it pulled to a halt at Mihaylavski Place. There, surrounded by flowers and candles, was the gray granite monument to the great famine of the 1930s.

Alex's vehicle stopped, which meant that the president's vehicle had stopped. She climbed out quickly and moved forward on foot, trying to draw as close to the memorial and the president as possible. She was within a moderate security area and from a distance of about twenty yards, she could see the president.

Security people gathered around him, including Robert. The president moved with slow dignified steps to the monument with the US ambassador, Jerome Drake. Alex positioned herself with a good view of what would follow.

The monument was a gray slab about six feet high, breathtaking and moving in its stark simplicity. The center had been cut away in the general shape of a cross with gentle contours. In the center of the cutout, there was the carved figure of a man, creating a silhouette. Within the cutout, another figure, presumably that of God, and within that a child's figure, the infant Jesus.

Alex moved slightly. She found a position just beyond the dignitaries.

The crowd was quiet now as one of the president's assistants handed over a large floral wreath. The president stepped away from Ambassador Drake and closer to the monument. Alex's gaze followed the president. For the first time, the great famine that she had heard so much about was a reality.

Several seconds passed in silence. Everyone around her was still. A strange series of emotions filled Alex. No matter what one thought of this president, at least the American leader was here to mark the significance of this monument. She felt a deep sorrow for the victims of the famine, the humans who had perished from starvation seventy years earlier in the bitter Ukrainian winter. She bit her lip.

Then, after another moment passed, jets roared low overhead, Mirage fighters, purchased from the French, followed by a quartet of aircraft from the United States. Everyone's eyes moved skyward, and there was a surge of talking in the crowd.

A second wave of planes passed overhead and again distracted the crowd.

The president was at the monument now, head bowed, Ambassador Drake a few feet behind. Robert and Reynolds Martin and several other Secret Service agents were only a few feet away, watching the crowd, nervous, eyes intent, poised for trouble.

The wreath was enormous, and carried by two US marines from the embassy. They laid the wreath at the base of the monument. The president leaned over and twitched the ribbons on them, thus symbolically "laying" them.

The president's head lowered itself for a moment in prayer, or whatever heads of state think about when they can't wait to get a photo-op done and start home.

Standing thirty yards away, Alex felt a vibration in her pocket. It was her cell phone. An incoming call. She pulled the phone from her pocket and she looked at the incoming number.

Federov! *What the—?*

Cupping her hand over it to keep her voice low, she answered.

"Move," he said in English.

"What?"

"Move from where you are!"

"Where are you?" she demanded.

"Doesn't matter. I can see you. Move!"

"To where?"

"Anywhere! Now!"

The line went dead, the call over. Perplexed, but alarmed, she took several steps from where she was, searching any windows she could see. The marksmen were on the rooftops and the helicopters were overhead. Security near the president was as thick as a Crimean blizzard.

Everything seemed fine. Tense but fine. The president was still at the monument, head bowed, making sure the world press got ample coverage.

And yet, and yet . . .

Beneath the freezing cold, Alex felt herself sweating.

What was wrong with this? What was wrong with this picture? It wasn't just that her guts were in a turmoil; every part of her was.

Her hand went to her weapon and rested upon it. She moved cautiously away from where she had stood, looking for hints as to what might be imminent, trying to figure what Federov might have known that she didn't. Had he been warning her or jerking her chain?

Then there was an ominous noise. A bang in the distance. Then another. She saw all the security people stiffen to alert. For a moment, everyone froze.

Then she realized.

More airplanes? No! Something from beyond the perimeter. Something that defied the most zealous of plans of protection.

More loud blasts in the distance, followed by another round, then quickly a third. She saw the members of the president's Secret Service escort cringe. Then there was a whistling in the air above.

Incoming projectiles!

Some of the security people quickly went for their own weapons. Then there were a series of explosions across the square. One, two, three, moving toward the presidential target with incredible precision.

Then all hell broke loose.

A few yards away, Alex saw a woman's throat burst open with a horrible gash. The woman staggered and blood flooded from her wound. She never knew what had hit her. Smiling one second, dead the next.

Then someone else was hit by something. Chaos everywhere. Bodies were falling and people were running. Explosives were coming into the square from what seemed like every direction. The entire entourage, the entire ceremony, was under attack from far beyond the square.

She heard someone yell in English. *"RPGs! RPGs!"*

Rocket-propelled grenades. Instinctively, Alex tightened her own security pass around her neck so everyone could see it. She ran toward her van and her presumed means of escape. But it was like running through a riot because everyone was fleeing in a different direction. She was knocked over twice and had to fight her way back to her feet.

An older Ukrainian man with an American flag ran across Alex's path. Before Alex's eyes, a piece of shrapnel hit the man in the face and blew his head open. Blood gushed from the wound, hot and wet, splattering everyone within a few feet. He reeled and went down.

Then another RPG landed and then another. Then she couldn't count any more because the rounds were on top of each other and coming in on top of the entourage.

Everything that happened seemed to happen simultaneously. The whole moment of terror was frozen into one frame of time.

A blizzard of bone, brains, and blood. Screams.

Cries of pain and terror.

Barked orders from the various security services.

Shots were fired from many directions. Alex couldn't tell if they were friendly or hostile.

Alex wanted to vomit. Her insides wanted to explode. Instead, she kept moving. She had lost sight of Robert. Americans were calling out, running. Ducking and darting. There was no logic except survival.

Alex continued toward the vehicle that had brought her. She searched the crowd madly for Robert but still couldn't find him. She thought she saw Reynolds on the ground with a wound, but when she altered her course and ran ten feet in that direction, the man rose and staggered with the help of another man. She was no longer sure what she had seen.

Someone gave a command for all American security people to show badges and ready weapons. She drew her handgun. She moved toward her car.

Then Alex saw that the presidential limousine had taken a direct hit. The driver writhed in the front seat. His face was covered in blood. She knew she couldn't do anything for him. Half his head was missing. He was still moving, but she knew he would die. She could do nothing.

She ran toward her own vehicle. Bullets were hitting everywhere. She spun around; the wreath lay under a body that looked Ukrainian. She turned in another direction and the complete lack of reality slammed home. Two agents whom she didn't know had the president between them. They had automatic weapons drawn and were looking for a car to use to escape. The president's own car had taken a devastating hit. So had the backup limo. They were within ten feet of her, then five, then ran smack into her.

"Here!" she screamed. "FBI!" she shouted, identifying herself. "Here! Here!"

They looked. There was the number-two armored Mercedes, abandoned by the Ukrainians. She threw open the door. The keys were in the ignition. She threw open the backdoor.

The Secret Service agents looked at her and understood. They abandoned their prearranged emergency routines. They just wanted the president out of there. They pushed the president in and covered the president's body with their bodies.

For a brief moment, Alex surmised that Ukrainian security had been infiltrated by traitors. The RPGs must have been the first line of attack. Gunmen on the ground would probably be the second.

American English: a man's voice. "Out of the way, lady! Out of the way!" A marine major in uniform — the driver for the Benz — blindsided her, grabbing her shoulder and yanking her out of the way. She hit the ground hard.

Just then, Alex discovered she was right. Combat between forces on the ground. Two men with automatic handguns and ski masks made a move toward the driver's side of the Benz, confronting the driver.

The marine whirled with his sidearm, but he wasn't fast enough.

The gunmen fired. The marine's eyes went wide in disbelief as the bullets threw him against the side of the car. The gunmen were only a few feet from the president.

Alex stared at the enemy for less than half a second, understanding the moment perfectly. She raised her Walther. They didn't expect that from a woman. They turned on her, but turned too late.

She was younger, faster, and smarter, and somehow God seemed to guide her hand. It was Colosimo's all over again, but this time for keeps.

She fired six shots, back and forth, back and forth, back and forth.

What happened would replay itself in her mind for the rest of her life, every surreal moment. Before either assassin could fire a shot at her, Alex saw her bullets shatter the front of the one man's face and rip a hole in his neck. His weapon flew from his hands and he sprawled backward.

She hit the second man in the sternum. He was heavier and stockier, but no match for a .9 mm round, even from her old Walther. He managed to squeeze the trigger of his weapon, but the shots flew into the sky.

Crimson pools burst from his chest as he fell.

She lurched quickly to her feet. The marine was dead on the ground beside her, the left side of his neck and face shot to pulp.

In every direction, everyone was running through a hornets' nest of automatic weapons fire and rockets. Remaining Secret Service agents closed in on the limousine. From behind her, in the backseat, two Secret Service agents huddled against the president, their weapons up.

One of them yelled, "Driver down! You! Get in!"

She knew this part of the drill too. Service procedure was to get Einstein out of the Red Zone as fast as possible. She turned and looked. The Service people meant her. She should drive.

For a split second, Alex could see the face of the president, as dazed and terrified as the guards. Like any battle, everything had gone exactly to plan until the first shot was fired.

She holstered her weapon and slid into the front seat of the vehicle. The front window was cracked but not shattered. It had been hit hard twice and showed the points of impact. But it had held. God bless Stuttgart engineering.

"I'm FBI!" she said to the agents in back.

"Get us moving!" one of them barked back. "*Drive!*"

Alex gunned the engine and found it responsive. "Hang on!" she ordered.

She remembered the route from the airport. She put the vehicle in gear. There was a crunching impact under the tires and she knew she was driving over the fallen bodies of the two men she had shot. In the backseat, radios crackled as the agents gave their location as well as Einstein's.

She sped out of the square. Other security vehicles fell in stride with her. She got out of the square and hit the main roads. There was still a mass of confusion, people dazed and gawking, others fleeing, some sitting by the highway in tears.

From somewhere there was a final explosion, and the car shuddered as if it had been hit again with fragments of metal. A new crack appeared on a rear window.

The vehicle now had a slight wobble to it, which told her that the wheels had been hit. She wrestled with the shuddering steering wheel. The car went into a skid at about fifty miles an hour, but she turned into it and pulled the vehicle out.

She hit a straight section on the motorway. The president started to sit up and look around, immensely shaken and surprised to be alive.

In the rearview mirror, other American vehicles were not far behind. Coming up on them, however, a brigade of four motorcycle riders. Friendly or enemy? No one knew.

"I got four outriders," she said to the agents behind her. "I don't know who they are!" She was doing seventy miles an hour and the riders were rapidly overtaking them. Four of them!

She heard the window go open directly behind her. The sound of the wind was deafening. Sirens blared everywhere. One of the Secret Service agents leaned out the vehicle from the chest up, brandishing his machine gun, looking for more trouble, waiting to see if there was the slightest hostile sign from the riders.

They were in Ukrainian military uniforms and were easily doing a hundred miles an hour. The radio in the car crackled.

"They're ours! They're friendlies!"

"I don't trust anyone," the second agent said.

The riders came up to the car. The agent leaning out the window had his automatic weapon trained on the nearest one. But the leader of the motorcyclists gave a friendly hand sign and pointed toward the airport. They were there to lead the way, or at least said they were. Alex maintained her speed. The motorcycles went on ahead and formed a wedge.

Gradually, the sound of gunfire ceased. Alex drove for seven minutes. She hit the access road to the airport. There, on a heavily guarded tarmac up ahead, sat the president's backup helicopter.

Uniformed American soldiers indicated the way for the limousine. Alex drove the vehicle directly toward the chopper and brought it to a halt fifty feet away. The rotors were already noisily spinning. The air was filled with the sound of engines, distant sirens, and violent curses.

The back doors of the limousine flew open. The Secret Service agents hustled the president out and quick-stepped to the chopper.

Alex stood by the driver's side of the door and watched the president disappear up the ramp. Her eyes drifted to the vehicle. Battered chassis, cracked windows, shredded tires. How had it had gotten there? And she realized she was trembling, at least inside. She looked everywhere for Robert but didn't see him. A horrible feeling swept her, a fear and anxiety unlike anything she had previously known.

"Oh, God, please . . . ," she heard herself mumbling

A man appeared next to her. He identified himself as the ranking Secret Service agent on the tarmac.

"You drove?" he asked.

"Yeah. I drove," she said flatly.

"Good job! Orders are to get all our people out of here as fast as possible. We're not waiting for anyone."

"I'll stay here. I — "

"Get in the chopper," he said.

"I — "

"Get your ass in the chopper! Orders! There's only one seat left!"

"Okay."

She took a step. He reached out and put a hard hand on her shoulder. "I've never seen you before, but you sure done good today."

"Thanks."

She turned and ran to the ramp. The ramp came up practically while she was still on it. She found the remaining seat on the helicopter and slid into it. Seconds later, the helo lifted off.

Her head was pounding. Her insides were ready to explode. Though no one could see it, fear riddled her and she kept repeating prayers in her head. The gun weighed heavily in her pocket and the images of the carnage on the ground in Kiev kept spiraling back to her, as did the visions of the two faceless men she had shot.

She closed her eyes, drew a breath, prayed that Robert had gotten out the same as she had, and she opened her eyes.

She hadn't realized it, but she was sitting right across from the president, who was staring at her.

The chopper lifted higher into the sky and headed for Air Force One, which was just a few minutes away at the international airport at Borispil.

Her heartbeat plunged back into double digits. The president nodded gently at her. "Thanks."

"Yeah," was all she could say.

She tried to look out the window but there was no visibility. She remembered the dark clouds that had covered Kiev on arrival and realized that was exactly where she was right now.

On the flight to the international airport, no one spoke. What was there that could be said after what everyone had witnessed, after what had happened?

Alex leaned back and closed her eyes. Her hand drifted to her neck, searching for the small cross to touch, to massage.

Somehow somewhere in all the horror, the chain must have broken. The cross was gone. It wasn't in her blouse or anywhere on her or on the floor of the chopper.

It was just plain gone.

FORTY-FOUR

The president boarded Air Force One at Borispil amidst vast confusion. Alexandra found a seat by herself in the passenger section.

She closed her eyes, and much as she had done before leaving on this trip, she tried to disappear into prayer, beseeching heaven that what had happened back in Kiev hadn't looked as bad as she thought it had.

Sometimes prayers are answered. Other times they are not.

Much of the time, human events have no order, no logic, no good side. They can only be as good as is made of them afterward.

So it was today.

The flight back to Washington was fourteen hours. Before arrival, news of the terrible toll on the ground in Kiev had made its way through those survivors on Air Force One.

There were already forty-two confirmed fatalities on the ground. Injuries were still being tabulated.

Seven were members of what appeared to be a *filorusski* assassination squad.

Twenty-three were Ukrainian civilians, including eleven Foreign Service nationals who worked for the embassy.

Twelve remaining casualties were American citizens.

Of those, seven were embassy employees whom Alex didn't know.

Then there were the five whose names did mean something to her.

The ambassador, Jerome Drake, was dead.

So was Richard Friedman, her control officer.

The note taker from the meetings, Ellen Higgins, had come out at the last minute to get a look at the president and take a photograph. She too had been killed.

So had Reynolds Martin, a.k.a., "Jimmy Neutron," who, along with another agent, had immediately blocked access to the president when the first RPG had landed.

That left one casualty, of which Alex was informed an hour before landing in Washington.

Special Agent Robert Timmons, partnered with Reynolds Martin, had been the other agent to immediately protect the president. He too had been hit with shrapnel at the outset of the attack. And he too had died on the spot.

FORTY-FIVE

In a private room at Josephs Air Force Base when Air Force One returned to Washington, spokespeople for various government agencies had sought to give out proper information updates and make some sense out of chaos and tragedy. Meanwhile, Secret Service agents in Washington, picking up the fallen standard, whisked the president to the well-fortified compound in the Catoctin Mountains of western Maryland.

In a first-floor corridor at Josephs, banners welcoming home the travelers were torn down and replaced with long sheets of paper. Magic markers were stuck with Velcro to the wall under the paper, so that anyone could write tributes to those who had died in Kiev.

Then, in the tragedy-numbed days after Kiev, Alex assumed the role of a widow to her late fiancé. She phoned his parents in Michigan and broke the horrible news to them, rather than have them hear it from someone they didn't know. She talked to a small crowd of distraught Secret Service employees who had gathered on the tarmac in Washington when Air Force One returned. The death of her own fiancé barely sinking in upon her, she shared what Robert had told her to say if disaster struck, that he had died doing what he had wanted to do, that he had given his life in service to a country he loved.

News media made much of Alex's personal story. They wanted to talk to her. So did the radio and TV talk shows. Publishers contacted her about possible books.

She wanted none of it. Fame, if that's what it was, had been thrust upon her at a terrible price. She declined all the offers. She tried to disappear from public view, but reporters waited for her at Treasury and at her apartment complex. With the loss of the man she had so deeply loved, all sense, color, and flooring dropped from her days.

She was put on mandatory administrative leave with full pay. She was debriefed several times, by Treasury, by the FBI, and by Michael Cerny.

Then, a week after her return to the United States, Alex flew to Michigan for Robert's funeral. Like Kiev on the day he died, it was bitterly cold. The arctic wind swept down from central Canada to drop the entire state well below freezing. But it felt even colder because Robert's parents had to do what no parent should ever have to do: bury a son.

Robert Timmons' parents stood in the front row of two hundred mourners at the graveside in a snowy Lutheran churchyard in Saginaw. The sky was clear, but the air was touched with ice. The sun ducked in and out from the occasional cloud.

Alex stood beside her slain fiancé's parents. Robert's father managed to hold his emotions together. His mother had stopped trying. Alex had cried so much in the last seven days that, for this day at least, for this particular service, she had no tears left. She still had a deep hollow feeling, one of shock and disbelief.

She felt betrayed. Betrayed by life, betrayed by God, betrayed even by the people she had worked for. Betrayed by her own emotions. She had allowed herself to love, and now, with the same passion that she had loved, she felt the loss of Robert.

A man had died. *Her* man had died. It pained her now to think what a poor part she had played in his life. It agonized her to wonder what she could have done differently in Kiev. Could she have done something that might have removed him from that terrible spot at that fatal moment?

Logic told her there was nothing. Her emotions pulled her in a different direction.

Alex was already living in what was to her the new reality, the one where someone's passing had left a hole in the heart and a deep wound in the soul. Back home in DC, there was no one on the other side of sofa for TV in the evening, no discussion of weekend plans, no one to discuss a new book with, watch some baseball or football, or to swap insights or rude remarks about the national news.

With Robert gone, there was no one next to her in the usual pew at church. No one with whom to plan a beautiful future. Instead, there were the lonely moments at home alone, reading and rereading the last email messages from Robert. "I can't wait to see you in Kiev! Let's sneak away and go out for vodka and caviar," he had written.

On some evenings the new reality was about gazing endlessly at the old photographs or not being able to look at them without breaking up. It was about hearing old messages on the answering machine and knowing she would never be able to erase them. "Hey, Alex. On our honeymoon, let's find a secluded beach on Maui and—"

She tore her thoughts away from the past and into the present.

The coffin was beside an open grave, draped with the fifty-star flag of the United States of America. The Timmons' family pastor presided. He wore an overcoat worthy of Kiev but was already frozen.

The minister spoke softly, rapidly muttering a prayer that no one could hear because of the harsh wind. Words danced on the icy air, brief and appropriate.

Alex stared at the flag that covered the coffin. Robert's mother clutched her hand. They exchanged squeezes. Alex's eyes drifted. A few places away from her, at graveside, there was an open space, where someone could have been standing but wasn't.

She pictured Robert there, young, strong, and handsome, as he would now always be in her memory.

"I love you so much," she said to him.

He nodded back. On his lips, she saw the same words.

She blinked back the tears and held them.

"You were such an all-American guy," she said to him. "And you know what your death certificate says?"

"What?" he answered.

"Place of death: Myhaylavski Platz, Kiev, Ukraine."

She saw him laugh. "But I'm in a good place now," he answered. "With God."

She nodded. His mother glanced in her direction, and she felt a squeeze of her hand again. Robert's spirit coming through his mother, she wondered? She preferred to believe so.

As his coffin was lowered into the earth, as mourners stepped forward to drop flowers into the grave after him, time stood still.

The fact that those who died were Secret Service agents would always be a piece of the equation for anyone who loved them. But for Alex, when it came down to the everyday reality of what happened, it was about life without Robert, not life without the Secret Service agent.

Robert had left so much of himself behind. Yes, he had died doing what he loved doing, serving his country, protecting the president. But her heartache was that she could no longer touch him. The unending heartache was that he was gone forever.

On the flight from Michigan back to Washington, Reynolds Martin's widow, who had brought her young daughter, Tina, to the memorial, sat with Alex. Tina sadly played with the *matryoshka* doll that her father had bought for her. As the airplane flew up out of Dulles and over the Atlantic, Tina suddenly started waving out the window.

"What are you doing?" Mrs. Martin had asked.

"I'm saying good-bye to Daddy," said Tina.

Somehow, maybe by coincidence, maybe not, she was waving in the right direction, eastward over the ocean, toward Kiev.

"How did you know the direction?" Alex asked.

"I saw him in the sky," the girl answered.

Alex put a hand across the girl's shoulders but had to look away.

It was then that Alex finally lost her composure.

FORTY-SIX

Two days later, back in Washington, Alex met again with Michael Cerny.

Cerny informed her that Yuri Federov had not been seen since the day of the attacks. No one knew if he was dead or alive or somewhere in between. The Caspian Group seemed to be continuing in business, but so had Howard Hughes' enterprises long after Hughes ceased to be a rational factor.

Alex hardly cared about any of this anymore. But Cerny took her over and over the small painful details of her time in Kiev. What had she seen, what had she felt? Was there anything—however small—that she might have neglected to mention? Mentally, she was now so blitzed that she couldn't handle the inquiry. She was beyond overload.

Cerny turned her over to other inquisitors, less gentle ones, including one whom she only knew as "Lee." Alex had the impression that she had been passed along to Cerny's higher-ups, or at least someone representing them,

Lee was a large, dour, nasty-looking man with a big head, long fingers, and remote blank eyes in a fleshy face. He was in his mid-forties and had a Marine Corps dishonorable discharge look to him. He came across as an articulate thug. She wondered if he had been assigned to her with some subtle physical intimidation in mind, the coarse six-four male debriefing the overeducated five-seven female.

Well, she decided quickly, if that was the game plan, if her own government was turning on her and holding her up to unnecessary scrutiny, she was having none of it. She would dish it right back.

The questions from Lee were interminable. He worked without notes or an assistant, which told her that they were being recorded. One grim debriefing session focused entirely on the subject of Ukrainian energy power plants, nuclear and otherwise, something that had hardly come up at all in the discussions Alex had had with Federov.

Q (Lee): Alex, do you feel he was avoiding the subject?

A (Alex): How could he avoid it if it didn't come up?

Q: Was there a reason you didn't steer things in that direction?

A: Yes. No one from this or any other department had asked me to.

Q: But you knew he had brokered a submarine to the Cali drug cartel.

A: What in God's name does that have to do with Ukrainian electricity?

Q: It's in the realm of exports.

A: So is vodka. So is caviar.

[*Pause noted*]

Q: Alex, you seem defensive. If there's something you may have neglected previously to mention, some scrap of information that might have seemed meaningless at the time, now would be a good time to —

A: [*Interrupting, manifesting anger*] Look! I was told to pursue him as a tax cheat. Those were my instructions. If there was another agenda —

Q: There was no other agenda. But we feel you may have learned or seen more than you realize you might have. [*Pause*] Did he mention anything about business with Asia?

A: Nothing of merit.

Q: Japan. China. Either Korea. Vietnam.

A: You're wasting your [*expletive deleted*] time! Am I under suspicion for something?

Q: Should you be?

A: Of course not!

Q: Then why would you be?

A: [*Expletive deleted*]

Q: What about his bodyguards? Kaspar and Anatoli?

A: What about them?

Q: Did they seem loyal to him, men he relied on?

A: I'm not sure he trusted anyone.

Q: Really? Why not?

A: If you were Federov, would *you* trust anyone?

Q: That's not the point of the question.

A: Then what is?

Q: Did he mention any attempts on his life?

A: Only in theory.

Q: Did he think the US was trying to kill him?

A: He gave me that impression.

Q: Why do you think he thought that?

A: Because he might have been right. I don't know.

Q: How was his health?

A: It seemed pretty good, even though he drank a lot and smoked a lot. But I'm not a doctor.

Q: By the way, what is Federov?

A: What do you mean, "what is he"?

Q: Russian? Ukrainian?

A: Don't you read your own files?

Q: I'm asking you. Set me straight.

A: [*impatience noted:*] The difference between being Ukrainian and Russian in Ukraine is one of ethnic identity. In the eastern provinces, everyone, Russians and Ukrainians alike, speaks Russian and the people live intermingled. But of two neighboring families, if one is ethnically Ukrainian and the other ethnically Russian they know it. That doesn't mean they can't be friends or intermarry. In Soviet times people had to carry "internal passports" and these listed one's ethnic nationality. I don't think this is listed on Ukrainian ID cards, but I'm not sure. So Federov would be an ethnic Russian but Ukrainian citizen.

Q: That's how he would describe himself?

A: Why don't you find him and ask him?

Q: You're making this more difficult. Why are you hostile to questions about Federov?

A: I'm not.

Q: Then answer mine.

A: How he would describe himself would depend on the circumstances of the question. If a foreigner asked, "Where are you from?" Federov would probably say, "I'm from

Ukraine." If he wanted to stress his ties to Ukraine he might say, "I'm a Ukrainian." Presumably he would be aware that the answer, "I'm Russian" without more ado would mislead the interlocutor into thinking he was a Russian citizen. If the question was ethnically focused, "I understand there are Russians and Ukrainians in Ukraine, Mr. Federov. Which are you?" he would presumably say, "I'm Russian, though a Ukrainian citizen."

Q: So even you aren't sure which he is?

A: [*pause, angrily*] That's my answer.

Q: I'll note that you didn't answer the question and we'll move on...

And so it went, the logic of the questions elliptical and constantly turning back upon itself, Alex's patience a thing of memory.

Lee pressed further on the subject of Anatoli and Kaspar. Who were these two associates who had turned up at her embassy meetings with Federov? Any unusual mannerisms? Were they cleared-eyed gunmen, or did they hide behind dark glasses? How did they sound? Like Russians? Ukrainians? Something of other origin?

She had no idea. Federov's humanoid bookends barely grunted, much less spoke, and aside from the fact that one seemed blinky from the dry air in the embassy, they seemed to see as well as anyone.

Who had she seen at the nightclub? What were the women like? Did they carry weapons to go with their Donna Karan suits and their Jimmy Choo shoes? By chance, had Alex gone to the ladies room and seen anything there of note?

No, Alex answered with an increasing edge, there was nothing special in the ladies' *pissoirs* unless unusually located tattoos or the latest in European lingerie was of interest to the interrogator. Or how about the fact that the ladies' room was dim and stank of Lysol? And as far as the clientele of the club, it was as unremarkable as that to be found at any other velvet-roped mob joint.

Was it a sex club? Lee wanted to know. Dancers? Topless?

It was nothing of the sort, Alex answered sharply. It was music, dining, and drinking, not necessarily in that order. Topless in this joint meant some Slavic wise guy wasn't wearing a shoulder holster.

"Did Federov try to seduce you?" Lee asked.

"Is the pope German?" she answered.

Could she look through some surveillance photos taken by contacts in Kiev?

She could and did.

Did she recognize anyone?

She didn't.

Not even Kaspar and Anatoli, Federov's two bodyguards?

Not even them.

Did she have last names on the bodyguards? Anything extra she might remember?

Nothing.

Did she see them the day of the RPG attacks?

No.

"So Federov would have been out without his bodyguards that day?" Lee pressed. "That seems strange."

"I can't say that I saw his two hoods that day," she retorted. "They might have been there, they might not have been. They may have been part of the attack, but so might have two million other people in Kiev. Why do we keep going over this? You've asked me the same question seven times! What is it with these two guys that you keep harping on?"

Lee declined to answer. Instead, he wanted to know her theory about the RPG attacks. Who had been behind them?

She had no special theory to accompany her, no special knowledge.

"Did Federov ever mention anything about an American couple named Peter Glick and Edythe Osuna?" Lee asked out of the blue late one afternoon.

The reference startled Alex.

"Yes. I *think* he did," she said after a moment's thought.

"You think? Either he did or he didn't."

"He did," she said. "He said they were a pair of American spies."

"What else did he say about them?"

She searched her mind. She had many memories of the night club in Kiev and could recall much of the conversation. But she was drawing a blank here. "They were assigned to kill him?" she asked.

"He might have thought so. What else did he say about them?" Lee pressed.

"Honestly, it was a boozy evening. I'm not remembering."

"Do you know who they are? Or who they were?"

"He said they were spies. I took everything Federov said with a few pounds of salt," Alex said, "but looking back, I haven't caught him in too many mistruths. If he said they were spies, my guess is they probably were."

Lee's finger was tapping lightly on the table, a little tic. "All right," he said quietly. Then he moved on. Why did she suppose Federov had tried to move her position in the final seconds before the attacks? Was he sweet on her and trying to get her out of harm's way? Or might he have been trying to move her *into* harm's way for maybe the same reason?

She had no idea and told her interrogators exactly that.

The questions drove her into the ground.

The sessions were relentless.

Remorseless. Didactic. Unapologetic. Endless.

The direction of the inquiries always seemed to point in one direction. The official policy of the United States was to find the people responsible for the RPG attacks and bring them to some sort of justice. If official help was not forthcoming or significant enough from Ukraine, justice would be sought in the back alleys of the world. In fact, Alex sensed that this was the real way questions were pointing, the desired way of American officials to address their issues.

The sessions went on nonstop each day and continued until, with no explanation, they stopped completely. That was how things worked in Washington. Truth was like the smile of the mythical Cheshire cat. It receded as one approached it.

She went to trauma counseling with a top Washington shrink three times the first week back. Then she stopped. It was her feeling that the visits to the doc only made things worse.

FORTY-SEVEN

Alex officially returned to her job at Treasury on Monday, March 2. She was offered a further paid leave of absence by her boss, Mike Gamburian. She declined it and tried to bury herself in Internet frauds.

Gamburian gave her a handful of new cases. Easy stuff. But nothing made sense.

Her focus was shot.

She would be driving and couldn't breathe. She would pull off the highway and gasp for breath. For a month, she couldn't sleep at night. But during the day, walking, in the office, in a supermarket, in a park, she would fall asleep on her feet. Twice she fell, helped up once by a passerby, another time by a suspicious cop who suspected she was a closet junkie.

At night, when she finally could doze off, her sleeping was safest on the living room floor. She had tried the sofa but kept falling off. At least on the floor, there was no falling off. She was convinced there was some high-pitched whine somewhere in the building. But she had greater worries than that.

A destructive voice within her became strident as the sorrowful days passed.

Why not end it all?

Why not be with Robert in heaven, if that's where he is?

Hey, you! Yes, you, Alex! Why not jump?

Your parents, your grandparents, everyone you love, hey, they're all waiting for you on the other side. Come on. Cross over. Death is as easy as a swinging gate in an old churchyard. Come on. What are you waiting for?

God is waiting. Do it!

Suicidal fantasies filled her days. The occasional homicidal one took up where the suicidal ones took a breather. She tried more therapy. It didn't help.

A friend brought her to a writers' group, but she kept writing the same thing over and over in a notebook: *I wish Robert were here.*

She'd watch TV for hours and would have no memory of what she'd seen. It was a living hell on earth, a fog that refused to lift.

Friends would phone. She jumped each time the phone rang, monitored the messages, rarely picking up, then erased them.

Friends from work.

Friends from the pickup basketball games at the gym.

Some of Robert's peers in Secret Service.

Her buddy Laura Chapman at the White House.

She avoided her friends and didn't want to be helped. At work, she quietly went through the motions, doing her job competently and engaging in no extra discussion. Soon, others would stop talking when she came into a room or an office. She had isolated herself well.

She went to church each Sunday, sitting alone, avoiding the pew she used to share with Robert. Sometimes she would go on Wednesdays. Absently she wrote his name in the prayer books and the hymnals that she found before her. She offered prayers and didn't hear answers.

Her pastor sought her out. They had discussions. No headway. The minister wanted to talk about God's love and Christ's forgiveness and her mission in life.

Her ears were deaf. She wasn't ready to hear any of it, much less consider it.

She was an emotional basket case and she knew it.

Sometimes Alex would find herself in the parish chapel and not remember how she got there or how long she'd been there. Once she realized that she had left her car running, ran out for the keys, found them gone. The parish assistant minister had taken them for her.

During the second week of March, on a Thursday night, she found the final handwritten note Robert had left. It was in blue ink in bold penmanship, and he had slipped it into a pair of her shoes. Red high heels. The sexiest footwear she owned. She only wore them for him and on special occasions. It said simply, "I love you and I always will."

FORTY-EIGHT

The phone call from Bernardo Santangelo came into Gian Antonio Rizzo's office at half past eight in the morning.

"Sorry to have not gotten back to you sooner," said the jolly keeper of cadavers at the city morgue. Today he didn't sound so jolly. His voice was quiet and he sounded shaken. "You asked me to alert you if anything unusual transpired with the bodies of those two Americans, the couple I showed you?"

Rizzo answered quickly, his senses on full alert.

"Yes?" he said.

"We've been friends for many years, you and I," he said. "So I'm doing you a favor. But you must never mention it."

"Go ahead," Rizzo said.

"Two things," said Santangelo, who added that he was calling from a café around the corner. "A security team from the American embassy came by and picked up the bodies. They had all the paperwork, personal and legal, to remove the bodies. This was two days ago. They seemed to be in a hurry. I believe the corpses have been repatriated to America now."

"And did you behave like their lap dog and give them all of the information that we have?" he asked.

"I had no other choice," came the response.

"Wonderful!" Rizzo said. "Bloody Americans! How do they always know these things? Spies, they have spies among us!"

Santangelo allowed his friend to rant, saying nothing.

"And what was the second thing?" insisted Rizzo. "Is it anywhere near as pleasant as the first?"

"Perhaps," said Santangelo. "I'm not supposed to give you any more information about the case," he said. "In fact, I've been served with papers from a federal court. I'm not even supposed to speak to you."

With that, he rang off, leaving Rizzo with a dial tone.

FORTY-NINE

Every once in a while, Alex almost felt human again.

Instead of running or going to the gym, she went for long walks, an unusual activity in her neighborhood. On a whim, she booked a trip to Puerto Rico and went for what she thought would be a week. She used the fake passport and driver's license that Cerny had issued because the government — with their usual bureaucratic diligence — had never asked for them back. She spent too much money and sat each day by a hotel swimming pool in huge dark glasses so she wouldn't be recognized.

In Puerto Rico she spent time in the bars and in the casinos. She played blackjack one night, lost more than a hundred dollars, then won it back the following night at the roulette wheel. Then she went up by several hundred dollars by playing the thirty-three, the "double trinity," as she thought of it. She drank way too much. The booze seemed to help even though deep down she knew it wasn't an answer. The double trinity hit on the thirty-third spin after she sat down to play.

She took three ten-dollar chips from her pile of winnings, placed it on the double zero, gave the dealer a smile and a shrug.

"One more spin and I get up and leave," she said.

"Good luck," the dealer said.

Alex smiled back.

The ball clicked around the rim of the wheel, clattered noisily and came to rest.

Double zero. Two hits in a row. The table buzzed.

"That's it. I'm done," she said.

She tipped the dealer lavishly and got up and left. She was ahead by six hundred dollars. She put four hundred aside and vowed to not put it back on the tables.

On the next night, she played roulette again, then some keno, then blackjack and broke even. At least it wasn't a loss. She must have looked much better than she felt because she was asked to dance by an attractive Canadian man. She obliged but declined to have dinner with him in his room, much to his disappointment.

"Something wrong with me?" he asked, teasing gently.

"No. Nothing wrong with you. My fiancé was killed in an accident recently."

"I'm sorry," he said.

"Yeah," she said.

"I understand," he said.

"Thank you."

"I'm not much good company for anyone, much less myself," she said.

"I understand that too," he answered. "Hey, if things ever change ..."

He handed her a business card. He was in film production in Toronto. She threw the card away.

Then she went upstairs and soon, inexplicably, found herself in tears again.

She came home a day early. Her home answering machine was loaded with twenty-six messages. She cleared it without listening to them. She felt as if she were about to hit bottom and fall through. She wasn't that far wrong.

Two nights later, toward ten in the evening, she took out her Glock 9 and placed it on the coffee table in front of her in her living room. She took out a pen and pad and loosely constructed a suicide note. She put a fresh clip of bullets in the magazine and slapped it into the butt of the weapon. She pulled back the slide. It snapped back on its spring, pulling a round from the magazine, leaving the round in the firing chamber and leaving the hammer cocked. She clicked the safety catch to "off." All that was needed now was a slight pull on the trigger.

Doggerel tiptoed across the fringes of her consciousness.

> *The time has come, the walrus said,*
>   *to speak of many things,*
> *Of loaded guns and obscene puns*
>   *and whether pigs have wings.*

Well, the time *had* come.

She walked her way through a suicide scenario. She set her suicide note aside on the table. She wondered if she was dressed appropriately to kill herself. She considered the mindless small details of who might find her. Or should she call the police first and then do it?

Alexandra's gaze fell upon a small mirror on the table. It was chipped from a time several weeks earlier when Robert, who had come over for an early dinner had knocked it off the table.

She saw the chip and emotions and associations took over. How long could anyone be expected to live with such grief? She looked away, purposefully avoiding her own reflection. The awful truth was in that mirror and she didn't need any reminders. Her skin was blotched with tension and fatigue. Her hair, which she hadn't washed in three days — or was it four? — was dirty and stuck to her cheek and neck.

God, I'm a mess. God, I can't deal with this. God, take me away from this.

She wished — she genuinely wished — she had died with Robert. Then they could have entered God's heaven together.

Then she thought of the other people who had been killed in Ukraine and another wave of despondency washed over her. She was wishing she were dead and those poor shattered families were wishing that their lost loved ones were alive. She felt further guilt for just being alive.

Okay ... she knew what she should do. This would be easier for everyone ...

She fingered the Glock. She hefted it. The gun felt heavy in her hand. Heavier than it normally did with a full magazine, even though that made no sense.

She'd just run through the scenario. Who would find her? Who would bury her?

Who would even miss her?

The answer was obvious.

No one.

She fingered the gun. Yup. Round in the chamber, hammer cocked, safety on "off."

Ready for business, as Robert used to say.

She had no family left. No parents, no children. She supported no one. She loved no one. No one depended on her.

She used to think she had come so far, done so well. It wasn't so long ago that all systems were *go* and the future looked beautiful.

Yeah, well that was a previous lifetime, wasn't it?

Previous lifetime. Her thoughts were skewed and out of kilter.

She reached for the little cross that she had for years worn around her neck and then, when it was gone, she was reminded why it was gone and what had happened. Ukraine had really ruined her, everything that had happened there, everything that she had lost. Her fiancé. Her religion. Her belief.

Her life? Just an afterthought. She had lost that in Ukraine too. This one single shot would merely be the final formality, the punctuation point that would complete the sentence.

She picked up the gun.

Her hand trembled. She turned it toward her temple.

Come on, Alex. Have the courage.

Do it. Do it!

She moved the nose of the pistol upward. She felt the cold black steel touch her temple.

She began a little countdown and the blessed eternal darkness became visible.

Five, four . . .

Time spiraled. So did thoughts. So did words.

She was a little girl again in Southern California, her mom and her dad nearby in the warm sunlight of Redondo Beach. Then she was a teenager in the south of France, riding a horse one summer.

Three, two . . .

Then she was in Russia, laughing with friends at the Café Pushkin. Then, finally, she was in Robert's arms for a final time. And he was holding her so tightly that for a split second it didn't seem like a fantasy anymore and she could actually hear his voice and he was telling her that he loved her and always would.

One . . . !

She could feel the touch of her finger against the trigger. Just a little more pressure and —

And then Robert was in front of her. And from somewhere he was talking to her, a voice as alive or real as anything in this room, telling her deep down what she knew he would tell her, what he would scream at her, if he could have seen her right now.

If anything should happen to me, if something bad, should happen, I never want you to be alone. Or unhappy.

You should go on ... you should go on ...

You must be brave and go on ...

I will send a guardian angel to protect you ...

Zero.

Her hand trembled horribly. Tears overtook her.

Her hand moved the Glock's deadly muzzle away from her head. She cried uncontrollably. She flicked the safety to "on." She pushed the eject button that popped the magazine partly out of the butt and took it the rest of the way by hand and tossed it across the room. She pulled back the slide and popped the round that had been chambered — the one that, if it hadn't been for Robert, would now be in her head — out of the ejection port. The gun empty like that, the slide stayed back. Just reinserting the magazine and pressing the release button would cause it to travel forward and put another round into the firing chamber, and the hammer was still in the firing position. With her thumb she pressed the release button and the slide came forward with a sharp snap. She pressed the trigger and the cocked hammer fell with another snap. The gun was now harmless.

She sobbed. *Oh God. Oh God. Oh Jesus ...*

It was a prayer, not a curse, an incantation, not a blasphemy.

She sat. She leaned back. She thought.

She cursed herself violently.

She couldn't even work up the courage to pull the trigger!

What a useless excuse for a human being she was, she thought.

She stood. She needed air.

That was it. Air.

She would go out for a breath of air. She would walk across the street to the Irish bar restaurant called Murphy's just two minutes away and knock back some drinks in the bar, summon up all the courage she could, and come back. Then she would finish things off.

That would do it. That would get the job done.

She pulled on her coat and went out the door. No sound from Don

Tomás across the hall. Well, who cared? Did he care enough about her? Maybe it would be Don Tomás who found her. Good for him.

She went downstairs, as bitter as she had ever been in her life. She was working up a rage again, against God, against everything and everyone, convinced that she could get this final job done tonight.

A few drinks and there would be no equivocating when she came back upstairs.

This is it for Alexandra LaDuca. No one lives forever, right?

She brushed past the concierge, barely nodding to him.

She went to the front door, her head down.

A large man with a pronounced limp was approaching, a duffel bag on his shoulder. She made no effort to get out of his way. At the last moment he saw her.

They collided. She threw a furious elbow at him. She connected solidly even though she was off balance.

She looked up, bitter and profane, ready to follow the elbow with a kick.

"Damn it!" she snapped. "Why don't you watch where—?"

"Hey, hey? *Alex?*" said a friendly voice, the man she had hit. An accent from the Carolinas. He laughed. "Hey, easy, woman, easy. What the heck? Wow, that's one nasty elbow you throw! Man!"

He reached out and steadied her with a strong arm.

"You okay?" he asked.

Two blinks. Then recognition.

"What are *you* doing here?" she asked.

A smile crossed his face. Concern with affection. "I was looking for you," he answered. "But I never thought I'd see you."

FIFTY

They stood together on the freezing sidewalk. "I was worried about you," Ben said. He pulled his gym bag off his shoulder and let it rest on the pavement. The bag was thick. He always carried his own basketball.

"Hey, we all know what happened. I can't tell you how sorry we are. You got notes from us, right?"

"I have a lot of mail I haven't opened," she said.

"We're all worried for you, Alex."

"Thanks. I'll be okay," she lied.

"Uh, huh," he said. "Well, I came over to make sure."

"Make sure of what?"

"That you're going to be okay."

"What are you, my guardian angel?" she asked, barely able to control the sarcasm.

"If I have to be, I will," Ben said steadily and without missing a beat. "I have a hunch you might need one right now," he said. "So here I am right here in front of you, minus the wings and the halo because those things aren't so fashionable these days."

She stood uncomfortably but felt herself give a slight smile.

"I promise you I'll be okay," Alex said.

"It's not that easy," he said. "The guys at the gym. We heard you were on leave from work, but this isn't right. We would all feel better if we saw you at the gym again. We're not going to all stop talking when you show up."

"I'm not feeling very social these days," she said.

"Yeah, I know. I know. Hey. You think I don't know maybe at least *a little bit* about being in a really stinking mental place? Heck!"

He reached down and rapped his knuckles on the prosthesis that connected his right knee with his sneaker. Then, "You had dinner yet?" he asked.

"I'm not hungry," she said.

"I didn't ask if you were hungry, I asked if you'd had dinner yet."

"What if I haven't?" she asked.

"Then, I haven't either, so why don't we have some together? Please don't say no."

A long pause again. Then, "Okay," she said. " Maybe I haven't had dinner."

"Want some? Plus a sympathetic ear. And how 'bout a drink?"

She thought of the Glock upstairs. It was waiting for her. All she had to do was pick up that magazine, slap it into the butt, pull back the slide and chamber a round, flick the safety off, and that little number would be a hundred percent ready for business, just like it had been minutes ago.

"No, look ..." she answered. "I — "

Ben motioned to the hotel across the street. "Come on. It's on me and my guess is you need it right now. Just don't walk too fast. I'm running out of legs, you know."

FIFTY-ONE

She ordered some soup. He ordered a burger. They both ordered pints of draft beer, he a Sam Adams, she a Boddingtons, an English beer that had been fizzed up for the American market.

"I was going to leave a note with your doorman to ask you to call," Ben finally said. "No one's heard from you in weeks."

A long pause from Alex.

"I was away," she said.

"That's no excuse. Your friends want to know you're okay. And if you're not okay, you got to let them know that, too."

Something in her throat caught. She couldn't answer. His gaze settled into her.

"I got to say, Alex, you look terrible right now."

"I feel terrible."

"Let me show you something," he said.

She waited. He reached down toward his bad leg, or more accurately, his missing leg, or, more accurately still, the fake leg. She heard him fiddle with a couple of straps and buckles. He brought the prosthesis, detached from his knee, up to lap level so she could see it.

He put it on the table. There was no surprise, but she realized she must have made a short gasp, because he reacted to it.

"There," he said. "How do you like that?"

"Would you put that back on!" she insisted. "People are staring."

The waiter passed by the table, did a double take, then fled.

"Let the folks stare," Ben said with a laugh. "It'll do 'em good. They want to stare some more, they can go over to Walter Reed and look at a lot of ex-soldiers, men and women a heck of a lot worse off than me. Some of them got three or four limbs gone, burns all over their bodies, eyes blown out of their heads, and brain injuries. Now, my basketball buddy Alex LaDuca," he asked with a smile, "how do you like my leg?"

"I like it. It's a nice fake leg."

"Want to try it on? It'll make you taller, on one side at least."

"Ben!" She already had her hand to her mouth, almost laughing. "Please!"

"Please what?"

"I like it better when it's strapped where it should be," she said.

"Thank you. That's the answer I wanted. So as a favor, just for you, I'll get dressed again. I'm going to need the leg to walk home."

She came out from hiding behind her hands.

"This is my 'Transformer moment,'" he continued. "A couple of straps and buckles and I'm half a robot."

She watched how quickly he buckled it back into place, dropping the trouser leg.

"I know what's going on with you," Ben said. "You never thought it would happen, but part of you is gone, just like part of what used to be me is gone. You woke up one day and looked around and something, *someone*, was missing that you never thought you could replace. And you still don't see how you will."

She felt something catch in her throat.

"You're where I was two years ago, Alex. You're hating life. It's a bad place to be."

"It's not like that," she said, her hand settling on the table.

"No? Look me in the eye and tell me that it's not like that."

She looked at him, opened her mouth to speak, then looked away.

Two beers arrived. The pints looked bigger than expected.

"When I lost my leg, I thought my life was over," Ben said. "I wanted to kill myself. Tell me that hasn't gone through your head."

She looked back to him after several seconds. She still couldn't speak. One of his strong hands settled on hers.

"It's gone through my head," she finally admitted.

"Has it gone *through* your head?" Ben asked. "Or is it still there?"

She didn't answer.

"It's there right now, isn't it? That 'I want to end it all' feeling."

"What makes you think so?"

"I know just by looking at you," he said. "Answer me."

"It's there."

"I can't make decisions for you," Ben said, "but, see, your life isn't over. Not by a long shot. You're on this earth for a reason. Right now, you need to get up off the floor and live the life God gave you."

"I miss Robert horribly," she said softly.

"Of course you do. You always will. My parents are both gone now. Think I don't miss them every day?"

"Mine are gone too," she said. "Long time ago."

"Brothers? Sisters?" he asked.

"None."

"That's where you're wrong," he said. "You come by and play some basketball tomorrow night. You'll see whether you have brothers and sisters or not."

She looked away for several more seconds as food arrived. She felt herself search for words and not find them. She was momentarily afraid to look back and didn't know why, but when it popped into her mind, what Robert had once said about a guardian angel, she managed to gather herself and focus.

"Are you always so smart?" she asked, turning back to him.

He laughed. "Heck, no! I was dumb enough to get my leg blown off in a stupid useless war. Know what? For six months I sat around being bitter, feeling sorry, feeling that I couldn't go on. I was a college dropout and just another wounded vet, battling with the VA for treatment. Well, you know what? I decided I wasn't going to be just another college-dropout wounded vet."

She found herself listening to him.

"When I lost my leg," he continued, "the pastor at my church in Durham used to phone me every day. Make sure my messed-up head was getting back together. Make sure I didn't go off the deep end. Know what I mean?"

"I know."

Ben shook his head. "I know it's corny, but my mom used to read the Psalms to us from the Bible. Three or four times a week, after dinner, we'd sit around the kitchen table; this is when I was growing up in Greensboro, and she'd read something from her family Bible. I always liked the psalm about lifting 'my eyes up unto the hills, from whence —'"

"'Cometh my strength,'" Alex responded softly.

"You know that one?" He was surprised.

"It's Psalm 121," she said. "I remember it from long ago. And, funny you should mention it, I had the occasion to use it myself in Kiev."

Her fingers went to her neck, where the jewelry used to be, then returned empty.

"Then you should practice it. What goes around comes around. Lift up your eyes. The loss is always going to be with you, Alex. Without Robert, you'll never walk quite the same way again. But you'll walk."

He paused. "Now here's where my pastor connects to you," he said. "After I was feeling better and got myself back into college, I called him up to thank him. He said, 'Thank me by taking the word forward. When you see someone else who needs that call each day, that supporting hand, *you* take that first step. *You* help *that* person.' That's why I'm here tonight, Alex," he said. "That's why I'm here in DC getting a college degree; that's why I'm here offering you a hand. You're not going to let my pastor down, are you?"

She smiled and pondered it.

"You're not going to let *me* down. Who'd throw me those great passes?" he asked.

"Suppose I did want to walk again?" she asked. "How do I do it?"

"One small step at a time," he said. "And keep your eyes lifted unto the hills. You're on this earth for a reason, and it's not just to throw me passes on the basketball court, though I wouldn't mind some of those real soon."

"I owe you," she said.

"Then get over for some basketball tomorrow. I'm averaging a lousy ten points a game since you've been missing."

"I'll be there," she said.

An hour later, she sat before the Glock on her living room table. Slowly, she lifted it.

She methodically removed the bullets from the magazine and put them in the cardboard box they came in. She placed the weapon back in its case and locked it. She put the empty magazine in a drawer in the kitchen that held odds and ends like packing tape and a nesting set of screwdrivers and an extension cord she didn't need. Not that she couldn't get it, but it would take effort and, more importantly, time and maybe reflection.

She walked back to the sofa, collapsed, and cried until there were no more tears.

She had promised. And she would go on.

The next day, she started going through the mail that had gathered for her. Her small mailbox in the lobby had filled up long ago, so the rest of her mail had been left at the desk. When the concierge gave it to her it filled a respectable-sized box.

The task took a while.

She played basketball again the next night. She received hugs and tearful embraces from everyone she knew. Never in her life had she so realized how valuable a network of friends could be.

She phoned her boss, Mike Gamburian, the following morning and told him she was ready to return.

There was a pause. "You're sure?" he asked.

"Tell me I can come back before I change my mind," she said. "Please, Mike?"

"You pick the day," he said.

On Wednesday, March 25, she returned to work at Treasury.

She was ready to learn to walk again, one step at a time.

PART TWO

FIFTY-TWO

At a few minutes past 7:00 p.m., Alex sat at her desk, delaying before going home. Springtime had finally come to Washington, and the city enjoyed its best weather of the year. Then the heat of the summer gripped the city in mid-June.

She stared at her two computers. The ice of Kiev seemed a world away, a bitter memory. But it still haunted her. Evenings were difficult. She was afraid of loneliness, afraid that missing a certain someone would overtake her.

She had started to work past her grief. Now she wanted answers.

How long had it been since Kiev? There had been times in the last few weeks when she could have instantly given the answer. It's been two days, it's been three. It's been a week, two weeks. A month. Then a second month. Then a third. Gradually, the story disappeared from the newspapers and the attention of the American public, replaced by other events, other intrigues.

This evening, on a whim, she entered her clearance for a secured Intranet site dedicated to the Kiev visit and the debacle that had transpired there. The screen went blank and she sighed. Then a dialogue box opened that asked for her name.

She entered it. If it was receptive to her name, no one could get on her case for getting access.

The dialogue window accepted her name. Surely someone had failed to purge her. But the next thing she knew, she was in the HUMINT — the human intelligence — leading up to the trip to Kiev.

Except, what was this she saw?

She leaned forward.

The file took new directions with new references. Surely further access codes would cut her off. But they didn't. She kept exploring.

For the next hour, the files attached to the presidential visit to Kiev took up the known story of what had happened and its aftermath. It was typical of the code of conduct of such things that, having been a principal player in the events of Kiev, she had received no subsequent briefings of how things had gone down or why. She had answered plenty of questions but had received no explanations.

She read report after report, analysis after analysis, of what had happened.

Something bothered her immediately.

Almost everything was written by investigators who had not been there.

She began to notice strange small discrepancies, none that made any significant difference by itself, but enough to bring to mind the principle that if you pushed together enough grains of sand, you would build a beach.

The attackers who had fired the rockets, their weapons and their vehicles, were described differently than she had remembered.

A small mistake? Maybe.

But she recalled that five men had charged the presidential limousine and found it recounted in several records that there were four. The Secret Service detail assigned to the president was listed as twenty-four. She knew there had been twenty-eight.

The official record had been tweaked. Why?

Leaning forward, she attacked the keyboard with more gusto. She referenced names including her own. She traveled through cyberspace to the personnel files and biographies of the government people who had attended the visit to Kiev.

Thirty-seven names in all. She scanned them, including her own again, to see if any backgrounds had been fudged. None had that she could see.

She went back and picked up the story. It was now past 8:00 in the evening. The disinformation was accelerating. She brought up her own name and factored in several cross references. She attempted to access the files that she herself had contributed in the lead-up to the trip, mindless low security stuff on trade delegations, black market currency issues, the penny-ante balance of payments stuff, and then the more substantial stuff on Federov.

She found these files had been tampered with too. With a rush, she then went after the reports that she herself had filed in the aftermath of Kiev. These were missing entirely.

She leaned back from her screen.

What was she looking at?

Typical Washington bureaucratic bungling? Or a far larger issue?

She tried to work around the files. She was typing furiously now. Her fiancé was dead and someone — or some agency — was playing fast and loose with the official version of truth.

She reaccessed her own name. She brought up her own reports via a different cyber thread. She found key parts had been deleted.

Her fingers froze again on the keyboard.

She paused. Now her mind was in overdrive. She had been around the government long enough to know that when something came up missing, particularly where the official version of events was concerned, there was never much in the way of coincidence. Bureaucratic incompetence was coin of the realm in government circles, but official tampering always smelled of a rat.

A big fat filthy rat.

She circled back. She reexamined every oblique inference. She went back to the accounting of security people on the trip and counted again. Something smelled wrong here too. She looked for the transcript of the endless interviews she had done with that sick ape named Lee. They were classified elsewhere. Technically, they had never happened, even though she knew they had.

They were like Lagos, Nigeria, and those lousy 419 frauds. She wouldn't have believed they existed except she had lived through them.

Then she looked for Michael Cerny's name. She had not seen him for six weeks now. She found no reference. No Olga Liashko, either. Instead, there was a reference to Gerstmann — which was contradicted one page later when the spelling changed and *Gerstmann* became *Gerstman* — who had been listed as her case officer before Kiev. In itself, that wouldn't have made much difference as frequently NSA or CIA people used their work names. It was just that they usually got the spelling of the name right.

She tried to access the work names, *Cerny, Gerstman,* and *Gerstmann.* It sounded like a law firm.

Nothing. The cyber-system returned her to "Start." She glanced at the time in the lower right corner of her computer screen. It was now past 9:00 p.m. She wasn't even hungry for dinner.

The Treasury corridors were quiet around her, aside from the cleaning crew. She looked up as one of the cleaning ladies went by. "*Buenas noches,*" she said.

"*Buenas noches, señorita,*" the cleaning lady said with a smile.

Then Alex jumped. Her computer, the small secure one, suddenly went down. She drew a breath, calmed herself, rebooted her computer and reaccessed her information system.

She had enough questions to fill a volume. Who could answer them? Who could even give her a clue?

She picked up her cell phone. She called the number she had for Michael Cerny. She would pick his mind, whatever his name was, Cerny or Gerstman or Gerstfogle or —

An electronic voice answered. It too startled her. The number she had for the man she had known as Cerny was invalid — a nonworking number.

Slowly, she put her cell phone back down on her desk.

She tried to be rational. Logical. Where was this leading?

A quite extraneous vision of herself assailed her. She pictured herself in Kiev with Robert, the night before he died. Now she kept trying to reconcile her own memory to what she read in the files. She felt a pounding headache creep up on her.

She plunged herself back into the darkest chambers of her memory and found herself sorting through the events of the previous February. She was in some of the worst reaches of her memory; when suicide scenarios tiptoed across her psyche every day.

"If I did die suddenly," Robert had said not long before his passing, "I would want you to pick up and go on. I would want you to have a life, a family, a soul mate, happiness."

It was almost as if he was in the room with her, invisible, a ghost, projecting such thoughts.

She glanced back to the monitor. It was alive again. She noticed a box concealed with the security issues. A menu item stared her in the eye: Operation Chuck and Susan.

She heard her own voice fill the room "What the — ?"

She tried to access it. Then the screen flashed again.

ACCESS DENIED.

She returned again to "Start" and attempted to retrace her path. But the security system blocked her from her first strokes. In terms of intelligence pertaining to Kiev, she might have lived it personally, but she was now locked out.

FIFTY-THREE

The next morning at 10:00 a.m., Alex knocked on the door to the office of her boss, Mike Gamburian.

"Got a minute?" she asked.

"Uh oh," he said. "Sure."

She entered. He motioned that she should close the door.

"I have to tell you," Alex said. "I think I came back here too soon."

"We can't blame you for trying," he said. "And God knows the president wouldn't be alive if you hadn't reacted the way you did. So your government and your employer owe you a big one."

She managed an ironic smile. "God knows a lot of things that I know," she said, "but God also knows a lot of things that I don't. Mind if I sit?"

"I can use the company," he said.

Alex sat. "Why am I a pariah?" she asked.

Mike Gamburian looked at her curiously. "What do you mean?" he asked.

"Don't play games, Mike. You're my boss. If my access to information has been curtailed, you would know about it. If you know about it, you would also know why. That's why I'm in your office right now, and that's why I'm going to present you with my resignation in one minute."

He sighed. "Let's go downstairs for a smoke," he said.

"Neither of us smoke," she said.

"I just started," he said. "Bad habit, I know. I need to quit. So let's go have a cigarette."

At the same time he made a gesture with his hand, pointing to the two of them and the doorway. She got it. They went down the elevator together in silence, not a single cigarette between them.

Then they stood on the outside of the front entrance of Treasury, standing a careful distance away from those who really were smoking.

They talked around the issue for several minutes.

"Look," Gamburian finally said, "the first thing . . . I'm your friend. You're a great woman and a fantastic employee. If you need to leave, I don't blame you, but I want you to know I'd hire you back in a flash any day of the week."

"I can't do my job if I can't access information, Mike. And I resent being excluded from an investigation of an incident that cost Robert his life. I want answers and I'm not getting them here."

"Okay," he said. "I understand. There's been some talk. Crap I can't do anything about. No one in the Western Hemisphere has a single negative thing to say about you. The way you handled things in Ukraine was beyond reproach. The first thing I need to tell you is that you can stay here. There'd be a promotion coming your way, added pay, the works."

"In a job with no responsibility, right? Where someone's going to be looking over my shoulder the whole time, right?"

He blew past her point.

"The second thing is that if you wanted to take more time off, with pay, that option is open to you too. No one's going to hold it against you." He paused. "I had a talk with the big boss. You could take up to a year if you wanted without a problem."

"You're talking in circles, Mike. If everything is hearts and flowers, *what is the problem?*"

"They think you know something," he said. "Something more than you're telling them."

"Why would I conceal anything?"

"That's what I asked them also."

"Who's 'them'?" she snapped. "Who are we talking about?"

"The powers that be."

"CIA? NSA? White House? Secret Service?"

He blinked twice. "I honestly can't answer that."

"You don't know or you can't answer?"

"I can't answer," he said crisply.

She seethed and stifled a profanity. "I've told them everything I know. Probably about three times with every detail I can remember."

"I'm sure you have," he said. "Thing is, they think you might know something that you're not even aware of."

"Have they questioned you?"

"Quite a bit."

She sighed. She nodded. "Okay," she finally said. "Then I want to clear out of here. I'll accept that leave of absence."

"Where will you go?"

"I received a message from Joseph Collins after Kiev. The businessman. You know who he is."

"*Everyone* knows who he is," Gamburian said. "He's like Donald Trump but without the funny hair."

"Mr. Collins has contacted me three times since Kiev."

"How do you know him?"

"I worked for him several years ago. He mentored me in a way. Summer of 2001."

Gamburian nodded.

"He's a decent man and a good employer. He has an offer he wants to make to me. A job. I don't know anything about it, but somehow he knew I might want to take leave of here."

"He's savvy to the ways of the world, Collins is, which is why he's so wealthy. He also knows how the government works."

"The job would take me back to New York. I should listen to what he has to say."

"You'd be a fool not to." Gamburian nodded sadly. "What type of job? Do you have any idea?"

"Mr. Collins is in his seventies now. He's been using a lot of his fortune to help the Christian churches fight poverty and disease in the Third World," she said. "That has its appeal to me right now. So I'm going to listen to what he has to offer, do some soul searching, look for some divine guidance if I can get some, and then see where I am."

Gamburian followed.

"Hopefully at the end of the day I'll be in the right place," she said.

"I have no doubt you will. No doubt at all."

He embraced her.

"I'm sorry it turned out like this here," he said. "Really, I am."

"Yeah," she said. "Me too."

FIFTY-FOUR

Lt. Rizzo finally was making progress. Or at least he thought he was.

He remained visibly furious that people from the US Embassy had removed the two bodies from the morgue and sent them back to America. But he was not about to let that stop his investigation. Inside, he didn't care much what they did with those corpses, but he was not shy about vocalizing his stated displeasure.

Allora bene, he thought to himself. Very well. If they wanted to block his direct access to resolving four murders by blockading his route to two of the bodies, he would pursue the matter from a different direction. Over the last decade, the Americans had been directed by a bunch of know-nothings who lacked the sophistication to understand how other countries, other governments, worked. He would fly under their radar, he told everyone he worked with, then bored everyone with another rant about American duplicity and interference.

Accordingly, his people had tracked down the drug-addled musician by going through pay receipts in the apartment where he had lived. Rizzo personally had interviewed the dead guitarist's disgusting band mates and the owners of the club where he had played. He had even found the marriage license of the girl who had died with him in the apartment and now knew her name was Lana Bissoni and she was indeed from Toronto.

From there he had the location of the wife's family back in Canada. Rizzo was not surprised to learn that they hadn't heard from her in five years. Nonetheless, Rizzo allowed her body to be shipped to Ontario.

Rizzo and his other detectives spent hours canvassing the building where the couple died and the club where the musicians had played. He knew that the key to any criminal investigation was talking to the day-to-day people who are in the same place every day. The people who see things and eventually tell you something.

From there he accessed some of the girl's friends and people who knew the couple from the nearby cafés. Apparently, Lana and her husband had had some fallings out of late. She hadn't been in the habit of showing up in the clubs where he was playing. In turn, she seemed to have fallen in with some of the Eastern European underworld that populated Rome.

Well, no wonder she "woke up one day and was dead," as Rizzo liked to say. You can't sleep with a dog without waking up with fleas. And certainly, in his opinion, many of these Eastern Europeans from the old Soviet republics were packs of mutts.

Now at least he had a direction to send his investigators.

He called another special meeting at his headquarters. He assembled all four of his newly acquired homicide people. They were each allowed to select one top assistant. So now he had eight people on this case, in addition to the *ragazzi* in the computer rooms, the interns, who acted as wild cards and who knew when they were going to come up with something good.

Then, finally, he used the extensive contacts he had with the underworld to make inquiries about the *mafia ucraina* in Rome. Had there been any special activity, he asked. Did anyone know of any shooters who had come into the city, done a job, then vanished? The local Italian hoods had no love for the foreigners who were coming into the city and cutting into their rackets. They hated the Russian and Ukrainian mobsters almost as much as Rizzo did. They would welcome the opportunity to put the heat on some of them.

But the inquiries turned up nothing. Whenever Rizzo and his people mentioned the Ukrainians, someone always changed the topic to the near-death of the American president in Kiev.

A lawless place and a lawless people, the Italians said. A true frontier of civilization. Dangerous.

FIFTY-FIVE

The Stanhope Hotel was on Fifth Avenue at Eighty-third Street, across the street from the Metropolitan Museum of Art. It was a regal old building dating from the 1920s, parked on some of the world's most expensive real estate. Its open-air terrace on street level stretched to the neighboring building that was every bit as distinguished.

The terrace was a relaxing place for drinks. In the middle was an island bar, surrounded by tables. Thick dark wood, accented by potted palms.

Alex arrived a few minutes before noon. Her one-time employer, the entrepreneur Joseph Collins, arrived almost simultaneously from the opposite direction, walking briskly.

Collins was a sturdy man for his age. He had led a good life, staying away from vices and excesses, active in the Methodist Church all his life. He had been married to the same woman for forty-two years, a woman whom he still referred to affectionately as "my best girl" and whom he described as "a cookie-baking Methodist."

The clean living showed. Collins possessed an easy grace. He kept one of his many residences a few blocks up Fifth Avenue, a co-op encompassing the top three floors of one of Manhattan's most exclusive buildings. He owned an even more impressive spread in London, and then there was his "little boat," as he liked to call it, the two-hundred-foot one, in Key Biscayne.

Mr. Collins's bodyguard, burly and pink-faced, in dark wraparound shades, a suit, and an open-collared shirt, took up an unobtrusive position by the front entrance, saying nothing. The bodyguard buried himself in a *New York Post* as he kept one eye on the entrance to the terrace. To Alex, the bodyguard had ex-NYPD written all over him. An even closer glance told her that he carried his weapon on the left side under the arm.

Alex and Joseph Collins found places at a reserved table on a far edge of the terrace, recessed back into a carefully secluded corner.

A waitress, young and pretty, cleared the extra place settings and brought them coffee. They ordered fruit and a plate of breakfast rolls. The waitress wore a name tag that said *Priscilla*. Her softly accented English suggested that she came from somewhere in the Caribbean.

"So," Alex said at length, turning to her former boss and breaking the ice, "normally when we meet you tell me ahead of time what's on your agenda."

"Well, first I wanted to know how you might be feeling, how you were recovering," Collins said. "God knows, you've been through hell and back, haven't you?"

"The answers are 'okay' and 'okay,'" she said.

"So I see," he answered.

"I appreciated the flowers and the notes. And the calls. Honestly, I did."

"The least I could do. I know how horrible it must have been," he said. "I'd be remiss if I didn't at least mention it."

"Thank you. I'm trying to move on."

"Is the government seeing after you?" Collins asked.

"To the extent that they ever do," she said. "There are some wrinkles."

"Anything I can help you with? I know the president personally, plus both of the current New York senators."

"I'll be okay," she said with a sigh. "It's just going to take me some time."

"What are you planning to doing with yourself other than meditate, haunt art galleries, and go to Yankee games while you're in New York?" he asked.

"It depends how long I can use your son's apartment. Very generous of you, by the way. Thank you."

"Don't mention it."

"He's away on one of his missionary visits?" she asked.

"Yes. We have a few places around the world, as you know. He's in Brazil right now. Rough posting. He brought it on himself. It's the work he *wants* to do."

She smiled.

"Okay," he finally said. "Let's talk about why you're here. *¿Qué tal tu español?*"

"*Buenísimo. Excelente. Hablo muy bien todavía. ¿Y por qué?*" Very good. Excellent. I still speak well, I think. Why?

"How do you feel about some travel?" he asked.

"To where?"

"South America. A trouble spot."

The waitress arrived with the fruit and the rolls. Alex appreciated the breather. Mini-Danishes and mini-croissants. Collins offered the plate to Alex before taking anything himself.

A noisy group of women, tourists, moved into a nearby table. One of them noticed Collins and nudged her acquaintances, a celebrity sighting in Manhattan.

"I know it's only been a few months since Kiev," he said. "That can seem like a short time or a long time. Do you think you're ready for something new?"

"I'm ready to listen," Alex said.

"Then I'm ready to make you an interesting offer," he answered. "Have you ever been to Venezuela?"

"A couple of times. When I was with the Treasury Department."

"Caracas?"

"That and Maracaibo."

Collins drew a breath and began. "I need someone to fly down to Venezuela and troubleshoot a problem for me. Someone who's good with people, speaks the language fluently, has good instincts for trouble, and most of all someone I can trust."

"I'm flattered."

"First class airfare, the proper support and security when you get there. Just meet some people, assess what's going on, come back, and report to me."

"Sounds easy," she said. "It couldn't possibly be."

"You're right. It won't be. I'd guess it would take you maybe a month to properly complete the assignment. I'd pay you twenty thousand dollars for the month, plus expenses. You'd need to go almost immediately. Sorry about the weather conditions this time of year. It's brutally hot." He smiled. "You're going to think you died and went to the wrong place. How's that sound? Miserable?"

"I'm still listening," she said.

"For almost five years, I've been financing a group of Christian missionaries who have been living among a large tribe of primitive indigenous people," Collin explained. "They're in a village named Barranco Lajoya. It's a very remote area south of the Orinoco River in the Guayana region. Very rugged area in the southeastern quadrant of the country, not far north of the border with Brazil. Not that there are signs posted in the jungle. Most of the region doesn't even have accurate maps yet."

"What are they doing, the missionaries?" she asked.

"They import medical care and are also trying to bring electricity to the area. They also support the local churches. Methodists, Episcopalians, and a cross section of evangelicals. Americans mostly, some Canadians, several others. Our people have also learned the indigenous language. It's mostly an Indian dialect, but with a lot of corrupted Spanish. They're translating the Bible into the indigenous language. That way they can bring the good news to the people. If they want it."

"Commendable," she said.

"I like to think so," he said. "My gift, if they choose to accept it. Look, it's not even that big an operation. The costs on the ground are quite minimal. I think my whole budget on this is maybe two hundred thousand dollars a year. Maybe two twenty-five. Small stuff."

"For you, maybe."

"Granted, for me. I've been blessed in my life, so I try to pass it along while I'm still on this earth. And this is also a pet project, you understand, translating the Bible into a new tongue. I'm convinced it's helping the people who are there, and the missionaries like what they're doing. I'd like to keep things going in the right direction."

"So what's the problem?" Alex asked.

"Well, after some considerable early success, we're being sabotaged. A lot of our work gets undone. There seems to be an effort coming from somewhere to discourage our people and drive the missionaries out of the country."

"That's unusual, isn't it?"

"Very. Most countries in Central and South America encourage missionaries even if they don't like them. They bring dollars and provide social services the governments are unwilling or unable to provide."

" 'An effort coming from somewhere,' " Alex repeated, thinking back a beat, framing Collins' own words. "What does that mean?"

"I don't know. Caracas. Washington. Maybe Havana." He paused. "There are a few ragtag guerrilla organizations in the area, but the army keeps them in check."

She sipped her coffee. "So interference with missionaries doesn't make sense."

"It's South America. It's Venezuela. It doesn't have to."

Collins produced a sealed manila envelope and handed it to her.

"Obviously, your ultimate job is to report back to me on where the problems are coming from. And what we can do about it, if anything."

She nodded.

"The Venezuelan government is hostile to us right now, as you know, I'm sure. And the country is almost as lawless as Colombia, next door."

She nodded. "I'll take your file with me today," she said. "Whatever is in it, I want to give it some thought."

"Fair enough," he said. He paused, then added, "I should mention one or two more things. Right up front."

She waited. From the nearby table, the tourists had stopped staring. They turned their attention to the menus.

"I sent someone down there seven weeks ago," Collins said. "A security man named Diego. Former marine. A very good man. Someone set him up with a mobile phone that was rigged as a bomb. In a hotel bar in Caracas. When he used the phone the first time, he was — how did they say it locally? — *decapitado.*"

A pause. "So someone's playing for keeps."

"Someone doesn't want us there, for whatever reason. And I fear that some of my missionaries and their villages are coming into the line of fire, too." He paused. "You'll need to wear a gun for protection. God forbid that you ever have to use it. But as I said, it's a rough area. Jungle cats. Poisonous bats. A lot of snakes."

"As well as the two-legged dangers," she said. "Correct?"

"I want to be right up front about what you might be getting into."

"Then I'll be up front with you," she said. "You're asking me to do

something for you and for the church. I'm appreciative of that. But
...." She paused. "You're talking to a woman whose faith ... is badly
shaken right now. I'm still recovering from Kiev and asking a whole
lot of questions about how God could let something like this happen
to me."

"I know that, Alex. But I also know what you're like. You need to
plunge right back into something." A shadow passed over his face. "Do
you know what Gandhi, a Hindu, said to some British army officers
during the battle for Indian independence?"

"What?" she asked.

"He said, 'Jesus was a good and moral man. The trouble with
many of you Christians is that you're nothing like him.' That's why
I keep the missions going, feeding the hungry, supplying medical
care, doing what I can to fight poverty and illiteracy. I asked myself
what Jesus would have done if he'd made all this money in hotels and
restaurants."

She laughed.

"And that was the answer that came to me. So these missions will
continue while I'm alive and afterward. I hope you can help."

"I'll do my reading tonight, Mr. Collins," she said.

She reached to her neck, where the gold cross used to be. Nervous tic time again. The jewelry was missing, of course, except in her
memory.

"If you're willing to go forward after you read the file," he said,
"I'm going to put you in touch with a man I've recently hired to advise
me on some Latin American issues. His name is Sam Deal. Ever heard
the name?"

"I might have. It rings a bell."

"Sam used to work for Washington. I've known him for many
years. He's no one's fool. He can give you an objective picture of what
you're getting into."

Alex nodded. Somewhere she had heard Deal's name. Then she
pegged it. Her friend Laura who worked at the White House had had
issues with him.

"I've tentatively arranged for you to meet with Sam tomorrow
morning at eleven if you wish to proceed. He's in town for a few days.
He has time to meet."

Alex nodded again.

"Sam would also be your weapons guy when you get to Caracas. You won't be able to fly with a gun, obviously, but I'll make sure you have protection as soon as you get there. Sam won't *be* in Caracas, but one of his people will arrange things. Don't worry about clothing for going out in the jungle. What size do you take?"

"Ten, American."

"I'll arrange for some gear. Shoes?"

"Nine. Wardrobe and firearms. You think of everything."

He laughed.

"If you don't mind my saying so, Mr. Collins," she said, "you can be a bit of a contradiction."

"How's that?"

"You want to send me on a mission of peace, but the first thing you do is supply armament."

"It's a cruel, mean world," he said. "I want you to be safe."

She smiled. "Sounds like *you* think I'm going."

"I rather have my hopes up," he said.

She grinned slightly and pushed back from the table. If nothing else, the offer was both flattering and exciting. But she wasn't sure how much flattery or excitement she was in the mood for these days.

"All right," she said. "I'll look at everything. Then I'll call you tomorrow."

From Collins's lips, she saw the trace of a grin.

"Thank you, Alex," he said.

By the entrance to the terrace, there was a sudden commotion that grabbed her attention. Outside on the sidewalk, a noisy homeless man accosted an older couple passing by. Alex watched as the man aggressively pursued them. The older couple hurried their pace. Alex rose to her feet. If no one else would do anything about it, she would.

Collins placed a gentle hand on her wrist. "Don't trouble yourself," he said.

"But—?"

Collins then nodded to his bodyguard. The bodyguard, obviously seeking any small piece of action he could find, moved with the grace and speed of a much younger man. He interposed himself between the couple and their assailant.

The panhandler attempted to shove the bodyguard in return. Bad idea. Mr. Collins's hired hand sent the vagrant hurtling in a different direction, and he disappeared.

FIFTY-SIX

Alex's apartment on East Twenty-first Street in Manhattan was a very quiet unimposing place, considering its location, and perfectly suited to her needs.

It was nestled into the back of a walk-up building first constructed in 1900, third floor rear, just twenty yards east of Second Avenue. The block itself was quiet, although traffic rumbled southbound on the avenue all day and all night.

Inside the furnished one-bedroom apartment, all windows overlooked a rear courtyard. The two rooms were a witch's brew of clashing wallpapers, lamp shades, aging furniture, and worn carpets. It reflected the lifestyle of Joseph Collins's son, Daniel, whose interests were far from the worldly or the run-of-the mill.

The younger Collins, single and about forty, had grown up wealthy, had worked in his father's businesses for many years, but had also gone to seminary at Southern Methodist. Alex had never met him but had spoken to him on the phone from time to time. At age thirty-five he had left his father's industries to help administer his father's Christian philanthropies. There were a collection of pictures on the walls and on tables of Daniel trotting the globe; in Africa, in central America, in South America, in New Mexico, and one — presumably to get a nasty dose of some colder climates — in Labrador.

The pictures showed the young man — these days forty was considered young — in various villages or cities. He looked content with his mission and his missions. Everyone should be so lucky.

Alex quickly took a measure of the other people in the building. The upstairs neighbor was an actor who was out of town, and the downstairs neighbor was the landlord, "Lady Dora" Rose, as she called herself.

"Lady Dora" was a quintessential New Yorker, an elf of a woman in her late sixties. She had been left a pair of brownstones including this one. But the story, as Alex heard it on arrival, got even better.

Lady Dora's late husband, Marvin, had owned a newsstand that had specialized in thoroughbred and harness racing tout sheets and sporting publications. His store also featured a telephone that never stopped ringing. Marvin, who was fifteen years older than Dora when they wed, had gone out for a walk one night in June 1977 and had never come back. Presumably he was still walking.

The "Rose" in Lady Dora's name was a truncation of "Rosenberg," which had been Marvin's name, and the "Lady" was a figment of her own inflated sense of grandeur.

"I made it up so I could be an interesting person," she told Alex when Alex asked about it. "Then for ninety-four dollars I had it legally added to my name."

Lady Dora showed Alex a New York State driver's license to prove it. Not that she drove or owned a car. Over the years, Lady Rose had also acquired a hint of a British accent, though more often than not the Brooklyn one she had been born with also surfaced. Lady Dora also introduced Alex to Sajit, the handyman, who came in for ten hours a week off the books to sweep the floors, fix the plumbing, and replace lightbulbs.

Sajit was from Sri Lanka. He was a slim, tiny, fastidiously neat man who always wore a white dress shirt with shiny black pants. Today was no exception. Under Lady Rose's critical eye, he set up a rickety card table with a pair of heavily dented metal folding chairs, the type often seen as props at wrestling matches.

"You will take good care of everything in Daniel's place, won't you?" Lady Rose asked. "Daniel's a wonderful young man. He has a famous father, you know."

"Daniel's father arranged with you to let me in," Alex said. "Remember?"

"Yes. Of course." Lady Dora shook her head. It was four in the afternoon the day that Alex had met with Joseph Collins at the Stanhope. The landlady was barefoot in the front vestibule and wore a pink bathrobe, her gray hair in bobby pins. She was on one of her daily rants. This one ended when she spotted the resident of 3-C, a self-proclaimed "documentary film maker" whose work was sold only over the Internet. Alex had a hunch that the man's oeuvre might be unsuitable for family viewing.

He was in trouble with Lady Dora for something, so Alex headed upstairs with the file in her hand and closed her door on the argument that ensued. It was at this moment that she made a note to phone Ben later that evening, just to vent. Calls between them were becoming more frequent. Alex appreciated the friendship more with each passing week.

That evening, Alex settled into this cozy atmosphere on East Twenty-first Street. She spread out some yogurt and fruit on the small dining table, turned it into her evening meal, and then repaired to the sofa in the living room to read.

Alex embarked upon her reading at a few minutes past eight in the evening.

For years, as the file explained in detail, Collins had been quietly financing the missionaries at a village named Barranco Lajoya in a mountainous region of southeastern Venezuela. The missionaries rotated in and out. There were several teams of them who worked in shifts ranging from six months to two years.

They had been living among a large tribe of primitive indigenous people, learning their language so that they could translate the Bible into it and bring the Christian faith to them. Some of the missionaries doing this work lived with the Indians for at least a year or two in order to learn the language and create an alphabet for it, and then translate the Bible. Some of them brought their families. Their children grew up in these remote villages. There had been considerable early success, first bringing literacy itself to these people, then bringing the Christian faith. And yet, after considerable early success, there then appeared to be an effort to destroy the missionaries' work and force them to leave the country.

A school built by the missionaries and the villagers had caught fire one night. Livestock had disappeared. The local streams, tributaries of the Rio Xycapo, had been polluted by industrial waste from a higher elevation. Yet there was no industry at higher elevations, and no known settlements. That meant that the waste had been brought in and dumped.

But why? The villagers had nothing that anyone would want. They were simple people who had been self-sufficient for centuries.

Why should anything change now? The people were so remote that who could care enough about them to victimize them?

Perhaps, conjectured the writer of this document, the interest of outsiders was enough by itself to put the small tribe on someone's list of enemies.

Alex began making notes in the margins, observations and questions to ask Mr. Collins when she reported back to him. She started to feel a pull toward these people. It was as if this was the path now intended for her. This mission to Venezuela emerged as something different than anything she had ever done in her life, exactly the type of thing she *wanted* to do. Against what she had expected, she was interested. An open mind could be dangerous.

She skipped ahead to a photo section. She scanned through several dozen photos of the village of Barranco Lajoya and its people; smiling faces of barefoot children, a classroom bringing literacy, a medical clinic set up, a joint Episcopal-Methodist-Baptist service in a small church. Kids playing soccer.

There were before-and-after shots of people who had received care from Collins's medical people. She was impressed. The man was doing good in corners of the world that badly needed benefactors. In return, he asked for nothing.

She waded through a background section on their village culture, then ran smack into an assessment of current-day Venezuela and its government.

The government of Venezuela was headed by President Hugo Chávez. His fanatically anti-American policies didn't make life any easier for Collins or his missionaries. Collins had had the foresight to send Christian workers with supposedly neutral passports — there were three Canadians, two Hondurans, and one English nurse there at the time that Alex read the dossier — all of whom spoke good-to-native-speaker Spanish. But the activities of foreigners in a village in the jungle aroused the ire and suspicion of paranoid rulers in Caracas.

Chávez, Alex knew, was a former paratrooper who staged an unsuccessful coup attempt in 1992. He was a latter-day blend of the populist Juan Perón and the totalitarian Fidel Castro. Chávez had assumed office of president democratically in 1998 after winning an election in which he ran on a populist platform. Chávez had long been convinced — not necessarily incorrectly and not that he hadn't brought it on himself — that the United States government had a hand in an unsuccessful coup attempt against him in 2002.

He remained obsessed with the idea that the US wanted to assassinate him. Given the long history of CIA involvement in almost all left-leaning countries in Latin America, there was a real rationale behind his fears. Castro had survived an exploding cigar, a booby-trapped conch shell, and a poisoned milk shake among numerous other "gifts" from the enterprising souls at various workshops in Langley, Virginia.

Further, as Chávez had already survived two attempts on his life, there was possibly something imminent to his assassination fears.

Chávez not only made no secret of his concern, but also paraded it regularly on his highly popular radio talk show, *Aló Presidente*, which was aimed at his power base, the poor and working-class people of Venezuela. Further, his overt hostility to the US, open admiration for Fidel Castro, close ties with the FARC — *las Fuerzas Armadas Revolucionarias de Colombia* — guerrillas in neighboring Colombia, and tight control over the huge Venezuelan oil industry, had made him a thorn in Washington's side.

Alex read carefully. The dossier continued.

Chávez recently seemed to have made overtures of toning down the anti-American rhetoric and making Venezuelan oil more accessible to North America. But he would do this only if the new US administration would cease both its efforts to undermine him and to isolate him from other Latin American countries.

The author of the document wrote: "The United States government is anxious for a shot at a more ready access to Venezuelan oil. We are ready to reconcile with him."

Yet next Alex ran into a set of political contradictions. While a US-Venezuelan rapprochement was in the offing, it still appeared that there were powers attempting to run the Indians off their land. Considering the mood of the two governments, who could have been behind that?

Chávez? Washington?

The international petroleum cartels?

Business interests would not have wanted to antagonize either government, and the local Indians didn't seem to have anything worth taking. They had no other tribes in the area that they were at war with, and there were no guerrilla activities in the area.

Applying what she knew about the area, the land, the political climate, and the geography, it was unlikely that there was any "spill over" activity from Colombia or Brazil. Was it just the proposition that Christianity was being spread to a native people that had antagonized someone?

Something was missing from the overall picture. As Joseph Collins had described it, it didn't make sense. She was forty pages into a forty-six page document and increasingly drawn to the assignment. After all, as Collins had suggested, her assignment was to go and observe.

To troubleshoot. To report back and not get involved.

She turned the page to the final section. And then suddenly, almost out of nowhere, she was smacked in the face by what she was reading.

An eerie series of events and associations began to come together.

A visit of the US secretary of state to Caracas was currently being planned for sometime in the following year.

Alex cringed and felt like slamming the file shut right there. The president had not left the United States since the bloody debacle in Kiev. The mission of the US secretary of state in Caracas was a test to see if potentially a US president could make a safe visit to a foreign country. American foreign policy had been so unpopular around the world in the last decade — the residual legacy of one particular US administration — that conventional wisdom suggested that the American president could no longer travel abroad. The catastrophe in Kiev was the event that was viewed as proof of this theory.

Yet despite Kiev, the new administration in Washington was pushing hard to distance itself from its predecessor. What influence did America have around the world if its heads of state couldn't make state visits? A successful visit by the secretary of state would be a key step toward reestablishing that position, just as new the administrations of Sarkozy in France and Brown in Britain had renewed French and British influence respectively, at least until the new leaders could muddy their own waters.

Alexandra's old instincts and skills started to kick in, even though she was in a "civilian" role now. To her it was obvious: in Venezuela, a massive security and diplomatic mess would confront the secretary of state.

And then another terrifying discovery presented itself.

As noted, Chávez had long been suspected of having ties to the FARC, the Marxist rebels in Colombia who finance themselves through the cocaine business. But Alex now read a short paper citing that these rebels, through major drug dealers, also had ties to the extensive Ukrainian Mafia. She thought back on how Federov had brokered a deal for a mothballed submarine to go to Colombian narcotics dealers.

She closed the file, shuddered, and wondered if her fears would keep her away from Venezuela. She hated to be intimidated by thinking a task was beyond her. And Mr. Collins was right: she *did* need to sink her teeth into something new.

And yet, there were two Kiev connections: a state visit and activity by the Ukrainian Mafia. In her line of work, there were no coincidences.

Were there?

She spent several moments in thought, then reached for her cell phone. She called Mr. Collins to confirm the meeting with Sam for eleven the next morning at a plush venue on New York's Central Park South.

Then she broke a beer out of the refrigerator, kicked back with some music, and phoned Ben in Washington, just to say hi and tell him, in vague terms, what was up and to hear a friendly reassuring voice.

It was only after she hung up, knowing herself as well as she did, that she realized there was yet another reason she had made the call. She was trying to get Kiev off her mind once again.

FIFTY-SEVEN

In Rome, Mimi had been doing excellent work.

Lt. Rizzo wrangled her some extra salary. He set her loose across the universe of cyberspace for hours. She hacked into much of the known information about the Ukrainian Mafia in Italy and even discovered that some of those missing weapons from the US Navy may have been trafficked by a shadowy outfit known as The Caspian Group.

As she was using the money to further her art studies, the dough came in handy. Rizzo used the young woman's information to focus on any of The Caspian Group's activities in Rome, including that of its leader and his bodyguards. Rizzo worked some theories: who was in Rome when the murders were committed? Who might have a grievance against the two couples who had been murdered? Using sources of the Roman police department, and some darker sources of his own that he had on the side, he went around to the people who had known the musician and his girlfriend.

He showed surveillance pictures. He focused on one of Federov's bodyguards, a man known only as Anatoli.

Then, with an eye toward cyberspace, he went back to Mimi. He set her to work researching Anatoli. Soon she had his cell phone number and dropped a tap on it.

One night after work, Rizzo asked Mimi if she could accompany him for a light dinner. He said the suggestion was purely professional, there was more work she could do, and it would be at a much higher salary. Rizzo also explained that he had someone he wanted her to meet, a guest from out of town.

She shrugged her shoulders and said, "Why not?"

An hour later, Mimi found herself with Lt. Rizzo at a dressy *trattoria* a few blocks from the government buildings and popular among foreigners. Dressed in her usual colorful blouse and micro-miniskirt, she felt herself somewhat out of place among all the expensive suits and designer clothes. She was the youngest female in the place. But she quickly got used to the attention she drew and enjoyed it.

She and Rizzo were met there by a man to whom Rizzo showed great deference, but whom Rizzo didn't introduce by name. He spoke Italian fluently but with a trace of an accent that she couldn't place. And there was something ominous about him.

Mimi was nobody's fool, so she studied the man very carefully as they engaged in conversation. She guessed that he and Rizzo underestimated her powers of everyday perception. The man's shoes looked American and he wore one of those rings — she thought it was a high school or college thing — that Americans wore. He had a wedding band too. But Rizzo had always been so vocally anti-American. It didn't make sense to her. So she tried something.

"You know," she said in English, "we could speak English if you like. My mother is American. I speak English well."

The stranger grinned. "*Grazie, pero, non,*" he said, remaining in Italian. Thank you but, no. We are in Rome, he explained, so we will speak as the Romans do.

She didn't press the point. Rizzo's friend moved quickly to a proposition he had for her, a one-time task. A special assignment for which she would be well compensated in cash. Lots of cash.

Anatoli was back in Rome, they said, and would be for another few days. They showed her a picture of him. He was a sturdy-looking Russian Ukrainian with dirty blond hair.

"Handsome, no?" Rizzo asked.

Mimi nodded. "You want me to seduce him?" she asked, more a routine inquiry than a opportunity to volunteer.

No, they said quickly, it wasn't exactly like that. It was more like a game of pin the tail on the donkey.

"What's that?" she asked.

The man with no name showed Mimi a small devise in a plastic case. It looked like a small needle with a flat head like a tack. They said they knew where Anatoli liked to go to party in Rome. They had a well-armed young man who would accompany her that night, but could she somehow see how close she could get to Anatoli ... and maybe stick the needle into his clothing somewhere.

She laughed.

"So it's a transmitting device, right?" She laughed with great enthusiasm.

The two men looked at each other, then back to Mimi.

"Possibly," said Rizzo.

"How am I supposed to get close enough to pin the device on him?" she asked.

"You're a pretty young woman, no?" Rizzo asked, stating the obvious. "I'm sure you'll find a way."

She thought about it. "I don't know," she began.

She was still thinking about it when they piled five hundred Euros on the table. "That's just for trying," Rizzo said. "There's another five hundred if you're successful."

"This Anatoli," she said. "He killed someone, yes?"

They didn't say no.

"Why don't you just arrest him?" she asked.

"Lack of evidence," Rizzo answered swiftly. "Life is like that, Mimi. Sometimes what we know to be true is not something that we can prove to be true. Equally, sometimes what *is* true *isn't* and what *isn't* true, in reality, *is*." Mimi blinked. Rizzo exited his philosophical riff almost more confused than when he had entered it, unless he wasn't. He paused and smiled at his own verbal gymnastics as his guest looked at him strangely. "Plus," he continued, "Anatoli and his friends are very bad men. There are other ways to take care of them other than a time-consuming and frustrating adherence to the letter of the law."

"What sort of 'other ways'?" she asked.

"*Many* other ways," Rizzo said.

Rizzo's friend reached into his jacket and piled another three hundred Euros on the table.

"And that's just for listening," he said. "Okay, Mimi?"

She smiled. "I'm all ears," she said, picking up the money and pocketing it. "This sounds like a blast!"

FIFTY-EIGHT

Alex liked to walk in New York, watching the neighborhoods change as she moved briskly at a pace with Manhattan. She found herself at Central Park South within half an hour of leaving her apartment. Sam Deal was seated outside on a terrace at the Café de la Paix.

Alex recognized Sam from a description Mr. Collins had given. He was a tall, thick man, gray-haired, pale-faced, with a neat moustache. He wore violet-hued wraparound sunglasses that looked far too young for him. The shades were more Brad Pitt than Tom Clancy, and Sam was definitely more of the latter than the former.

Alex studied Sam as she approached. He was glancing at his watch. Then he turned toward her, and his eyes settled, wandering up and down. His glasses were low across a nose that looked as if it had been broken more than once. His hands were on the table, unmoving, not far from a drink and a pack of smokes. A copy of the *New York Daily News* was open in front of him, and Sam appeared to have been immersed in the sports section, soaking up the previous evening's boxing at Sunnyside Garden, a card of Irish and Italians against Puerto Ricans and Mexicans.

She approached him. "I'm Alex LaDuca."

"Ah," he said. "Good. Great."

Sam stood. He extended a big raw hand and shook hers. "I'm Sam Deal," he said. "Call me Sam. That's what my parents called me."

Alex sat down and ordered a sparkling water. From the get-go, as she sipped her drink, she didn't like Sam. He looked and sounded like the kind of guy who, as a kid, would have stolen other kids' lunch money in third grade.

"So you're going to South America, huh? For Mr. Collins?" he asked at length.

"That's right. Venezuela. If I take the assignment."

"What did you say your name was?"

She gave it again.

"You any relation to the former Mets catcher, Paul LoDuca?"

"That's my husband," she said.

"The ballplayer ain't married," he answered.

"That's right. LoDuca and LaDuca. It's spelled different. No relation at all, but I like the player. Outstanding catcher, dependable hitter."

Sam laughed. "I'm impressed. You got some sass to you."

"Thanks."

"And you work for Mr. Collins?"

"That's correct. For Mr. Collins."

"Well, that's a great thing too," he said. "We both work for him. So I better be polite to you and tell you what I know. Tell me, you interested in coming back from this assignment alive?"

The question took her completely off guard. "I was hoping to," she answered.

"Well, good start," he said. "See, I got this attitude toward Latin America. My feeling is we should blow up Cuba and stuff it into the Panama Canal. How's that?"

"Write to your senator and suggest it."

"Well, no matter," he said. "Look, let's get out of here, and Sam will tell you everything you need to know. Shouldn't take more than thirty minutes. Let's walk."

Sam downed a full gin and tonic and popped a straw hat on his head that reminded Alex of *The Buena Vista Social Club*. On the hat was a football booster's pin that Sam was quick to explain without being asked.

SEC. Ole Miss.

Sam's boy played football, he explained. "He's a big dumb kid but he's a great linebacker," Sam said. "Got a shot at the pros."

"Congratulations."

Sam said he was planning to get down to Oxford, Mississippi, for all the home games.

They crossed the street and were about to enter Central Park. "Hey. Let's do this." He pointed at the stand of horse-drawn carriages. "I've always wanted to do this with a pretty lady. Let's go for a ride and we'll talk."

He hailed the first carriage in line along the north side of Central

Park South. Alex nodded. Sam addressed the driver in Spanish, and the driver was pleased to reciprocate.

Sam offered her a hand to help her. She accepted it out of courtesy, not need. She stepped up into the carriage, and she caught Sam eyeing her legs for half a second.

Okay, a carriage ride in Central Park. She had never done this. For a moment, a wave of sadness was upon her. It was a beautiful day. Joggers and strollers filled the park. She missed Robert.

Sam waited till the carriage entered the park. Then, "So," Sam said, "I assume you're a practicing Christian like Mr. Collins. That's all he hires."

"Then that would also make you one, right?" she said.

He sniffed. " 'Kill a Commie for Christ,' and all that? I'll buy that part of it."

"That's not exactly my direction," she said.

"Oh yeah? Are there some other directions I should know about?"

"I could list a few. Eradicating AIDS. Hunger. Poverty."

"Whatever," Sam muttered. "Look. You look like a smart girl," Sam said. "So before you get going on a lot of squishy soft do-good stuff, let me give you the template for American foreign policy in this hemisphere." When it came to charm school, Sam was a proud dropout. "You know anything about Rafael Trujillo?" he asked.

"I know he was the dictator in *la República Dominicana* for, what, thirty years?"

In the background, the clop of the horse's hooves kept beat with Sam's voice.

"Thirty-one," Sam said. "Lemme get you the quick backstory. In 1930 General Trujillo placed himself on the ballot for president and then used goon squads to terrorize the voters. When the elections were held, ninety-nine percent voted for Trujillo. *Viva la democracia,* huh? The thugs had done their job."

Sam pulled a cigar from his inside jacket pocket. Romeo y Julieta. A fine Cuban, of all things. "You don't mind if Sam smokes, do you?" he asked.

"I don't care if Sam burns."

"Good answer," he snorted. "No one else does, either."

Sam produced a Dunhill lighter and threw up a flame worthy of the Olympic torch. He lit his cigar as the horse turned north on the east side of the park.

"So late in 1930," Sam continued, "Santo Domingo got knocked flat as a tortilla by a hurricane. Trujillo suspended the constitution to speed along the cleanup. Any unidentified bodies were cremated. So Trujillo decided that what his island needed was even *more* unidentified bodies, as long as he could decide who they would be. This coincides with the vanishing of several political enemies. Get it?"

"Got it," she said.

"When Santo Domingo was rebuilt, it was also renamed. *Ciudad Trujillo.* Trujillo City. Can you imagine that? From there, Trujillo received support from Washington for three decades. His methods for suppressing dissent were torture and mass murder. Know what FDR said? He said, 'Trujillo is an SOB, but at least he's *our* SOB.'" Sam laughed. "I always liked that," he said.

Behind the glasses, behind the cigar smoke, Sam was enjoying this. The clop of the horse's hooves patterned nicely on the walkway. At this hour on a weekday, the park was closed to motor vehicles.

"Flash forward to the 1950s and '60s" Sam said. "The press was controlled, so was the judiciary, so were the unions. Trujillo personally took over some state monopolies. Salt, insurance, milk, beef, tobacco, the lottery, newspapers, and he had a big chunk of the sugar industry. The only thing he didn't have was bananas and tobacco, and that's because the US companies had those. By 1958 he was personally worth about $500,000,000. Then when it started to look like Castro would take over Cuba, the US began to worry that Trujillo might inspire a similar revolution. So the CIA began plotting Trujillo's assassination in 1958."

"Which was before Castro took over Cuba," she said.

"Correct," Sam said. "And not a coincidence."

"CIA agents made contact with once-loyal Trujillistas who were plotting an assassination. They were wealthy Dominicans who had personal grudges or who had family who had suffered. The CIA supplied several carbine rifles for the hit on Trujillo, and they promised US support for the new regime once the dictator was dead."

They stopped at an intersection. Sam relit his cigar.

"You've heard of the Monroe Doctrine, the Marshall Plan, the Good Neighbor Policy?" Sam said. "I got to laugh at all that crap. Know what we used to call the John F. Kennedy Doctrine?"

The light changed. They continued.

"JFK once told the CIA, referring to the Dominican Republic, 'There are three possibilities ... a decent democratic regime, a continuation of the Trujillo regime, or a Castro regime. We ought to aim at the first, but we really can't renounce the second until we are sure that we can avoid the third.' How's that for situational ethics?"

She nodded. "Not bad. How's the cigar?"

"It's good. You want one? I know ladies smoke them these days."

"Not this lady."

"Ever tried cigars?"

"Yes. I don't mind if a man smokes a good one, but I don't care for them, myself."

"I think a lady with a petit corona is kinda sexy. Let me buy you one."

"Finish your story, Sam, okay?"

"Okay, well, Trujillo got whacked in May 1961 on a deserted patch of highway. A sniper picked off his driver from a thousand meters away, the car crashed and gunmen came out of the bushes with handguns to finish him off. The coup didn't have traction, though. The assassins were rounded up along with their families and friends. Some committed suicide. The rest were taken to Trujillo's hacienda. They were tied to trees, shot, cut up, and fed to sharks at a nearby beach. Eventually the US Atlantic Fleet arrived in Santo Domingo's harbor to try to keep the lid from blowing off the place.

"The 1962 elections brought a physician and writer named Juan Bosch to power. Bosch was anti-Communist, but hey, he was a reformer, which is a damned fool thing to be in Latin America 'cause you're gonna get hit by one side or the other. Anyway, Bosch was dedicated to land reform, low-rent housing, and public works projects. He was deposed by a CIA-backed coup after seven months. When a popular countercoup tried to restore Bosch to power in 1965, the US Marines paid a visit."

Sam moved toward conclusion and his point.

"It's all about oil, money, international relations, and corruption in South America, same as Eastern Europe, Middle East, you name it. It's very simple, we put them in, and we take them out. From Trujillo to Saddam Hussein."

"You're not telling me anything new, Sam."

The carriage had arrived at the East Seventy-second Street Plaza. Alex was ready to depart.

"No. I'm not," he said. "But here's what you have to remember in Latin America. The US screws around with the politics, but the alternative is ten times worse. The world works at the behest of the banks and corporations, and policy is enforced at the point of the gun. Because of that, you and I can walk free and are privileged to pay six bucks a gallon for gas. If it ever works the other way, it means the Islamofascists have defeated us, and they'd rape a nice-looking educated girl like you or hide you in a burka or burn you at the stake. So think of it as the binary system for world politics. You have two choices. Where would you rather live today? Cuba or the Dominican?"

He didn't wait for an answer. "That's your poli sci lesson, and that's why Chávez's options are clear. He can be a world outlaw, or we'll take him out."

He let his lesson settle.

"When are you leaving for Caracas?" Sam asked.

"I haven't even decided if I'm going," Alex answered.

"Of course you have," Sam said. "I'll make sure you have a weapon and a contact when you get there. Be sure to go to the doctor and get some antimalaria meds. If the heat, the gators, and the snakes don't kill you, malaria might." He eyed her as she stepped down from the carriage. "That's a nice skirt, by the way. I like it. Looks good on you. You got the legs for it."

"Thanks."

"Want to have dinner later?"

"So long, Sam."

She hopped out of the parked carriage and didn't look back as she walked toward Fifth Avenue. Before she reached her apartment, she had pulled her cell phone out of her skirt pocket and phoned Joseph Collins. She would make the trip to Venezuela. That same evening, she phoned her friend, Don Tomás, in Washington. He had been the Counselor for Political Affairs at the US Embassy in Caracas. It had been his last tour with the Foreign Service, capping a distinguished career. He had even been there during the unsuccessful coup.

From his usual skeptical perspective, he gave her a rundown on current Venezuelan politics, particularly as affected by the current-day demagogue, Chávez.

"Venezuela has turned into a very dangerous place," he said. "Almost as bad as Colombia next door."

"I know," she said.

"If you must go," he said, "avoid the many bad areas of the city. My cleaning lady asked me that her schedule ensure that she would be able to get to her home in daylight. She lived in this hillside slum named Petrare. Governmental authority and social services only reached halfway up the hill. Toward dusk and after dark, hoodlums swaggered about with their guns exposed. Of course, there was always the threat of vigilante justice. Sometimes neighbors got really fed up with it and Petrare would 'smell of kerosene,' the favorite lynching tool. Police intervention was nonexistent."

"Charming," she said.

"Aside from that, travel safely and good luck."

"Thanks. Should I carry a gun?" she asked.

"A woman on assignment in *that* part of the world?" he answered with a laugh. "You'd be a fool not to carry *two* guns."

FIFTY-NINE

Mimi was dressed to kill when she arrived at the Club San Remo shortly before midnight. Sailor Moon all the way. Blue and white blouse. Red shoes and knee-high red socks. She wore a blue miniskirt, which normally was eight inches above the knee but she had used pins to take it up another two inches. Two ponytails, one to each side. Blue tint in her hair. The works.

Her escort was a handsome young plainclothes member of the *carabinieri*, a guy named Enrico. If he was going to get paid for escorting girls to clubs like this, well, he had the best job in the world. And Mimi, she liked the looks of her escort right away. He wasn't the smartest guy she'd ever met, much less the most sophisticated. But he sure was well put together. She had hit the daily double on this assignment, she reasoned. She would get paid *and* have some fun.

They had another man in the club to watch their backs, but Mimi never even knew who he was. All she knew was what her job was, how to dress so a guy couldn't miss her, much less say no, and then how to get the job done.

Enrico worked a cell phone once they were inside the club. The contact had been shadowing Anatoli all day.

Enrico sat at a table with Mimi and they sipped scotches. Mimi kept crossing and uncrossing her legs, enjoying the growing attention from her escort. Finally, Enrico turned to her.

"That's him," he said, indicating to his left. "That's Anatoli."

Enrico closed his phone. Mimi leaned over and put an arm on Enrico's shoulder, but her real intent was to look past him and get a better view of her mark.

Anatoli, Federov's onetime sidekick and bodyguard, sat at a corner table with two beautiful young women. He wore a leather jacket, his hair was cut short, almost an old-style KGB cut.

"He's nice looking," Mimi said in Italian. She recognized him from his picture.

"What did he do?" Enrico asked. "Why are we watching him?"

"I think he killed someone."

"Oh," Enrico said. "After we're finished here, want to go get some food?"

She looked at Enrico. She smiled. "Sure," she said. The nice thing about Enrico to Mimi, aside from how good looking he was, was that he was with the national police, so if he had killed anyone it was probably legal and he wasn't in any trouble for it. Unlike Anatoli.

"Then let's get this done and let's get out of here," Enrico said.

"You don't like the music?"

"No."

"You don't like the drinks?"

"They're okay."

"But you do like me?" she laughed.

"A lot. Let's go somewhere."

"Your place?"

"Maybe."

"Okay," she said. "Keep me covered."

She gave him a kiss on the cheek and went to work.

She fingered the small tacklike transmitter that she had concealed at the waist of her skirt. She pulled out a change purse that was filled with small coins. She unzipped it partially and stood.

She worked her way toward the ladies room, which, by good fortune, took her past Anatoli's table. As she passed the table, she unzipped the purse. The contents, entirely coins, spilled out. As they fell, in the erratic light of the club, she whacked them so that they'd roll under Anatoli's table.

Mimi then let loose with a loud profanity in Italian. Now she had Anatoli's attention. He stared at her as did the women at his table. She had *everyone's* attention now.

Her hands went to her face as she surveyed the loss of her coins with feigned horror. Anatoli, checking her out, slowly started to smile.

"*Oh, scusi, scusi, scusi!*" she pleaded.

Anatoli laughed. He didn't speak much Italian. He gestured with his hands that it wasn't a problem.

More sign language. Mimi pointed to herself and then under the table. "*Voi permette?*" she asked. She gave him her sexiest most excited smile. Could she maybe crawl underneath and pick things up?

Anatoli nodded. Mimi went down to her hands and knees, a flurry of bare arms and legs, and disappeared headfirst under the table to retrieve the coins and conduct her larger bit of business.

She crawled around between four bare female legs and two male legs in jeans. Working quickly, she picked up coin after coin. She got Anatoli and his two female friends quickly conditioned to feeling her movements, brushing against them, reaching past their shoes and boots. Anatoli was predictably amused and fresh, giving Mimi a solid pinch on her butt. She gave his hand a playful slap, which only encouraged him more. Then his hand came to rest on her butt and gave it a squeeze.

Perfect timing, just what she wanted. It gave her the opportunity to "retaliate" by holding his foot. At exactly the same moment he was examining her backside, she withdrew the little homing device from her waist and shoved it firmly into the heel of his boot. Then she wriggled free and emerged with a laugh from beneath the table.

The two women with Anatoli glared at her. But he was all hearts and flowers.

"*Va bene?*" he asked. Find everything?

"*Suffisamente,*" she answered. Enough. "*Grazie mille.*"

"*Prego.*" He answered.

She turned and sauntered back to Enrico, feeling Anatoli's eyes on her backside as she left. She slid into the seat next to Enrico.

"Got him," she said. She wasn't nervous at all. Inside, she felt remarkably cool. "We can get out of here," she said.

"No, no," Enrico answered. "We wait a few minutes. No reason to make him suspicious if he sees you leave right away."

"Then I'll have another scotch," she said.

In fact, she had two of them. Both doubles.

Thirty minutes later, they were back out on the street. They walked a block. There they found Rizzo in a car, waiting. He was just putting down a cell phone when they approached.

"Perfect," he said. "The signal is strong."

"It's in the heel of his right boot," she said.

"I won't ask how you did that," Rizzo said.

"Use your imagination."

"Mimi, you're a genius. And I love your outfit."

He handed her an envelope. Impetuously, she opened it. There were five hundred Euros in it in cash, ten bills of fifty Euros each.

"Anytime," she said. This was the easiest money she'd ever made.

"I'm off duty now?" Enrico asked Rizzo.

He gave the handsome young man a nod. "Just see that Mimi gets home safely," he said. "Eventually."

"Eventually," Mimi said, hanging on Enrico's arm now.

They all laughed.

Rizzo pulled away from the curb. Enrico took Mimi under his arm, and, mission accomplished, they went their own way for the rest of the night.

SIXTY

The formal way for the US government to persuade a foreign government to do something is through a *démarche*, which can be made either in Washington to the foreign embassy or in its capital or in both places at once.

It can be done at any level, up to and including "calling in" the foreign country's ambassador for a senior state official to deliver the request or having the US ambassador approach the host country foreign minister or even prime minister.

In the case of the American couple who had been shot to death on a cold evening in January, the American government needed to be coy in its handling of the case. The Italians were already fuming over American handling of several intelligence issues, and there were still warrants out for several CIA agents concerning "renditions" carried out in Italy. Worse, the Italians knew that the CIA had embedded some excellent contacts in Rome right under their noses within the various Italian police agencies.

Hence, a prickly problem it was. The CIA station chief in Rome informally approached his contacts in Italian intelligence and began to exert whatever informal influence could be brought to bear upon the Roman police. The scandals about CIA flights with disappeared persons transiting Italian airspace did not make this any easier. Similar contacts were made in Washington through the Italian ambassador.

An additional complication was that the Italian government was, as always, a delicate coalition. Such requests reaching the public, or at least certain members of parliament, could actually blow apart the ruling coalition.

Nonetheless, the matter of Lt. Rizzo's investigation went through the usual back channels. Rizzo felt he had made highly praiseworthy progress on the case. So when he found himself summoned to the office of the minister of the interior, he should have beamed with pride, expecting to be congratulated upon his fine work. But one never knew which way these meetings with bosses would go. Nor, in any way, could he expect to know where his investigation would be headed next.

SIXTY-ONE

Monday morning. Alex stood in the security line at JFK in New York, waiting to check in for her flight.

Time for everyone to be searched. She read all the signs. Every bag to be X-rayed. Take off your jacket. Take off your socks and shoes. High risk of terrorist attack. Drop your slightly used undergarments in a one-pint ziplock and turn them over to the baggage handlers.

Hey, got a steel pin in your hip? Take it out so we can check it.

What nonsense. Okay, okay. She knew she was anxious over this new trip, and she tried to cool it. But what was her country coming to? Give me your tired, your poor, your teeming masses, your fingerprints.

Signs, signs. Everywhere there were signs, as the old pop song went. Messing up the view. Messing up everyone's mind. No cigarette lighters on the aircraft. No scissors. No knives. No booze. How about a numchuck or a Tai Chi sword?

Yeah. Long-haired freaky people didn't need to apply, but they were actually going though the security line just fine. A woman who looked like someone's great grandmother was being searched, however. A security person was examining her roll of lipstick. Alex sipped from a fresh bottle of cold water that she knew she was going to have to relinquish.

The fear had taken root all over America by now, planted by excessively reckless people in the government. Having been in Ukraine on the day of the RPG attacks, having had to fire lethal weapons at other human beings and shoot her way out, she knew what real fear was. She knew what it was like to be scared, to understand what a true threat feels like, to be a moment away from a painful death or perhaps permanent disfigurement if she acted wrong or was just plain unlucky. She knew what it was like to lose someone she loved in an attack that made no sense.

But on American soil, she didn't want to live in constant fear.

She resented the signs. Who the heck was going to make a bomb out of Scope and Pepsodent, anyway?

Alex took off her shoes, belt, and jacket and put them in one bin. Her computer came out of her backpack and went into another while the backpack itself went into a third. Then she dumped her wallet, change, keys, passport, and boarding pass into a fourth. Then she graduated to the hallowed grounds of a "five binner" as she dropped the black duffel bag stuffed with a week's worth of clothes in the fifth.

A security person watched her uneasily, and she was ready for him to say something. She preempted him. "Why don't we all just wear transparent plastic raincoats when we travel," she said. "It would speed things up and make things much easier, wouldn't it?"

He looked at her and muttered something about regulations. He was about to wave her through when a TSA agent stopped the screening counter.

"We'll need to search this backpack," he said to Alex. "Is this yours?

"What's the problem?" she asked.

Whatever it was, it drew a second TSA person, a supervisor. They opened the bag and pulled the rest of her things off the carrier. How she longed right then to have a Federal ID, her old Treasury Department or FBI identification. But she was as naked and vulnerable as any other American.

The first agent reached in and pulled out a half-finished bottle of Diet 7-Up. He smiled, shrugged, and tossed it into a bin that was already overflowing with other half-dead plastics of liquid.

She smiled back. "Oops. Sorry," Alex said.

"It happens all day," the guy said. A job well done, that capture of a 7-Up bottle.

She repacked and pulled her backpack onto her shoulder.

What was the last thought of that song? *Thank you, Lord, for thinking of me, but I think I'm doing fine.*

Trouble was, Alex wasn't so sure how her country was doing. Billions spent to inconvenience travelers, and where was the real fight against the real enemies of modern civilization? Just one woman's opinion as she grabbed her duffel and hooked her backpack onto her left shoulder. She turned toward her gate.

At a newsstand on the way, she bought another drink and a paperback novel in Spanish, one of those Nobel Prize – winning South American works where the women turn into butterflies. Might as well get into the mood.

SIXTY-TWO

A few hours into the flight to Caracas, as the aircraft passed above the Caribbean, the pilot announced that passengers on the right of the plane could see Cuba. Alex glanced out her window, and sure enough, there it was, nestled in the blue water about a hundred miles to the east.

She had never been there, wished she'd be able to visit sometime, and took a long look as her plane passed. It was hard to believe the political issues at play. She felt sorry for the Cuban people, who had been under one oppressive regime or another for more than a century. When would the world again be able to celebrate the classic poetry of José Martí or the music of the modern-day Cuban *trovador* Silvio Rodríguez?

Christian missionaries were not allowed to visit the island, for example, even to bring clothing or medical assistance. The Cuban people deserved better, as did all the people of Central and South America. Having had a mother from Mexico, Alex felt very close to these people. She made a note to include them in her prayers.

The island passed. The jet continued its path southward over the Caribbean. Alex slipped into headphones and dozed. She missed Robert horribly. A wave of sadness remained, but at least she felt she was moving forward, starting to get a grip again on her life. She wondered how Ben was doing as well as her pals at the gym.

Note to self. Work my way back into basketball when and if I get back to Washington. She slipped off into a light nap.

She drifted. She opened her eyes. It had seemed like only a few minutes, but she had fallen asleep for the better part of an hour.

The plane was descending now into Maiquetía, Caracas's airport. The airport was called that after the village that once stood there, rather than "Simón Bolívar International Airport," its real name.

The aircraft went into a sharp bank as it angled in from the sea, with mountains on one side. The aisle-seat passenger in Alex's row was an older woman who gave a nervous glance at her seatmate. She shook her head. "Scary, no?" she asked. She looked to Alex for comfort as well.

Alex smiled.

"And you haven't flown into *La Carlota*," the man in the middle seat said. He spoke with a Spanish accent.

"Where's *La Carlota*?" Alex asked.

"The old downtown airport in Caracas. It's mostly used for general aviation now. Coming in you're almost kissing the Ávila, the mountain range that forms the southern border of Caracas. As a young man I remember coming in there in fog. You felt the pilots were just sensing where the Ávila was."

Alex nodded and shook her head. The aircraft eased into a further descent.

"President Chávez often still flies out of there," the other passenger said. "Hopefully one day his pilot will get it wrong."

Moments later, they were on the ground, taxiing to the terminal.

Maiquetía airport was astonishingly modern. Alex retrieved her bags and cleared customs easily. Outside the gates, the steamy Venezuelan heat was waiting for her. She was struck by the contrast with Kiev, where everything had been frozen. The clothing she had worn from New York was already uncomfortably heavy.

She scanned a crowd waiting for arriving passengers. There was a well-dressed man with a sign that had her name on it.

Alex approached him in Spanish. "*Buenas tardes. Soy Señorita LaDuca.*"

"*Mucho gusto,*" he answered.

They continued in Spanish. Alex slipped into the flow of it with ease.

"I'm José Mardariaga of the Mardariaga limousine service," he said. "I've been sent by Señor Collins to pick you up. Let me take your bags."

The man took her to a new Lexus with air conditioning that worked. A blessing.

"Is it always this hot this time of year?" she asked, making conversation.

"Down here on the coast, *sí, claro!*" Señor Mardariaga said. "But

not in Caracas, which is up high. The Spaniards usually built their colonial capitals in the mountains away from the coast for this reason.
For instance in Chile, I'm a Chilean myself, the port is El Paraíso, but
the capital of Santiago de Chile is inland, in the mountains."

"Nice airport."

"There's even a TGI Friday's," the driver said, as if that was the
height of current civilization. Perhaps it was, Alex reflected.

"Chávez's doing?" she asked.

"Not a bit of it! The project of replacing the old airport terminal
predates him."

Hearing him, Alex thought back to her phone conversation with
her friend Don Tomás, just before leaving. He had discussed attitudes
toward Hugo Chávez based on social class.

Venezuelan sociologists traditionally divided society into five
classes. A, B, C, D, and E. A were the rich, B were those who could
have an American middle-class lifestyle, C were people what the Venezuelans called "middle class" but had an American lower-middle-
class lifestyle at best. D's were working class people with very modest
income but steady work, and E's were the people on the bottom.

Seventy percent of Venezuelans were D's and E's. They were
Chávez's unconditional supporters. The C's were torn, but many were
anti-Chávez, if for no other reason than the classic desire of their class
to seek to distinguish itself from the classes below. The A's and B's
loathed Chávez. The B's were in the toughest position, because this
was the country they were stuck with. The A's, the truly wealthy, already had their bolt-holes in Miami and their assets stashed in American and Swiss banks.

Clearly, Alex thought, her driver with his own limousine service
was an anti-Chávez C.

The ride to the city went quickly. Alex came out of her daydream
as they went through a tunnel, and then on the other side they were
on the expressway that ran the length of the long, narrow city. Before
her, Alex saw high-rise office buildings and, on some of the hills, obvious condos. But on other hills there were cinderblock shacks piled
one on top of the other.

"*Estoy curiosa. ¿Dondé está Petrare?*" Alex asked, remembering
Don Tomás's description of the city. Where's Petrare?

"That hill right in front, in the distance. You won't want to go there," the driver said.

"I know," she said. "A friend warned me."

The car turned off the elevated freeway onto the parallel street running under it. The driver executed a hair-raising U-turn in the middle of traffic, then turned right up a well-manicured driveway with palms in the center strip.

The Lexus came to a plaza with a white, low-lying building and stopped at the door. "*El Tamanaco*." the driver announced. "*Su hotel, Señorita*."

Alex checked in. She found a suitcase waiting for her in her room, courtesy of Sam and his operatives. Jungle clothing and a weapon. Shirts, hiking boots, shorts, a rain slicker, and a Beretta. She tried things on. She checked the weapon. She also found a small digital camera and three extra memory cards. A thoughtful addition.

She showered, ordered a light meal from room service, and realized she was exhausted. Toward ten in the evening, she collapsed into bed and slept.

SIXTY-THREE

The meeting at the Justice Ministry in Rome had not gone exactly the way Rizzo had planned. He had excluded his assistant DiPetri, the worthless one, because why should the worthless one be allowed to show up when the laurels were being awarded? The worthless one hadn't done anything helpful, for example, except possibly just keeping his foolish hands out of the way. So why should he get any credit?

But twenty minutes into the meeting with the minister, Rizzo wished he had brought DiPetri along to take some of the heat. In response to the minister's questions, Rizzo found himself giving a step-by-step recapitulation of his two investigations, from the commission of the crime, through their linkage, through trips to the *obitorio*, through the official meddling by the Americans in the custody of the bodies, through his Sailor Moon linkage of the crimes to Ukrainian Mafia.

Unimpressed, the minister sat at a wide desk with his eyes downcast, a secretary recording Rizzo's explanation.

After several minutes, despite his years of professionalism, Rizzo got as jittery as a dozen scared cats. There had been much in the press recently about CIA agents embedded within the Roman police. The minister had no reason to suspect Rizzo of such collusion, of serving two masters like that, but Rizzo didn't know whether he might come under accusation, anyway. Things like that happened sometimes.

Rizzo finally came to his conclusion. "And that is where we are today," he finally said.

The minister looked up.

"Do you feel that any arrests are imminent?"

"Arrests, *Signore*?"

"Arrests," the minister said in a tired voice. "Surely you know what arrests are because I'm certain you've made a few in your long career."

"Arrests in Rome are unlikely," Rizzo said, "as I strongly suspect that the gunmen have fled the country by now. As to identifying them and asking one of the other police agencies in Europe to effect the arrests, well, that — "

"Let's save the wishful thinking for later, shall we?" the minister said, cutting him off. "Are there any Ukrainian or Russian gangsters in Rome now whom you feel that we could pin this upon?"

Rizzo's eyes widened, clearly ill at ease with the notion.

"Pin?" he asked. "As in 'frame'?"

He became conscious of a slow tapping on the table by the minister's right hand.

"I believe that's what you would call it."

Rizzo stared at the political appointee in front of him. His eyes were fixed and steady. In a flash, he put much of the reasoning together and didn't like this one bit. After spending twenty-two years with the homicide brigades in Rome, he was going to be asked to fudge evidence, to squander the case, to perjure himself before a magistrate, just to ease a politician out of some sort of squeeze. And if the whole thing backfired, well, his own career would crash down, he could go to prison, there would go his pension, and Sophie would end up in bed with some young musician punk like the ones he was in the habit of arresting.

He thought quickly. "No, *signore*," he answered. "I know of no such criminal who would fit our needs so conveniently," he said.

The minister looked at him with thinly veiled dismay. "Very well," he finally said. "We will take another approach. How many detectives do you have working with you on this case?"

"Four of the best in Rome," he said.

"And I assume each of them has an assistant?"

"That would be true, *signore*."

"So that makes nine of you. What is your individual caseload?"

Rizzo did some quick math. "I would guess, each of us might have twenty, give or take. So somewhere between one hundred fifty and two hundred among all the detectives involved."

"*Bene*," said the minister. "Put them all back to work on their other cases."

"Excuse me?"

"I think you heard me, Rizzo. And I think you understood me. Reassign everyone and make no further efforts on this case yourself."

"I'm afraid I don't understand."

"I'm afraid you don't either, Gian Antonio. This case will most likely conclude itself. Remain available. You will need to liaison with an American agent sometime within the very near future."

The minister motioned to the newspaper. There was a copy of *Il Messaggero* on the table, the headlines blaring about Kiev.

"Do you speak English?" the minister asked. "Well enough to liaise with an American?"

"Not very well, sir. I understand a little, but — "

"Strange," the minister said. "Your file says that your father was in an American POW camp after the war. Your father spoke it quite well."

"The memory of spoken English was not pleasant to my father," Rizzo said. "We spoke Italian in our home."

"Yes. Of course. What else would Italians speak, correct?"

"Latin, maybe," Rizzo answered.

"Your sense of humor is not appreciated right now," the minister said.

"I do have someone in my department, an intern, who could be of service with English," Rizzo said.

"What about French, Rizzo? Do you speak French?"

"French?"

"Yes. It's what they speak in France."

"*Si, signore*," Rizzo answered.

"Good. That's all. Remain ready."

Rizzo opened his mouth to ask for more details, more of an explanation. But the minister cut him off.

"Do you like art, Gian Antonio?" the minister asked, changing the subject.

Rizzo was perplexed. "Art?"

"Italian art! The works of Bernardo Cavallino, for example. Guido Reni. Seventeenth century. Ever heard of them?"

Rizzo had never heard of either. Nor did he care to. "Of course I have," he said.

"If so, you're the first policeman I've ever met who has. Do you think the works should be in Italy?"

"If they're Italian, of course."

"I agree. That is all, Rizzo. *Grazie mille.*"

The double doors opened. The minister's guards barged in to escort Rizzo out. He left without a protest.

SIXTY-FOUR

Alex had not been to the Venezuelan capital for six years. She found it much as she had remembered it, hemmed in by green forested hills that rose to each side of the city. Caracas squeezed the tremendously wealthy and the desperately poor into a single chaotic metropolis. The fascinating disorder was reflected in the gravity-defying skyscrapers at the center of the city, which were a short walk from the teetering shantytowns that covered the surrounding hills.

In the evening, a Señor Calderón presented himself at the hotel. He was a lanky Venezuelan in his twenties. He was an emissary of Mr. Collins and worked for Collins's foundations in South America.

They spoke Spanish. He asked her to call him by his first name, Manuel.

Manuel Calderón would be her guide to the village of Barranco Lajoya. He would pick her up the next morning at 9:00 a.m. and take her to a small private airport east of Caracas. A private helicopter would take her and Calderón to Santa Yniez, which was a small clearing in the jungle. Calderón explained that the airfield had been built by smugglers who brought cocaine into Venezuela from Colombia and Brazil. But it had then been seized by the government in the 1980s following the collapse of Pablo Escobar's empire and had been sold to pro-Western business interests. President Chávez kept threatening to nationalize it, but so far, he hadn't.

"Pack your jungle gear in the backpack and have your weapon accessible just in case," Manuel said. "Dress accordingly. Temperatures will probably be a hundred, at least."

"Will the gun be a problem at the airfield?" she asked.

Calderón laughed. "You're in Venezuela," he said. "Everyone has a gun."

The next morning, Calderón led her to the airfield, which was on the edge of the city. They found their way to a rickety old helicopter, a thirty-year old Soviet SU-456. They buckled in for a flight to Canaimo.

Two members of the national police joined them, needing a lift to Santa Yniez. One of them was in his forties, the younger one in his twenties.

The early morning heat was already stifling. Alex needed only a tan T-shirt and cargo shorts. She wore new hiking shoes and heavy socks. Before leaving the hotel, she had applied DEET to her neck, arms, and legs and packed her digital camera in a convenient pocket.

The two national police officers seemed perplexed, even amused, that a good-looking woman was to be on the flight. She could tell they were trying to figure her out. She engaged them in a conversation in Spanish and kept deflecting their questions about her nationality, as they waited to take off.

"As police, we could ask to see your passport," one of them said, quite amiably.

"*Mi madre fue mexicana*," she said, trying to deflect it further. "*En realidad, chilanga.*"

"*Así, ¿usted es mexicana?*" one asked.

She took a chance and showed them her American passport. She told them that she was on her way to visit friends who were among the missionaries at Barranco Lajoya. This, plus her excellent command of Spanish, seemed to appease them. They didn't bat an eyelash when she pulled her Beretta out of her bag and strapped the holster to her waist. If anything, they were amused.

Then they began to ask more questions. They asked her why she was carrying a gun. She answered, why not carry a gun? They laughed and accepted the answer.

"The last time we were in this aircraft, we took seven bullets from rebels," the younger one said, making conversation. "But we were flying over near Colombia that day. Today we go southeast toward Brazil."

"Yes, I know," she said.

The older cop added that once they had sufficient altitude, small arms fire couldn't touch them. And if it did, it wouldn't penetrate. And if it did penetrate, it would be spent. And if it were spent, they could pick it up and throw it out the door.

"And if it *did* wound someone, the wound wouldn't be too bad, *sí*?"

Alex asked, picking up their facetious tone. "And if the wound *was* bad, we'd fly to a hospital."

They laughed again. "*¡Claro, claro!*" they said.

She swatted at a pair of mosquitoes that had somehow followed them into the aircraft. The policemen watched her as she reapplied some DEET lotion to her legs, even though she was already breaking a sweat. She caught them looking at her and gave them a smile. She felt she had won them over.

The helicopter lifted off into the low mist that covered the city, then broke through the clouds and hovered near the mountains, the aircraft listing to its port side dramatically. She held tightly to her seatbelt with one hand and her seat with the other. At one point, she reckoned, they were no more than two hundred feet above the treetops, and her heart gave a huge surge when a downdraft brought them half that distance lower.

The pilot righted the craft with a sudden jerky motion. They listed starboard violently, as if swinging in a gondola on a cable. Then the mountaintops became distant and they were well above them. The chopper banked and headed south. Alex kept track of directions by their relation to the sun.

The interior of the helicopter was stuffy and hot. Twenty minutes into the flight, Manuel pushed open the side door to the helicopter. "You'll get a better view this way," he said. "Plus, we'll get more air."

He was right. The open door cooled the helicopter. She and Manuel sat strapped into seats at the open door. There was a gun turret there also, but no weapon. The policemen retreated to a corner, broke out a deck of cards and started to play, having no interest in what lay below. Alex guessed they had seen it a thousand times. That, or they didn't want their uniforms to serve as airborne target practice.

They flew low between gaps in the mountains over breathlessly rugged undisturbed scenery. They crossed a long, wide savanna and then a blue river; then the jungle below thickened, though it was criss-crossed with rivers and lakes. The journey was hot, and the motor of the helicopter was thunderous.

Below, green stretched in every direction beneath a low haze. At one point they came to a clearing where there were modern houses and communities. Alex scanned carefully. She saw few vehicles and no people.

"Who lives out here?" she said.

She took out the digital camera and began taking random pictures.

Manuel answered. "*Nadie*. No one any more. There were merchants here. Rubber merchants. But it's no longer safe."

"Rebels?" she asked.

"*Bandidos*."

Alex nodded.

After ninety minutes, the chopper flew over one of the most beautiful areas of the country, the Canaima lagoon and its surroundings. The lagoon was fed by several small waterfalls. Mist hung above the falls. She was surprised by the changing color of the water and sand. In several places, both took on a reddish hue. In some paces the sand was a light pink because of the presence of quartz. She took out the digital camera and recorded what she saw.

Beyond that, they passed over several flattop mountains. Several mining settlements had dug in. She could see machinery and movement on the ground, plus big gouges in the forests and earth. She took more photographs.

They arrived in La Paragua after a two-hour flight. A Jeep was there for them, along with a driver named José. He was a young man, maybe eighteen, with a handsome smile and an Argentine accent. A lunch of chicken, beans, and rice waited in the car, along with chilled bottled water in a crate with ice. Alex quickly won José's approval by talking about the ins and outs of Argentine soccer.

The police departed in their own direction, giving Alex a final glance as they departed, admiration mixed with approval and a hint of subdued lechery.

Manuel, Alex, and José then began a three-hour trek over bumpy roads as they drew closer to Barranco Lajoya. The men rode in the front. Alex preferred to have more room to herself by sitting in the rear, but she continued to chat up both her driver and guide.

In some areas, mud on the road was so deep that it sucked at the tires of the vehicle. In one area, one entire lane of the road had been washed away by a mudslide. The road hadn't been repaired, but the line in the middle had been redrawn. At another area, there was a one-lane "bridge" that was nothing more than a sheet of metal dragged across a fifteen-foot crater. Manuel and Alex got out of the Jeep and crossed the bridge on foot in advance of the Jeep in case the vehicle tumbled.

The roads weren't bad, they were hideous. To make it worse, Manuel kept looking at the side rearview mirror. Alex asked twice if for any reason he thought they were being followed. Both times, Manuel answered only with a shrug.

"These days in Venezuela," Manuel finally grumbled, "anything is possible."

SIXTY-FIVE

The Jeep halted at the side of a clearing. Beyond, a narrow path wound up the mountain between trees and rocks. The path was deeply rutted, the ruts flooded with water.

José stopped the vehicle and they all stepped out.

The late afternoon was so hot that steam rose from the mud. Low swarms of flies and gnats settled into little clouds above the mud. Alex fixed her hair into a ponytail, put on a cap to protect her head, and plastered herself with DEET for the third time.

"Barranco Lajoya is about a mile up the mountain," Manuel said. "From here we go on foot. When God made this place, he must have been in a bad mood."

She might have hiked up the mountain in long pants, despite the constant risk of insect or snake bits, but the heat ruled that out. Malaria was also rampant, so was rabies, and anything that flew or crawled had a good chance of being poisonous. She hoisted her pack onto her back and adjusted the weapon in her holster. The sheath with the knife was arranged on her left hip.

"The climb is steep," Manuel said. "Take plenty of water."

She put two one-liter bottles in her backpack and tied a fresh canteen at her waist.

"*Los machetes*," José reminded them. *"Tigritos, ¿ustedes saben?"*

She frowned. José explained. There were occasionally jaguars on the mountain, he said. They tended not to attack during the day, but one never knew. If the big cats were hungry enough, they would go after anything. Manuel took a machete with him, for protection as much as slashing through the underbrush. Alex at first declined, then took one.

Both Alex and Manuel checked the ammunition in their sidearms. If they needed the pistols, they might need them in a hurry. With a final gesture, José produced a pair of bracelets, suitable for ankle or wrist. They were made out of light wood, slatted with thin but strong wires running through connecting the beads. He proposed that they each wear one. Within one of the slats on each was a variation on a SIM card, a small directional chip.

"In case someone needs to go looking for a body?" Alex said.

"We try to think of everything," he said in Spanish.

Then they were ready and began their ascent.

They crossed a barbed wire fence that belonged to a local rancher. Then they trudged several hundred yards through a half-shaded path through the jungle. The DEET worked and kept the biting flies at bay. Above them was a canopy of leaves, which provided some shade but also held the humidity across the floor of the jungle.

The hike was steep, like a march through a giant terrarium. Sweat rolled off her. They stopped for water after a quarter mile and had all the water they wanted when they came to a wide stream with a hard rushing current.

They picked up sturdy fallen branches from the zimba trees and fashioned walking sticks out of them. The path across the first stream was across a series of rocks that some Good Samaritan had put in place but which the force of the current had loosened.

Some of the rocks were submerged. Manuel crossed first and offered a hand back to Alex. There were fifteen steps, then they were at a soggy little island in the middle of the stream. The ground below their feet was soft like quicksand, so they kept moving.

The other side was a deeper ford. There was no choice but to wade through it. Manuel led the way. The water was past her ankles, then up to her knees, then almost touching the hem of her hiking shorts. Then they came up to the other side. They dried off as much as they could, re-applied the insecticides and continued. Alex felt as if her boots would be wet for days, but forged ahead. Fortunately, she had two pairs.

This was like a different planet.

Twenty minutes later, before her was another makeshift bridge of stepping stones, twice as wide and perilous as the first set. The stick was useless now, the water was too deep and the stream swelled into a small unfriendly river right before her eyes.

Manuel, becoming unsteady, crossed ten feet ahead of her. She was on her own. She kept the stick and used it as a balance, as a tightrope walker might.

An insect hit her in the throat and she slapped at it, hitting herself hard on the neck. The rocks below her left foot wobbled and she fought wildly to retain her balance, waving her arms, trying to keep the stick centered. She managed.

Manuel arrived on the other side. She stayed focused. Nine more stones. Then eight. She counted them down. The river narrowed and became shallower. Her confidence swelled. She had made it. Two more steps. Then one.

Manuel extended a hand. "*¡Aquí, señorita, aquí!*" he said, above the rustle of the current. She grasped his hand and he pulled. She took the final step with a neat jump and landed on the soft riverbank.

"That was the toughest part," he said.

They stopped to drink, catch their breath, and gather themselves. They found some shade and stopped again where the path was halfway up the mountain. At one point, Manuel took out a pair of binoculars and scanned downward to an area where they could see part of the path they had taken. "What are you watching?" she asked.

"*¡Mira!* Three men with rifles," he said.

Her heart jumped. She said nothing. Manuel handed her the field glasses and showed her.

She trained the glasses on them and felt her heart leap a second time. There were indeed three strong dark-skinned men in jungle pants and T-shirts. All three were armed with rifles. The guns were old but could kill nonetheless. One of them also had a sidearm. She scanned all parts of the path to see if there were any more than three, but those were the only ones she saw.

They were following them up the same path about half a mile below. Startled and fearful, she handed the glasses back to Manuel. Obviously, he read the anxiety on her face because he laughed.

"Don't be alarmed," he said. "About two miles from here there's a rancher. His livestock escapes sometimes, and he sends out his *hombres* to bring back what is his."

"They need all that artillery to track down goats?" she asked.

"The region is peaceful these days," Manuel said, "but it is still too dangerous to wander around by oneself or unarmed. About a year ago, a man named Luis was upset because his wife had fled his village. He sat around drinking all day, then attacked some friends for no reason with his machete. He killed a child. The people in his village had to take things into their own hands."

"What did they do?"

Manuel wouldn't say.

"Please tell me," she pressed.

"It was not pleasant. And it is not good to speak of it to outsiders," he said.

"I want to know," she said. "There is no one else here. You can say it aloud to the mountain, as if I'm not listening."

He paused, then spoke slowly.

"They attacked him with heavy hammers and clubs," he said. "They broke his legs. Then they the tied him to a tree and left him for three days. By the time they returned, he was dead. Wild animals had feasted on the body, perhaps when he was still alive."

At length, she said, "I see."

"There is no justice out here other than what people make for themselves," he said. Luis's remains had received a proper burial under four feet of dirt, a pile of stones, and a primitive wooden cross on a remote part of the mountain.

"God will be his judge, as he will judge all of us," the guide said.

Alex nodded and asked nothing further about the incident. Her gaze drifted back down the mountain. Manuel's eyes followed her gaze.

"Anyway, there is no reason to be alarmed right now," he said, looking back down the mountain. "Those men down there are looking for the pigs and goats that belong to *su jefe*. I know those men. They are friends. Let's continue."

"Good idea," she said.

They rose and continued their hike. The path narrowed again and headed into heavy brush under a stand of trees. It continued that way for another few hundred yards, then came to a clearing and began to wind steeply through a rocky area that required climbing.

She was thankful she'd worn good footwear, solid mountain hiking stuff. The gun and the machete hung heavily at her side and reminded her constantly of the extra danger from wildlife.

Then she was out of breath. They stopped. She found a rock and she sat, panting to get her wind back. Manuel seemed midway between concerned and amused.

The time passed slowly and heavily. There was a rustle in the underbrush. Alex's hand went for her weapon as she thought of the jaguars. But when a beast emerged it was only a wild pig, a descendant of an escapee from a nearby ranch. Future prey for *los tigritos*. The animal gave them a curiously indignant look and scooted off into the heavy brush.

"*¿Está bien?*" Manuel asked.

"*Estoy bien*," she answered. "I'm okay."

"One more push to Barranco Lajoya," he said.

She nodded and stood. He led the way after a final warning to look out for snakes, which could be up to six feet long. "The rattlers are the worst," he said. "And you don't always hear the rattle before they strike."

The last part was free of rocks. From somewhere there was even a breeze. A hot breeze, but a breeze nonetheless. She became short of breath again, but Manuel urged her on, promising that the rest of the way was short and if she stopped at this altitude it could sometimes prove impossible to get back into gear.

Then, up ahead, she heard an incongruous sound.

Chickens.

When you heard the chickens you were close to the village, Manuel said. A final few hundred feet and she came to a clearing. The contours of a wood and plaster roof came into view, and then there was the sound of children shouting. Manuel walked ahead of her a few more strides, and a minute later a clearing opened before them. When they stepped out of it, there was the village of Barranco Lajoya.

The path didn't end so much as it disappeared into a rambling battered mishmash of rundown huts and shacks. Walls were made of scrap metal, as were roofs. Some roofs were thatched, others had gaping holes in them. There were hammocks for sleeping on small overhangs to some of the huts, attempts at porches, and a few primitive colorful murals that attempted to make things look better. Some of the better homes had mosquito netting on the windows. The majority didn't. The windows were just open. Alex saw one car, an old blue Citroen with an ornate grill. It must have been forty years old and have spent part of its early life in the old French colony of Guyana, to the east. She wondered how it could have gotten there and guessed that the path must have been more passable in the past.

There seemed to be one store, which operated out of a window in someone's hut. Barefoot children played soccer in a field cluttered with litter. A hand-painted sign on the side of one building said *Iglesia Christiana*. The church. The building would have been considered an eyesore and a slum in most American towns, but here it was one of the better buildings. It was white stucco, shuttered windows and large wooden doors that locked. Beside it, adjacent to a porch, was a gasoline-powered generator. Electricity had not yet come to Barranco Lajoya, nor had telephones. In Barranco Lajoya the modern world didn't exist.

A crowd began to gather. Moments later, a small middle-aged man with slick hair, a round face, and a pleasant smile came forth from the church. He introduced himself as Father Martin. He was a Cuban American from Miami, who spoke English and Spanish.

"*¡Bienvenida! Por favor, acompáñame,*" he said. Welcome and come with me. I will take you to the other missionaries.

SIXTY-SIX

In London, Anatoli felt safe. Honest to God, he had never committed even the slightest crime in the United Kingdom. And he wouldn't. He rather liked the place, the pubs, the football, the girls. Like the cute redhead with whom he had spent the previous night. The trashy blue collar fun of Oxford Street and Picadilly Circus. London was a great place to be for a young man from one of the old Soviet republics. Much better than Rome, from which he had arrived a week earlier.

He stepped out of the shiny black taxi at the foot of Edgerton Gardens in Kensington. It was a mild morning. He would walk the rest of the way home, pass by a pub for an early pint maybe, then go home and sleep off the previous evening.

He sighed to himself. He blinked against the unusual bright sunlight of London in April. He put on a pair of sunglasses.

First rain, then sun, then more rain, then more sun. He blinked. How did these English ever get used to it? It wasn't like Ukraine where things were steadier.

He skipped the pub. He had been out late the night before and needed a long nap. He turned onto his block of red brick flats and saw nothing unusual.

He entered his building. The lift was out of order again. Well, he only lived three flights up. He took the steps two by two. He clutched an old metal key in his hand.

He looked at his door. The little splinter that he'd left above the lock was still in place. No one had entered while he was out. Either that, he mused to himself, or whoever had entered was so good that they looked for the little marks like that and fixed them.

The floor was silent. Anatoli opened the door and stepped inside.

The lunging, swinging metal baseball bat came from his blind side and was aimed straight at his kneecap. It missed slightly, but smashed the bone of his shin with a sickening crack. At the same time, doors to the apartment behind him opened and men in London police uniforms rushed toward him. They hit him hard from behind and shoved him forward into his own apartment.

Anatoli went berserk. He fought like a wild man. If there were two things he knew in life, one was fighting. The other was killing. Now he knew a third thing: if he were taken prisoner, he wouldn't see freedom until he was a very old man, if then.

He threw his powerful elbows at the men behind him, caught one in the jaw and one in the gut. He clenched a fist, threw a backward punch at the same man and caught him in the groin. The man howled profanely and loosened his grip.

The man with the bat hammered at Anatoli's knee again and caught it. Anatoli screamed, then cursed in Ukrainian. Those he fought cursed him in English.

Anatoli started to go down. But he managed to get a hand to the gun he carried under the left armpit of his leather jacket. He moved the gun at one of his assailants. He counted *six* of them now, plus one that was smaller, older, who was standing back. He pulled the trigger, once, twice.

One bullet flew wildly. But the other tore part of the left hand off one of the men who was trying to take his freedom away. The man spun away with a loud screech, blood splattering in every direction like a shattered bottle of ketchup. Anatoli saw a curled pinky finger hit the floor.

Then the bat hit Anatoli's wrist. The gun flew away from him. Anatoli's hand and wrist were then rendered nerveless and paralyzed from a second blow.

"Bring him down! *Down!*" the leader said from outside the fight.

One of the intruders had a police club and used it with remarkable efficiency. He walloped Anatoli on the left side of the temple so hard that it crushed the cartilage in his ear. Another blow to the midpoint of his face broke his nose. Then there was one to his groin that took much of the fight out of him.

Anatoli went down hard onto his face, overpowered. The fight had taken a full minute. Championship bouts one-on-one often took less.

Anatoli lay stunned but not unconscious on the old Pakistani carpet that covered the floor. Someone grabbed him by the hair, lifted his head, and slammed it down again. He felt his hands pulled behind his back and cuffed. His mouth was hot and salty, and little shards of his teeth floated on his tongue. His physical fight was gone but a rage still surged within him. If he ever got out of here, he swore to himself, he would find all these men and kill them.

He was still breathing hard, clinging to consciousness, wondering how he could have been so careless or who had betrayed him. He wondered if the redhead had been a setup to get him out of his apartment. And how had they found him?

Voices. Voices in the room. A voice talking on a cell phone: the man who had stayed back from the fight. He was obviously the leader. Even dazed and defeated, Anatoli knew how these things worked.

"Yeah, we got him," the voice said.

There was a pause. Then it continued. Same guy.

"Are you kidding me? *Of course* he fought, you moron. He fought like a stuck hog. What'd you expect ... that he'd come to tea with us at Fortnum's?"

There was another pause. Then, "One of my men got clubbed in the balls. Another got a bullet wound. We need some doctors fast."

In the background Anatoli could hear the man he had shot wailing and crying. Anatoli wished to hell he had killed him.

"Should I put him down, Mark?" Anatoli heard someone say.

"Put him down," the commander said in response.

Anatoli hadn't been in America often and his English wasn't strong. But it seemed like most of these men who had attacked him were English.

They looked it. They smelled it. They sounded it.

But their leader, Mark, the one with the cell phone, the one who had stayed clear of things until the dirty work was done, was American. Anatoli could tell by the accent. If he'd known his American accents better, he would have recognized the soft strains of the Tidewater region of Virginia.

Through a broken nose, shattered teeth, and a fractured jaw, Anatoli cursed his captors. But there was no physical fight left in him now. Darkness came down on him like a collapsing brick wall.

Everything hurt. Consciousness faded. And even as darkness descended, his right eye twitched uncontrollably, even more than usual.

Then one of the assailants pressed something to the side of his head. The nose of a pistol, it felt like. A few seconds later, there was a tremendous explosion and darkness.

SIXTY-SEVEN

From the day she arrived in Barranco Lajoya, Alex kept her eyes and ears open on behalf of her employer, Joseph Collins. Her assignment had been to take a good look at things and report back. What's being done right? What might be done better? And above all, see who might be trying to push these poor indigenous people off their land.

Identify who and report back.

To that end, Alex embedded herself in the everyday life of the village, the better to catch the pace and feel of the place. The better to observe.

Father Martin installed her in a thatched hut located behind the church. Some of the wives from the village, accompanied by their daughters, had scrubbed the concrete floor of the hut with a heavy bleach and disinfectant before Alex's arrival. As noxious as the smell was, it kept the insects at bay, though when she lay down to sleep, she could see the insects crawling above her, through the leaves and branches of the roof. There was also a small supply of citronella candles on a wooden table and a small can of insecticide.

Bedding was a thin foam mattress spread on the floor, plus a sheet and mosquito netting. There was a ring of chili powder around the sleeping area, which kept most of the crawling spiders, lice, and red ants away. In the evening, two candles lit the room, and Alex was cautioned to leave one on at night to deter the occasional small snake that might intrude. Rattlers, she was reminded, could sense the body heat of their prey and would strike in complete darkness.

The best plumbing in town was also in the back of the church, in an attached shed, but this was in a single open room where food supplies were also kept. When Alex used it, two of the women from the town, whom she quickly befriended, "stood guard" for her so that no men would walk in. The village men were too well mannered, or intimidated, to burst in on her, but accidents could happen.

Bathing was rudimentary, too. About a hundred yards through the woods there was a mountain stream which was about twenty feet wide where it ran past the village. The women of Barranco Lajoya considered it safe in terms of pollution and wildlife. They had been using it to bathe and wash laundry for many generations.

The men tended to be away during the day, so the women would go together in the late afternoon before dusk, maybe ten to fifteen at a time, usually with many children. Alex tended to go to the river with the younger women, the wives who were sometimes barely older than sixteen, but mostly in their twenties.

They would disrobe completely, leave their clothes in neat piles on the riverbank and move quickly into a meter of rushing water. They would scrub themselves with bars of a strong Mexican soap. The water came from a great elevation and was surprisingly refreshing. A strong current kept it clean.

Alex was hesitant at the procedure at first and reluctant to undress in front of the women of the village, though the venue was really no more than an outdoor version of a women's locker room. But she quickly got used to the procedure. In a strange primal way she felt at one with God's nature when she waded into the cool stream and then slowly submerged herself. It occurred to her that the topography here had probably not changed much in two thousand years, since the time of Christ. People had probably been bathing in this tributary for just as long. Before many days had passed, she looked forward to the daily ritual.

She had heard that sometimes soldiers came through the area and would stand on the opposite riverbank, watch the women, and shout to them. Sometimes the soldiers would even take pictures. The men of the village tolerated this. They knew better than to challenge the soldiers. Everyone in Venezuela knew better than to challenge groups of military.

Alex kept an eye out for the soldiers. She had no inclination to put on a show for them. But she did see them once. Two of the younger soldiers were taking pictures from the opposite shore while Alex and three others were bathing in knee-deep water.

Surprisingly to Alex, the women bathing made no effort to cover themselves and actually waved to the men in uniform. One blew kisses.

Later one of the women explained. "We are safer when the soldiers come by to watch us," she said. "Because we bathe in the river, the soldiers pass by our village. If they didn't pass by, we would be at the complete mercy of bandits."

To bathe, the women also needed to wear rubber sandals. The thongs protected the soles of the feet from microscopic dangers that lurked on the bed of the stream. It was through the soles of the feet that parasites, some of which could be fatal, might enter the body. A woman named Inéz who was always accompanied by three small children, gave Alex a pair of black rubber thongs made from an old tire.

Two weeks after Alex arrived, a medical mission from Maracaibo visited Barranco Lajoya. With the exception of Mr. Collins's missionaries, foreign visits were a rarity in the little town perched three thousand feet above the valley floor. The scenery may have been Aspen-caliber, but there were no ski lifts here, no businesses. There weren't even toilets outside of the church. On one side of the town, the drop on the mountain was so steep that one could fall off. Sometimes children did.

The people of the town were endlessly grateful when the doctors and nurses arrived. If residents of Barranco Lajoya got sick, they usually had to hope they would get better on their own. Some didn't even bother to do that. They had learned to live with pain and infection, and sometimes die with it.

"The worst thing that can happen to a human being is to lose hope," Father Martin said one morning. "A lot of people here feel hopeless."

On the first day of the visit, the missionaries turned the town's church into a medical clinic in a matter of minutes. Two doctors from Maracaibo set up shop behind little-kid-style desks. Other missionaries set up stations to take blood pressure and test adults for diabetes. Bags of pills and medical supplies were stashed behind the altar of the church. Outside on the playground, the cluster of townspeople was organized into a line and missionaries registered every single person. They wrote down names, ages, and complaints, which ranged from hacking coughs and stomach aches to limbs rotting from blood poisoning.

What followed wasn't textbook medicine. The doctors made diagnoses on the fly, seeing ten times the number of patients they would on a typical day in the US. The little pills that Americans took for granted made a huge difference in Barranco Lajoya. They could whip lingering infections and knock out the stomach parasites that could starve even a well-fed child.

Alex used her fluent Spanish to help counsel some patients. She saw one ten-year-old girl who had been suffering from a sore throat that made her wince every time she swallowed.

She asked how long the girl had been in pain.

The girl's response: "*Seis años.*" Six years.

The doctor prescribed antibiotics but told the girl's mother she would need to take her to one of the hospitals on the distant coast to have her tonsils removed. She wasn't sure that would happen. The medical brigade like this was like a strobe flash in the dark. The stomach parasites were going to come back, blood pressure medicine would eventually run out, lice would again infest the children. Suspected cancers would go untreated. But temporarily suffering had been lessened. At least those who brought in help from the outside had done *something*.

"I'd like to think that we weren't just giving a dose of an antiparasitic but also a little dose of optimism," Father Martin said at the end of the day. "And yet there are those who would take even that away from these people."

As the first month passed, Alex watched as the resident missionaries went about their work, which consisted mostly of trying to establish a school, or at best literacy, and a small medical clinic. These activities took place in the church, which was close to a hundred degrees during the day.

Alex rose with each lemony dawn, sometimes watching the last of the men begin their daily trek down the mountain. She then set out to explore the region, trying to figure out what could be there that would cause someone to want to drive the missionaries away. If anything.

Some days she would hike on foot. On other days, burros were available. She would never travel alone, never travel unarmed. On her journeys, the most striking thing in Alex's eyes was the magnificent raw beauty of the countryside, rivers and waterfalls, thick jungle, and endless unspoiled vistas. Always, she took photographs. Her digital equipment had enough memory for two thousand shots. She fired away liberally, then cleared out the clinkers in the evening.

Twice, Manuel returned to Barranco Lajoya to take her on explorations by air.

Each time, he guided her back down the mountain and drove her to a nearby landing field that could accommodate helicopters but not airplanes. From there she took off and surveyed the region by air.

On the first trip, the pilot took her all around the area to the east and northeast, all the way out to the Rio Amacura delta on the coastline and the blue Caribbean. She could see Trinidad and Tobago in the hazy distance. Then on another day, a different pilot flew her westward down over the Amazon jungle to Puerto Ayacucho, which was the capital of the Venezuelan state of Amazonas.

"The army has a huge base here," Manuel explained. "We cannot fly too close to it or they will shoot at us. For sport, if for no other reason. They conduct a continuous campaign against drug runners from Colombia, yet some of them also take payoffs from the drug runners."

Alex nodded. Then they continued south to one of the world's great natural wonders, the Casiquare canal, a waterway that linked South America's two greatest river systems, the Amazon and the Orinoco. By air for the first time, it was breathtaking, much like going over Niagara Falls and the Mississippi at the same time.

"When we return," Alex asked, "can we fly north over Barranco Lajoya? I'd like to see the summit of our mountain."

"We can do that," Manuel answered.

The aircraft then guided Alex over her village by air. She took more pictures. She then had the pilot trace the route of the river until they found the places where the water came out of the ground. She could see no place where pollution could have begun, as once reported.

On foot, and on the backs of donkeys, Alex learned enough about the surrounding areas to take hikes on some days through paths in the jungle, never neglecting her sidearm, always accompanied by men with rifles from Barranco Lajoya. Her daily outfit — boots, fresh socks that she'd wash each night, hiking shorts, a T-shirt, a red bandana, and cap—became her work clothes. She clipped the compass to one of the belt loops on her shorts and it remained there.

Her "school uniform," as she thought of it. Her arms and legs tanned within a week. Her stomach flattened even more than usual, and her legs grew stronger than ever from the rugged hiking and climbing. Her local guides showed her to clearings where she could see horizons that were hundreds of miles away on a clear day. On other days they showed her lush orchards that they had planted on their own. The guides often trekked fifty pound bags of fruit by donkey down the path and sent the produce to market. On another day, she was led past the area when the women bathed to where the stream merged with a much larger body of water. There were three dugout canoes waiting, and her guides took her on a journey upstream about ten miles by paddle. They stopped at a quarry where the men picked up about twenty pounds each of smooth flat rock, a distinctive local granite with a quartz content that, like the sand in some of the river beds, gave the rock a pink hue.

"What are those for?" Alex asked.

Both men smiled. "*Mi sobrina*," said one of them. "My niece. And some of the other girls."

"What do they do with them?" Alex asked, intrigued.

"We'll show you later," the girl's uncle said.

Then, when the boats were loaded, they allowed the current to bring them back. It took the better part of a day.

That same evening, Alex received the answer to her question about the stones. The granite substance was not just unique for its color, but also for its density and durability. When Alex examined the stones, she was amazed how hard they were. They were like little pieces of natural iron. As a result, the young girls in the village used hammers and chisels on them and created jewelry of all designs. The jewelry was then sent to markets in the cities to sell to tourists. For a pendant that took many hours to create, a girl would receive a few pennies. But it was better than nothing.

A sweet sixteen-year-old girl named Paulina, the niece of one of the boat guides, had accepted Christianity. She was a very plain girl with mocha skin and dark hair that she wore pulled back. She had delicate brown eyes and worked small miracles with the granite, making boldly carved crosses onto circular stones. Paulina's designs were the best of any village girl. They sold well as far away as Ciudad Guyana, Alex learned.

The first time Alex saw one of the Paulina's works, she gasped at how skilled the artistry was. It was akin to hearing a gifted child sit down and play Mozart on the piano.

In reaction, Alex's hand subconsciously went to her neck where her father's gold cross had been for many years.

Paulina giggled.

"Why did you do that? You're not wearing anything at your neck," she asked.

"I used to. But I lost it," Alex said.

"Oh."

Alex grinned and selected one of the girl's pieces. It was a flat round stone, graying pink, slightly smaller than an old American fifty-cent piece, but twice as thick. The cross had been carefully cut into the center of the stone. The stone was heavy for a piece of jewelry but had a slight hole at the top where a fine strand of leather was threaded through.

Alex put it on right away.

"It will protect you," the girl said engagingly.

"Of course it will," Alex said. Impetuously, she hugged the child. The asking price was less than fifty cents American. Alex gave the girl the equivalent of five dollars. Then she bought two smaller ones for friends back home.

The stone crosses were, Alex reasoned, the perfect souvenirs of her stay at Barranco Lajoya. For some reason, it made her feel complete again, as if she had found something that had been missing. Even when bathing in the river, even when washing her hair in the river with the coarse Mexican soap, it was the one thing she never removed.

A fifth week passed. Then a sixth.

She thought of Robert many times during these days, his smile, his sense of humor, his kindness, his body, his warmth. She still was resentful for one aspect of her life, angry with God so to speak, over Robert's abrupt departure from this world, without even a word of farewell. How could *that* have been in the plan of an almighty and forgiving God?

But she mentioned this to no one. Being so far away from her normal life, all her past experiences, allowed her to think, to put things in perspective, to turn new emotional corners.

Curiously, she also realized that she had no remorse about the men she had shot and presumably killed in Kiev while defending herself. She kept all of this locked up inside her, and went about her daily business in her remote venue, even while no answers were coming forth for Mr. Collins. She had been sent here to observe, to develop a theory about who would want these indigenous people off their land and want the missionaries gone. She had by now spent several weeks studying the area from the ground, from the air, and occasionally by water. And there were no suggestions of anything amiss.

She began to wonder if she had made this trip for nothing.

SIXTY-EIGHT

Then there were the events of late July.

They began when the young girl, Paulina, who had sold Alex her new pendant, had traveled halfway down the mountain path one morning with two other girls. The three girls came running back in terror around noon.

Alex was one of the first to see them. *"¿De qué se trata?"* Alex asked the breathless girls. *"¿Quién es?"* What's this about? Who is it?

A group from the village gathered, including the missionaries.

The girls explained. "Strange men," Paulina said. "A whole band of them!"

"¿Dondé estan?" Alex asked. Where are they?

"At the clearing. Halfway down the mountain," said a second girl, trembling with fright. The men, the girls said when they came breathlessly back to the village, were heavily armed and had threatened them. They had tried to capture the youngest and prettiest of the three girls, but the girls had run.

"¿Qüantos?" Alex asked. How many men?

Maybe a dozen of them, the girls answered. Men they had never seen before, at one of the clearings. Men who had no good business in this area.

"¿Cazadores? ¿Banditos? ¿Soldados?" Alex pressed. Hunters? Bandits? Soldiers?

"¡No sé, no sé!" Paulina said, starting to cry. The girls couldn't tell. They only knew enough to be frightened of this band of outsiders.

"Did they follow you?" Alex asked.

"No," Paulina said. "They looked like they were scouting. They didn't follow."

Alex embraced Paulina and turned to the men of Barranco Lajoya. "We should go have a look," she said.

Several men from the village went into their homes. They emerged with rifles and an array of handguns. Alex went back to her own hut and strapped the holster with the Beretta around her waist. The pistol hung on her right side. She tucked an extra clip of bullets in her pocket. She brought a canteen of water, also, as well as a compact pair of binoculars.

A group of angry men waited for her when she emerged. They looked at her oddly.

"You are going with us?" one of them questioned. "*¿Una mujer?*" A woman?

"I'm going with you," she said steadfastly in Spanish. "*¡Claro! ¡Si! ¡Una mujer!*"

The men looked at each other, then nodded, all in accord. There were no further questions. They brought with them every rifle in Barranco Lajoya.

In a burning sun, they went back down the mountain to take a look. Paulina went along, staying close to Alex. They tried to find the place where the strange group of intruders had been seen.

Alex expected the worst. Her heart was like a drumbeat as the group from the village descended the rugged mountain trail. She wondered whether this event would throw some light on what she had been sent here to discover. She wondered what Robert would have thought if he could have seen her here now with these people. He would have been proud of her, she thought to herself.

After a march of half an hour, they found the spot where the girls had seen the men. "They were here," Paulina said. But no one was there now, other than the party from the village.

Alex stepped slightly off the path near the clearing. She examined the thick underbrush. It had recently been trampled, but that indicated nothing. She looked for other signs of human activity, food wrappers, cigarettes, bullet casings, but found nothing.

"There were men here. I swear," Paulina said to Alex.

Alex placed a hand on the girl's shoulder. "*Yo sé. Te creo*," she answered. I know. I believe you.

A moment later, there was a sudden noise in the brush about fifty feet away. Reflexively, Alex's hand went to her pistol. She drew it and instinctively went down to one knee. The men of the village turned toward the sound with their rifles. And then a wild ram emerged slowly from a thicket. The beast looked at them in contempt, chewing on something, then turned its head and disappeared.

Alex put her gun back into its holster.

"We shouldn't return home until we've had a thorough look around," she said.

There was agreement. The group from the village split in two and followed two paths that led away from the clearing, about a dozen individuals in each group. They searched the area, found vantage points that allowed them to look across clearings up and down the mountain. At her locations, when she could, Alex used her binoculars to scan in every direction. But she saw nothing.

The two groups made a rendezvous back at the larger clearing an hour later, hot and exhausted. The blazing summer sun was starting to sink in the sky by this time. Alex glanced at her watch. It was past 5:00 p.m.

The search party returned to the village without a shot fired. Several men had the nagging suspicion that for whatever reason the teenage girls had made up a tall tale.

Alex quickly grew tired of listening to them. Quietly, she slipped away from everyone and disappeared to a secluded cove in the river with a change of clothing. She wanted to bathe and wash the day's sweat from her body as well as rinse the shorts, T-shirt, and underwear she had worn that day. Alone and undressed, she was careful to go only knee deep in the water and keep her pistol within quick reach on the riverbank.

She washed quickly, herself and her clothes, then stepped out of the water, dried off, and dressed in a clean shirt and shorts. Her only witnesses were a flock of noisy parrots who kept her company overhead. She welcomed the presence of the birds, as they formed a primitive sentry system. She had already learned that the birds' chatter changed when strangers approached.

In the evening, after dinner, the men from the search party grumbled loudly about the hike down the mountain. They didn't feel the story Paulina and her friends had told was reliable. Later, many of them buried their complaints in warm beer on an outdoor patio.

Alex could hear them and understand them as she lay on her own foam mattress, reading a novel in Spanish by Isabel Allende by the light from two candles.

Alex wasn't so sure that the girls had made up their story. Why would they? And the trampled underbrush suggested larger bodies, and several of them.

Alex had fallen into the habit of sleeping in her clothing, except for the socks and shoes. She also kept her pistol loaded and at her bedside.

Tonight was no exception. Yet the night was calm, the darkness deep in the jungle around the small enclave. The only noise, distantly, were the normal jungle sounds of the feral creatures that lived by night. And the only sounds nearby were the occasional mutterings of some of the village men, slumped on front doorsteps drunk on *guarapo*, the local cane-sugar liquor.

SIXTY-NINE

Many of the residents of the Barranco Lajoya left each morning before dawn to make the long trek down the mountain. A jitney, a rusting old minivan with missing windows, would pick them up at daybreak at the base where Manuel had parked his Jeep. The van would take them to either the nearby ranch or a more distant one where they would work in the fields of sugar cane. There they worked for the equivalent of three dollars a day, plus a lunch of beans and rice. This they would do seven days a week for ten hours a day in the torrential subtropical rainy seasons of the winter as well as the sweltering heat of the summer. These were the lucky ones.

The ranchers also owned some of the water rights in the area, excluding the native people from one of their few resources, except in the higher elevations. The people here were used to having nothing and expecting nothing. So when missionaries came in, they were grateful but knew the generosity could end any day and their schools and minimal clinics could disappear. It had been this way for as long as anyone could remember. The armies of Spain had come through in the seventeenth and eighteenth centuries and had tortured and crushed everyone. Bolivar, *el libertador*, had lived at the end of the eighteenth century and the beginning of the nineteenth and had managed to create an independence based on the ideals of the American independence. Now everything in Venezuela was still named after Bolivar. You even paid with a Bolivar if you had any money. But for three quarters of the people, nothing had really changed. There remained poverty and oppression. The people learned not to complain. Once again, the little that these people had could disappear with no warning.

"A couple of years ago," Father Martin said one evening, "there was an incident at another village named Barranco Yopal." Martin spoke as he shared a fish dinner by candlelight with the other resident missionaries inside the church. "President Chávez ordered a Christian missionary group working with indigenous tribes to leave the country. They were mostly American from a group based in Florida."

"Why did Chávez want them out?" Alex asked.

Father Martin laughed ruefully and shook his head. "Chávez accused the missionaries of 'imperialist infiltration' and links to the CIA."

"Was there any truth to it?" she asked.

"No, Chávez was being a demagogue," the priest said. "The missionaries at Barranco Yopal were dedicated people. They spent several years living among the tribes in order to learn the language, creating a written form for it, and translating the Bible into it. Then they taught Christianity to the people. The missionaries brought along their families. Their kids grew among the native children and didn't interfere with native culture. All they wanted to do was bring Christ and the Word of God to the people. They dedicated years of their lives to this. Then Chávez turned up one day with his military uniform and his red beret and held a ceremony to denounce 'colonialism.' He presented property titles to several indigenous groups. He gave them title to land that they had been on anyway. Title to something that they already had. He came off as a hero and, in truth, hadn't really done anything."

Around the table, people shook their heads.

"Chávez accused the missionaries of building luxurious camps next to poor Indian villages," Father Martin continued. "He accused them of circumventing Venezuelan customs authorities as they freely flew in and out on private planes. The missionaries had built their own compound, but it was hardly luxurious. And they flew their own aircraft in and out so that their supplies wouldn't be stolen. The most efficient thieves in any South American country are the customs officials, the police, and the army."

One of the female missionaries at the table, a nurse from Toronto, chipped in. "There are people who resent us for philosophical reasons," she said. "In primitive societies, there's no separation of religion and the rest of the society. We are among people who for centuries have followed rituals intended to make the corn grow, bring rain, and remain healthy. The people who criticize us claim that by bringing

Christianity to them, even if we leave their own rituals alone, we've rendered meaningless the core of the native culture."

"But we're here to help them," someone said.

"All cultures are in transition," Father Martin added. "We feel we've given them something new and joyous."

"We're accused of acting the same way the Spaniards and Catholic Church did with less remote Indians when the *conquistadores* came through," the nurse said.

"Except the Spaniards and the Catholic Church didn't try to bring them electricity and health care," another missionary chipped in.

There was laughter.

"It's incredible," Father Martin said. "As soon as you try to bring these people anything, people try to stop you, to take it away. Why?"

Alex had no answer. To the obvious next question of *who* was undercutting the missionaries' work there, there remained no easy answer, either.

Leaving dinner that night, Alex watched a group of men assembled on the edge of the field that was contiguous to the village. The men were watching their children, teenage boys for the most part, compete in a soccer game in the dying daylight.

Despite the efforts on the missionaries, everyone she saw was destined for a life of poverty. These men would work in the distant fields, swelter in the sunshine and the humidity, and barely get by day to day, grateful for any small crumbs from life's table.

She went to bed fitfully that night. Very early the next morning, in the midst of a pleasant dream, she awoke to the staccato sound of gunfire.

The little village of Barranco Lajoya was under attack.

SEVENTY

Alex threw off the mosquito netting that covered her and sprang to her feet. She grabbed her gun belt, which had both her Beretta and her knife hitched to it. She strapped it over her hiking shorts. She shoved her feet into her boots without bothering with socks and went quickly to the window of her hut.

It was just past dawn. She could hear a terrible commotion but couldn't see it. There was sporadic gunfire and people screaming. She saw people of the village running in every direction, fleeing into the woods.

She drew her Beretta. Then she moved quickly to her door, opened it slightly, saw that it was safe to leave, and stepped out. The commotion was coming from the center of the village. She headed toward it, her weapon aloft, moving along the wall of the church.

Screaming became louder. Voices pleading. People fleeing past her. She reached the corner and looked around it.

At first she thought that a gang of bandits had invaded. When she looked closer, a greater fear coursed through her. These were soldiers of some paramilitary organization, some local militia, she guessed. Maybe they were the men the girls had seen on the mountain. There was no way of knowing.

There must have been a dozen of them, just that Alex could see. Everything was happening too fast, too chaotically. It was Kiev all over again, except this time in Spanish, in the heat, and just after dawn.

More shouts and screams. The gunmen wore masks. They fired rifles and pistols into the air. They were using clubs and huge sledgehammers to strike at houses and structures. Residents, some of them barely clad, fled into the woods around the village.

Then she saw some of the gunmen drag Father Martin and his family out of their residence. Father Martin's hands were raised and he looked terrified. He was pleading with the invaders. They kept yelling at him.

"¿Dónde está?" their leader screamed to Father Martin. *"¿Dónde? ¿Dónde? ¿Dónde?"*

Where, where, where? They wanted to know where something was. Something they wanted. They threw Father Martin to the ground. He shook his head. Whatever the secret was, he wasn't telling. They let his family flee.

They meant to kill him.

A local boy came out of a hut with a rifle to defend the priest, and the attackers shot him from two different directions. When a woman came to the door behind him, his mother, she too was dropped by gunfire.

Alex watched transfixed, her horror so deep that she could barely assimilate what was happening. But she pinpointed the gunmen who had shot the boy and his mother.

Reflexively, she knelt down low into a firing position, partially concealed by the wall. In a fury, she fired at one of the men who had shot the boy and his mother.

She saw the weapon fly from the man's hands. The man clutched his chest and went to a knee, stunned.

Alex had hit him in the middle of his gut. She turned her pistol toward the other gunman, who had suddenly realized they were under fire. Alex fired two shots at him. The first one spun him, the second one dropped him.

Then she heard another popping sound. Then a second. Father Martin lay motionless on the ground. His killer stood over him. Then he turned toward Alex.

Alex stood and, against all logic, in a blind rage, stepped out from cover. She held her Beretta forward, steadied it and fired twice. The first shot hit Father Martin's killer in the upper chest, the second hit him full in the face. Then she heard a bullet whistle past her and smack into the stucco of the church.

She stepped back under cover. She knew the rest of the invading party would now come for her. Some of them would circle the church and try to come up behind her.

Before they could, she fled. She ran at full speed past her cottage and into heavy foliage beyond, a sickening horror still in her gut, but an instinct for survival pushing her onward. She reached the heavy foliage beyond the back of the church. She kept herself low as she ran in a zigzag pattern, pushing and pulling her way through the brush. Brambles and small branches struck at her bare legs, scratching her badly.

She kept going. Occasional shots came after her.

She stopped behind a tree. She could see slightly through a clearing. She needed to slow down her pursuers. She saw one gunman who had a teenage girl from the village by the arm. He was about forty yards away. Then she realized it was Paulina he was threatening.

Alex raised her Beretta. It was a risky shot, almost worthy of a sniper with a pistol, but she could hold her hands steady and shoot from cover.

She took the shot. She hit him full in the chest. She watched him reel backward and go down. She saw Paulina flee. Alex put a second bullet into him for good measure.

Alex knew that she would be followed. She ran deeper into the jungle. A barrage of bullets from automatic weapons ripped through the brush on different sides of her. One shot, the closest, tore into the bark of a tree about ten feet away.

But she knew they were firing wildly now. She kept herself low, her heart pounding, her adrenaline racing, her heart in her throat.

She didn't return fire. Her only instinct was to get as far into the jungle as possible, change directions, and escape.

She kept moving. In the distance, she could hear them coming after her.

SEVENTY-ONE

Lt. Rizzo had had a horrid week.

First, Mimi, his favorite intern and Sailor Moon girl, had changed her course of studies at the university. Because of this, her schedule at the university had changed. She had signed up for a series of art and design courses that conflicted with her internship with the city police department. Hence, she had resigned her position with the Roman police. The irony of all this was that she and her new boyfriend, Enrico, were inseparable in their off hours.

An even worse disaster had occurred with Sophie. Rizzo might have known that no long-term good could come from her working at one of those chic designer clothing places on the via Condotti. Flouncing around in there each day, modeling the chic dresses, designer jeans, sheer blouses, and snug miniskirts, it was a matter of time before the wrong pair of male eyes settled upon her.

In this case, the wrong pair of eyes belonged to an American pop singer who went by the stage name of Billy-O. He was a guy in his thirties who had limited musical range but was a first-class piece of eye candy. His music producers in Los Angeles pushed him heavily and were currently getting him into some films. They had even hired a hack Hollywood TV writer to usher in a new script for him.

Thus Billy-O's income resembled the GNP of a small hot country, even though he personally had more fun than a small hot country. In his public life, he played the part of a white working-class rocker-rapper up against the establishment, and his music matched that image. The truth was, he was a spoiled kid from the New York suburbs. Sammy Newman was his real name. He was a young man who dragged three broken marriages behind him, dozens of affairs, and a couple of attaché cases filled with lawsuits. But he still was one of the great lotharios of his generation. The man was a known bad boy; no one ever came out of a relationship with him better off than they'd gone in. But women couldn't resist him. Sophie was his latest. They had met in the clothing shop, and now she had taken a few vacation days to spend a long weekend with *il cretino*, as Rizzo thought of him, in Monte Carlo.

So much for the lot of a career policeman when some Hollywood music Adonis rolled into Rome and started to flash a limitless bankroll.

All of this left Rizzo in a thoroughly rotten mood as summer finally arrived in Rome and the month of July progressed. It also gave him more than a bit of a rotten attitude. So when his captain phoned him on a Monday in the middle of the month and requested that he assemble all the papers and documents he had on the two abandoned murder cases, he met the request with a subservient growl. Rizzo was to assemble all his information and prepare for a meeting with some law-enforcement agents of another nation.

When he learned through the grapevine that the agents he would meet with were American, he pondered the possibilities and complications before him.

He wondered, in his best passive-aggressive manner, how he could make the most of what was obviously a wonderful opportunity.

He looked at the calendar. Two weeks till retirement. Well, he would do some administrative finagling and maybe push back retirement for another sixty days. There were some strings that needed to be pulled, some contacts who needed to take care of a few things. The Roman police were understaffed right now anyway. No one would mind much if he remained on to take care of some pressing open cases.

Mimi and Enrico, he mused to himself as he assembled everything on the four murders. Sophie and Billy-O. What was the world coming to?

SEVENTY-TWO

Alex lay perfectly still in the underbrush, feeling the insects in a cloud around her face, feeling the humidity of the jungle drench her clothing. She had maintained her position for several hours.

She lay low on her right side against a small embankment of rocks, a tangle of branches and leaves pulled over her to conceal her. Her bare legs extended into the tall grass for cover. She was dripping with sweat, lying on her side, listening carefully to hear if any of the enemy assassins were near. Twice they had passed within ten feet of her. She had kept her pistol raised and even had one of the men in her sights. But they hadn't seen her. So she hadn't betrayed her position by firing.

She tried to separate the sounds of the jungle from the sounds of human pursuers. She listened for voices. She heard none. She had put the weapon away. Then she heard movement somewhere.

She moved her hand to her weapon and again pulled the Beretta from her holster. She positioned the weapon close to her, leaning on one elbow, keeping both hands on the gun. Her heart started to race again. Almost every sound seemed like the enemy. Who were these people and why would they have attacked peaceful missionaries and an isolated village? Yet in the forefront of her mind, all she could think of was her own survival.

At this point, it was defend yourself or be killed.

Just like Kiev.

She wished the world weren't like this, but it was. Nervous tic time again. As she leaned on one elbow, one hand strayed from the pistol and went to her neck. Instead of finding the little gold cross that she had felt there for twenty years, she found the pendant Paulina had made for her. She messaged it. It felt cool and reassuring in her hand. Somehow it made her feel better.

She could still hear her own heart pounding. She tried to pace her breathing to let things settle. The underbrush that concealed her was settling around her. Her bare legs stung where they had picked up some scrapes and small cuts. She would soon have to clean the cuts and apply a strong disinfectant, but how?

Blood poisoning in this part of the world could be instant and horrific. It could paralyze a man or woman with a systemic infection within two or three days. It could kill a person in four. She would need water soon, too. Her mouth was parched. She knew where the streams sliced through the jungle, but it would have to be safe before she could move. No point taking a bullet in the back, even though water meant survival.

She reckoned that she was positioned about five hundred yards from the village. She had carefully noted the position of the sun as she had moved to one point of concealment after another, and she also had her compass.

She hatched out a plan. She would move at dusk, she reasoned, and try to find water. Then she would hide again overnight and try to creep back toward the village near dawn. She guessed that the raid on the village was a hit and run. But she was guessing.

Something in the tall grass shifted, underbrush she guessed, near the lower part of her body. Whatever it was, it pressed against her leg.

Look out for tarantulas, she reminded herself. She moved her legs slightly. Well, too big for a giant spider. It wasn't small and crawly whatever was pressing against her. It felt like a branch or a vine.

Her heart settled slightly. She heard no voices pursuing, though she knew her pursuers would be quiet. Her heart settled more.

Time passed interminably. The tedium alone, combined with the building thirst, was enough to kill a woman.

Then she felt the pressure on her leg. The "vine" was moving, sliding. Then she felt it slide itself across her legs. At the same time she heard a distinctive rattle. The snake was already upon her bare skin, exploring.

Every instinct within her told her to jerk her leg away. But simultaneously, she knew she was dead if she moved. The snake had already entwined her. If she budged, it would strike. If it struck, she was dead.

The sweat rolled off her with a new fury. She heard the rattle again and felt the body of the rattlesnake coiled itself in a tightening grip around her leg. She had a knife but couldn't reach for it.

She moved her head slowly. The serpent was firmly around her calf now and working its way up her leg. Then it was past the knee. Then it was on her thigh a few inches above her right knee.

If she fired a shot, she would draw the attention of her attackers. But at least she would be alive to fight. She would have to kill the snake within the next minute before it sank its fangs into the flesh of her bare thigh.

She couldn't even see it yet. The tall grass hid it. She moved her gun slowly, positioning its nose in the direction of the snake. She would have one shot to try to save her life, but if the bullet from her own gun blew her foot off, that would be akin to a death sentence out here, too.

A prayer kept repeating itself in her mind.

Oh, my Lord. Oh, my Lord. Protect me now if you ever have before!

She was in tall grass so thick that she couldn't see past her waist. A little breeze rustled the grass. The snake was still climbing her, staking her out, claiming her.

Alex guessed it might be four feet long because it was coiled around her from her ankle till past her knee, and she couldn't feel the head or neck of it.

Then the grass moved slightly, and like a small dark ghost emerging from a pale green cloud, the head of the snake poked through, skin glimmering with scales, its small black eyes alive with menace, small black bifurcated tongue flickering in and out.

The rattler was a creature of horror and beauty at the same time. The head was silvery gray, and a row of diamond shaped markings with brown centers outlined in yellow spanned downward from the head to the body. Beyond it, as the grass moved and the snake advanced toward her upper body, its head lifted, Alex could see the tail, lightly striped with brown and yellow.

She gazed at its eyes, elliptical pupils centered by black irises. For a moment it opened its mouth slightly, showing the venomous fangs that could kill her as easily as a jungle fighter's bullet.

The head was now about eighteen inches away from the nose of her pistol. It seemed to be looking her right in the eye, almost freezing her.

The head continued forward. In the back of her mind, she suspected that it was instinctively going for her throat.

Closer.

It was now about a foot from the nose of her gun.

She figured she had one shot. Maybe two if the first one wasn't a clean hit.

She steadied her wrists as best she could. There would be a kickback to the pistol, enough so that a second shot would be questionable.

The snake moved forward another inch or two, exploring. Then it stopped.

The tongue continued to flick.

She knew. It was ready to strike at her flesh, either her arm or her neck.

Now or never.

The heat pounded her, and the sweat rolled off her so furiously that she felt as if a fat person were lying on top of her.

A final prayer and . . .

Now! She pulled the trigger.

The weapon erupted with a powerful bang.

The impact upon the snake's head was instantaneous. The bullet took the snake's head off with precision, smashing it into oblivion, leaving a writhing decapitated creature spasming and unraveling on her, spilling its reddish yellow guts onto her clothing. The rest of the snake's upper body, the part that wasn't coiled around her, flew backward toward the grass, the neck oozing with blood and intestines.

Alex felt the snake's body go limp around her leg.

She felt a deep sickness in her stomach and wanted to vomit. But she fought back. She reached through the grass and grabbed the remains of the carcass where it was wrapped around her leg. She pulled it off her and flung it away.

She slid forward.

Cautiously, she got to her feet. Both her legs were red and cross hatched from scrapes. She gasped for her breath, breathing hard, the gun still in her hand at her side. She looked in every direction and saw no enemy. Maybe they had departed already. Many people had fled into the jungle, perhaps the attackers had given up and departed. She prayed that was the case.

She guessed the direction of one of the streams. She went five minutes through some heavy foliage, then heard the water. She reasoned that she was about three hundred yards downstream from where the women of Barranco Latoya were used to bathing.

The water there would be safe, she reasoned. And it might be a terrain she knew better than the attackers.

She found the stream. She holstered her gun. She picked a secluded place and removed her shoes and socks. She waded in and drank. Never had water felt so good, satisfied so deeply. She washed the cuts and scrapes on her legs. The abrasions stung but the water soothed. She caught her breath. Then she washed her arms and her face.

She kept up her vigil. She saw no one else. No raiders, no survivors from the village. She wondered if she should creep closer to the village but reasoned that if any gunmen had been left behind, that's what they would be looking for her to do. So she didn't. She would maintain her plan to return at the next dawn.

She found some wild roots and berries that she knew to be edible. She had enough nourishment to sustain her. She was still in shock over what had happened, what she had seen, at having been under fire. But she was alive, rallying her spirit and still ready to fight back.

Her hand went to the stone at her neck again, then left.

She moved another hundred yards downstream, measuring the distance with paces, using the position of the sun to verify her direction. She then tailed off into the woods. She found a vantage point and settled in again. She covered herself with leaves and branches and kept her back to a rocky slope.

More time went by. An intense exhaustion began to grip her, then possessed her completely. She closed her eyes, unable to keep them open. Her pistol was in her hand, on her lap. It must have been four in the afternoon when she drifted off.

She opened her eyes again a few hours later. There was still some daylight and some of her camouflage had been pulled away.

She blinked awake, startled, as someone grabbed the pistol from her. The dying sunlight of the day cast severe shadows among the trees. But she did see the large heavy silhouettes of three men, all in military green and brown camouflage-style uniforms, with beige coiled braids on the right side. All three had automatic rifles.

One of the rifles was pointed straight at her face, inches away. A second man poked her in the shoulder with the nose of his rifle. The third one held her Beretta. He tucked it into his belt. The leader appeared to be about thirty. The two younger men were barely out of their teens. They stared at her as if she had arrived from outer space.

"*¡Levántese!*" the rifleman ordered. Get up.

Slowly, raising her hands in the air in surrender, she stood.

SEVENTY-THREE

"*¿Quién es?*" one of them asked. Who are you?

She assessed quickly. On their chests they wore nameplates, on their lapels and shoulders, they wore ranks. Militias didn't do that. On their heads, they wore the floppy hats of regular army units assigned to the mountains.

They were soldiers of the Venezuelan army. The leader was a trim *comandante* named Ramírez, equivalent to a major. His two men appeared to be privates.

The leader held her at gunpoint and one of the others took her knife away. Then they started patting her down, a frisk and a grope at the same time. Across her body, across her breasts, between her legs. She cringed and pushed back. In return, the groper held her arm tightly, shook her and threatened her with worse if she didn't cooperate.

She refused to answer them.

The indignities continued. One of the men pushed his hand within her T-shirt and continued to explore. She pulled back angrily, throwing an elbow.

"*¡Párense!*" she snapped. Stop! "*Soy norteamericana,*" she said. "I was in the village when it was raided. I fled."

Ramírez looked her in the eye. The other two studied her up and down.

"*¿Cuál pueblito?*" the comandante asked. What village?

"Barranco Lajoya."

They looked at each other.

"Barranco Lajoya was destroyed," he said in Spanish. "There was a massacre."

She felt her spirits plummet, her heart going with them. Her friends. The missionaries. More than ever she was conscious of the pendant she wore around her neck. But was it doing anything, protecting anyone? Where was God when she needed God?

"How bad was it? The massacre?" she asked.

"If you're an American, why is your Spanish so good?" Ramírez asked, ignoring the question. "Americans don't speak Spanish without an accent."

"My mother was *mexicana*. What happened to the village? I was with the missionaries. How bad was the attack?"

The soldiers relaxed very slightly. "Prove that you're American," the leader said.

She reached slowly to the side pocket of her shorts. She pulled out her passport and handed it to them.

One of the younger soldiers took it and gave it to the major. They kept their guns trained on her. She had no chance to run, she knew. She would have been cut down within a few feet if they chose to kill her.

Major Ramírez looked at the passport and looked at her. Then he examined the passport again and stared at Alex's face. He closed the passport and handed it back to her. He told his private to return her weapons.

"*Venga con nosotros,*" the captain said. Come with us. We're very sorry.

They led her through several thickets, the young soldiers hacking their way with machetes. They came to a path and fell in with other soldiers. Other people from the village had been rounded up too. The sad tragic trek through the forest took half an hour. Then they came to a clearing and then what remained of Barranco Lajoya.

Nothing in her experience could have prepared Alex for what she saw, not even the violence and obscenities from her experience in Ukraine.

There were bodies still lying on the ground, men and women and children, awaiting body bags. The straw roofs of several buildings had been torn off, cement and concrete buildings had been smashed. The raiding party had shown no mercy. Walls were down on almost all buildings, the generator had been smashed into oblivion, and the muddy unpaved streets of the town were strewn with the shattered remnants of the buildings. The village looked as if it had been bombed.

The soldiers led Alex into a small littered clearing behind another hut, and there on the floor were several sheets and canvas coverings. It was a makeshift morgue. There were so many bodies that Alex didn't think to count them.

Major Ramírez removed his hat and led Alex to a viewing area, which was no different from any other area except it was a small cleared patch of ground.

The *comandante* looked at her with sorrow in his eyes. Then he reached down to one of the sheets.

She braced herself. Ramírez lifted the first of several gray blankets so that she could see. Against her will, against all the training she had received at the FBI Academy, against even the horror of what she had witnessed in Kiev, she gasped and retched.

On the ground were the bullet smashed corpses of the six missionaries who had served in this village, four men and two women. These were the people she had known personally and worked with. Their bodies were caked in blood, their limbs and heads twisted at impossible angles and folded back together.

Some of their faces had been hammered into pulp by the force of the bullets. One woman's head, the one closest to Alex, had star fractures in both eyes and a lower jaw blown off. One man's upper torso had been hit by so many bullets that the soldiers had had to tie it closed with rope and canvas.

The executions, she could tell, had taken place at close range and without the slightest sign of mercy. This was the earthly reward that these kind people had received for trying to bring some good to this small tough patch of the world.

Alex stared at the obscenity before her. She wondered: had the invaders come for the missionaries? Or could she have been the ultimate target? But if the raiders had known she was among them, why had she been the only foreigner to defend herself and to have escaped?

Plenty of questions. No answers.

"*Ya está bien*," she said softly to Ramírez. "*Más que suficiente*." More than enough. Enough for the moment. Enough for a lifetime.

Ramírez gave a terse signal to his soldiers. They covered the bodies again. Alex turned away and left the room. A few feet away, she sat down on the ground, too shocked to even cry. Insects buzzed around her and the heat was relentless. She no longer cared.

On the morning of the next day, she oversaw the simple funerals of the people of the village. A military chaplain presided. The dead were interred beneath wooden crosses on a mountainside that overlooked the valley. The missionaries who had lived with them were buried with them and, presumably, would remain with them for eternity. How long, Alex wondered, would the ghosts of those slain haunt this place?

That afternoon, Alex watched as Venezuelan Red Cross workers came in and led a long march of survivors down the mountainside to waiting vans. The village was no more. The survivors were to be relocated.

That same evening, Major Ramírez appeared and spoke to her. "I have my further orders," he said. "You are to leave the country immediately."

"It's not like I was planning to stay after what happened," she said sullenly.

"Your contact will find you in Caracas," he said.

"What contact?" she demanded.

"I only know my instructions," he said, "and I've just related them to you." He paused. "And if I were you," he said, "I would leave quickly, before the government of Venezuela changes its mind."

That evening before sunset, she returned to La Paragua and flew back to Caracas by army helicopter. Three soldiers accompanied her, obviously under orders, saying nothing, only staring. The personal items she had left at the hotel had been safely stored for her. She retrieved them easily upon her return to Caracas.

The horrors of Barranco Lajoya hung heavily on her. She phoned Joseph Collins in New York with the intention of relating what had happened. But word had already reached him. He inquired only about her safety. She assured him that the Venezuelan army had treated her properly.

They agreed to meet in New York as soon as possible. Then, that evening, she found a Methodist church not far from her hotel and spent time in prayer and meditation — seeking answers and guidance and not finding much of either — until an elderly pastor appeared and closed the doors to the church at midnight.

SEVENTY-FOUR

Alex walked the few blocks back to her hotel from the church.
The blocks were quiet and shadowy, South American cities being lit at night nowhere as well as North American ones. She had her Beretta with her and examined every shadow as she approached it.

She returned safely to her hotel. But in her room, there was a man waiting, a visitor. She was not altogether shocked to see him. She had almost been expecting his reappearance. In the darkest corners of her mind, things were starting to fall into place, no matter how much she wished to reject the meaning of recent events.

"I wouldn't get too comfortable here," the visitor said, standing as she entered her own room. "We have a long trip ahead of us."

"Go to hell, Michael!" She glared at him and suppressed an even more violent and profane run of obscenities.

"No, really," Michael Cerny said evenly. "I know what you've been through. I know what you're thinking. But we're going to iron everything out by the end of the day."

"What I'm thinking is that there's a black cloud following me around. And you're it. I ought to shoot you."

"That doesn't sound very Christian to me," he said, "nor very charitable."

"Then I ought to shoot you twice," she said.

"Let's go," Cerny said. "We're on our way to Paris."

"Not a chance!" she answered.

"You might want to change your mind," he said. "Don't you realize what the militia attack on Barranco Lajoya was about?"

"No, I don't," she answered. "Mr. Collins sent me there to troubleshoot. To find out what someone had against these people. So why don't you tell me? Then we'll both know!"

"The attack on the village had nothing to do with the village itself," he said. "But it was made to look that way. You honestly don't understand what they were after, what they were looking for?"

She could see Father Martin being thrown to the ground again. The insistent voice of his murderer as he stood above him.

¿Dónde, dónde, dónde? Where, where, where?

What had they been seeking?

"It hasn't occurred to you?" he asked.

It had. "They were looking for me," she said.

"You," said Cerny. "The Ukrainian Mafia sent people looking for you. They wish to kill you or kidnap you and take you back to Ukraine."

"*What?*"

"Don't be so surprised. The Ukrainian underworld has a million dollar contract out on your life. They followed you to Venezuela but the people in Barranco Lajoya wouldn't give you up."

Still in shock, she asked, "How could they even have known where I was, the Ukrainians?"

Cerny shrugged. "There are all sorts of theories," he said. "We can discuss them eventually." He paused. "Did you ever discover why the village was being harassed in the first place?"

"All sorts of theories," she said quietly. "Local ranchers. People who want to poach the wood from the forests. Venezuelan nationalists who don't believe the missionaries should "pollute" local culture. The government in Caracas who thinks we're all a bunch of imperialist agents. Plenty of theories and not one that will hold together. Not yet, anyway."

"We're going to New York first," Cerny said. "You'll have an evening to talk to Mr. Collins. That would probably be a good idea. Then we're headed back to Europe."

"I thought I was finished with the Ukrainians. At least for a few years," Alex muttered.

She felt a deep surge of fear inside her. That, and a lack of comprehension. What had she been, other than a bystander, one who lost something precious, her fiancé, and might have lost her own life too, if things had gone any differently. "How could they possibly care about me?" she asked.

"That's what we'd like to know as well. You must have learned something, witnessed something, had access to something in Kiev. All we know is, your life is marked."

She simmered.

"Anyway, you might want to help us get them before they get you," he said. "Federov and his one remaining bodyguard. We're flying Air France to Paris, you and I. Business class if it makes you feel any better."

"I'm not going anywhere other than back to New York," she said. "And I'm not going anywhere with you."

"Alex, don't be foolish," he said. "By this point, you don't have much choice."

This time, as it sank in, she didn't spare him the expletives.

SEVENTY-FIVE

Gian Antonio Rizzo was planning a trip as well. He had reassembled everything he had on the two spiked murder investigations, but as far as his bosses in Rome were concerned, he was warning everyone that he was prepared to be as difficult and obtuse as possible.

"Lousy meddlesome Americans!" he complained to anyone who would listen. "They come in and steal your work time after time. When will it end?"

Rizzo's political distaste for the Americans was beyond discussion. He cursed them profanely whenever he could. He'd gone on and on about it so much that it wasn't that anyone could question it any more; no one even wanted to hear about it.

Then suddenly life's random events broke in his favor, reversing a recent trend. Sophie was back from Monte Carlo, contrite as could be, and asking her policeman to forgive her and take her back. The American actor, Billy-O, Sophie now told him, wasn't much more than a pretty face, wasn't even that much in private, and as a singer could barely hum a tune. Plus he was a financially askew hophead, she told him, traveling with a least a dozen illegal prescriptions in his medicine kit, including a small packet of cannabis and thousands of dollars sewn into the lining of his luggage. Sophie knew since she'd been in his hotel room for two days and saw everything.

"Why are you even telling me this?" Rizzo grumbled, sounding bored and hurt. "To incite me? To make me jealous?"

"I don't know," she answered. "So you know how sorry I am. So you know that I made a bad mistake and that you're a better man than he'll ever be."

"I don't want to know anything about him," Rizzo said, cutting her off with a wave of his hand. "Nothing would make me dislike Americans more than I already do."

There was no disputing that part by anyone who had listened to Rizzo over the last several years. But Sophie would not shut up. There might have been something to those rumors that he, Billy-O, danced at the other end of the ballroom, as the English would say. In fact, Sophie had been treated wretchedly in Monte Carlo and said she wouldn't mind at all if Gian Antonio could pull a few police strings and make life miserable for that Hollywood punk while he was on the continent.

"What can I do?" Rizzo scoffed. "What authority do I have? These Hollywood types have all the money and know all the right people. Who do I know? The minister of justice and he can't stand me."

In fact, Rizzo had a good idea that he might want to get out of town, lie low for a short while. He had some other things to attend to, a side business as it were. His bosses told him that he could take a week off if he wished. He wished. He had the time coming and his juice within the Roman police department was diminishing day by day, even with the recently approved sixty-day extension of his duties.

He thought about the whole situation. Sophie. The actor. The minister. What he could use, he decided, was a good reason for being out of town.

So he asked Sophie if she might want to accompany him on a business trip. He would be busy for much of the time. There was some highly confidential stuff in a neighboring European capital. She would need to let him go there for a few days, then join him. He had some work to accomplish, some people to meet. But thereafter they could get reacquainted, let bygones be bygones, and he might even be able to let the memory of that American musical nuisance fade away.

Sophie took the bait. She said yes.

So a trip to Paris for two was on, Rizzo to go ahead first, Sophie to join him in three days. They would relax and get to know each other again. Billy-O had given an entirely new meaning to the term "one hit wonder."

Rizzo's peers in the police department in Rome all envied him for so flagrantly going off to patch things up with his lady friend in the middle of the week. Some guys had all the luck, as Rod Stewart might have sung.

Meanwhile, Rizzo made a few phone calls to some people he knew. They would arrange for Billy-O to eventually draw the receipt he deserved.

SEVENTY-SIX

Alex and Michael Cerny flew to Miami via American Airlines, then connected to New York. They stayed overnight in the city.

That evening, Alex met with Collins for an hour at his home, giving him her grave in-person account of what had transpired at Barranco Lajoya. She gave him all the photographs and notes she had taken. He listened quietly and seemed overcome by a great sadness.

Then he stood from behind a desk. They were in his study, a room that was high-ceilinged and elegantly furnished. With a stiff walk Collins crossed the room to a wide plate glass window that looked down upon Fifth Avenue. He stared downward for several seconds in silence, as if the view might give him some explanation of the craziness and brutality of the contemporary world.

There was no indication that it did.

The silence continued. There was a sag to Collins' shoulders, one she had not seen before. She wondered what he might be thinking. "Presumably the Ukrainians had no intention to harm Barranco Lajoya before I sent you there," Collins said softly. "So it seems my best of intentions have contributed to a tragedy, a catastrophe. There's blood on my hands."

"No one could have foreseen this, Mr. Collins," she said. "No one."

"Generous of you to say so, Alex," he said, turning back toward her. "But I can draw my own conclusions and I'll have to live with them." He paused. "Call me a foolish old man," he said, "but I feel I will now have a debt to those people from that village for as long as I live. I don't consider the books closed on that place."

"If it's not presumptuous," she said, "I feel much the same way."

"You do?"

"At the appropriate time," Alex said. "I'd like to return. Unfinished business."

An ironic smile crossed his face. "Unfinished business," he said.

"Yes, we agree. You seem drawn to unfinished business, don't you, Alex? Venezuela. Ukraine...."

"That does seem to be the path that's before me right now," she said. "It's not where I thought I'd be right now, but it's where I am."

He nodded.

"I know how that works," he said. "Show me someone for whom that isn't the case, and I'll show you someone who sat back in life and never took chances, never tried to do the right thing. I admire you."

"Thank you, sir."

"Be careful in Ukraine," he said. "I've heard it's a godless place."

"I'll do my best," she said.

"I know that," he answered. "Just while you're doing your best, be careful also." He moved back to his desk. "I have a check for you for your work in South America. I've rounded it up to fifty thousand dollars. Don't protest. Try to find some time to enjoy it and a place to relax with it," he said.

She accepted it in an unmarked envelope, which she wouldn't open till later in the day when she would mail it to her bank in Washington.

"I'll do my best," she said again.

A few minutes later, she was out of his apartment and back down on Fifth Avenue, walking home slowly, enjoying the anonymity that a crowded New York sidewalk always afforded her.

SEVENTY-SEVEN

The next morning, Alex and Michael Cerny were on an Air France flight from New York to Paris. Two hours into the flight, sitting side by side in business class, Cerny took out his Palm Pilot. He applied his fingerprint to the security section and powered it up.

"I want you to read some files," Cerny said. "CIA and NSA stuff. They'll tell you more about why we're going to Paris."

"Full disclosure?" she asked with an edge.

"Call it what you want," Cerny said. "You need to know some backstory."

He handed the Palm Pilot to Alex. She began with a CIA file that was, as much as anything, a continuation of what she had read on Yuri Federov back in January. But it added to her knowledge.

Federov had been on a CIA list for several months as a foreign national in whom the Agency had taken a "special interest." At the same time, Federov had developed a long list of enemies in the underworlds of North America, South America, and Europe. So many, that fear of his enemies had impeded his movements for years. Thus from time to time, Federov had been in the habit of traveling through Europe in the guise of a priest.

But within the last eighteen months, Federov had taken the guise one step further. He had hired a double, a retired actor from the National Theater of Hungary. The double was a friend named Daniel Katzman. Katzman bore a resemblance to him. Hence Katzman traveled as Father Daniel, a Federov decoy-within-a-decoy so that Federov himself could move about the world more freely.

Daniel turned out to be in the role of a lifetime, or, more accurately, the last role of his lifetime. A pair of assassins shot him to death in a French café named *L'etincelle* during the first days of the new year. Alex noted the date. January 2. The French police were still working on the case, the file said, the one of the man in priestly garb shot dead over a cognac and a cigar at a café in the Marais.

From the shooting, a triple riddle posed itself:

Q1: When is a dead priest not really a dead priest?

A1: When the dead Russian mobster is not a Russian mobster either.

Q2: Then when is a dead Russian mobster not really a dead Russian mobster?

A2: When he wasn't even a priest either. He was an actor and a friend of the man who was supposed to be shot.

And then the biggest question of all:

Q3: When is an underworld "hit" not an underworld "hit"?

A3: When neither the victim nor the perps are members of the underworld.

The electronic file ended abruptly. Cerny guided Alex to a second one that discussed a pair of agents who worked for the CIA, and not with great efficiency. Their names were Peter Glick and Edythe Osuna. They were married to each other, or seemed to be, but didn't work at it very hard. They had picked up a trail that they felt belonged to Federov by monitoring flights from Kiev to the capitals of Western Europe, notably London, Paris, Madrid, and Geneva, places where Federov either had business interests, money stashed, or both.

They tracked their target to Paris and asked for permission from Langley to proceed with an "intervention." The request went all the way up to cabinet level. Permission was granted. They acted. Next thing anyone knew, the secure faxes and phone lines were exploding between Langley and Paris and Langley and Rome.

Edythe and Peter fled to Madrid after Paris, then Rome. Yet for people who should have been disappearing into the background, they were reckless, physically incapable of keeping a low profile. Nor were they upstanding citizens. They moved in a shadowy world of illegal gun dealers, smugglers, swindlers, sexual merchants, and con artists. They frequented nightclubs in Paris and Rome where couples paired off with strangers. They lived on the social and political edge of the world.

They picked up a trail for Federov. But they picked up the wrong trail, one that was set out as a trap.

As soon as Alex saw those names, a bell rang within her. Her mind flashed back to the club in Kiev, her quasi-sober conversation with Federov, as well as the suggestive questions posed by her.

Federov, in Russian: "Have you ever heard of a pair of Americans named Peter Glick and Edythe Osuna?"

Alex: "New names on me. Should I know them?"

Federov: Maybe. They are involved in this visit by your president."

Alex: "Part of the delegation?"

Her favorite gangster: "No. They're a pair of American spies. They were recently retired."

So the tale that followed made sense. Edythe and Peter established a procedure for a hit on Federov in Paris. They quickly wired Washington and Langley for approval. No one ever asked them if they were sure their target was who they thought it was. Accuracy of that sort was the least of the details attended to. Like much CIA intelligence over the last decade, it wasn't just faulty, it had so many holes in it that a truck could have driven through it with its doors open.

Peter and Edythe were known in security circles in Europe and known by the underworld also. They were recognized to be Western operatives, most likely American.

After the mistaken killing in Paris, they were ripe for a setup.

Alex continued to read.

The setup came when Federov wanted to strike back. First, he had set up his old friend Katzman possibly to be whacked in his place. Then he took it as a personal insult that Katzman had been so victimized.

From his own experiences in European nightlife, Federov knew a young woman for the job. One night in Rome, Peter and Edythe met a young woman named Lana Bassoni who lived in Rome. She was very pretty, a sometime model and sometime artist's model. But she was married to a musician who wasn't going anywhere. There was also another detail about Lana that Peter and Edythe would never had guessed until it was too late. She had once worked for Federov at one of the after-hours mob joints he ran in New York. She had been a hostess-plus-a-bit-more, depending how much a client had to spend and what a client wanted. It all made sense.

The meeting at the club in Rome — Lana, Peter, and Edythe — was made to look like a coincidence. But it was anything but. About an hour after meeting, Peter and Edythe disappeared for a while. The next morning, Lana did too.

Alex looked up from the Palm Pilot. "I assume there's more," she said to Cerny.

"Of course," he said. "Short and sweet. Do you want to read it in English or Italian?"

"Doesn't matter," she said. "Give me both in case I sense something wrong with the translations."

"Smart girl," he said. "That's why you're here."

She took back the Palm Pilot. "If I were *really* smart, I *wouldn't* be here."

She opened the final files. There were a pair of homicide reports from the Roman newspapers from January, including that of a musician and his girlfriend found dead in their flat in Rome. Then some follow-ups from several weeks later. The final entry had to do with a pair of bodies found in the sandy bogs near Villa di Plinio. Two bodies had been found, not yet identified.

The file ended, as did the information Cerny accessed in his Pilot. He took the device back and tucked it away.

"Well?" he asked.

"Well what?"

"Show me that lightning intellect," he said. "What do you make of all that?"

"Tie it together, you mean?"

"If you can."

"But you know the correct answers already?" she said.

"I know answers that I believe to be correct," he said. "There's a difference. So put your thesis to me, and I'll let you know if you're in the right line of work or not."

"I'll give you a scenario that works," she said. "Just as it came to me as I was reading."

"Please do," Cerny answered above the drone of the aircraft's engines.

"First off, someone in Washington was dumb enough to order a hit on Federov. Someone wanted him killed, for whatever reason."

"I could argue that by saying we don't do things like that."

"And I'd argue back that I know that you do, same as we never used to employ torture until we got caught doing it."

"Keep going."

"Peter and Edythe had the assignment to hit Federov. But they blew it and whacked his double, his imposter, instead. Since his double was his pal, Federov was pretty angry. He hit back. He had his moll Lena set up Peter and Edythe in Rome. My guess is they got hit by some Ukrainian gunmen that night on the via Trafficante. Do I know the principals?" Alex asked. "I'm guessing I do."

"Twitchy Eye, that's Anatoli," Cerny said. "Then there's Non-twitchy Eye, which is Kaspar."

"And they killed Lana, why?" Alex asked. "To eradicate any links back to them? Keep her from ever talking?"

"It appears that way," Cerny said.

"Federov ordered it?"

"The Ukrainians are not always so well disciplined. Anatoli and Kaspar could have been acting on their own when they took Lena out.

"Lena's boyfriend? Collateral damage?" she asked.

"Apparently. Tough for him," Cerny said. "But that completed the cycle of four deaths in twelve hours."

Alex hit the end of her files. She looked up. Cerny was looking at her.

"So," she said. "If I mentioned something called 'Operation Chuck and Susan' to you, presumably you'd know what I was talking about."

"What do you want to know?"

"I already know," she said. "Operation Chuck and Susan. My computer crashed when I tried to access that file. And it was related to Kiev. My guess is that Chuck and Susan were Peter and Edythe. And you were trying to keep it from me for as long as possible that you wanted to kill Federov. Who knows? Maybe he didn't lift a finger to stop the attack on the president because he felt the United States kept trying to kill him."

"We need to take him out," Cerny said. "For all the reasons you know, plus the ones that I know, plus probably several more that neither of us know. Is that sufficient?"

"If we know all this, why are we going to Europe?"

"To put the final pieces in place," he said, "and to finally eliminate Federov. As long as he's alive, he's a threat to you and to the United States."

"What sort of threat to me?" she asked.

"For starters, he wants you dead."

She thought about it. "I'm not sure I believe that," she said.

"What are you saying? You didn't see what happened in Venezuela?"

"I saw what happened," she answered angrily. "For God's sake, I was there, remember? I'm just not sure I'm buying that Federov was behind it."

Cerny rolled his eyes. "You're telling me that you know more than we do?"

"Maybe I do."

"Don't count on it."

"I know how to judge a man. One of those first RPGs in Kiev hit right where I had been standing. Federov moved me away from that place."

"Proof that he knew there was going to be an attack."

"Everyone in the city knew of the possibility of an attack!" she snapped back. "If anyone in authority had had any common sense, the president would have skipped the memorial, citing security considerations. And then the president would have gotten out of the country as fast as possible. But I'm just an underling. I don't plan these things. I had no opinion worth hearing at the time, right?"

"Sounds like I'm hearing one now," he said.

"Yeah. You are."

She handed the Palm Pilot back to him. He pressed his finger to its security patch, let it read his fingerprint, and shut it down.

"When we get to Paris," he said an hour later, "we'll deal with this. We have a meeting the day after arrival. One of our local people who's familiar with the case."

"What sort of 'local people'?" she asked, fatigue in her voice. "Who is he?"

"You'll like him," Cerny answered, without giving a name. "He's embedded with one of the European police agencies."

"CIA?" she asked.

"Naturally."

"French?"

"No," Cerny said. "As a matter of fact, he's Italian."

SEVENTY-EIGHT

Lt. Rizzo was the first to arrive, dressed sharply in a new suit, his hardcopy files under his arm.

The meeting was in the United States embassy in Paris just off the Place de la Concorde, in a secure room on the third floor. Cerny arrived with Alex. They took seats at a small conference table. A third man there was Mark McKinnon, who was the CIA station chief in Rome. He had made the trip separately from Rizzo so they would not be seen together. They had, in fact, not seen each other in person since talking over a glass of wine at the dark San Christoforo bar in the Trastevere neighborhood in Rome.

Cerny handled the introductions. An embassy observer was present also, a young man fluent in English, French, and Italian.

"Signor Rizzo has been with the Roman police for twenty-two years," Michael Cerny said to Alex. They spoke English. "Seventeen on the *brigata omicidia*."

"Rough work," Alex allowed.

"Gian Antonio has been a CIA asset for at last the last fifteen of those years," McKinnon added. "High quality material, almost always accurate."

"Thank you, Michael," Rizzo said in perfect English. "Almost?" he laughed.

"No one's perfect," Mark McKinnon said. "Not in our line of work."

Cerny looked to Alex. "I brought Ms. LaDuca up to speed on the flight over, vis-à-vis the two murder investigations in Rome," Cerny said. "In terms of Federov and his bodyguards, where are we now?"

McKinnon opened a file and slid a photograph across the table to Alex. "Recognize this guy?" he asked.

She glanced at it. "That's one of the men who came to the embassy in Ukraine with Federov," she said.

"He's one of Federov's bodyguards," McKinnon said. "He's actually the remaining one."

"Remaining?" she asked.

"The other one is currently deceased," McKinnon said. "He had an accident in his home in London. Fell and hit his head."

She shuddered.

"Yeah, right," she said. "Careless of him." She returned the photo. "That's definitely the man, right? In the photo?" McKinnon asked. "From Kiev."

"That's him."

McKinnon placed the photograph back in the file. "He's in Paris right now," he said. "His name is Kaspar Rodzienko. Ukrainian-born Russian. It's our feeling that he and his boss were instrumental in the attacks on the president in Kiev. We'd like to wrap him up as quickly as possible. For that, we need bait for him to come forward."

"And that would be me," she assumed evenly. "The target for Comrade Kaspar."

"That would be you," McKinnon said.

"We'd rather get him here in Europe than have him find his way into the US and come after you there," Cerny said.

Alex looked at the three men at the table, plus the observer, and gave them an ironic shake of the head. "What are you asking me to do now?" she asked.

McKinnon looked to Rizzo.

"We have some informers among the Ukrainians in the local underworld," he said. "We have the ability to let Kaspar know you're in Paris. We've already done that. The information he received indicated that you're on a trade mission for the Treasury Department. We have a safe apartment for you to stay in. Near rue Mazarine. Fine neighborhood, about a two-minute walk to the river. We'd set a security ring around you. When he comes looking for you, we hit him."

"So you've made me a target," she said. "Again."

Silence around the room. "Not much we can do about it at this point, LaDuca," McKinnon said. "You'll be compensated well for this."

"Well or posthumously?" she asked, her displeasure growing.

"Better to get him on our terms rather than his own," Cerny said.

"We think he's here for maybe two more days. If he knows you're here and where you might be found, he'll come into our view. Then we strike."

"What about Federov?" she asked.

"We have no idea where he is now. He's kept a low profile since Kiev. We can't account for how many passports he might have."

"Or what names they're under," McKinnon added.

In her mind, she was putting it together. "The date of the 'hit' in Paris, when someone was killed by our people under a false identity. Wasn't that January second?"

Cerny answered. "Yes, it was."

"And the file came to me four days later in Washington," she said. "So that was the start of your next attempt to get Federov?"

Cerny again. "You could call it that."

"Then six weeks later, the president is in Kiev, I'm supposed to keep tabs on Federov, and we're trying to look like we're negotiating a peace with him. And you guys are looking for new ways to hit him, but he beats you and takes a shot at the president instead. Lucky for you he missed."

"Well," Cerny said, "you know what they say. If the shoe fits, wear it."

Alex considered her part in the near endgame, that of the bait in a trap. "And my alternative is?" Alex asked.

"As we said, wait for months, years. You never know where he'll turn up."

Cerny, McKinnon, and Rizzo escorted Alex to her lodging, which was a small two-room apartment on the rue Guénégaud in the sixth *arrondissement*. The apartment was toward the middle of the block in an old building with two huge blue doors at street level. The River Seine was a hundred yards to the north and the intersection with the rue Mazarine a hundred feet to the south.

They went there in the late afternoon. Alex studied the logistics, not a bad idea since her life depended on them. Two flights to walk up, one key to open the door. The door was reinforced from the inside, steel slabs that would bolt all the way across, a steel frame reinforcing the security from within.

There were shutters that would close on the two windows that overlooked the street. No point to be a target from across the street or a rooftop. When Alex inspected them, she saw that they too were reinforced with metal.

She put her foot to the ragged carpet in the apartment to test the floorboards. The wooden floor and steps in the hallway outside had creaked and sung like a choir with every footfall. The floor under the carpet was stable. She could have jumped on it and it wouldn't have given a vibration.

"Concrete?" she asked.

"Above and below."

That didn't protect her from a bomb, but it definitely made one impractical. She checked the rear window. It was barred, though the bars could be unbolted from inside in case of fire. Cerny also explained that there was no access to the building from the roof. No exit from that direction either.

McKinnon gave her a new cell phone, specially designed. Someone on her surveillance team would be on it twenty-four seven. She didn't even have to dial. Just open it and talk. It had a camera and a tracking device. She may have been a target, but she was a high-tech one.

"I'll warn you," Cerny said. "We'd put you in body armor, but then any shooter who detected it would sense the trap and aim for the head. So what good would that do?"

"We think he'll come after you right away, LaDuca," McKinnon said. "Probably tomorrow, maybe even during the day. For whatever reason, there seems to be some urgency in getting you killed."

"I'm flattered," she said with irony. "What in God's name is it they think I know that even I don't know?"

"We have no idea," McKinnon said.

"What if he comes after me tonight?"

"We're ready," Cerny said. "We have backup teams all over the city. Stay in touch by phone and we'll lead you to the nearest help if you need it."

"It doesn't take more than a second or two to fire a bullet," she said.

"But it takes a while to set up a shot on a moving target in a city," McKinnon said. "Kaspar is not on a suicide mission. He wants to hit you and get away. That makes him vulnerable. Even more vulnerable than you since he's not watching for us."

She was to go out to dinner with Lt. Rizzo that evening in Montparnasse at La Coupole, the atmospheric old haunt of Hemingway and the expatriate American writers of the 1920s. He would pick her up by car and drop her off after dinner. Rizzo would be her escort and act as her bodyguard also.

In the evening Cerny introduced her to a Frenchman named Maurice, a lanky Parisian cop who did extracurricular stuff the same way Rizzo did. Maurice was unshaven in a leather jacket and jeans. He didn't seem to be the brightest man she'd ever met.

In any case, Maurice would be posted in the entrance foyer of her building, keeping an eye on whoever went in and out, while another local guy named Jean, whom she met at the same time, would watch the entrance at the restaurant. At the end of their twelve-hour shifts, others would rotate on and off.

"Do I get a weapon to defend myself in case you guys screw up again?" she asked.

Cerny reached to his attaché case. He pulled out a box and handed it to Alex.

She opened it and found a Glock 9 with twenty-one rounds of ammunition, enough for a full clip plus a half dozen for good luck. She hefted it in her hand and looked around the table.

"Looks exactly like mine," she said suspiciously. "The one I own back in Washington." She continued to examine it. "Even has the same little nicks as mine. Imagine that."

"What could make you feel more secure than having your own weapon?"

She looked at them angrily, not surprised. "If I knew you were going to burglarize me, I could have used some clothing changes too."

They weren't sure whether she was joking or not.

"You guys better know what you're doing this time," she said. "I can only be shot at so many times before I get hit."

She clipped the holster to her waist of her skirt on the right side. There seemed no end to what had been put in motion in January.

SEVENTY-NINE

At La Coupole, Alex sat across the table from Lt. Rizzo. The restaurant, which dated from the twenties, was pure art deco, with characteristic light fixtures on the many square pillars that held up the ceiling of the large, not-very-intimate room. Above the light fixtures were paintings that had been done by local artists in exchange for food and, more probably, drink all those decades ago. Alex wondered which, if any, of them had lived full, happy lives pursuing their muse.

She wore a black skirt, cut well above the knee, comfortable and flexible in case she needed to run for her life later. A light rain fell outside and added a gloss to the Boulevard Montparnasse. Against the rain she wore a pair of chic leather boots, which she had bought late that afternoon in a shop across the street from her lodgings. The boots were supple and flexible while still looking sharp.

They spoke Italian. "LaDuca" meant "the duchess" in Italian, Rizzo noted, a quirk he liked. He asked about the origin of her name. She explained about her father. She shied away from other personal information, however, and he did too; one never knew when a listening device had been dropped. But he did speak of his boyhood, growing up in the slums of Rome, learning English from his father who had been in a POW camp and how he had done his own stint in the Italian army. He amused her with a tale of blowing up a bridge in Spain in the 1970s, part of a prearranged NATO training exercise, but no one had warned the Spanish police.

"It all got blamed on the Basques," he said with a snort, following an account of how his brigade of Italians had to hightail it to France in their socks.

In return, she told him about Venezuela and the slaughter in Barranco Lajoya. He listened seriously and offered condolences. They did not discuss Kiev. He knew the details of her loss and stayed away from the subject.

Things were playing out in her mind in three dimensions now. The first was the present, in a nostalgia-laden restaurant on Paris's Left Bank where the relics of eighty years ago — in addition to the painting on the pillars, portraits of Hemingway, Gertrude Stein, Pablo Picasso, Scott and Zelda Fitzgerald, Kiki of Montparnasse, Man Ray, and Foujita — haunted the walls. Amidst this, Jean sat near the door, poised and intent, his eyes fixed on comings and goings.

The second dimension was one step beyond the immediate present, the notion that at any given moment a bullet could find her, putting her into the same earthly blackness that had consumed Robert. For the first time, she *really* considered what death would be like. It occurred to her that she might have just days, hours, or minutes to live.

But beyond that, even as she conversed with Rizzo in the forefront of her mind, her mind played out its own recent memories. This evening had taken on its own madness and it gripped her. She thought of Robert and his funeral, of the chaos in Kiev, and the massacre in Barranco Lajoya, and she thought of the six slain missionaries, Father Martin, and her friends back in Washington who would probably be playing basketball that night.

Then dinner was finished. She was conscious of the Glock she wore on her hip, concealed carefully under a light jacket.

She reminded herself that she had loaded the weapon and even chambered the first round. The Glock had a concealed hammer, but it was there, back and ready to fall and fire the round. All that prevented it doing so was the safety catch, which she could snap to "fire" with her thumb as she drew the weapon. This practice was dangerous, but the second or two needed for the operation of the slide to chamber the first round might make all the difference between — it was best not to think about what came after "between." In her mind she went through the reflexive motions of using it.

She ordered a Caesar salad, while he had a *blanquette de veau*, thus confirming her suspicion that Italians largely lived on veal. He matched her stereotype for stereotype, and neither was completely wrong.

"*Voi americane sempre mangiano delle insalate, perché non vogliono ingrassare,*" he said with a smile. You American women always eat salads because you don't want to get fat. *"Ma è chiarissimo que per Lei non c'è pericolo a proposito di quello"* — but it is clear that you're in no danger of that.

"That's because we do eat salads," she answered with a laugh.

For a moment Alex wondered if he was hitting on her, but from his expression it was simply a compliment, and she felt flattered. Of course, she realized that any compliment of a young woman by an Italian male was at least a potential hit.

It didn't bother her. In some ways, it made her felt normal again. And shortly after, Rizzo began to speak affectionately of his own lady friend, Sophie, who would be joining him in three days.

Coffee, the check, and then they were out the door, leaving. Jean had her back and Rizzo found a taxi.

The driver took them back to the apartment building on the rue Guénéguad.

Rizzo stepped out first and scanned the quiet block.

"Check your telephone," he said to her. "I'll check mine."

They both checked. The devices worked. Then, as they stood there, a shadow moved in a sturdy black Peugeot that was jammed into a parking spot twenty feet from her front door.

In a light rain, a window on the driver's side descended.

Startled, Alex's hand went to her gun.

"Va bene," Rizzo said in Italian. It's okay.

From the driver's seat in the car, Michael Cerny gave Alex a small and almost playful salute. "The block is clear," he said. "You're fine."

"Maurice is inside the building?" she asked.

"Talked to him ten minutes ago," he said.

"And he was alive when he was talking to you?" she needled.

"He sounded like he was," trying to make light of it. "I didn't specifically ask, though."

"Very funny," she said. But she relaxed slightly.

Rizzo gave her an embrace. She walked the rest of the way down the street to her door, tuned into the sound of her own footsteps on the sidewalk.

She stopped, tried to take a sense of the situation, and arrived at the big blue double doors that led into her building.

A nagging instinct told her that all hell was about to break loose. She looked back and saw Cerny give her another wave.

To enter she punched a numeric code on one of those keypads that all Paris apartments now had — the days of the concièrge who lived next to the door and let people in who rang were long gone — and pushed the door open.

Quiet as the grave, she thought as she stepped inside, *and if I'm not careful, only once removed from one.*

EIGHTY

She pushed her way in and the light clicked on. The doors closed behind her. There was coolness to the stairway. She waited a moment and then realized why. Someone had left the window open on the first floor landing, one flight up.

Probably Maurice. But where was Maurice?

She paused for a moment, her senses alert to possible danger. Then she continued to the steps. An open window had allowed some rain to fall inside and the effect was soothing. It had been stuffy earlier in the stairwell.

She started up the steps. The sound of her footsteps echoed on the plaster walls and the wooden stairs. Lord, she was tired. Her brain buzzed with the events of the day.

She arrived on the first floor landing.

The floor was damp from the rain and she made a note to speak to Maurice. She could give him some friendly advice on home maintenance.

Well, no matter. The building was quiet.

Too quiet?

On the landing one flight up, she pushed the window shut and locked it. There was water on the floor. Someone was going to slip. She had been told that Maurice kept towels and mops in the closets on the landing. She decided to do her good deed for the day. She would drop a towel and quickly glide it over the floor with her foot, lest the next resident slip on this mess.

She stepped to the closet.

The door was stuck.

Her gaze gravitated downward. She caught the faint outline of crimson that was flowing from under the closet door.

She yanked the door open. Maurice, or what remained of him, slumped forward from a crouched lying position to a sprawling one. Her eyes riveted on the hole in his head just between the eyes. Then, she quickly took in the two bullet wounds to the chest. The gunshot wounds to the body were probably the first ones, followed by the head wound, which was the *coup de grâce*.

The bullet had passed through his skull and exited from the rear and into the wall, bringing some inevitable blood, fragments of bone, and brain splatter with it. His face was smashed in from the force of the bullet, which was probably point blank. From the size of the hole, it was clear that the bullet had been high powered.

Suddenly, the lights went off. Her first impression was that she had taken too long to climb the stairs and that the lights, as they did in European hallways, had turned off automatically. But then she realized someone had manually cut the power.

Meaning, someone was waiting for her. She had walked into a trap. Her left hand went fast for her gun, snapping the safety catch to "fire."

In the darkness, the door to her own apartment opened one flight above. She heard the heavy footsteps of a man rush outward. Simultaneously, the blue doors down below opened and she heard someone else rush in.

Cerny? Rizzo?

She was in the middle, trapped in the darkness. Was the intruder below her savior or assassin? From above there was a flash and a brutally loud retort. A bullet crashed into the woodwork of the steps a few feet from her. Then there was a second shot at her and then a third.

Her hand whipped upward as she ducked away from where she had stood. She went into a low crouch, pointed her weapon upwards, and pulled the trigger. Either God guided her hand or just plain dumb luck prevailed.

Or maybe it was her years of training, because the agonized profane scream from the top of the stairs, followed by a torrent of obscenity in Russian — not Ukrainian but Russian! — told her that she had hit her target.

Alex heard the man's body slump toward the wall. Then in the darkness she saw the erratic wavering flash of his pistol and heard the ear-splitting "bang" as he fired twice rapidly again and still tried to kill her.

The bullets shattered against the wall above her. One hit several feet above her head. The other passed so close to her right ear that she felt it go by. The impact sprayed powdered wood and concrete from the wall.

She steadied her own weapon. She could see a silhouette in the darkness and fired twice at the midpoint of it. She hit the target, heard the impact of the bullets and then heard the tumbling crashing sound of the man's body on the stairs. All this rose above the sound of other heavy footsteps rushing upward from below.

She shifted her position, standing now. She leaned flat, her back to the wall.

"Rizzo? Cerny?" she asked.

Mistake. The response was the repetitive flash and loud bang of an automatic weapon and more shots impacting against the wall behind her.

She lowered her own weapon, fired toward her second assailant, and scored another hit. She heard a howl of pain and the clunk of his weapon hitting the floor, followed by the heavier thud of his body, followed by groans and cursing.

She heard the weapon rattle across the wooden floor and drop down two or three steps. She moved toward her only possible escape. She raced down the stairs and tried to step past the fallen body. The man who had tried to kill her cursed profanely and grabbed at her. Clearly she had not hit him in a vital spot.

He slashed at her body. With a powerful arm, he brought her down.

She fell hard to a knee. He cursed her in Russian. He had one strong hand on the shoulder of her jacket. His other hand, wet with blood, pushed at her throat. She threw an elbow at him and made contact. But he still fought, cursing in Russian that he would kill her. She could tell that the other hand was grasping for his gun.

She swung downward again with an elbow and smashed at him with the hand that held her gun. Both blows landed hard, catching him on the side of the face, then on the side of the skull. She felt his grip on her weaken. She swung hard again with the hand that held her weapon. It cracked across his forehead.

His grip on her shoulder weakened. She followed with the same elbow crashing downward, pile-driver style, onto the top of his skull.

She fought and pulled away. She struggled to her feet. In the dim light from the outside, she then saw him access his gun. Alex had no choice. She pushed her Glock to the man's chest and pulled the trigger. The bang was enormous, and she could feel the spray of blood as his body tumbled away and sprawled backward.

She felt sickened but kept moving.

She found her way to the door, swung it open, and found the street blocked by another huge man. For an inexplicable second they glared each other in the eye.

"Kaspar," she said, recognizing him from Kiev.

"Alex LaDuca," he said calmly.

Once again, Alex was faster. She brought her knee up and caught him hard between the legs. He bellowed and reached for his weapon. She hit him again, chopped at his hand to freeze it. She knew he had a huge advantage in physical force. If she gave him the slightest chance to overpower her, she was dead. In turn, she knew she had the advantage of speed and surprise: he hadn't expected her to survive the trap inside the building. She kicked him in the shins, then the kneecap. Somehow she thought of Robert and the carnage in Kiev as she was fighting.

Where was Rizzo? Where was Cerny?

Kaspar staggered. He slumped slightly.

She smashed him across the back of the neck, and with all the strength that remained in her, she shoved at him. He staggered backward into a car but rebounded like a tiger. He kicked at her and got lucky, catching her in the wrist, sending her Glock flying from her hand. Her wrist was hit so hard that it felt frozen. Her fingers wouldn't move. Kaspar lunged at her gun. She chopped him hard behind the neck then followed with a kick to the ribs. Momentarily he blocked her access to her own gun.

Then she turned and ran like the devil himself was chasing her.

She dashed toward Cerny's car. And then she saw what had happened. The front windshield had been riddled with bullets, probably from a silencer-equipped automatic. She saw Cerny's body in the front seat, slumped on the wheel, blood all over his skull.

She would have been sick. But there wasn't time. She ran past his car, ran faster than she had run in years. She heard the profane shouting of Kaspar struggling up from the sidewalk behind her.

Something hit a parked car nearby as she fled. She knew it was a bullet, fired by a pistol equipped with a silencer, probably the same one that had dispatched Cerny.

She ducked and wove between parked cars.

In front of her, the rear window exploded on another parked car. It was a good thing that even in trained hands the best handgun was only accurate — in terms of hitting a human sized target — to about seventy yards. Obviously she had inflicted some pain on her assailant; his aim was wildly inaccurate.

She kept low, zigzagged, and wove. At one point she slipped and was thankful that she was wearing boots, otherwise she could have torn up an ankle.

Another silent round smashed into the bricks above her head. She heard yet another one smash into a plate-glass shop window.

The *police judiciaire* were going to have a ball with this one, she thought for no good reason.

Then she turned the corner.

She was on the Quai Conti by the river. Some isolated traffic passed.

Then there was a shout from a doorway, a crash of some heavy glass shattering a few feet away. A human form. A man. Rising to his feet, moving toward her.

Alex nearly expired from heart failure and figured this was the end of her life. She was about to be killed unless she somehow eluded him.

She stepped up her pace. No traffic, the skyline of nighttime Paris across the river, Notre Dame Cathedral illuminated like a giant wedding cake.

Her legs felt strong. She ran on the wet pavement and turned the next corner. She breathed heavily and leaned against the wall.

Good. No one had seemed to follow. Yet she knew from long experience that there was no substitute for getting as far away as quickly as possible from any place of trouble. She reached into her coat pocket, gripped the cell phone and opened it. She waited. And waited. No answer.

She turned left and ran into the dark Paris night, not yet knowing where to run, just wanting to escape.

Come on, Rizzo! Answer, answer, answer!

Please pick up, please pick up, please pick up.

Then Rizzo did answer.

Her mind scrambled. It rejected Italian. They spoke French.

"C'est moi! Alex!" she blurted out. It's me, Alex, she said, breathlessly.

"Qu'est-ce qui ne va pas?" Rizzo asked. What's wrong?

"Tout!" Everything, she said, continuing to run.

She turned slightly as she moved and saw Kaspar in pursuit.

She turned westward. She stepped out into the busy traffic. Her ankle caught on something, twisted, and she went down. A taxi blared its horn, swerved, and sped by, barely missing her. She pulled herself back up, her ankle throbbing, a knee bleeding. She gathered up her cell phone and stumbled back onto the sidewalk.

She ran hard. She turned toward him and saw he was limping badly too. But Kaspar must have packed another clip into his weapon. The sidewalks and asphalt around her exploded with the pattern of bullets that just missed her on each side.

Her heart was pounding in her throat and she ran for her life as the Ukrainian assassin followed.

EIGHTY-ONE

She flipped open the cell phone. Rizzo was still there.

"Find your way to the Métro," Rizzo said, referring to the Parisian subway. "Then get to the Odéon station. That was the closest stop to your apartment. We have a team of people there," he said.

She knew her way around Paris but in her haste to escape had run in exactly the wrong direction to get to the Odéon stop. She now would have to take a circuitous route.

"Or do you want them to abandon their positions and come find you?" Rizzo asked.

"No. They'll never find me," she said breathlessly. "I'll get there."

She tried to assimilate everything that had happened, but the horror of it acted as a block. She wondered about the men she had shot.

Had she left them dead? Dying?

Who knew, though she was sure she'd be reading about it in the newspapers, if not watching it on the news. A wave of disgust overcame her, quickly followed by an urge to survive.

Her thoughts were punctuated by police sirens. The distinctive European ones, like the ones in the open car of police going to round up "the usual suspects" at the beginning of *Casablanca*.

The traffic was heavy on the *quai*. But she darted into it, barely missing a car, then another. She was on the bank of the paved promenade above the river. The floodlit Cathedral of Notre Dame was behind her. One of the great views in the Western world, and she was scared out of her mind. No time to be a tourist.

Heavy drops of rain were falling. A gift from heaven maybe. If Kaspar was trailing her, it would make her more difficult to see. She kept her head down. She couldn't see the rain but she could feel it on her face. What she could see was her breath against the humid mist of the night, that and the recurring image of Maurice's body tumbling out of the closet.

She moved as fast as she could on a bad ankle, urging herself to run and resisting the urge at the same time. She broke into a fierce sweat and crossed the river on the Pont du Carrousel. The massive Musée du Louvre loomed on the other side. She came off the bridge and was on the right bank.

Alex looked over her shoulder and thought she saw Kaspar's dark figure still crossing the bridge, limping badly also, following her.

Suddenly a police car approached, its siren wailing, its blue light flashing, heading in the way she had come. She tried to flag it down, but in the rain the gendarmes didn't see her. They kept going. So did she.

She limped two blocks eastward, keeping Rizzo on the phone. She could see the lights of the Place de la Concorde up ahead. She knew there was a Métro station there and she figured it would be crowded. From Concorde, there would be a short ride to safety. It was too risky to cross a bridge again on foot. A perfect route? No, but she prayed it would work.

Alex picked up her pace. The rain intensified as she passed the gardens of the Tuileries. She cursed her original decision to run north, not south, when she fled the scene of the shooting.

Her body trembled. Within minutes, she arrived at the busy Place de la Concorde and, looking over her shoulder, still saw Kaspar in pursuit. She darted through the maniacal traffic and accessed an entrance to the Métro.

Alex ran down the old concrete steps to the platform. Her footsteps echoed noisily. She slipped badly on the wet stairs. She skinned her other knee and her ankle wailed in pain. But she struggled up to her feet and continued.

She found the Number 12 line southbound. She had thrown Kaspar, at least for a few moments. Without seeing her, he would have no idea which line and which platform she had fled to. Where was he? She was torn between leading him to the Odéon stop and losing him completely. She wished now she had worn a bulletproof vest. What would protect her if he tried to pick her off?

She went to the far end of the platform. She kept her head down, her eyes on the steps. Then, amidst the crowd on the other side of the platform, waiting for a train in the opposite direction, there stood Kaspar.

From a distance of about fifty feet, directly across the tracks, their eyes met. He had a clear shot now, across the tracks. In the distance, she heard the sound of a train approaching the station.

Kaspar glared at her, reached for his weapon but then realized the train rumbling into the station would take his shot away. So he turned and ran. He was trying to cross over.

A train roared into the station. A crowd flowed off the train and another crowd surged on. It was almost midnight but the subway was moderately busy.

She stepped onto the last car. Just before she boarded, she saw Kaspar descend the distant steps in pursuit. She couldn't see whether he had gotten on or not. She assumed he had. She turned against the wall of the subway car. She wished she had recovered her gun. The empty holster made her feel naked.

The train rumbled along. Why did these Parisian subways have to zigzag like snakes beneath the city? Stations were often only two hundred yards apart.

One stop. Two. She got off and switched cars, trying to throw her pursuer. The train arrived at the Sèvres Babylone station.

She stepped off, stayed in the crowd, and transferred to the Number 10 line going east to the Gare d'Austerlitz, the ancient train station. The 10 would take her to Odéon within two minutes.

She finally started to catch her breath. Under her clothing, her body was soaked. Sweat rolled off her. This train was crowded too. She kept waiting to see if Kaspar would come through looking for her. The doors between the cars were only for emergency use but were unlocked in case emergency use was required.

She took out her phone again. She found Rizzo on the other end.

"Where are you?" he asked.

She told him.

"Still got Kaspar after you?" he asked.

"Probably. I haven't seen him for several minutes."

"We're ready for you," he said. "When you arrive at Odéon, get off as quickly as possible. You'll see some musicians playing. Walk toward them as quickly as possible."

"Where will you be?" she asked.

"Watching," he said.

In ninety seconds, the train arrived at Odéon.

She stepped out at the south end of the platform. Her ankle continued to kill her.

This station too was busy. But she could hear some street musicians, a small band playing for change in the subways. Accordion, violin, and sax until 1:30 in the morning. Only in Paris. They were at the other end of the platform, about a hundred feet away. It was strange they were playing so late.

She looked in every direction.

She saw no help. She spoke into her phone.

"I don't see anyone," she said.

"We've got you," came the answer from Rizzo.

"What do you mean you've 'got' me?"

"We see you. We're watching."

"Who's watching?"

"Get past the musicians," Rizzo said.

"I don't see Kaspar," she said.

"You must have lost him."

"I don't think—"

"He's behind you!" Rizzo said. "Get moving!"

She turned. Eye contact immediately. His gaze again ran smack into hers simultaneously. She saw him reach for something under his jacket. He was about fifty feet behind her.

"Get moving!" Rizzo repeated. "Get away from him!" barked Rizzo's voice on the phone.

She had never felt slower in her life. Her ankle wouldn't obey. She cursed the boots and wished she'd had sneakers. She bumped into a couple that was kissing and the contact nearly knocked her over. Kaspar was gaining.

"I can't move fast! My ankle!"

"Get past the musicians!"

"I can't. He'll catch me first." The words in her phone barked at her. "Move! Move!" they demanded. "You'll be safe!"

"Why don't you shoot him?" she demanded. "Just shoot him!"

"We can't! Not yet!"

"He's going to kill me!"

"Keep moving!" Rizzo barked. "Now! Move!"

It was the endgame and she knew it. She zigzagged through the crowd. She had never felt slower in her life. She heard excited voices and she heard the assassin steps behind her. And she heard the music, which got louder and louder as she lurched toward it. How was she going to get out of here? She eyed the *sortie*, the exit, on the other side of the players.

Kaspar must have drawn his gun because she heard a woman yell and scream. Then there was chaos behind her.

She broke into a final attempt at a run. She edged past people and Kaspar was on the run behind her.

Then her earphone thundered again. "Get down! He's got a gun!"

She tried to move, but her ankle turned again. She fell and went down hard. She knew she was a goner. She got up and stumbled past the musicians, fell hard again. The musicians stopped playing.

She got past them. The accordion player reached into his pocket. So did the violin player. She saw from the corner of her eye. She tried to stand.

Then she saw what the trap was, what this was all about. Like Anatoli in London, Kaspar had stepped into his own hell on earth.

The violin player raised a black pistol at the same time. The accordion player pulled one out also. Kaspar raised his own weapon and the Métro platform was a flurry of bullets.

The violinist aimed right at Kaspar's gut and put two shots into him. The assassin staggered for a moment, and his eyes went wide in pain and in the realization that death was at hand. He flailed and fired two shots wildly. Kaspar staggered, his hand snapped back, and he fired his own gun upward instead of downward.

There was a flurry on the Métro platform and bullets rang in every direction.

Alex felt something wallop her hard in the midpoint of the chest, just above the breast bone, at the center where her stone medallion hung.

She saw the accordion player reach forward and put a bullet into Kaspar's head. Then a second. But she barely saw that, because she felt something wet and sticky on her chest. Blood. She had been hit by a bullet in the midpoint of the chest. The feeling first was numbness, then the pain radiated, as did the shock.

"Oh, God. Oh, God," was all she could say.

Alex had a bullet wound in the center of her chest. She was bleeding.

Unreal. But she knew how quickly it could be fatal.

She clutched the area. She lay on the ground in shock, wondering how everything since January had led to this time, this place. The pain was spreading now and so was the blood. From the corner of her eye, she could see Kaspar lying on the ground, his skull torn open by a team of assassins.

One of them stayed over her and cradled her head.

"I'm dying," she said. "I'm dying." The pain was radiating out from a center point in her chest. Shivers turned to convulsions. She put an unsteady hand to the area where she had been hit. She felt warm wetness, the blood, and the broken pieces of the stone pendant from Barranco Lajoya.

It was surreal. The accordion player-gunman ripped off the sleeve of his shirt and pressed it to her chest. She drifted. Consciousness departed, then returned halfway.

Then there were the sounds of police over her. Her eyes flickered and she didn't know how much time had passed. She only knew that the musician had disappeared.

Strange faces, noisy men and women in Parisian police uniforms, hovered over her. They barked orders and tried to help. She could no longer understand the language. They worked on her with bandages, tubes, and breathing devices. She felt herself tumbling deeper into shock. Or into something or some place she didn't understand.

Then everything went from white to black then back to white again, and she was thinking, "If this is dying, it's easier than I ever thought. Much easier . . ."

A cloudy painless whiteness enveloped her.

Two minutes later, her heart stopped.

EIGHTY-TWO

The heavyset woman came down the stairs of her apartment building in a hurry. She carried one large suitcase and struggled with it. Three flights down the back stairs and she was sweating beneath her tan raincoat. But she had been sweating since before she had finished backing.

Short notice, long trip. But a big payoff. It would all be worth it. She was going to get a new passport, a new identity. And a free trip out of the country. She would get more money in cash in the next few hours than she would by keeping her lousy government job for another twenty years. So it hadn't been much of a decision when she had made it several years ago.

Still she was nervous. She had heard horror stories about people who got involved in this type of thing. But there was no turning back now.

It was nearly midnight.

She stepped out from the front door of her middle class building in Alexandria, Virginia. A few parking spaces down, in front of a hydrant, a car engine started up. The car slid forward a few parking spots and gently came to a halt.

She recognized two of the men in the front seat. The front window rolled down.

Handsome men. Smiling faces. The faces of her homeland.

"Hello, Olga," the man in the shotgun seat said.

She answered in Ukrainian. "Do you have the money? Do you have my passport?" she demanded.

The man opened an envelope that sat on his lap. There were some huge bricks of money and some banking information where the rest could be found. He handed her a Brazilian passport.

"See if you like your picture," the man answered. "But I wouldn't advise you to stay too much longer. FBI. They're probably on their way."

The mere mention of American police was enough to make her heart jump. She had known of other CIA employees who had sold out over the years. Most of them went to federal prisons and didn't emerge until they were very old or until some other more patriotic prisoner stuck a shiv in their backs.

Olga glanced at the passport. Her picture. A new name. She was now Helen Tamshenko and she was a resident of São Paulo.

Good enough. She reached for the back door and slid into the car. She slumped low. No one would spot her as a passenger.

The driver pulled away from the curb. An oncoming pair of headlights swept the street. Then a second. Two big unmarked Buicks, traveling fast.

"Just in time," the driver said softly. "That's the FBI now."

Olga stayed low. She preferred not to see. Her car proceeded without incident. They went to the intersection and turned. She watched the driver as he glanced in his rear view mirror. He moved quickly and deftly into traffic so it would be difficult to follow.

"We're okay," he said, continuing in Ukrainian.

The man on the shotgun side turned his head halfway around to talk to his passenger. "You're a lucky lady tonight, Olga. Real lucky."

Both men laughed.

They drove across the Key Bridge back into Washington. They navigated carefully through traffic. Olga sat up a little to watch where they were going. Within another few minutes, they entered Rock Creek Park. Its roads were dark and quiet at this late hour, which was what everyone there wanted.

"I'll tell you what's going to happen, Olga. We're going to move you to another car. You're going to drive through the night. Your next driver will take you to Montreal and you'll fly to Mexico. From there to Cuba. The Americans will lose track of you in Havana. But you'll connect there for Brazil."

The driver glanced at him and smiled.

Olga remained nervous.

"Where's the money?" she asked.

From the front seat came the rest of her package. The nice plump packs of money. Enough to get her started. She was breathing a little easier, but not by much.

Olga's vehicle pulled off the road. She looked around. Sure enough, there was another car waiting, its lights off.

The driver of Olga's car flashed its lights. The driver from the other car gave a slight wave of recognition. A passenger side guard stepped out to cover the situation. Olga assumed everyone was armed. Well, that was fine because she was, too.

"There you go," said the driver. "Don't say we didn't do anything for you. You're on your way."

"I'm on my way," she nodded.

She checked her new passport again and stuffed the money in her purse. She stepped out of the car and closed the door behind her.

"Bye, Olga," the man in front said pleasantly. "Good luck."

She was too tense to answer. She gave a nod to the car that had brought her here as it pulled away. She started toward the other car. The rear door opened and the driver beckoned to her again.

EIGHTY-THREE

One of the grand boulevards of Paris that leads to and from the Arc de Triomphe in Paris is the Avenue de la Grande Armée, directly opposite the Champs Elysées. It travels eastward from Place de l'Etoile, where the arc stands, and rolls through expensive neighborhoods till it arrives in the wealthy suburb of Neuilly-sur-Seine.

If a traveler stays on the boulevard, he or she passes majestic apartment buildings and mansions that smell of the money of all nations. One will also come to the American Hospital of Paris, which was where Alex arrived thirty minutes after the shooting incident in the Parisian Métro. Not only was there a wound in her chest from a bullet, but she had gone into cardiac arrest.

An intensive care unit in a hospital outside one's native country is never a cheerful place. But the American Hospital of Paris has been an institution for a century. In a country of exemplary medical care, it remains one of the leading hospitals.

Hit in the center of the chest by a bullet, Alex's body was moved there from the Métro's Odéon station by ambulance. Her body was motionless beneath a sheet and a blanket, covered to the shoulders. Medics on the scene looked at the wound and tried to close off the blood, but given the force of the hit, they shook their heads.

The ambulance technicians who transported Alex to the American Hospital saw that her vital signs were almost nonexistent. When her heart stopped, electrical cardioversion was applied. Electrode paddles were applied to her chest and a single shock was administered.

She was unconscious at the time, somewhere between life and death, prepared to go either way. In the ambulance on the way to the hospital, her heart flickered again. If she had been gone — wherever souls go to — she was back.

Or trying to get back.

She was admitted to an emergency room, where the bizarre nature of her injury was properly assessed for the first time. The bullet that had hit her had ricocheted off the Métro wall. Its impact had been greatly defused. And somehow, in the center of her chest, right above her breastbone, the bullet had scored a direct hit on the stone pendant that she had bought in Barranco Lajoya.

The stone had broken under the impact of the bullet, but it had defused the damage from the fired round. While there was a flesh wound and severe trauma to the breastbone, including a hairline fracture, the bullet had not broken through beyond the flesh at the surface. Contrary to how it appeared in the Métro, it had not entered her body.

Detectives who inspected the crime scene in the hours after the shooting found the spent bullet in the center of the tracks, in the spot to which it had been deflected.

The stone had saved her life.

On her first day in the hospital, she lay by herself in a private room under heavy sedation. She was groggy. She was on heavy pain-relief medication and an IV fed into her arm. Her chest throbbed. Under the bandages, the skin of her chest had turned the color of an eggplant. Every breath hurt. She was afraid to look at her wound. And above all, she was surprised to be alive.

On the second day she felt better. It was only then that she wondered whether anyone knew where she was, much less who she was. She inquired of one of her nurses.

The nurse informed her that people from the American embassy had arranged for her care, including the private room. Nonetheless, the pain and discomfort persisted. She was too distracted mentally and zonked out on medication even to read. She left the television on 24/7, the remote control at her bedside. All she had the energy to do was flick stations back and forth, the usual French fare — NYPD Blue reruns dubbed in French and a cheesy Gallic clone of The Jerry Springer Show were her grudging favorites — plus odd channels from CNN to Al Jazeera.

Her third day in the hospital was the first day when visitors were allowed. Mark McKinnon, the CIA station chief from Rome, was the first to see her.

McKinnon pulled a chair toward her bed and sat down.

"How are you feeling, LaDuca?" he asked.

"Surprised to be here."

"You got very lucky," he said. "Somebody sure is watching over you."

"You could conclude that," she said. Her chest still hurt. There were small burns where the electrode paddles had been applied. "Sometimes I wonder."

She was also still groggy. The medication remained at its original strength.

"A bullet on a ricochet can kill someone," McKinnon said. "Apparently you had some sort of pendant there on your chest? That's what the doctors told me."

"A pendant that I got in South America," she said. "Very hard stone. It took the brunt of the impact. So they tell me."

McKinnon was shaking his head.

"Lucky," he said.

"Lucky," she answered.

"What are the odds of that happening?" he asked.

"You tell me. I don't have any answers anymore."

He smiled and gave her shoulder a pat.

"I understand you'll be here for a little while more," he said. "Just rest, get your strength back. Eventually, the police are going to want to ask you questions. But we're taking care of everything. Back channels."

"Back channels," she said. "Wonderful way to do things."

He didn't miss her irony.

"Banner year you're having, huh?"

"Yeah," she said.

He paused. "There's still some outstanding business," he said. "Yuri Federov may be dead. We don't know. We have to assume that he's still out there somewhere. You're not completely safe until he's completely out of business."

"Killed, you mean."

"That's another word for it."

"And that all ties into Kiev, doesn't it?"

"Absolutely," he said.

"Which in turn ties in how and why my fiancé got killed."

He nodded.

"Someone betrayed me, didn't they?" she said. "That's why Maurice got killed. And Cerny. There's a traitor somewhere on our side, and he's got allegiances to the Ukrainian mob."

"That's a subject for future discussion," McKinnon said.

"So the answer is *yes*?" she said.

McKinnon nodded.

"We had a leak in Washington," McKinnon said. "Poor Mike Cerny. Cynical chap that he was, he hadn't vetted all his assistants as well as he should have. Everything was getting to Federov almost before it happened."

"Olga?" Alex asked.

"You said it. I didn't."

Alex shook her head in disgust.

"Anyway. Olga is someone you won't be seeing again."

"Arrested?"

"The opposition got to her first." McKinnon said. "But we'll discuss this later."

"When I'm healthy enough," she said, "we'll go back at Federov, assuming he's alive. And we'll find any other traitor too. How's that?"

"Federov is out of business, at least," McKinnon said.

"How do you mean that?"

"He was deposed from his own businesses by his own peers," McKinnon said. "That's how it always works in the underworld. He drew too much attention to himself. If he's not dead, he's in deep cover. Like back into one of his priest outfits or something."

"I'm sure," she said, not really meaning it.

"One thing's certain. *You'll* never see him again."

"I'm grateful," she said.

"Federov's still on our lists, though. Retired or not, if he's alive we'll go after him. But as I said, it's no longer your problem, Alex."

There was a pause while she remained silent. McKinnon stood. "The French have posted an extra pair of their police in the lobby," he explained. "*Policiers en civil.* Plainclothes. They look like a pair of bouncers. Then we've posted two of our own as guards on this floor also. Don't know whether you've seen them."

"I haven't been out of this room since they wheeled me in," she said.

"Of course."

She gave everything some thought.

"I have some unfinished business in Venezuela too," she said. "Barranco Lajoya. Those people. I'd like to do something."

"Tough to accomplish much in that part of the world, isn't it?" he commiserated.

She shook her head, the images of the carnage relentlessly replaying themselves in her mind's eye. "Before I die, I want to go back and do what I can for those people. They deserve better."

"You know what your boss, Mr. Collins, would say," McKinnon said out of nowhere. "He'd say that's where Jesus would be. Comforting the downtrodden and the desperate."

She nodded. It suddenly hurt too much to speak.

"We've had discussions with Mr. Collins about Barranco Lajoya, by the way. Something may already be in the works. He's willing to chip in heavily on an international relief effort."

"God bless him," she said.

"I know he's going to phone you in the next few days."

"That's good," she said. "We can talk."

A nurse appeared. She looked at McKinnon, shook her head and tapped her wristwatch.

"I guess that's my five minutes," McKinnon said.

"And I guess I have a lot of work to do when I get out of here," she said.

McKinnon left a calling card, a nondescript CIA thing with a fake name, a fake title, and a real phone number. The card cited him as a cultural attaché to the embassy in Paris, with an office in Rome. His cover job was overseeing the exchange of French and Italian filmmakers and American filmmakers.

She was left with a lot of time to think. Too much time, really, but no one ever remarked that time went quickly in a hospital. Federov played over and over in her mind, as did Barranco Lajoya.

Here she was alive again. Why?

What was she to do with the extra years she had been given?

EIGHTY-FOUR

In a private search chamber at New York's John F. Kennedy Airport, Sammy Newman — better known to the world as the singer Billy-O — stood with his hands in his inside-out emptied pockets and wondered how things could have gone so terribly wrong.

In front of him, two US customs agents, with their mulish dedication to their job, went through every bit of his luggage, examining the linings, his dirty socks, and underwear. One was a no-nonsense guy with a trim moustache and glasses. The other was an even-less-nonsense female with a big midsection and pinned-back hair. They said nothing as they methodically disassembled his luggage. A Beatles tune, "Yellow Submarine," mutilated into Muzak, played softly over the sound system.

Meanwhile, Sammy could have used a yellow submarine to get out of there. The flight from Nice, *première classe* all the way on Air France, had been a sweetheart. Hardly a bump, great food, and there had been two flight attendants who had caught his eye, beautiful Gallic girls with dark eyes, slender builds, and sultry legs. They had pushed their phone numbers into his hands. Sammy had booked a week at the Carlyle in New York and was thinking of inviting both girls over and extending the stay to two weeks. He had some fun planned before having to return to Los Angeles and finding out what his agent had lined up as his next film.

But now, *this!*

He was breaking a major sweat.

The agents had gone through the lining of his leather suitcase and had found the extra twenty-thousand dollars that he always carried, a violation of currency transfer regulations. He met that with a shrug. He knew his lawyer could get him out of that one.

"Hey. It's dangerous to show a lot of cash these days," he said. "Know what I mean?"

"Currency transfer violation, sir," the male agent said. "Sorry."

"Aren't you from this area?" the woman asked. "New Jersey or something?"

"Westbury, Long Island."

"Oh, yeah," she said. "Knew it was something."

She then returned to her business of putting Sammy in jail.

The money was just the small stuff. Now, as the perspiration moved from his brow to the side of his face, and as it flooded from his palms, these lousy agents were invading his medicine kit.

He watched. They opened his pill containers and examined the contents. They showed the contents to each other. They glanced at him and didn't say anything.

"I got a prescription somewhere for everything," Sammy said, "even if some of the pills got messed up. You know, wrong bottles."

The agents didn't say anything.

Sammy was already wondering which of his lawyers he would call, or maybe his manager Adam Winters in Santa Monica, when and if they gave him his phone back. Actually, he pondered, thinking it through further, he might need someone in New York. And fast.

Then Sammy's spirits hit the floor and shattered. The female agent found what would be the grand prize for her today.

She opened a small vial that was within a larger prescription vial. In the smaller container, there were two little tightly folded packets of aluminum foil, thick and plump, and double wrapped.

"Hey. Gimme a break, could you?" Sammy asked. "Please?"

The agents unwrapped the foil. The contents of the first packet looked like oregano. Or catnip. The agents sniffed. It didn't appear to be catnip or oregano and it wasn't basil, either. Well, a pot bust was a pot bust. Worse things could happen.

Then a worst thing did. The second agent unwrapped a smaller packet that had escaped notice at first. The contents this time was a single small cube.

"I don't know how that got there," Sammy tried meekly.

"Right," the male agent said.

The female reached for a pair of handcuffs. All three of them knew what hashish looked like when they saw it. And they saw it right now.

"Sorry, Billy," she said. "And you know what? This is a real shame. I always liked your music."

EIGHTY-FIVE

Woman's body found in Rock Creek Park

POSTED: 4:55 p.m. EST August 21
UPDATED: 7:33 p.m. EST August 21

WASHINGTON (The Washington Post) — A woman was found dead in Rock Creek Park near Walter Reed Hospital on Thursday. Police familiar to the case confirm that it was a homicide from gunshot wounds.

The body was found by a jogger at 9:12 a.m. It was about 30 yards off Sherill Drive near 16th and Aspen streets in Northwest.

Police said the woman appeared to be in her late 50s and was of European descent. She was wearing a tan raincoat and appeared to have a valid passport from a South American country.

"A possibility is that the individual came into the woods to walk and was met by a robber. There were no other signs of trauma other than the gunshot. Her purse was open and there was no money or identification in it, other than her passport," DC Police Inspector Jerome Myles said. "We just don't know any more at this time."

Police said they are awaiting further results from the medical examiner and are attempting to locate any relatives of the woman. Her name has not yet been publicly disclosed.

EIGHTY-SIX

On the morning of the next day, the doctors at the American hospital moved Alex out of critical care into a private room on a regular ward. Late that same afternoon, a nurse came in with a name on a piece of paper to see if she would recognize, to see if a prospective visitor would be allowed.

She recognized the name and was very pleasantly surprised. "*Oui, bien sûr*," Alex answered.

"*Cinq minutes seulement*," the nurse said, limiting the visit to five minutes.

"*Oh, mais pour lui, dix?*" she asked. For him, ten? "*S'il vous plaît?*"

The nurse rolled her eyes, gave a slight smile, and shrugged, which meant, yes, okay.

The nurse left. A moment later the door eased open. A large man with a slight limp entered the room, carrying a huge bouquet of fresh flowers and a small shopping bag. He wore a dark suit and a dress shirt open at the collar and was a day or two unshaven. More importantly, he was walking very well on one real leg and one fake one.

Alex sat up in the bed and thought of pickup games of basketball back in Washington for the first time in several days, not to mention the dark in March when this same man had deterred her suicide.

"Oh my," she said. "You sure show up at the strangest times."

"Hope you don't mind," Ben answered.

"Not at all."

Impetuously, he leaned down and gave her a kiss on the cheek. She accepted it. They exchanged as much of a hug as IV tubes would allow. He stepped back and placed the flowers at her bedside table.

"You sure know how to find trouble, no matter where you go," he said.

"It finds me. What are you doing here?"

"Right now," he said, "I'm visiting you in the hospital."

She laughed for the first time in days. It hurt.

"I can see that much," she said, "but why are you in Paris?"

"I'm visiting you in the hospital," he repeated.

"I don't follow," she said.

It was very simple, he explained. The group that she played basketball with back in Washington, the family at the gym, had heard that Alex had been hospitalized in Paris.

Critical condition, but improving.

"Who did you here that from?" she asked.

"Laura. Laura Chapman."

"Ah. Of course." It made sense. Laura would know through government channels.

"Did Laura mention what happened?" she asked.

"No," he answered hesitantly. "What *did* happen? Some sort of accident in the subway?"

"You could call it that," Alex said. Then she shook her head. "Long story, actually. For another time, okay?" She motioned to a chair.

"Okay," he answered.

"Well, anyway," he continued, sitting down. "There are about fifteen of us regulars who you play with. Dave. Matt. Eric. Laura. A couple of guys whose names you don't know but who you'd recognize. We all sat around talking a couple of nights ago after a game. I said someone should go visit. So we each dropped a hundred bucks into someone's sweaty gym bag."

Alex could feel herself smiling.

"We called it our 'Alex fund,'" he said. "We put everyone's name in another bag. Whoever's name got drawn would make the visit, the 'fund' covering the expense of the trip, time lost from work, and so on. Since it had been my idea, I was selected to make the draw."

She laughed. "And you drew your own name?"

Hesitantly, he said, "Yeah. I drew my own name."

"The hand of God?" she asked.

He smiled. "Nope. I cheated. I palmed the slip of paper with my own name. I wanted to make the trip."

She laughed. "Good of you," she said.

"Look at this," he said, reaching into the bag.

He pulled out a miniature basketball hoop and a foam ball. The hoop was about six inches across, the ball about four inches in diameter. It was one of those $4.98 toys that one sees in offices or children's rooms.

She laughed again when she saw it, and laughed harder when he stuck it up to the wall and flipped her the ball.

"Should I pass to you so you can dunk it or should I shoot?" she asked.

"Oh, by all means," he said, "go for the three pointer."

Her arm hurt too much to raise it. So she threw a random under-hand shot up against the wall, about six feet away. It hit the front of the hoop, flew upward, then dropped straight down.

It swished.

"Whoa!" he said. "The hand of God?"

"I'm sure God is too busy to busy to worry about three-point shots in hospital rooms," she said.

She looked across the room. "See that window over there?" she asked.

"I see it."

"I'd like to get to it. Will you help me?"

"I'd be honored."

She slid her legs around so she could slide off the side of the bed. Ben helped her stand, steadying her as she stood. She ached all over. She was again conscious of how she must have fallen because there were bad bruises on her legs and elbows. In a hospital gown she could still see the scratches on her legs from the brambles in the Venezuelan mountains, as well as the hard fall in the French subway.

She looked as if she had been beaten up.

"I don't know how many individual injuries I have," she said, "but you know all about stuff like that, right?"

"We're all wounded in some way. We're all mutilated. You know that old Paul Simon song, 'An American Tune'? Goes something like, 'Don't know a soul who ain't been battered, ain't got a friend who feels at ease . . .'"

"I know it," she said.

"One step at a time," he said, helping her walk. "This is great. You're doing fine." He helped the IV-pole trail her.

She nodded and continued the faint tune as he acted as her support.

"Don't know a dream that's not been shattered," she sang softly. "Or driven to its knees."

They sang together. "But it's all right, it's all right."

She hung on his arm, got stronger with each pace, and traveled the dozen steps to the window. She gazed out on the courtyard. Over the roof of the hospital, in the distance, she could see part of the Parisian skyline.

"Well, I'm alive," she said.

"You're alive," he answered. "Against the odds, we both are."

She nodded. He helped her back to the bed. She sat down, then lay down. Her energy was already gone.

He sat in the chair by the bed for the remaining minutes of his visit. She felt weak but inside she started to feel good. He looked at a small object in a dish by the bedside.

He reached to it. "May I?" he asked.

"Sure."

He picked up the remains of the stone pendant that had saved her life. It was in three pieces. The center of it had been smashed into dust by the ricocheting bullet so that, if the pieces were pushed back together, one could see, right where the engraved cross came together, a deep gouge. Aside from that, the three pieces fit together perfectly, as if designed by a master carver.

"What's this?" he asked.

She smiled.

"Come back tomorrow and I'll tell you," she said.

He put the pendant back into the dish and then back onto the table. The pieces fit themselves back together. She admired the small cross that Paulina had carved in the stone, thousands of miles away — the small carving that had saved her life.

Distantly, she thought of Paulina.

"It's a deal," Ben said. "I'll come back tomorrow. And you can tell me."

A few minutes after Ben left, Alex's strength again ebbed. She settled again into a comfortable sleep.

EIGHTY-SEVEN

The following morning, for the first time since her arrival at the hospital, Alex felt good enough to sit up and read. Her physician passed by at about 8:00 a.m. There were newspapers in French and a few books at her bedside. Ben's bouquet sat at her bedside, and now a second one did too, from her former coworkers at Treasury in Washington. Word either traveled fast or not at all these days.

She reached for the papers and began to glance through them. A nurse came by shortly after ten.

"*Il y a encore un visiteur,*" the nurse announced. Another visitor.

"*C'est qui?*" Alex asked.

"*Un médecin étranger, je crois,*" the nurse answered. A foreign doctor.

Alex shrugged. "*Bien. Pourquoi pas?*" she said. Well, why not? The more medical advice, the better. Or, she wondered, was the opposite true? Well, she would listen.

She set aside her newspapers and leaned back in her bed. She drew a deep breath as the nurse left the room.

She reached to the side table and pulled out a hand mirror. She glanced into it. To her mind, she looked tired. But, she now realized, she would survive.

Ben's visit the previous day and the gifts he had brought from America had done more to rally her spirits than she could have imagined. For the first time since arriving there, she began to entertain a restless spirit. How long would she be in the hospital? How long before she could be discharged and go home? How long before she could resume a normal life?

She brushed at her hair with her fingers, instinctively sprucing up for her visitor, even if it was a doctor. Plus, Ben would come by later. The pain in her chest had subsided. Maybe, she wondered, if Ben were staying a few days, he could help her pack her things and return to Washington.

The door opened and a man in a white lab coat entered, his physician's ID clipped to his lapel. Alex saw him first out of the corner of her eye.

The visitor was tall, strikingly tall, maybe six foot three. He was sturdy with a slight beard, about a week's worth, and wore a tie. He almost looked like an old priest and he had a faint smell of cigarettes about him. And what type of doctor smells of cigarettes?

She put down the mirror, looked at him, and smiled.

He spoke softly in Russian. "*Zdrastvuyeeti. Dobraye utro.*" Hello. Good morning.

"*Dobraye utro,*" she answered instinctively. Good morning in return.

"How are you feeling?"

"Better today, doctor," she began. "I—"

She looked into his eyes. With a surge of horror, she pegged the face.

"That's very good, hey," he said. "Glad to hear it."

She sputtered in Russian. "What are you doing here? How did you—?"

She reached for the alarm button to call the nurse. "Please don't make a sound," Yuri Federov said. He reached under his lab coat and pulled a gun from his hip. She eyed it. It was a small compact piece, snub nosed and sleek. Chinese.

Fear shot through her. Her hand froze.

"Your security people need to do a better job," he continued. "Both the Americans and the French. I showed the French police a fraudulent physician's ID badge," he said, motioning to the one he wore. "And I walked right past them. And your American guards are down at the nurse's station, flirting with the pretty French girls, trying to get home phone numbers. What kind of security is that?"

"So you're here to kill me?" she asked.

"It's not that simple," he said.

"No? Then why is your hand still on your gun?"

"Because it's not that simple."

He went back to the door and locked it. Then he walked slowly to the window and peered out, downward to the courtyard, as if he were looking for someone or trying to determine if he had been followed.

"Your two bodyguards are dead," she said. "Anatoli and Kaspar. I'm sure you know that."

"At the time of their deaths," Federov said, "they no longer worked for me. They betrayed me."

"Could have fooled me," she said.

He scoffed, turning back to her. "I wouldn't have given the order to kill you, hey? You should know that," he said. "My competitors in the underworld purchased the loyalty of those around me," he said. "Anatoli and Kaspar were hired away by those who wanted me out of a position of influence. I was not upset with their deaths."

"Americans?"

"Maybe. Who knows?"

He turned back from the window.

"Who attacked me in Venezuela?" she asked.

"My competitors," he said. "To keep the heat on me. So that your government would continue to hunt me, as they do to this day. They don't know where I am. They don't know what I do. They are endlessly stupid. It will take them five years to figure out I've withdrawn from my businesses."

"No, they already know that," she said.

"They tell you that," Federov said, "but they think otherwise."

She pondered it. "Why should I believe you?"

"I don't know. Why should you? Maybe because I'm here. Maybe because I saved your life at least once."

"What about the attack in Kiev?" she asked. "The attack on the president."

"I told you at the time. Not my people. *Filorusski*, but not my people."

"But you knew?"

"Everyone knew. Even your president knew. But your leader was a camera-whore who persisted with the visit." He paused. "Don't you realize that you were part of a conspiracy to get *me* killed?" he asked. He coughed. "That's where the conspiracy began. You were to be next to me. If they knew where you were, they had a sniper ready to get me. So I moved. Can you blame me? They wouldn't have cared much if they had killed you too!"

"Prove it," she said.

"Why should I? You already know I'm telling you the truth."

"You sure you're not crazy?"

"I'm not crazy like that! I'm Russian. Now I'll prove both. Insanity, plus a flair for the grand dramatic gesture."

He raised the gun with startling speed and spun it in his right hand. He removed the loaded clip, checked it, and slammed it back into the magazine again.

"Don't be afraid," he said.

He reversed his grip on the pistol and held it by the barrel. Then he handed it to her.

"Take it," he said. "With guards like yours, you'll need it."

"What?"

"Take it! This is your opportunity," he said. She reached out and took the pistol from him. She aimed it at the midpoint of his chest.

"Very good," he said, stepping back half a pace to not crowd her. "If you feel you need to kill me," he said, "do it now. If you feel I'm responsible for your fiancé's death, avenge yourself. I'm in here illegally. Your story would be that I threatened you. No one would question further. This is my gift to you, a chance to set everything even."

For what seemed like a long, long while, she held the gun on him.

"But if you do not pull the trigger, I will be out of France by nightfall. I am going somewhere to keep my money warm."

"Switzerland?"

"Somewhere," he said. "Hey." On a piece of notepaper, he wrote down the names of a hotel and a restaurant in Geneva. He handed it to her. "If I can ever do you a favor," he said, "come visit. Go to the restaurant and ask for me. But come alone."

She held the weapon steady. She set the notepaper aside.

"I should be going," he said.

"You should be going," she agreed.

Yuri Federov, onetime kingpin of crime in Ukraine, turned and walked to the door. At that moment, as if on cue, someone tried the door from the other side and, finding it locked, rapped sharply. A male voice from the other side called out in English.

"Alex? You in there? You okay in there?"

A beat and she answered.

"I'm okay, Ben," she said.

She pushed the weapon under her top sheet.

"Go," she said to Federov. "Now."

Federov unlocked the door. The door opened. Ben stepped in. Federov gave him a nod. Ben gave him a nod in return.

"Sorry," Ben said with a shrug. He labored in an alien tongue. *"Je ne parle pas français."* I don't speak French.

"And I don't speak English," Federov lied quickly in English. He turned back to Alex. He smiled. *"Dasvidania,"* he said. Good-bye.

"Uvidimsia," she answered. See you.

He gave her a final grin and a nod. *"Da. Uvidimsia,"* he agreed. See you.

Federov clasped Ben on the shoulder for a moment and gave him a nod. Then Federov left the chamber.

Ben came in and sat down. He looked at the door, then back to Alex.

"So?" he finally asked. "Who was that?"

A moment passed.

Then, "A friend," she finally said. "An unlikely friend, but a friend."

ACKNOWLEDGMENTS

In addition to conversations with selected personal sources, the author is grateful to many sources for background and research on Kiev, the Orange Revolution, and the political histories of North, Central, and South America. Among them, *The New York Times*, *The Washington Post*, The United States Department of Justice, Wikipedia, *The Columbia Encyclopedia*, and *The Encyclopedia Britannica*.

The author welcomes comments and correspondence from readers either through the Zondervan website or at NH1212f@yahoo.com.

> **"Loaded with fascinating details....
> A muscular story with great bones."**
>
> —*USA Today*

NOEL HYND

THE ENEMY WITHIN

Laura Chapman, a Secret Service agent assigned to the White House, is put on a case that borders on the unthinkable: an assassination plot against the new president, with the trigger man a member of the United States Secret Service. Since it is known that the assassin is male, Laura is not a suspect, but as her investigation proceeds, she cannot shake the suspicion that she is being set up. In her increasing moments of paranoia, she wonders: Am I going to be the next Lee Harvey Oswald?

> **"*The Enemy Within* is a great story, written intelligently and introducing a very sympathetic main character."** —*The Dallas Morning News*

> **"[A] high-octane thriller."** —*Booklist*

www.tor-forge.com/theenemywithin

978-0-7653-4509-7 • 0-7653-4509-9 • Paperback

Share Your Thoughts

With the Author: Your comments will be forwarded to the author when you send them to *zauthor@zondervan.com*.

With Zondervan: Submit your review of this book by writing to *zreview@zondervan.com*.

Free Online Resources at
www.zondervan.com

Zondervan AuthorTracker: Be notified whenever your favorite authors publish new books, go on tour, or post an update about what's happening in their lives.

Daily Bible Verses and Devotions: Enrich your life with daily Bible verses or devotions that help you start every morning focused on God.

Free Email Publications: Sign up for newsletters on fiction, Christian living, church ministry, parenting, and more.

Zondervan Bible Search: Find and compare Bible passages in a variety of translations at www.zondervanbiblesearch.com.

Other Benefits: Register yourself to receive online benefits like coupons and special offers, or to participate in research.